NEBULA AWARDS SHOWCASE #55

Outstanding Science Fiction and Fantasy

Edited by
Catherynne M. Valente

Print Edition

Excerpt from *Riverland* by Fran Wilde, copyright © 2019 by Fran Wilde. Published by Harry N. Abrams. Reprinted by permission of the author.

Excerpt(s) from EXHALATION: STORIES by Ted Chiang, compilation copyright © 2019 by Ted Chiang. Used by permission of Alfred A. Knopf, an imprint of the Knopf Doubleday Publishing Group, a division of Penguin Random House LLC. All rights reserved.

Excerpt from *The Haunting of Tram Car 015* by P. Djèlí Clark, copyright © 2019 by P. Djèlí Clark. Published by *Tor.com*. Reprinted by permission of the author.

Excerpt from *This Is How You Lose the Time War* by Amal El-Mohtar & Max Gladstone, copyright © 2019 by Amal El-Mohtar & Max Gladstone. Published by Gallery / Saga Press. Reprinted by permission of the authors.

Excerpt from "Her Silhouette, Drawn in Water" by Vylar Kaftan, copyright © 2019 by Vylar Kaftan. Published by *Tor.com*. Reprinted by permission of the author.

Excerpt from *The Deep* by Rivers Solomon, with Daveed Diggs, William Hutson & Jonathan Snipes, copyright © 2019 by Rivers Solomon, with Daveed Diggs, William Hutson & Jonathan Snipes. Published by Gallery / Saga Press. Reprinted by permission of the author.

Excerpt from *Catfish Lullaby* by A.C. Wise, copyright © 2019 by A.C. Wise. Published by Broken Eye Books. Reprinted by permission of the author.

Table of Contents

Introduction
by Catherynne Valente ix

"The Best of Twines, the Worst of Rhymes: A Tale of Two C++ies (or, Why Game Writing Is Bad And Great)"
by Seth Dickinson 1

"Queering Chaos"
by Foz Meadows 9

"Lois McMaster Bujold and Being a Grand Master"
by LaShawn Wanak 13

"Give the Family My Love"
by A. T. Greenblatt
(Nebula Award Winner, Best Short Story),
published by *Clarkesworld* 17

"The Dead, In Their Uncontrollable Power"
by Karen Osborne, published by *Uncanny* 37

"And Now His Lordship Is Laughing"
by Shiv Ramdas, published by Strange *Horizons* 55

"Ten Excerpts from an Annotated Bibliography on the Cannibal Women of Ratnabar Island"
by Nibedita Sen, published by *Nightmare Magazine* 77

"A Catalog of Storms"
by Fran Wilde, published by *Uncanny* 83

"How the Trick Is Done"
by A.C. Wise, published by *Uncanny* 99

"A Strange Uncertain Light"
by G. V. Anderson,
published by *The Magazine of Fantasy and Science Fiction*. 125

"For He Can Creep"
by Siobhan Carroll, published by *Tor.com* 173

"His Footsteps, Through Darkness and Light"
by Mimi Mondal, published by *Tor.com*.............................. 201

"The Blur in the Corner of Your Eye"
by Sarah Pinsker, published by *Uncanny*............................ 225

Excerpt: "Carpe Glitter"
by Cat Rambo (Nebula Award Winner, Best Novelette),
published by Meerkat Shorts 253

"The Archronology of Love"
by Caroline M. Yoachim, published by *Lightspeed*............. 265

Excerpt: *A Song for a New Day*
by Sarah Pinsker, published by Berkley
(Nebula Award Winner, Best Novel) 297

Excerpt: *Riverland*
by Fran Wilde, published by Abrams
(Andre Norton Nebula Award winner) 311

Excerpt: "Anxiety Is the Dizziness of Freedom"
by Ted Chiang, published by Knopf.................................. 331

Excerpt: *The Haunting of Tram Car 015*
by P. Djèlí Clark, published by *Tor.com*............................. 351

Excerpt: *This Is How You Lose the Time War*
by Amal El-Mohtar and Max Gladstone
(Nebula Award Winner, Best Novella),
published by Gallery and Saga Press............................... 367

Excerpt: "Her Silhouette, Drawn in Water"
by Vylar Kaftan, published by *Tor.com* 393

Excerpt: *The Deep* by Rivers Solomon, Daveed Diggs, William Hutson, and Jonathan Snipes, published by Gallery and Saga Press 417

Excerpt: *Catfish Lullaby* by A.C. Wise, published by Broken Eye Books 439

Biographies 459

About the Science Fiction and Fantasy Writers of America (SFWA) 467

About the Nebula Awards ® 469

Introduction

Greetings, people of Earth.

This is a moment in time, crystallized and trapped between two covers. A moment in the history and evolution of science fiction and fantasy, a moment in the social, economic, and technological progression of a vast variety of cultures. A moment of experience, of interpretation, of performance, of perception, of witness.

This is what we were like then. By the time you sit down to read this, it will already be in the past. It is a photograph, sun-faded, but preserved indefinitely. A photograph of people, of ambition, of achievement, of community. These are the stories we valued, that surprised and confronted us, that comforted and bonded us, that showed us the way forward and back. Each slate of award winners is a little time capsule, hurled into the future, to note, with extremely shiny markers, who we were.

For a moment.

Science fiction has been part of my life since before I was born. It was part of my family before I ever set foot in a convention or on an awards dais. And when science fiction has been part of, not just your life, but your whole lens through which to understand the world, for that long, you don't even remember a time when you didn't know what the Nebulas were. The honor and prestige attached to the awards reached my little mind, I suspect, quite awhile before I fully understood the astronomical phenomenon. This is a beautiful award with a long and lovely history, bringing together each generation of young trailblazers and old legends to uncover the best the field has to offer.

For a moment.

And every year is its own moment, frozen under glass no less than the orbs and glitter of the award itself.

This was 2019's moment.

It's almost incalculable to me how much the world of science fiction and fantasy has changed since I took my first hesitant steps toward becoming a part of it in 2004. I'm not just speaking about representation, though that is, of course, a profound and ongoing shift. The variety of voices, techniques, choices, and forms that make their way to the forefront of the Great Conversation and are lauded by awards is so much vaster now than it was then, in that moment, in that time, in that sun-faded photograph. We have come so far; we are telling so many different stories now, stories about ourselves and others and worlds both possible and long vanished. We are confronting injustice, ignorance, and inertia in the very real world around us and defying it with every syllable of our narratives.

Here, you will find that variety brilliantly expressed. From avant-garde time-traveling lovers of *This Is How You Lose the Time War* to the eerily prescient pandemic and illegal concerts of *A Song for a New Day,* to the strange adventure that belonging to a family truly is, so achingly on display in *Riverland, Give the Family My Love,* and *Carpe Glitter.* And a look toward beloved classics finding new forms with the *Good Omens* television series, the golden age feel of *The Outer Worlds* game, and the towering lifetime achievement of this year's grandmaster, Lois McMaster Bujold.

What I see in this photograph, in this moment, is a confrontation of and deep concern for time and family. These works were, of course, all written before 2020 shattered the familial bonds of nearly everyone on this poor traumatized blue jewel in the sky, which makes it all the more incredible

how, by chance, but not really by chance, no cultural trend is every truly blind luck, each of these works fundamentally build themselves around what it means to form bonds, create togetherness our of separateness, connect to one's own past in order to survive in the immediate disaster of the future, and find the desperately needed salvation not so much in a revelatory technology that deuses our machinas, but in each other, in our choices and connections, in a refusal to sacrifice those very precious things to the great machine.

For a moment, at least.

I tell you what, the kids are all right.

I invite you into this moment. Whether you are reading this hot off the delivery truck or in 2041 and wondering what the literary field was like in those days that seem so innocent and carefree now, but were, and I promise you this is the truth, anything but when they were our immediate reality, our precarious present. So many of these excerpts are telling you the story of 2020 and beyond before 2020 every happened. They are telling you stories about family and time. About how to not fall apart in a broken world. About how to live to see that beyond. We didn't know...except that, it seems, some of us did. Which is the great duty of a science fiction writer. To know. To see. To seem, though each work in reality came by the skin of its teeth in the rough and tumble madness of publishing and editing and publicity and just trying, *trying* to create something real and good in this world, as though they knew how things would turn out the whole time.

A beautiful act, repeated yearly, as long as that world lets us.

So come in, people of Earth, people of tomorrow, people of always. Read this moment. Run your fingertips over the dog-eared corners of this golden photograph. Remember, or learn, what it was to live and work and create at the end of the second decade of the twenty-first century.

This was the best of us then. The effort and soul and intellect contained in this volume is truly staggering. And here, in these pages, we have brought it all together to coalesce into something more. Into a gorgeous image for you to interpret.

Out of dust.

Out of hope.

Out of passion.

Out of hydrogen and helium.

Out of art and fear and imagination.

Out of clouds of color and light.

Out of so many stars.

This is a moment. This is a book. This is love and work and human souls pulled together, for a moment, by the gravity of thought, into pillars of creation.

This is a nebula.

Come in, and see how it glows.

The Best of Twines, the Worst of Rhymes: A Tale of Two C++ies (or, Why Game Writing Is Bad And Great)

by Seth Dickinson

Video games, like all fiction, depend on our emotional inability to distinguish reality from exciting lies. We know games aren't real but our *brains* don't know, if you follow me. Imagine if we were hyperrational super-beings with no response to fake stuff. Games would bore us; fiction would be an intellectual exercise, useful only for working out how we'd respond to some future situation. It would suck. On the other hand, we wouldn't spend thirty World of Warships Boat Bucks on a Biz Markie skin and authentic 'Just A Friend' horn for KMS *Bismarck.* (This essay is in no way affiliated with Lesta Studio, Wargaming.net, or the great artist Marcel Theo Hall.)

Fortunately, or otherwise, we are human beings. And human beings are a lot like video games—absolute design clusterfucks, hacked together in panic and last-minute desperation, thick patches of compromise slathered on top of technical debt caked over legacy work from the dawn of time. No time to do what's best, so just do what's least bad: the motto of natural selection and bug triage committees.

And there's no documentation, so if you want to know how it works you'll need an MRI, or a wizard.

One of the few consolations of being human is that we are not alone. This is the best and worst part of writing for video games.

It is the worst part because a game writer does not usually get the absolute control of a novelist or a poet; you cannot align everything, from sentence rhythm all the way up to character arcs and macro plot structure, into a single crystalline structure of pure genius. (Let's pretend we are pure genius.) A lot of game writing is difficult interpersonal politics. A lot of it is convincing people to listen to you, or at least reassuring them you're listening to them, especially when they plead with you to stop making their lives harder. Your leads may be too busy to give you the direction you need; your game may be changing so quickly that no one can commit to any firm answers to the big questions, like 'who is the protagonist' or 'what's going on with that giant horse in the skybox, anyway.' (Answer: the art team thought it looked cool.)

Unless you are a brave one-person developer, you must also remember that there are people downstream of you, localisation teams and editors and lawyers, whose lives you will fill with regret if you don't take their needs into account. You must take direction, and you must do your very best to execute ideas you won't always believe in. You may not own your own labor. Your characters and ideas may become corporate property, and even if you find them plucked from the depths of some codex entry you wrote to headline the entire IP years later, you won't see a dime for it. In fact, team turnover might mean no one even *knows* you created those characters. Talk about estrangement from our labor!

But you can *talk* to people. With any luck you will be surrounded by other human beings who are heads down in the same project as you and who find both use and delight in your imagination. In an industry where editors and agents are increasingly too overworked for regular check-ins, novelists work alone. But a game writer always has someone to reach out to, if only to share your misery. And that emotional and mental support isn't one-way. You can make an artist's job easier, you can give a designer a decaying heap of prose and watch them pluck gameplay concepts from the compost. Nothing is more wonderful than someone bouncing your idea back with a twist you never could've twisted on your own. What is the opposite of loneliness if not knowing others are thinking about you better than you can think about yourself?

Everyone is some kind of storyteller. This can be difficult for writers, because it means everyone thinks they know how to write—nobody imagines they're fluent in C++ or Autodesk Maya without years of training, but everyone speaks a language, and so everyone likes to think they can write stories well. Your job is not to be the One True Storyteller. Your job is to help everyone turn their story into words.

Is writing for games a job I would recommend? Not unconditionally. Even if you're lucky enough to land on a team that values writing as more than a fill-in-the-blanks exercise, turning all their placeholder strings into 'the good version', you may face crunch. Crunch, the practice of working massive overtime for weeks or months on end in order to hit immovable deadlines, is life-destroying. Part of what makes it life-destroying is that it doesn't sound so bad at first. It sounds like something you can do. I love going all in on a creative project, so what could be so bad about getting paid to do that? A lot. Writing is not hard physical labor, and it is not physically risky in the way that, say, ice road truckin' would be. But if I can say one thing in favor of hard physical labor (I got my own start working in kitchens, then college summers loading FedEx trucks), at least it releases some dopamine. At least you can put it away when you go home for the day. Game writing can be soul-witheringly hollow. It can mean staring at a screen for a hundred hours a week, trying to fill a spreadsheet of item descriptions without any idea what the items look like, what they do, or, in fact, whether anyone on your team except the poor souls in QA will ever read your work. Human beings need meaning. If you can't find some meaning in what you're doing, you will get lost. Especially in modern game development, where 'shipping' a game is just a signal to move on to working on DLC and live service updates, the crunch really may never end. Nobody wants it to be this way, but it ends up this way. If you end up in this situation, *get out*. There is nothing in that cave worth dying for.

(Indie development may come with its own kind of self-imposed crunch, especially when you've put your whole life on hold to commit to a passion project in a crowded market with 4132849 other games competing for visibility. And it can be harder to quit when the project is, in a profound way, part of you. I will say that some of the best times I've ever had in game development involved crunching on small projects with equally small audiences. But that crunch was totally voluntary, and it was work I really believed in, work I felt I had a personal stake in. All to say: game developers need unions.)

A game writer's experience strongly depends on the people around them. The games industry receives a constant influx of bright young talents who are willing to accept shitty working conditions for the chance to do what they love. This makes everyone replaceable. And oh, man, will you see replacement. (My first day at my first professional game gig, the two people sitting to my left asked me if I knew what was going on; then they were called into a corner office and I never saw them again.) In a world of constant turnover, uncertain advancement, and personal insecurity, good people can turn very. You may not be rewarded for your work if you don't fight to be seen, and fighting can get you labeled as a problem. This is harder if you're not a white man. Even at studios with strong commitments to diversity, it's inevitable that racism, sexism, and all the other intersections of prejudice creep into interpersonal interaction, often without any conscious intent. Whether we acknowledge it or not, it's those interpersonal interactions which can make the difference between a new job and a no-hire, or a comfortable happy team and a sullen bog of learned helplessness.

All this adds up to a monumental and unsolved challenge. Games are a young art, and untamed. No one *knows* how to make video games in the way that we, say, know how to write novels or short stories. There's no firm set of best practices, no clear workflow, no unified format for delivery (not compared, to, say, the conventional format of stringing sentences into paragraphs and paragraphs into scenes and scenes into a story). Any game that ships with a coherent story is a minor miracle. Any game with a truly ambitious narrative, one coherent meaning that seeps down from high-level themes right into the basic mechanics, is the proverbial airliner assembled by a tornado: except this was a tornado of people all trying their damndest to make the beast fly.

So there are reasons to love game writing, too.

People won't just read your work, they'll *do* it. They'll act based on the way you make them feel. The key trait of a game, even one that's simply about walking through and studying an environment, is feedback between the game and the player's choices—game and player each trying to model each other, and to make decisions that will help both of them work right. A reader thinks about a novel and brings it to life in their mind—but the novel can't answer in real time. A game is a live, two-way conversation. Together with art, design, audio, and the engineers that make it all work, you get the chance to dance with the player. They'll make decisions—not just big scripted ones, but subtle tactical and emotional choices about what to fear, cherish, protect and explore—influenced by the stories you've told them. The human mind is for modeling the world, and you get to help another human being build that model. Learning a game is the same as falling in love: it's about reading the choices someone else has made, and putting them in your head, and coming to know what those choices say.

I once made a Discord channel full of game modders very angry by suggesting that the most game-ish game, the True Platonic Game, would have no words at all. I'm not sure it would even have art or sound. Every aspect of its story would be delivered through decisions and mechanics. I think I still stand by this, even if such a game is sort of a silly thought experiment.

But this Ultimate Game would still have *writing*. Even without words or images, it would speak. And someone would have to write that story.

If our ability to enjoy games is an exaptive accident, a pleasant side effect of our need to imagine how future situations might play out and how others might behave, then in a very deep sense the true purpose of storytelling is to guide our choices. When you write for a game—when you add that line of flavor text which makes a player hang on to an item rather than sell it, or spare an enemy they might have killed—you are, for a moment, both a wizard and an MRI machine. You have entered their brain state and altered it. You have cast a spell and compelled a choice.

In the first Destiny game, released in 2014, I included a short vignette about a character striking a brief truce with one of the alien Fallen as they both fought off a more terrible foe. It ended sadly, but that moment of connection with an alien (who, in the game world of Destiny 1, we only met as an implacably hostile foe) struck a chord. As I type this, Destiny 2's ongoing story sees the player's city accepting Fallen who want to live in peace and work for reconciliation. You can go into the game world and find them. Artists modeled them, animators rigged them, audio gave them voice, engineers made them render and network properly. People on social media are even now (quite viciously) arguing over the ethics and practical concerns of living alongside a species who've for so long been a genocidal antagonist.

I had nothing to do with this story. I did not decide on it, write it, produce it, or anything else. But I do believe that it has roots in that brief vignette I told in a few paragraphs of text in Destiny 1. My little contribution was picked up and greatened by writers and artists and investment designers and the producers who keep them all afloat and by everyone at the studio who ever touched this work and even by the player who loved the idea of sympathetic Fallen and spent years asking for more. It is not mine any more. It is ours.

That is the best part of game writing.

Queering Chaos

By Foz Meadows

At some point during my teens, I stumbled on a quote which, courtesy of the early noughties internet, was misattributed to Voltaire: *Without order, nothing can exist – without chaos, nothing can evolve*. Now as then, it's a sentiment I find compelling, and as I watched the opening sequence of *Good Omens*, episode 3: Hard Times, which documents the 6000-year-long association between the demon Crowley and the angel Aziraphale, it came instantly to mind. As depicted in *Good Omens*, heaven is the source of order and hell the source of chaos; and yet, despite the opposition of their respective sides, it's through the initially pragmatic friendship of Crowley and Aziraphale that affairs on Earth progress in what is ultimately a very human fashion. As, too, does their relationship, which is played as a romance without ever being explicitly confirmed as one – which makes it all the more pleasing to learn that the quote of which they'd reminded me is, in fact, the work of Oscar Wilde.

Or so says the internet of 2021, at least; this may well be another inaccuracy. Either way, the line itself remains applicable, winking at the same cheerful blasphemy (as some will see it) which characterizes both the *Good Omens* TV series and the novel of the same name. Which is more scandalous: the idea of an angel/demon romance, or one in which both participants present as male? As a queer atheist with considerably more than one foot in the world of SFF, my default is to see nothing wrong with either – and yet the idea that either option should be taboo is what the narrative sets out, gently, humorously, to challenge. By definition, heaven and hell should be absolutes, and while *Good Omens* offers us glimpses of them as such, they are more frequently – and compellingly – depicted as *hierarchies*, an achingly human concept which is nonetheless (in the literal, Biblical sense) canonical to their functioning.

The narrative leap from *hierarchy* to *bureaucracy* feels entirely natural: who amongst us hasn't had to deal with one masquerading as the other? It only makes sense that, as comparatively junior members of their respective hierarchies, both of whom are pushing them for updates on and progress regarding dominion over Earth, Crowley and Aziraphale would end up having more in common with each other than with their bosses. That it's all done with a comedic touch does nothing to undermine the quiet relatability of Aziraphale's fear of heavenly paperwork, Crowley's wariness of retribution. And yet there's a romance to it, too, adding a layer of tenderness to what might otherwise be a very well-executed panto: what does it mean, to love someone you've been emphatically told you shouldn't? In *Good Omens*, the metaphor is literalised along multiple axes, which takes some doing: when Aziraphale severs ties with Crowley at the end of Hard Times, it plays in every respect like a queer breakup, where one party (Aziraphale) is still wrestling with the internalized shame and fear that comes from fraternizing with (wanting) another man (Crowley) who represents everything he's ever been warned away from. Present the exact same scene with the Biblical/SFFnal context removed, and there are still those who'd instinctively cast one man as an angel in rightful fear of demonic temptation.

And hanging over it all, the knowledge that the world will

end – that even heaven wants it to end, to wash out the evils and start again. More than once during their flashback sequence, Crowley remarks that some act of divine retribution or other endorsed by god seems more hellish than divine. "Not kids, you can't kill kids," he says, horrified, as Noah fills the Ark, a sentiment later paralleled by his argument with Aziraphale over what, exactly should happen to Adam Young, the prepubescent antichrist. Aziraphale wants Crowley to kill him, so that heaven won't have blood on its hands (the great flood, of course, doesn't count) – and what does it mean, really, to trust unquestioning in the goodness of even a heavenly hierarchy? When and why should obedience be valued more than knowledge?

In *Good Omens*, the world exists because of the order of heaven, but by the end of the show, it's saved by the chaos of hell. Adam Young – "half angel, half devil, all human," as the child antichrist is described in the book – opts not to break reality. Like Crowley and Aziraphale, he is fond of the world, and the great ineffable plan for a holy war ultimately weighs less than a child's desire to see his friends grow up, and to grow up in turn. To *evolve*, as Wilde said (or as someone said), and in so doing right the wrongs of those who came before him, like the nuclear reactors Adam vanishes in his sleep. It's Anathema Device, inheritor of the Nice and Accurate Prophecies of Agnes Nutter, who tells Adam about nuclear reactors, along with other man-made evils, prompting him, however subconsciously, to change a world he has otherwise been intent on keeping static, as we learn through the research of witchfinder army apprentice Newton Pulsifer. Adam's hometown of Tadfield has always had perfect weather for the time of year, the landscape bending to Adam's subliminal, childish desire to keep things ideal. Perfect. Unchanging – until, like the looming specter of adolescence, the apocalypse comes and lets the chaos in.

But chaos is not the end of all things; at least, not when leashed by intention. Balance is restored, and in this new, same-yet-different world, Aziraphale and Crowley return to their same-yet-different romance. It's difficult for a single episode of any show to perfectly encapsulate the themes of the whole – that is, by and large, why shows require episodes, plural – but Hard Times comes very close.

I think Oscar Wilde would've liked it.

Lois McMaster Bujold and Being a Grand Master

By LaShawn Wanak

I am going to let you in on a secret. I haven't figured out what it means to be a successful writer yet.

Success in genre fiction can be measured in a multitude of ways. The number of sales of a debut novel. Subsequent reprintings of said novel. 5-starred reviews on Amazon Awards. Name recognition. Name recognition of the writer's significant characters. Fanfiction made in the writer's universe.

In between the financial and the popularity successes, only one success is actually controlled by the writer. This is craft. Mastering craft allows a writer to shape sentences together into ideas, characters and environments that only exist in a reader's mind. A writer specializing in our field of science fiction and fantasy must know how to turn phrases, chart dialogue, paint environments, wrangle creatures of their own making, and do it all in a way to so that readers stays riveted until they reach the very last page and they stumble back into their own realities, blinking and stunned.

We writers are told that we can only control what we write. We can't control anything else beyond that. Whether our works will be picked up by publishers. Whether it would be actually read. All we can control is putting our butts in chairs, finishing our work, and sending it out. And then do it again. And again. Ad infinitum. This is where most of us are, myself included.

A Grand Master, then, is someone who has not only done this throughout their writing career, but their work help shape and define the SF/F genre as a whole.

Lois McMaster Bujold exemplifies this, which is why she was chosen to become the 36th Grand Master for the 2020 Nebulas. She is best known for her space opera *Vorkosigan Saga*, which follows the life of her most significant character Miles Vokosigan; his life and those connected to him span over more than twenty-five novels, including omnibuses. She is also known for her *World of the Five Gods* series, as well as her more recent tetralogy, *The Sharing Knife*. Her books had garnered seven Hugos, and she has won Nebulas for *Falling Free, The Mountains of Mourning,* and *Paladin of Souls*. Her works has been translated into over twenty languages, and by becoming a grand master, she joins other notable women (though still a scant few) blessed with that title: Andre Norton, Ursula K Le Guin, Anne McCaffrey, Connie Willis, Jane Yolen, and for 2021, Nalo Hopkinson.

In the above paragraph, what I have not mentioned is the *work* Bujold put in. What we don't see are the submissions and the waiting, the books that sold less than others. In her 2020 interview with Clarkesworld, she briefly mentions the slumps and snags she encountered, but over time managed to overcome.

But it's more than just the writing. If craft was all that was needed to sell books, we'd all be rich. What makes our genre unique is that we are not just writing to entertain. Science fiction, fantasy, and all the permutations of other genres—romance, horror, western, even (gasp!) literary – are more than just stories. They are ways for us to discuss events in our world, imaginary sandboxes for us to dream, metaphorical conversations. Bujold noted in her Worldcon

Speech in 2008 that "To my mind, a genre is "any group of works in close conversation with one another." I like this definition for its inclusiveness–because there are genres in painting and architecture and music and a host of other human arts as well. This is also a working definition with the emphasis on the working part, genre from the creators' point of view."

Writing stories give us the chance to have those conversations. Even painful ones. Bujold paved the way for voices who are underheard, the marginalized. Women, BIPOC, disabled. Those who have been shut out of writing SF/F are now coming into our own. BIPOC and queer writers are being published. But in order to do so, we need to continue doing so for years. We must be willing to not just contribute to the conversation, but to do so on an ongoing basis.

As a writer, this terrifies me. Not be willing to have the conversation even when one is tired or bruised by the ongoing conflict happening on social media, or the latest controversy. To be able to despite all and dealing with that to *continue writing and making stories.*

To be a Grand Master is to have tenacity. The will, despite it all, to continue to write, and sending work out, saying under our breaths, *if this doesn't sell, it doesn't matter. Maybe the next one* will. And keep doing it over and over. Even if publishing methods change. Even if people criticize and badmouth the work. Write and submit. Rinse and repeat. And continue to add your voice to the conversation.

These days, Bujold continues to write. Nowadays she focuses on novellas. She stays in contact with her fans through Goodreads and has adapted to the fluctuating changes in the publishing world by publishing through Amazon. One day, once the pandemic is over (because Bujold was awarded Grand Master in 2020, so of course I have to mention the pandemic) I hope to sit down with her.

We'll bond, I'm sure, over the joys of anime and fanfiction, and I would ask her how writers like me could continue the conversation and continue to write stories. My guess is her answer would be similar to the one she gave in Clarkesworld, "I don't see science fiction as being a platonic ideal toward which all works and writers should convergently aspire. I see it as a tapestry of many individual writers' threads which, taken together, give the illusion of a picture. I only spin my own thread."

Then again, she may give an entirely different answer. From one successful writer to another.

Give the Family My Love

By A. T. Greenblatt

I'm beginning to regret my life choices, Saul. Also, hello from the edge of the galaxy.

Also, surprise! I know this isn't what you had in mind when you said "Keep in touch, Hazel" but this planet doesn't exactly invoke the muse of letter writing. The muse of extremely long voice messages however . . .

So. Want to know what's this world's like? Rocky, empty, and bleak in all directions, except one. The sky's so stormy and green it looks like I'm trudging through the bottom of an algae-infested pond. I've got this 85-million-dollar suit between me and the outside, but I swear, I'm suffocating on the atmosphere. Also, I'm 900 meters away from where I need to be with no vehicle to get me there except my own two legs.

So here I am. Walking.

Sorry to do this to you, Saul, but if I don't talk to someone—well, freak out at someone—I'm not going to make it to the Library. And like hell I'm going to send a message like this back to the boys on the program. You, at least, won't think less of me for this. You know that emotional meltdowns are part of my process.

850 meters. I should have listened to you, Saul.

And yes, I know how cliché that sounds. I've been to enough dinner parties and heard enough dinner party stories, especially once people learned that I'm possibly the last astronaut ever. At least now I have an excellent excuse for turning down invitations. "I'd *love* to come, but I'm currently thirty-two and a half lightyears away from Earth. Give your family my love."

Of course, they won't get the message until six months too late.

Wow, that's depressing. See, this is why I told the people in R&D not to give me too many facts and figures, but they're nerds, you know? They can't help themselves. Despite best intentions, it sort of spills out of them sometimes.

And it's not like I can forget.

750 meters.

The good news is I can actually see the Library. So if I died here 742 meters from the entrance, I can expire knowing I was the first human to set eyes on this massive infrastructure of information in person.

Oh god. I might actually die out here, Saul. Not that the thought hasn't crossed my mind before, but the possibility becomes a lot more tangible when you're *walking* across an inhospitable alien landscape.

Also, my fancy astronaut suit is making some worrying noises. I don't think it's supposed to sound like it's wheezing.

675 meters. God, Saul, I really hope this mission is worth it.

Have I told about the Library, yet? No, I haven't, have I? And I've only been talking about this, for what, years now? Well, you should know, it's not what I expected. Which is stupid because alien structures are supposed to be alien and not castles or temples, like with steeples and everything. Shut up, Saul. (I know you're laughing, or will be laughing at this six months from now.) I don't regret reading all those fantasy sagas when we were kids. Only that I didn't get to read more.

But you want to know what the Library looks like. Well, I've climbed mountains that feel like anthills next to this building. It sort of looks like a mountain too. An ugly misshapen mountain, full of weird windows and jutting walls. It's shiny and smooth from some angles and gritty and dull from others. It gives me the shivers.

Which is not really surprising. This is an alien world with alien architecture full of all that alien and not so alien knowledge just waiting to be learned. More information than the starry-eyed Homo sapiens ever dreamed there was possible to know.

500 meters.

Saul, I'm getting concerned about my suit. My left arm isn't bending at the elbow anymore. Not that I need my left arm to keep walking, but it's a bit disquieting, in a panic-inducing sort of way. God, this was so much easier when all I had to do was rely on the Librarians' technology to get me here. Now, I have to rely on humanity's own questionable designs to get me this last kilometer. But that's the Librarians' rules for getting in. "You have to get your representative to our entrance safely through a most unforgiving landscape." Turns out that outside of my very expensive outfit there's an absurdly high atmospheric pressure, corrosive gases, wild temperature fluctuations between shady and light patches, et cetera, et cetera. Also, the ground is just rocky enough to surprise you.

I don't want to think about what'll happen if I trip. Can't think about it. I wasn't a physics major before, and this is not the time to start.

350 meters.

I mean, I *knew* the dangers signing up. I *knew* this was going to be the hardest part of the trip. (I mean, how could it not be? The Librarians figured out how to travel lightyears in a matter of months. And that's just for starters.) But I was the best candidate for the job and I had to do *something*, Saul. I know you think otherwise, but I haven't given up on humanity. This isn't running away.

I wish I could run right now because now there seems to be a layer of fine dust coating the inside of my suit. Oh my god.

250 meters.

Shut up, Saul. I can hear you telling me in that big brother voice of yours: "It's okay if you freak out, Hazel, just not right now" like you did when we were kids. And you're right, I can't freak out, because the worst thing that could happen right now, aside from dying, is having an asthma attack from the dust. Okay, okay, okay. I just need to keep calm, keep focused, keep moving.

175 meters.

There's definitely something wrong with my suit. The coating of dust in my suit has gone from "minimal" to "dense" and I have no idea which piece of equipment I'm breathing in.

Don't panic, Hazel.

Don't panic, don't panic, don't panic.

Can't panic. I'm picturing the R&D nerds when I tell them about this. They're going to completely melt down when they hear that their precious design didn't hold up as well as planned. Good, retaliation hyperventilating. Because that's what happens when your best candidate for the job is an asthmatic anthropologist.

100 meters.

Okay, I'm almost there. I can see the door. This faulty, pathetic excuse for a space suit only has to last me a few more minutes. I just need to keep walking. Soon I'll be safely inside and reunited with my beautiful, beautiful inhaler.

75 meters.

Well. Hopefully, they let me in.

So . . . here's the thing Saul. The Librarians never actually gave us a guarantee that they would admit me. They said it was up to the Librarians who live in the Library. (Apparently, they are a different sect from the explorer Librarians that I met and traveled with and well, the two sects don't always agree.) But the explorer faction gave me a ride here, so that's got to count for something, right?

Thing is, this *stupid* suit was supposed to withstand a walk to the Library and back to the ship if I needed it. Looks like my safety net isn't catching much now.

25 meters.

I'm sorry I didn't tell you this before I left, but I'm not sorry either. The knowledge that I can potentially gain here is worth the risk. It's worth every cent of that 85 million and if I'm going to die on the steps, well that sucks. But okay, at least we tried.

10 meters.

I'm not sorry, Saul. Just scared.

Hopefully the Librarians let me in, but if you don't get another transmission from me, you know what happened. Give the rest of the family my love.

Okay. Here we go.

• • •

Have you ever been in love, Saul?

Yes, I know you love Huang. I've seen the way you look at her and she looks at you. But remember the moment when you looked at her like that for the first time and you thought, "Holy crap. This is it. I've finally found it."

Yeah. The Library, Saul, is magnificent.

And . . . difficult to describe. It's sort of like the outside of the Library. It changes depending on what angle you look at it from.

When I left the decontamination chamber (at least, I think that's what it was?), I stepped into the main room and everything was dimly lit and quiet. The Library's Librarians—which I later learned preferred to be called the Archivists because they are *not* the Librarians who travel the universe—were milling around the massive room. They looked similar to the explorer Librarians we met on Earth; tall, lanky, humanoid-like bodies. But they all had long, shimmering whiskers that the explorer Librarians didn't (couldn't?) grow out. Their whiskers went all the way down to their splayed, ten fingered feet.

The room was surprisingly empty except for these installations in the middle of the room that could either have been art or furniture. So you know, sort of like university libraries back home.

I was just starting to breathe easier, my inhaler *finally* kicking in after that walk from hell, when the light changed and suddenly I was standing next to this fern/skyscraper thing that smelled weirdly like hops and was a violent shade of purple. It became ridiculously humid and the room was filled with what I can only assume were plants. Even the Librarians—I mean, Archivists—changed. Now, they had four legs and two arms and were covered in this lush white hair.

I reached out and touched one of the ferns next to me and it was like touching a prickly soap bubble, which was not what I was expecting. But then again, I wasn't expecting it to reach out and tap me back on the forehead either.

I think I swore. I'm not sure because everything changed again. Suddenly, I was shivering and standing on something like a frozen ocean that's trapped an aurora in the floe. The air was nosebleed dry and smelled like rust and I could see pale things moving underneath the ice. The Archivists themselves had become round and translucent, floating a meter in the air.

And the room kept changing. It was terrifying . . . and completely amazing, Saul.

So there I was, gaping like an idiot, simultaneously too afraid to move and too busy trying to take all of it in. In my slack-jawed stupidity, it took me far too long to notice that two things didn't change. First, the Archivists always kept their rubbery fluidity and their whiskers. And those little lights never moved.

Crap, I'm not describing this well. I forgot to mention the lights. There were thousands of them, like miniature stars, scattered seemingly at random around the room, drifting, hanging out in midair. I think they were what made everything change, because when an Archivist would go up and touch one with their long whiskers, bam! new setting.

So get this: When I finally mustered up a little courage and asked a passing Archivist what those lights were, they said: "Every known solar system worth learning about."

I would say I've died and gone to a better place, but I've used up my quota of terrible clichés just getting here.

Wait, that's not true. I still have one awful one left.

I stood in that room for a while, longer than I should have, but the truth is I was trying to work up the nerve to introduce myself to the head Archivist. But I never did because eventually they came up and greeted me. It was one of the most nerve-wracking conversations I've ever had. Between the steroids from my inhaler and pure, uncut anxiety, my hands were like a nine on the Richter scale.

You see, Saul, the Archivists are not to be messed with. Like seriously. Do not contradict them, raise your voice, be anything less than painfully respectful. They may look squishy, but they can dismantle you down to your atoms, capture you in a memory tablet, and put your unbelieving ass on a shelf where they keep all of the boring information that no one ever checks out. And they'll keep you sentient too.

Or sentient enough. I hope.

Fortunately, my interview was fairly short. The head Archivist found me worthy enough, I guess, and gave me very, *very* limited access to the Library. When they led me to the section with our solar system, I sort of wished you were here Saul, so you could have taken a picture of my expression at that moment. Pretty sure you would qualify it as "priceless." Because the size of this room, you could fit a small town in here.

And get this, the Archivist was *apologetic*. "We've only just begun to study you and we thought you would prefer to see our research in physical form," they said, "Hopefully you can find what you need in our meager collection."

Except, here's the thing. They probably have more information on us than we have on ourselves.

Actually, I'm counting on it.

• • •

Everything here is so strange, Saul. The light is too colorless and the air tastes weird. The walls and the shelves seem to bend slightly. It's all new and deeply alien.

It's wonderful.

The Archivists have set up something that's not too different from a studio apartment in the corner of the section on sea coral. It has running water and artificial sunlight and all eleven seasons of *M*A*S*H* on a TV that looks like it came from the 1980s. I have this theory that my living quarters are part of some junior Archivist's final thesis project, but I'm probably just culturally projecting. On the bright side, if they picked the 80s, they could have done much worse than *M*A*S*H*.

I'm sure in a few weeks I'll start having terrible bouts of homesickness and will send you even longer, possibly more rambling messages questioning every life decision leading up to this point. But right now, being in the Library is sort of liberating. In a let's-call-my-big-brother-because-my-new-studio-home-is-way-too-quiet sort of way.

Oh. I got your first message today. Remember the one you recorded six months ago, about three days after I left? I knew you were pissed, but wow, Saul. A backstabbing, alien-loving, wheezing, useless coward? You had three whole days to think of something and *that's* the best you could do?

I know you didn't mean it. I know you're only half angry at me, half angry at our dying planet, and half angry at, well . . .

I got a message from Huang too. She told me about the most recent miscarriage. I'm so sorry, Saul. One day the two of you are going to be the world's best parents. I believe that more than I believe in your international reforestation project, which is definitely going to work.

And I get how you think I'm abandoning you and Earth for a sterile, stable library, but I needed to come here. I have this working theory about the Librarians. Wanna hear it? Too bad, I'm going to tell you anyway.

See, the more time I spend with them, the more I'm convinced Librarians could have obliterated us if they wanted to. But they haven't. In fact, they've put a painstaking amount of effort into studying us and making first contact with all the right people. Asking those people just the right questions like: "We managed to save the information before this university archive burned or this datacenter got flooded. Would you like to retrieve it?" Questions that convinced us to put this mission together.

Which leads me to believe they're trying to help us.

I know you're rolling your eyes, Saul. Have I ever told you that you always look like a moody teenager when you do that? Yeah, I know I have. But hear me out, I'm trying to tell you something important.

Please.

Do you remember our first big argument over this mission? You said that anyone who comes to Earth while in the middle of an environmental collapse can't be trusted. I agree. Except, the first Librarian I ever met told me that the Library was built as a beacon for all sentient life in the universe. A place where researchers could come and learn about lost discoveries. And past mistakes.

I can hear you saying: "And you were naïve enough to blindly trust them, Hazel?" No, Saul, I'm not. Before I was picked for this crazy mission, I was just there to help first contact go smoothly, being one of the few remaining anthropologists who have studied interactions between vastly different cultures. I had zero interest in becoming an astronaut; space travel always seemed too risky and uncomfortable to me. But the Librarians were impressed by my commitment to cultural preservation. The space program was impressed by my ridiculously good memory. And I became convinced that if I didn't go, someone else would eventually slip and we'd be adding "total societal collapse" along with "environmental disaster" to the list of humanity's problems.

You see, Saul, there's so much that I'm witnessing in the Library that I'm not telling you, because the Librarians' advanced tech would devastate our underdeveloped society.

Which didn't stop the people in R&D from telling me over and over again to take careful notes on everything I observe and send them the information on the down low, of course. I was sent here to reclaim any research and history that could help us save ourselves, but I think they're hoping that I'll learn about useful alien tech too. I'm tempted to send them a report that says: Sorry nerds, it's all just magic.

No, Saul, not really. My official reports are going to be *way* more straightforward and professional. You know, double the facts and half the amount of sarcasm. But I think I'm going to keep sending these messages to you, for a while at least. All this is not actually why I "ran away" from home.

Really, it was just a good excuse to get out of commuting in Chicago traffic.

Just kidding. It was the Great Plains fires. There's only so much smoke and ash an asthmatic researcher can deal with before she ships out.

Only sort of kidding.

I have a list of things I need to investigate for the scientists back home, but for now, I think I'm going to call it a day. Looking at the amazing amount of information around me makes me realize how much we've lost. How the Librarians managed to recover all this is a mystery I don't intend to solve, but hopefully they managed to save the research I'm looking for.

Have I mentioned how much of this is mission is chalked up to hope?

• • •

Hello, Saul, I'm lost. No, that's not true, my memory won't let me get lost, but I imagine this is what it feels like. The rows of memory tablets are identical, if you don't pay attention to the Archivists' annotations at every turn. I can't actually read them because they just look like miniature sculptures, but I remember the small differences. The Archivists were kind enough to give me a basic map with a basic translation of where to find things. But Librarians' basics and human basics are not the same thing.

God, I thought finding the research would be the easy part of this trip, but I might never find my way out of the single-celled organism section. So, give the family my love.

I know what you're thinking. Yes, I do. You're thinking:

"How about you come home then, Hazel, and help me with these seedlings?" because we've been having this argument for what, ten years now?

No, not quite. Nine years, 10 months, and twenty-seven days, since that first fight over dinner.

Yeah, Saul. My memory is my own worst enemy sometimes.

By the way, I got your second message today. Apology accepted. But I can't come back, Saul. I barely started my information recovery project. Some good stuff got destroyed this last decade.

Like Dr. Ryu's research. If I can find it. If it's here at all.

God, this message is depressing. Hey, here's something cool I learned today; the kitchen cabinets produce whatever food I'm thinking about and the twenty some blank books in the living room become whatever I want to read. It really is like magic. Everything a human needs and all the books a girl can want.

I'm not coming home, Saul.

• • •

Well, it's been a week and while I *still* haven't found Dr. Ryu's research, I've found plenty of other interesting things here. Like patents and working concepts of solar powered vehicles and papers on regenerating corn seed that needs two times the amount of CO2 for photosynthesis. We had so many opportunities to stop things before they got terrible, Saul. And we missed them all.

Honestly, the wealth of information here is mind-blowing. The Librarians are like the universe's most organized hoarders. They've saved everything from road construction projects to packing and advertising protocols for the garment industry. And get this, every time I activate a memory table, the information is projected around me. Sometimes the entire aisle transforms and I literally get lost in my work. Which is why there's been a long gap since my last message. Sorry about that, Saul.

Don't laugh, but I spent all of yesterday in the children's literature section. All the stories there came to life too; old houses covered in vines and chocolate factories and little engines that could. It was fantastic, Saul. And completely depressing. Because as I sat there surrounded by those hopeful stories, it hit me that your grandchildren might not even know these stories exist. Yes, I know you disagree. But I'm a learned anthropologist and a general pessimist and I'm scared.

I asked an Archivist if this is how they store all their information. They asked if I'd be offended if they laughed and showed me the memory tablet that contained all the knowledge of the Library. It was about the size of paperback romance novel.

"Our information would be inaccessible to you otherwise," the Archivist explained. "All of your search engines are either too crude or too biased."

"But didn't this take you forever to build?"

"No," they said, but I must not have looked convinced. "Magic," they added.

Saul, I think the alien race of information scientists are listening to these recordings. So whatever you do, don't reply back with anything you don't want recorded for posterity.

"Why is the Library so large then?" I asked.

And here's where the story gets really depressing, Saul.

They told me that once this planet, the inhospitable place that's just a wasteland and a massive Library now, was full of life. There were once billions of Librarians. Now, there's only a few thousand. Before they became the masters of information science of the known universe, the Librarians ended up destroying their planet too.

The first Librarians I ever met told me the Library is a beacon for sentient life in the galaxy, except now I know it's not just a beacon for other species. The reason why the Library's so big, Saul, is that most of the Archivists and Librarians live here too.

They couldn't save their planet either.

I can hear you asking me why I bothered coming here if I'm going to be stubbornly bleak about the future and it's not an easy thing you demanded, brother mine, and I'm trying to tell you in my circular, rambling way, that I . . .

I . . .

Saul. I need to call you back. I think I finally found Dr. Ryu's research.

• • •

I've got it, oh my god, I'm so relieved. It was a fight to get it, though. No, Saul, I'm not exaggerating. Stop rolling your eyes.

Remember when I said the Archivists could keep their information sentient? Well, she was sentient enough, Saul.

When I accessed the memory tablet, the researcher herself appeared so real and sharp I could see the gray strands in her hair and the clear gloss on her fingernails. She didn't look thrilled to see me and I should've taken it as a warning, but I was way too excited.

"Are you Dr. Yumi Ryu?" I asked. (Gushed would be more accurate.)

"Up to the age of 53," she answered.

"Amazing! It's great to finally meet you, Dr. Ryu. I want to ask you everything. What's it like being archived by the Librarians? No, wait, can you tell me about your reforesting research first?"

For some reason, Saul, my rambling didn't put her at ease. "Why?" she asked, her expression suspicious.

"Um, well, because the news back home isn't good. Most of the North Pacific rain forest has been destroyed by a combination of drought and wildfires. Including your original research at UBC."

She didn't seem surprised by this, just sad. "And where is your team, Ms. . . . ?"

"Hazel Smith. It's just me."

She frowned, the suspicion on her face growing. "They sent a single astronaut? Why?"

"Resources and funds. Both are extremely limited these days."

"Why you then?"

"Because I'm a researcher too, Dr. Ryu, and I'm dedicated to preserving human society. Also, because I have an extraordinary memory, especially for data and details, and don't need batteries."

Ryu arched an eyebrow. Out of nowhere, a memory tablet about the size of a romance novel appeared in her hands. She stared it intently.

"What are you doing?" I asked, not getting a good vibe from this.

"Reading your articles, academic and otherwise. Being part of the Library, Ms., excuse me, Dr. Smith, means I can check out materials too."

Suddenly, I knew how this conversation would go. It would be like those awful dinner parties that ended in silent awkwardness when people asked why I didn't have kids. But there was nothing I could do, except try not to chew on my fingernails. In all of human culture, there's nothing more uncomfortable than standing there while someone else reads your work.

But if anthropology has taught me anything, Saul, it is

that human beings can always surprise you.

"Wow," Dr. Ryu said and the tablet disappeared from her hands. "You have a depressing view on human nature."

I've always hated having this conversation, so I stuck my hand in my pockets and said: "I'm just going off history."

She nodded. "For what it's worth, I agree."

Color me stunned, Saul. "So will you tell me about your research?"

Ryu stared at me hard, with that critical eye that only people who spend too much time in labs analyzing details can pull off.

"No," she said.

No. That's what she really said. After traveling thirty-two and a half lightyears for research like this. I won't lie, Saul, for a brief second I considered smashing the memory tablet.

"You serious?" I said.

"Yes, Dr. Smith. I've spent most of my professional career fighting politicians, big businesses, home developers, farmers. Anyone who didn't like the idea of giving up their land and returning it to forests, to try to reverse some of the damage we've done. I can't tell you how many times people tried to destroy this research."

"I'm not here to destroy anything, Dr. Ryu. I've given up too much for that."

"And what did you give up, Dr. Smith?"

"Earth. Everyone I know and love. I've risked my life for this information!" I said. In hindsight, maybe a little too defensively.

"No, that's running away," she replied. Yeah, she really said that to me, Saul. "Why are you really here?"

I sighed and used your classic line. "Because it's hope for the future that keeps us going."

"And who do you have hope for, Dr. Smith? Because from

what I've read, you don't paint a hopeful picture."

I didn't know what else to do. So, I told her, Saul. Everything I've been trying to tell you.

• • •

There aren't many defining moments in my life. Mostly, I think defining moments are clichés in hindsight. So maybe this is too, but do you remember that summer, ten years ago, when everything burned? Yeah, hard to forget.

I'd just gotten my first master's degree and wildfires in northern Washington were raging, and there was a trail you could take up a mountain that was still a safe distance away, but you could witness the worst fires in history firsthand. It was only an hour drive from campus. And I was frustrated and scared, but also curious. So I figured what the hell.

I took this guy with me. No, you've never met him, Saul.

We walked up that mountain together, though the ash made for awful traction.

It wasn't love and we both knew it. That was one of the many, many rules I broke to myself that summer. But I liked him and he liked me. And in that moment, that was enough. Good enough. The world was on fire and right then, I was too grateful to have someone who would climb a mountain with me just to watch the world ending.

Mortality makes you reckless sometimes, Saul.

Eventually the smoke got so bad that my asthma couldn't take it. He practically carried me back down.

Two months later, he went back home to Colorado, where there were a few trees left and I spent that fall sobbing and wheezing. Which made sense when I took a pregnancy test.

I chose. And I don't regret that choice, Saul. Except three days, eighteen hours, and twelve minutes later, you called and told me about the first child you and Huang wouldn't have after all.

I'm sorry I didn't tell you before, Saul. But I'm not sorry either. I was twenty-three, and though I could repeat back textbooks verbatim, I consistently lost my keys and forgot to eat. And after that summer, it was hard to see myself with a future and much less, a future for a kid. I know you're disappointed in me because you believe that no opportunity should be wasted. You think every life, even the cockroaches in the shed, should have a go at it. You've always believed in a future on Earth, Saul. Where I saw ashes, you saw fertile soil.

That's what I told Dr. Ryu. I told her all about you and Huang and your relentless perseverance and hope. I think she saw a kindred spirit in you or maybe just the right strain of stubbornness. So, she agreed to share her research with you. We're going to transcribe a little every day. Her memory tablet makes the Library's aisles transform into thriving forests. It is truly beautiful.

Consider this part one of my gift to you, Saul, because like hell am I going to apologize for the choices that brought me here.

Part two is that one of the benefits of becoming the last astronaut was getting a ridiculous stipend from the government. Well, more like a life insurance payout, because I'm going to be here for a long time. Hopefully not forever, but there's a lot of lost information here and the Archivists apparently are used to long-term guests.

I told you I had one last, terrible cliché and it's the worst one of all. The one where the astronaut doesn't come home.

Saul, I want you to use that money to start that family you and Huang always wanted.

Honestly, I'm still not convinced we can save Earth, but you are, and that works for me. So, I'll keep searching and sending home the information I find and maybe, between the two of us, that'll be enough.

So, give the family my love.

The Dead, In Their Uncontrollable Power

by Karen Osborne

The funeral is nearly over when the dead captain explodes.

Roses turn to shrapnel. The cathedral is lost in fire. I am drenched in blood. Bone buries itself in the wall next to my head, my arm, my howling, open mouth. I am standing at the back of the room where a sin-eater's child belongs, and that is why I live when everyone else dies.

I used to be a girl. Now I am a *hundred.* The dead whisper me awake and stay with me while I dream. The oldest have forgotten their names, but never their rage or their jealousy. The newest bicker in my brain like they're still alive: blood-stained Madelon, scandal-tongued Pyar, power-mad Absolon, all of them captains of our broken and beautiful spacebound Home.

My destiny was always this: to drink the sin-cup and to hold the sins of the captains in my body where they cannot harm our people on their journey to Paradise. I can stand in the cathedral under the wheeling stars until my feet give out, or pray until my throat shreds with the effort, but truth is truth. The captains must be sinless. They must lead our generation ship with confidence, with a mind tuned to moral truth. Our new captain, Bethen, is responsible for the hundred thousand lives that breathe inside the hull and all the lives that will come after. Someone else must take her family's sins upon herself, lest the dead walk and breach our hurtling world to black vacuum. Someone else must rock themselves to sleep, white-knuckled, licking spittle from their lips, so Bethen can lead.

That someone is me.

This is the bombing: I am covered in blood. In chunks of wet meat. My own memories of this horror will still be worse than anything broken Absolon shows me. I wipe my face, my hands, my hair, but there is blood everywhere. There are rose petals, shredded, still burning, at my feet. My hands are shaking. I am not sure they are my hands. I am screaming. I am not sure it is my voice. I look around for my father.

I cannot find my father.

Gossip rules steerage in the days following the bombing. Those of us who survived drink too much, trying to kill the memories. Police from first class sweep through the steerage dormitory where I used to live, flipping mattresses and shoving workers against the walls. A mutiny, an assassination, plain and able terrorism: this abomination is unheard of inside the hull of Home. There has never been an uprising against the dazzling mercy of first class. Why would there be, when the captain of our ship sees only the truth of beautiful things?

We wonder. But here in steerage, we can do little more than that. So we eat. We talk. We sleep. We work, in hydroponics and the maintenance gangs. The elders are merciful, and even let me go back to the deck-scrub team for a while, until the sins in my bloodstream find their way to my brain and I can no longer control the things I do and say. I open my mouth to warn them: *you cannot trust the captains, there* have *been mutinies, there* have *been so many deaths, I have seen children pushed from airlocks—*

—but then Absolon fills my mouth with obscenities instead of truth and Madelon makes me piss my pants in the middle of the workday. The elders tell me I am scaring the children and put me out of the common dormitory. I try to scrawl my bloody truths on paper so everyone can know what is really going on, but Pyar slips his fingers into mine, and all that comes out are drawings of stuffed animals with knife-cut throats and bouquets of broken roses, and then he makes me rip it all into small chunks and eat it anyway.

The people in steerage know I have the truth burning an abyss in my head. Why do they turn away? Why can't they listen?

Why do they think I can handle it when they cannot?

I dream about this day. The bombing.

I dream about this day all the time.

"Mey."

The sacristan is bleeding from his belly, but he knows his duty even through his pain; he knows what he must do. He was kind to me before all this. He takes my hand; it is wet with blood, and he tugs me towards the ruined altar, under the windowed canopy, under the streaking stars. Somewhere in the part of my brain that is not screaming, I know this is what must be done. He is a sacristan and this is a funeral and I am the last sin-eater.

I know I am the last, because the bloody mess he has just asked me to step over used to be my father.

My father didn't mean to have me. He wanted to end the cycle. He never wanted to know that a child of his would have to go through the horrors he experienced. I was a mistake. My father did love me, though, and before he died he taught me to paint the sin-eye on my forehead—the red lid, the white iris, the black center—and live at the mercy of steerage, of old friends from school who avert their eyes as they drop rations in my lap. *Things have changed,* they whisper. *My mother will not let me see you anymore. My father is afraid of the things you might do.*

I am afraid of the things I might do, too.

Things settle down after steerage is searched. The police question me, too, hoping that the dead captains saw something I did not. I tell them: *I do not know who set off the bomb. I do not even know who would have the strength to try.*

Whenever I get the courage to tell them anything more, Absolon delights in silencing me. The words feel like broken glass against my tongue. He shows me one particular mutiny, over and over again, thrilling at my reaction, the way I cannot look away, the way I squirm at the blood. He knows I cannot stand it. He shows me how he shot seven men and women in a light-soaked steerage chapel, as alien light poured through an emerald window onto a beautiful planet below. He shows me how easily that could happen to me. Had I not known that we had not yet reached Paradise, I would have guessed he was already there.

The conversation at the end of the scene would always go the same way. "Find a place to put the bodies," Absolon would say to the second-class constable, who would nod, his chin stiff, and mention the *sacristy*.

I teach myself to handle Absolon's torture by concentrating on the details of the chapel in the background: the beautiful stained-glass window, the waystop world beyond. The window in my vision is a smaller twin of the one in the cathedral, emerald-green swirled through with marshy azure, a forgotten artist's representation of our future Paradise, and the world below is lush and green. Beyond, I see the sin-eye painted on the bow of the starship, in an angle that could only be seen from steerage.

The window looks familiar.

I try to tell the others about the vision that evening in the mess, but Absolon twists a knife in my head, and the pain is so much that my words come out in tongue-tripped babble. The others respond with shaking heads, moving their trays to eat somewhere else.

Of course they won't listen. I smell like onions and sweat and oil and shit. I am graceless. I totter and I yank myself around and fight the voices in my head. I think myself mad for a long time, until I realize where I have seen the window before.

Captain Pyar's family is dead. Their graceful words and golden robes did not protect them from the bomb: from having their stomachs opened, their skin blackened, their eyes burned out. The only survivor is Bethen, the youngest. She is my age. Black hair, thin hands, skin bright like the hull of our ship. She is on her knees. Her robes are on fire, but she does not seem to notice.

She holds the virtue-cup in her left hand, and the sin-cup in her right. Somehow, she has saved the sacrament inside. I can see the nanobots squirming in the black liquid—the good memories for her, the sins for me.

We just stare at each other. I don't think she wants to do it. I sure as hell don't.

"You must drink," pleads the sacristan.

Bethen holds a calming hand in his direction and drinks. What else can she do? She is Pyar's only surviving child. She is the captain now.

There is an unused storage room in the loudest quarter of steerage, near the compartment where the engines whine and whirl and scream. My old scrub-team boss keeps broken cleaning tools there and extra chemicals for the deck ablutions, and I'd spent a decent amount of time there over the years stocking and restocking tall grey boxes. It takes me a few minutes to navigate through the towers of boxes to the dark green glass, and a few minutes more to move the stack in front of the window, but then I am face-to-face with Absolon's dream, seeing the truth for the first time.

The window is shrouded in decades-old breachcloth that hangs careless and open at the bottom. I feel the rough stained glass under my dirty fingers, searching for the telltale language of a repaired hull breach: rivets, autosealant, desperate chill. There is no evidence of a hull breach underneath the cloth—just the darkness of tough grey metal on the other side, covering the window so no alien sun could ever light it again.

I yank the breachcloth away. The window is just as I remembered from Absolon's bloody memories: an artist's rendition of green, azure, life waiting for the faithful. A chapel window, like the ones in second class.

First class had the cathedral. Second class had a smaller church. Here in steerage, work was our worship.

But this had been a chapel.

A space of our own.

My vision goes grey, and then bloody—Absolon is showing me the execution again. I know by now that he means to distract me from my investigation with this blank horror, but I have seen this memory so many times by now that I can use it for research instead. In my head, Absolon kills the mutineers again, then tells his functionary to hide the bodies, and then the man asks about the sacristy.

The sacristy.

I push aside some dusty chairs, running my hands along the tight angle where the wall meets the decking. I know I am moving in the right direction, because Madelon takes my breath and hangs it from her dead fingers until I see stars. I claw at the sides of my head to make the pain stop. I feel like passing out. Darkness is pooling in the corners of my eyes when I find the door I am looking for, a thin square flush with the wall—just like the one in the cathedral.

None of the dead want me to go in.

So I go in.

This is what happens:

The tradition of the sin-eater goes back almost as far as our memories of the burning homeworld itself. When a captain dies, their blood is removed and scrubbed of the nanobots that have been circulating in their body since they took the throne, collecting their memories like drops of water on a leaf in hydroponics.

The captains know this. The sin-eaters know this. The people do not. The captains won't let me tell them. The truth is lost in the babble I sing. But does it not make sense, now that you think about it? You can't expect all these people to live quietly in a tin can their entire lives and not dream or wish or explode or rub themselves up against the truth or want something more than what they have. The solution is simple: if you know the leader rules with grace, if you are sure *they are benevolent, you can more easily live with your quiet submission.*

In the moment after the bombing, with the blood of hundreds dripping through the strands of my hair, on my shoulders, over my lips, into my eyes, with the sin-cup extended, with my father gone—I am still like my friends back in steerage. I am complicit with my own repression and more frightened than I've ever been.

I still believe all of this is necessary.

Going inside the sacristy is like going back in time. The air is stale and gritty and tastes of dust and rot. It is dark, and once my eyes adjust, shapes form around the column of light let in by the storage room: cabinets, closets, closed drawers, all made of rough wood from the homeworld. I check the closet for the golden robes of the captain's family, but find only green jumpsuits so delicate they fall apart at my touch—green jumpsuits, those most ancient of sacred robes, in the style that we had all thought lost with time. I look for cups, laid out for sacrament and sin-eating, but there is nothing in the drawers.

I am moving over to the cabinets when I trip over a pile of bones.

Absolon laughs at me, the bastard.

The bones have been left in an unkempt, haphazard jumble, like the bodies they'd once belonged to had been shoved together quickly and dropped one on top of another. I count seven skulls, each with its own little round hole in the center of its forehead. I run my thumb over the smallest, and one of the elder ghosts—one of the nameless, from the nameless time—imagines what my head would look like if it had been treated like that.

I drop the skull, my fingers suddenly numb. When I go to pick it up again, I see something new.

Under the lattice of ribs is a *photograph*.

I have only seen photographs in school. This one is old—faded, covered in dust, barely legible. I push the bones aside, making sure to be respectful, because respect for these long-dead mutineers makes Madelon *so* angry—and pick it up. This is a picture of a group of seven people in green jumpsuits, with joyous smiles like welcoming stars on their faces, standing on the bridge of *Home*, holding hands, the yawning window overlooking a green planet as familiar as a fever dream. I know all seven faces. I have seen these seven faces murdered by Captain Absolon over and over again, and their bones are scattered at my feet.

Above are obtuse, boxy lines I know to be *words*, because I have seen words written in the missals the first class use in the cathedral.

The world in the photograph is Paradise.

I can tell it is Paradise because it looks exactly like the artists' renderings they showed us in school. I can tell it is Paradise because Absolon is screaming. Because Madelon has taken my breath for her own. Because my eyes are needles and my body is burning. Because Pyar has my courage in his dead hands. But I can still think. They try to take the truth away from me, but like all truth, it is there in my head, it speaks in tongues, it is loud as a sunrise: *we have already been to Paradise.*

We have already been to Paradise and we left.

My friends can argue with my words all they like, but they will not be able to argue with this kind of evidence.

Rip it up, Absolon screams. *Rip it up and eat it and—*

I pick up the photograph and run as fast as I can.

In the cathedral, after the bombing, Bethen puts the virtue-cup down, and hands the sin-cup to the sacristan. Her eyes turn towards mine. She wants to say something, but she can't. The virtues are multiplying in her head.

The sacristan sees my nervous tremor and gulps, his Adam's apple wavering. Does he think I will attack him and make him drink the sin-cup?

Should I?

It must be you, *he says.* You are the last of your line.

Pick someone else, *I say.* I do not want this.

The sacristan tips the sin-cup against my lips hard enough to bruise me, like I need more sin, like there isn't enough here in the broken, bloody cathedral. I taste my father's blood—dusky like fear, tangy like metal, the nanobots that supported our society thrilling against my lips. I gag. Once I drink, nobody will be able to touch me, lest my blood transfer the sin to them as well.

Your father is dead, *he responds.* Nobody cares what *you* want.

I have to drink. I have no choice. I am the last sin-eater.

Somehow, I reach the steerage mess without tearing the photograph in half. I know everyone here—every face, every soul, everything they said about me before I became sin-eater and most of the things they said afterward. There is obscenity on my tongue and babble stuck in my teeth, but everyone is so used to this by now that very few of them look up.

My old scrub-team is seated by the door. I knock the

spoon out of my old boss's left hand and drop the photograph in her lap. Soup splatters her face, and she stands, angry. The attention of the room follows, a hundred people rubbernecking to gawk at the sin-eater getting a sin-eater's due.

"Look," I say, and point to the photograph. I cannot say more. Absolon is sitting on my throat.

I am afraid for a moment, but she sees the truth like I saw the truth; she stares, and moves very slowly, picking up the photograph and staring at it with a silent, intent gaze. Tears glisten at the corners of her eyes.

"This can't be true," she whispers. "The captains can't lie. They can't lie. They only know grace."

"Knowing grace doesn't make you incapable of doing evil," I manage. It feels like speaking through dark glass, from the darkness outside an airlock.

She stares for five long seconds, then looks up, scanning the crowd. She walks over to the table where the schoolteacher sits—the only one of us who was born in second class, the only one of us who can read. She hands it to him, and he mutters under his breath as he runs his finger over the words scrawled at the top, the faces of the shining, smiling people wearing the ancient sigils of Home.

My teacher speaks slowly. The room is so quiet now that you can hear nothing but the humming of the engines and your own heartbeat. "A com-mem-or-a-tiv eh-dish-un uh-pun the ar-rival of tha fee-nix to pare-a-dyse—"

The room erupts in screaming.

They say new sin-eaters go crazy from the very first moment of the very first touch of sin on their tongue.

Before the bombing, I alone knew this was untrue. My father would hold me at night and rock me back and forth, whispering terrible things in my ear, but his touch was always tender and his tears were always hot and real. I knew what was truth. He only looked insane. Others told of his actions, but I told of his heart. And now that I can speak of Absolon and Madelon and Pyar and the others, I know he was stronger than any of them.

In the cathedral, surrounded by so much death, I vowed to be stronger than him.

The police come immediately, of course. The bridge is always watching for unrest. The police wrest me from the grasp of my boss, my teacher, my friends, and shove me towards the cathedral. They are wearing gloves. Of course they are wearing gloves. They always wear gloves. They are scared of touching me.

They have guns at their waists, the kind of guns that Absolon used to make bones of the mutineers in my memory. I wonder if they will make a little hole in my forehead and shove me in a sacristy myself. So I ask them what I have done wrong. I want to tell them *I am no mutineer, I simply found a photograph, I don't know what it means.*

They just hear screaming.

They open the doors to the cathedral, and I choke on the smell of old death. The scrub-teams have made progress on removing the blood from the carpet, but some stains remain. The walls are still scorched where the fire snacked on the old homeworld wood.

Captain Bethen presides over the ruined space in a great velvet chair where her father's bier had lain, her fingers laden with titanium rings and her hair wound through with roses from steerage hydroponics. She is swimming in her father's robes. She has not yet had them cut down for her smaller frame. The light of the star coming through great emerald window behind her make her look even less human than I remembered.

One of the policewomen walks the photograph to Bethen and lays it in her lap. The room is tied in desperate silence as she stares at it, reads the words, her eyes darting from detail to detail.

Her hand is shaking.

Finally, when I think I can stand no more, she puts the photograph aside and arranges her hands on her lap. "I was wondering when you'd get here. My father said they all come eventually. No, don't kneel."

When I try to answer, I hear the babble building at the back of my throat. The pain behind my eyes, so bright I can hardly see.

"Be quiet, Grandfather," Bethen snaps. "Let my sin-eater speak."

I meet her eyes.

"I understand so little. Some of the things I do, I cannot countenance, but they seem right... and that seems wrong, after the cathedral, you know? After all those people died? And now this photograph. What brought you here?" Her lips glint emerald in the starlight. She slides her shaking hand into her robes so that I cannot see it. She is too late for that.

"Absolon. And the people he killed."

Bethen blinks. "He killed no one. I would know."

"He—" Absolon's fingers grab my throat and twist, and I cannot speak for the shock of it.

"Grandfather," Bethen snaps.

I feel a rush of freedom, and the words come like runoff from an open valve. "I can show you the bones. He killed them all. He shot them point-blank in the head and then put them in the sacristy and closed steerage off from the stars. But you don't know that. Of *course* you don't know that," I say.

Bethen rises from her chair. The starlight catches in her earrings. Her robes are a mess of sound—clanging and rustling and chiming, metal on metal on silk. My heart bangs against my ribs. My muscles ache.

"My sin-eater," she says. "You see a massacre. I see a

victory, a necessary one. Yet, I—" She falters. "I only *know* that it was a victory. I feel happy about it. I feel... the rush of power he felt, the certainty that it had to be done. Not *what* was done. It makes me sick to not know, to only suspect—"

My stomach churns. *How dare she.* "I'm your sin-eater, not your confessor."

Bethen looks away.

She had asked me not to kneel, but inside my chest, the *hundred* are screaming for it, to give Bethen and the ghosts in her head the respect none of them deserve. I refuse them; I will not kneel here, not in my father's own blood, not in the place where he died, not to the person who would justify it as *good*. This causes Absolon to rail in my lungs, in my throat, in my veins, to cause me to shake, to scream. I fight. The floor feels like a magnet, full of the *hundred* telling me to kneel, to *fall*. Finally, my body betrays me. My knee hits the ground at a bad angle, and I cry out in pain.

"I'm sorry," says Bethen, her voice hasty and kind, her hands still laced together against the gold of her bodice. "Do you know what they're telling me to tell you right now? That this—you on the ground, me up here—is how our world must function. They ask me if I want the ship to fall apart. If I want a civil war. If I want blood in the cathedral. If I do not want my children to rest quietly in Paradise. It is *deafening*."

I stop fighting and Absolon lets me shiver on the ground.

"Do you believe them?"

"I don't know."

"Have you tried to talk to them?" I ask.

"I—tell them that there has already been enough blood in the cathedral," Bethen says.

My voice wavers. It is difficult to speak. "You saw the photograph. You know as well as I do that we have already rejected Paradise. And steerage knows, too. Do you think they will not come for you?"

Her voice is faint. "If Absolon chose to take us away from Paradise, there has to be a very good reason."

I do not feel well. I look around at the bloodstains, the ruined cathedral, the emerald light from the new star choking everything in green. Bethen's voice echoes: *My father said they all come eventually.* Had my father had this conversation with Captain Pyar, and *his* father with Captain Carelon and on and on back to Edrime and Absolon and the nameless ghosts who never stopped screaming? Is this why his every step was made in despair?

"They asked him to give up his power," I manage to say.

Bethen shakes her head. "But he was the *captain*."

I stare. I writhe. "Not on the planet, he wasn't."

"He *had* to leave. Because of the steerage rebellion that kept us on the ship—"

"Why would we rebel? We dream of *nothing* but Paradise!"

Bethen paces the edge of the sanctuary, her shoes jingling with the sound of bells. "There must have been a reason," she repeated. "Absolon is so sure. He is so sure that no one could take care of Home better than him. And, now, he tells me there is no one that can do that better than me—"

I drag myself to a sitting position. The anger chokes me more than Absolon's fingers at my throat. "He kept us all enslaved here because he did not wish to give up his power! His stained conscience! Stars, Captain! You're just like him!"

In my head, Absolon laughs.

And laughs.

And *laughs*.

Speaking feels like death now, but I cannot stop my words. No dead thing will silence me. I cannot make a bomb. All I have are my words. "You know, Bethen, it must be incredible. Being you. Never doubting your place. Not even for a *second*. Your clear conscience. What kind of sins are you going to commit? How many people are you going to kill, knowing that my children are going to be there to absolve you? That you are not going to have to remember what you've done? That you can just make *me* choke it down? Are you looking forward to that?"

Bethen fixes her eyes on the place where my father knelt.

Her hands are shaking.

One last memory of the bombing.

This one is mine. There are so few of those now that every single one is precious.

We are in the cathedral. We are singing. It is seconds before the bombing. The sacristans are escorting my father to the front of the aisle, where he will take the dead captain's sin-cup. He has already been sin-eater for fourteen years. I barely remember a time before he ranted and raved and called himself Absolon. Madelon. Edrime. Carelon.

Of course it is my father who made the bomb. Of course he would have the strength. Maybe I would, too, after so long a time hearing their filth.

Fourteen years of pushing through the sins he sees to find the only solution he can manage, after drinking down all of that hate. Hate matched with hate. He thinks he will kill them all. That killing will be the thing that actually stops this. He has spent so much time listening to the captains that he sees no other way.

He turns around. He smiles at me. He has a bright, round thing in his hand. He mouths: "For you, Mey."

Then: the fire.

There must be another way. But what choice did he have?

"I don't want to kill," Bethen says. "Don't you understand what I am saying? Don't you understand how *alone* I am?"

The golden captain with the power of life and death, reaching out to the sin-eater who has not showered in a week, asking her to understand what loneliness feels like? It is a marvel that I do not spit at her feet.

"You're *a hundred,* just like me," I cough. "You are never alone."

Bethen sweeps her hand over the dead cathedral. Over the dead, in their uncontrollable power: in the air, in my blood, in hers.

"They tell me everything is worth the captain's chair. The deaths. The decisions. The long journey that will never end, now. But that photograph, and this cathedral, and all those dead people—to justify this? I don't understand. I need to see the truth. Absolon and the others—they won't let me turn around, they won't let me go back to Paradise, and I do not know why." She plucks at her robes and her voice breaks. She is crying.

For that moment, she is just a girl.

The steerage-rat in me, the one who works through hunger, that stares out portholes, that dreams of a better life. She is the one that speaks.

"My father should have showed you," I whisper. "I can *show* you."

"How?"

I offer her my wrist.

I can hardly breathe.

Bethen's eyes are flint at the offer, and she squats next to me, her eyes going up and down my body. The sweat on my forehead. The memories under my skin. Absolon and the others come to realize what I'm offering her, and my mind becomes a writhing sea of the worst things they've ever shown me. I see blood spurting from the foreheads of mutineers. My mother dying. The cathedral bomb. Two girls in the cold black outside, their mouths gasping at nonexistent air, their eyes popping like grapes in a vise.

Show me Paradise, I rage at them. And they do. They show me Paradise: the crystal seas, wind rustling the leaves of blue trees. The knowledge that here, he would be no better than anyone else. That he would have to give up the gold, the salutes, the best food, the *power*. I am seized with jealousy. Rage. Covetous anger. *What would the steerage-rats do, if not for my paternal guidance?*

If I cannot convince you, he says, *I will take you. You are not so powerful.*

I no longer have control over my breath. My fingers.

He is in my bowel, in my brain.

I cannot stop the darkness.

"Captain," I gasp, "please."

"I'll see everything?" Bethen steadies herself by placing her hand on my sweating forehead, smearing the sin-eye I drew there this morning. "I'll see the truth?"

For a moment, I think she might slap me.

"Get a knife," I manage to say. I gasp for breath. "And the cups. I'll drink your truth. You'll drink mine."

There is a wailing silence.

"Do what she says." Bethen barks the order at the policemen in the back like she's been giving them her entire life. Like she's been giving them for a thousand years. And once they shuffle out, fear tightening their shoulders, she turns back to me, and slides her arm under mine, helping me stand.

"Show me," she says.

Bethen writhes.

It is the first memory we share together.

Before Bethen marries me, I draw the sin-eye on my forehead in red and black and show her how to do it, as well. She walks down the aisle in emerald green, roses in her hair. We drink together from both cups and vow to be together until we die. It is a political marriage to keep the peace, but her eyes are dark and lovely and her body is warm, and I feel something bright and new whenever she smiles.

We will need the strength of two if we are to overcome the *hundred*, the uncontrollable dead, the voices that whisper their ancient hate so loud we can hear it in our own world, where they do not belong. And as she takes my hand under the streaming stars, our ship turns around and aims for Paradise.

When we die, we will turn Home—the *Fee-nix*, the ancients used to call it, but my spelling might be wrong, I am still learning to read—over to someone new, someone who will never hear Absolon. They had their time. Bethen and I will ensure the descendants have theirs.

And then it will be their choice: how they live, how they sin, where they go.

And Now His Lordship Is Laughing

By Shiv Ramdas

When the first breeze of the morning whistles over the green tips of the paddy-stalks to kiss the tawny jute thatching of the bungalow roof, Apa is already out on the verandah. It's still dark but that doesn't matter, it's been more than twoscore years since she's needed light to work by. All she needs is the jute and her tools. Needle and twine, knife and lime, all have their place and in Apa's hands that place is to give form to thought. Beneath those hands the strands strain, first to oppose her coaxing, and then, bit by bit, to obey her bidding. Once or twice, a sharp fibre-edge pricks her finger and she silently shakes the droplets of blood aside with practiced ease, careful not to let any spill on the jute, even as the material in her grasp twists in apology.

Before the rosy arms of the sun reach out from the dark to embrace Midnapore in another new day, she's already been at work for several hours. Her deft, callused fingers move quickly, expertly, back and forth, one fold up, another stitch down. As she works, she hums her shukro-sangeet, a song of thanks to the jute, for what it has been and what it will be. No matter how many times she works and weaves it, Apa never ceases to wonder at the miracle of this material, the most special, versatile crop there is. You can wear it, build with it, eat it and feed with it; there's almost nothing in which you can't use it. And it grows everywhere, Bengal's ubiquitous treasure. Yet, despite what people say, jute has no magic, no mystery or secrets; what you ask of it is what it gives. Even if it does carry memories; each generation of crop remembering what its parents have done, so each fresh time you mould it, it proves easier than the last. All you need is enough of yourself to put into it, and the knowledge that both you and the jute are in this together, not master and dasa, but two friends working side by side.

By the time Nilesh comes out onto the verandah to stand behind her, the golden strands in her grasp have already begun to take the shape they will spend the rest of their existence in. A small hand reaches out, tapping her on the shoulder, and Apa turns, to be met by a pair of accusing black eyes.

"You said I could help!"

"I said if you finished your milk you could help."

"But Grandma, I did!"

He holds out his hand, brandishing a tumbler, then overturns it. A solitary white drop clings to the rim, then falls free, landing on the verandah floor.

"See? See?"

Apa laughs. "All right then. Sit down next to me, and go through all these jute bits I have dropped. I need you to find the two biggest ones and set them aside."

He beams, plonking himself down beside her with a loud thud.

"Be careful! You'll hurt yourself!"

He giggles but doesn't answer, rummaging through the discarded scraps of jute, the pink tip of his tongue peeping out from the side of his mouth, brow scrunched up in concentration. Silence falls over the verandah for a while, punctuated only by Nilesh's periodic exclamations and grunts. Apa pays them little heed: the jute demands all her attention. She sits there, head bent down, sunbeams dancing off her silvery hair, hands still flashing first one way, then another, as the fibres she holds in her fingers come together as only Apa can make them. And as she finishes, the final fibrous form resting in her lap, Nilesh leaps to his feet, handing her two pieces of jute.

"These were the biggest ones, Apa."

"Thank you, Nilesh. Yes, these are exactly what I need."

"What is it? What doll have you made today?"

"Patience, patience."

She twists the scraps around the doll's waist, using the very tip of the knife to shape them. Then a dab of lime to hold them in place.

Nilesh's eyes widen. "It's wearing a dhoti now! I made the dhoti!"

He claps delightedly, and then squeals as the doll claps along with him.

"It's a hattali'r putul! A clapping doll!"

She smiles. "No, it's a Nilesh Putul."

"It's me? It's for me?"

She smiles again. "Yes and yes. Do you like it?"

He leans forward, planting a big, sloppy kiss on her weathered cheek, and then does a little dance, whooping excitedly. A slight frown creases her brow as she watches him; his eagerness for everything doll-related is a bittersweet reminder of what used to be. Where once it was common for children to gather gawking at her while she worked, or for villagers to stop by the house and ask her about taking on so-and-so as an apprentice, it's now been years since anyone has. Today's young people have other things they want to do with their lives, things that do not require them to spend decades hunched over with needle in hand, nor pay ever-increasing levies and taxes. Apa sighs. But then there's Nilesh, always so eager to help her in her work. Perhaps he will be the exception, and when he's old enough she'll teach him the craft, and maybe the art of Midnapore dollweaving will outlive her after all.

He's still dancing away happily even as the doll kicks its feet in perfect unison with his. Apa watches them both, her heart now sowing fields without a thought for the reaping.

Until the sound of hoofbeats rends the air, growing louder as the horse trots down the path towards the bungalow verandah. Now they see him, the uniformed Englishman sitting upright in the saddle. Apa keeps her eyes on him all the way, her new creation now held tightly in her hands.

"Nilesh. Go inside. Hurry, now."

"But why, Apa?" he protests. "I want to hear what he says too!"

Apa half-turns, fixing the boy with her eye. "I said, now."

He darts back inside, as anyone would have, because no one in Midnapore disobeys Apa. As the horse draws to a halt, the old woman rises to her feet.

The Englishman dismounts, flicks the sweat from his brow, and stands before the verandah.

"Matriarch of Midnapore. Captain Frederick Bolton, of the Calcutta Presidency Battalion."

He sounds like most of his countrymen, flat-toned and steady. She often wonders how the English have come by their belief that the inability to emote is a virtue. It seems so unnatural.

"I remember you."

She speaks in English, because it hurts her ears to hear them try to speak Bangla. Although more often than not, what they speak is Hindi in what they think is a Bengali accent.

"I come as the emissary of His Grace, Sir John Arthur Herbert, Governor of Bengal, Representative of Her Gracious Majesty Victoria, Queen of India and the Empire."

"What do you want this time?"

He smiles. "Oh, you know what His Grace wishes for. He's asked you for it on more than one occasion. One of your dolls for Her Ladyship."

"No."

"I would urge you to reconsider."

"There is nothing to reconsider. Your master is, as you say, Governor of Bengal. He can have almost any toy he wants."

"What he wants is one of yours. His Grace says he has never seen another dollmaker whose work compares to yours. None of the others have your magic."

"He might have seen many more of us if he hadn't made it a point to drive so many out of work with duties and levies every time the wind changes and those schools where you tell our children how backward our ways are. And I have no magic. I am but a means to an end."

"Come now, His Grace is willing to be generous."

She gestures at the thick paddy and jute fields encircling the bungalow, green and lush, gently swaying in the summer breeze.

"Look around you, Captain. I have no need of his generosity."

"I strongly recommend you do not choose this path. Your Governor is not a man used to being denied. Especially by a native. See, you even hold a doll as we speak. All you need to do is simply hand it to me, and you can name your price."

"My putuls are not for sale. I give them to those whom I choose, and I do not choose those who demand them at the point of a bayonet. Be off with you."

He sighs. "I fear you may come to regret this, Matriarch."

"All of Midnapore, nay, all of Bengal regrets the day your kind came here. What is one more regret? If you turn your horse around, you will find the path leads back just as surely as it led you here. I would urge you to take it."

She could swear she sees his eyes blaze, but just as suddenly, the anger is gone and he's taking a deep breath. Had she imagined it? When he speaks, his voice is even.

"I will convey your message to His Grace."

With that, he leaps back on his horse and gallops away.

Apa stands erect, watching until man and horse are out of sight, vanished among the towering crops on either side of the road. He might be gone, but the dark cloud of his unspoken promise still lingers. An additional crease lines her already-wrinkled brow; she twists the jute doll in her hands.

For as she well knows, just like jute, the white man has a long memory, and unlike the jute, he does not mind the blood.

• • •

Under the relentless gaze of the sun, the scorched earth shimmers. Through the haze, the shriveled, blackened stumps of what had been the jute-field protrude upwards. From the verandah, Apa stares unblinkingly at them. As she watches, a charred wisp dances off one, carried by the breeze to fall in the burnt, dried-out remains of what had been one of the paddy plots. Next to it, a host of flies buzz above something lying there. A dead bullock, or, more likely, a person. The British have already taken all the bullocks, right after they took all the rice. Every last grain.

It's been almost four days since she lost Nilesh. Mercifully, he'd stopped crying towards the end, so for the last couple of days he'd just lain there, hands over his bloated belly, eyes staring sightlessly at something in the distance that nobody else could see. For a brief, interminable while, she'd wondered what he'd felt during those final days, but she knows the answer now. Nothing.

Despite what Apa had always thought starvation would

be like, the hunger isn't even the worst part. The pangs don't last as long as one would imagine; by the fourth day they're almost entirely gone. It isn't even the weakness, terrible as that is. No, it's the lethargy, the constant feeling that nothing matters, not food, not movement, not brushing away the flies circling overhead and settling on one, unwilling to even afford one the dignity of being truly dead before they move in. It's the sense of lying there, waiting to shut down, but being unable to do even that, as the mind refuses to accept what the body is telling it, that this journey has come to an end. Time comes and goes in strange, fluid stretches; a leaf taking hours to fall to the ground, the span between sunrise and sunset vanishing in the time it takes to blink. Blinking is the one thing that seems unchanged, as though her brain has a special rapport with the eyelids that it never developed with the rest of her body. What is strangest of all is thought itself. Her mind doesn't seem foggy. Thoughts appear with what feels like increased clarity, even as she watches her body wasting away, as though her brain is cannibalising the rest of her to feed itself.

As if on cue, a fly buzzes around her head, coming to settle on her nose. She blinks to drive it off, but it ignores her efforts. It's there to stay, welcome or not. Must be British. She thinks about brushing it away, but her limbs are heavy and belong to someone else, and it doesn't seem that important anyway. She blinks again, and in the instant her eyes are shut, she hears a sound, no, a series of sounds, words, coming from very far away. She opens her eyes again on the other side of the blink, and the man comes into focus.

He's in front of the verandah, still astride his horse, moving his mouth, making the sounds. He looks familiar. Can it be, yes, it is indeed him, the British soldier who keeps coming here unbidden, like one of those flies. What's his name again? Bol, Ball, something like that. What does it matter?

Behind him, also on horseback, three more men. They don't matter either. Maybe if she shuts her eyes again they'll go away.

She closes them, and then she feels hands, one pulling her head backwards, the other forcing her mouth open, tipping something into her mouth. A steady stream of something, thin, yet mushy. She chokes, deep racking retches, spluttering the food back out, looking up through watering eyes. Two of the men are crouched over her, one holding her, the other holding a spoon and a bowl of watery-looking rice gruel. Spoon Man is wiping the regurgitations off the unhappy expression on his face. He looks back at his companions. The familiar-looking soldier says something to his men. The feeder grimaces and she feels rough hands grab her head again, tilting it backwards, as the spoon closes in once again.

• • •

She sits on the verandah, cross-legged, ignoring the soldier beside her, waiting for the other one to come with the evening bowl of gruel. They no longer feed her now that she's strong enough to do it for herself, but at least one of them hovers nearby at all times. At first she's unable to keep any food down, as though her stomach now considers rice a foreign object it wants nothing to do with, but they persist, and slowly, her body has learnt how to eat again. She still doesn't know why: they haven't said a word to her since. They do, however, talk to each other. From listening, she learns that one is called Willis, the other McKissic, that someone called Sir Winston has ordered the governor to take all the rice, and it is happening all over Bengal.

Every so often, slowly, gingerly, she runs her tongue along the inside of her gums, wincing a bit. Her teeth and mouth hurt all the time now, why she doesn't know. From the force-feeding? Or maybe that's merely the part of her that was being eaten from the inside out when the soldiers returned to the bungalow.

The sun is lower than usual when McKissic returns with the gruel, and this time he isn't alone. Four more mounted soldiers accompany him, and riding at their head is that captain again. With an effort, Apa recalls his name. Bolton. He reins in his horse, dismounts, and stands before the verandah, riding crop still in one hand. He jerks his head at one of the other men. This individual crouches down over Apa and proceeds to hold her wrist, then touch her neck, look in her mouth, and run a hand over her still-distended belly as she sits there silently. Finally, he stands up.

"She'll be fine."

"Strong enough for the job?"

"I'd venture to say so, yes."

"Excellent. Thank you, Doctor." Bolton looks at Apa. "I told you no good would come of your defiance. It's a good thing I got here in time, isn't it?"

He smiles at her, waiting for a response, while she stares back at him, stony-faced. For a slow, long time, silence spreads its wings over the verandah. Until eventually, the captain cracks.

"His Grace is, however, still willing to be generous. He offers you a bargain. Food for you and whatever others are yet alive here."

Others, he says. How long has it been now since Agni took her Nilesh? She isn't even sure any more. All she remembers is how small, how frail he'd looked on the pyre. How hard it had been just to force the doll she'd made for him into his tiny, stiff hands before she'd lit the flame. Fire had been his protector, doing what she no longer has the strength to. It had made sure that nobody would attempt to strip the corpse of its clothes, as she heard has been happening all over Midnapore. Clothes are fibre and fibre can be food. She's also heard news of even worse horrors: children attempting to eat their deceased parents, parents their dead children. And even worse, whispers that, in some places, there are those who aren't even waiting for others to die. Then, silence, no news of anything for days before she too had fallen into the starvation-stupor. That had been the one good thing about it, the inability to think of Nilesh, all the others she'll never see again, about any of it.

Despite her best efforts, the tear burns its way out, dangling on the rim of her eye for a moment, before it falls to the dusty verandah floor with a loud plop. She looks up at his hateful face.

"There are no others here."

"What a pity."

Her face must be showing some of what she's thinking, because he immediately goes on.

"Look, don't blame me for this. I'm just doing my job here."

"Just ... doing your job."

"Yes and what's more, I'm trying to help you here. As is the Governor. We're on your side, you know. Think about it. Food and drink for you, and in return, all His Grace asks is that you give him something in return. A doll for her Ladyship."

She feels a stirring within her, a white-hot core of rage in her belly, growing, spreading outwards.

"He did all this ... for a doll?"

At this, he laughs aloud. "You know, sometimes you natives really are full of yourselves. No, the Denial of Rice Policy is so much bigger than you, or this state. It's been a huge help to supplying the war effort. Ever heard of the Axis? No, of course you haven't. Be glad—that's who we're protecting you from."

"Protecting."

"Yes, protecting. The Prime Minister himself has written to Sir John, commending him for his success in ensuring continued food and supplies for the Allied troops. Instead of complaining, you should be proud of the role Bengal is playing in saving the world. As is the rest of India. Anyway, enough of this. I didn't come all the way out here to the boondocks to discuss global politics with you. Won't you just see reason, for your own sake? Just make that damned doll and we can all be done with this song and dance. Here, McKissic, give her some more of that stuff. Maybe the taste of food will straighten her mind out."

She feels rather than sees the bowl being thrust into her hands. All she can hear is what he's said, echoing in her head, over and over. Once again, the white-hot rage surges through her, going from kernel to spreading flame so quickly that she scarcely remembers how it began. She raises her hand, to throw the bowl of gruel back in his face, and as she does, one particular sentence bounces around inside her mind again.

"....the rest of India."

Then the rage is gone, replaced by something else, harder, colder, so alien and frightening, so different from any feeling she's ever known that it couldn't possibly have come from her. But it's inside her.

She lowers the bowl. "I need materials, and tools."

He nods, pleased, although there's something else there as well. Relief? "I thought you might see the light. I have jute here. What tools?"

"Lime, a needle, some thread, and a knife. Her eyes are blue?"

He stares at her. "What if they are?

"Then I will also need some indigo. For the dye."

"You shall have whatever you need."

Then he pauses. "You'll have to be supervised, of course. Can't have you using that knife to do some mischief to someone. Or yourself. Willis, McKissic, I'm afraid your vigil continues. Give her everything she wants. At least until—how long before it's done, now?"

"I don't know. Two days, maybe three. It is not an exact science. I need to feel the shape in the jute before I can set it free."

"You lot and your mumbo-jumbo, I tell you. No matter. You want three days, you'll have them. But before I go, I'd like you to understand ..."

He leans forward, grabbing her shoulder so powerfully she cries out. His face is inches from her own, so close she can feel his warm, moist breath when he speaks. His voice is a whisper, harsh and chilling, travelling right through her.

"When I come back three days from now, I expect to find Her Ladyship's doll. Do not disappoint me, old woman."

He steps back, smiling. "Three days," he says again.

With that, he leaps back up into the saddle, and rides away, leaving behind Apa and the two soldiers on the verandah.

Apa takes a deep breath, raises the bowl to her lips with shaking hands, and slurps up the thin, flavourless gruel. She's going to need all her strength for what is to come.

• • •

Needle, twine, knife, and lime. One fold up, one stitch down. She'd forgotten how good it feels to weave, to just be holding the jute once more, an old, lost friend, now returned home.

"I missed you," she whispers, head bent down. From sunrise to sunset she sits cross-legged on the verandah, working, only ever stopping for food and ablutions. When she needs a break, she looks at the banyan tree. With the fields all gone, she can see further from the verandah than ever before, all the way to the tree. It used to be the sabha sthal, where the villagers congregated for Panchayat meetings under the broad, dangling roots. Now it's something else entirely. Vultures peck at the swaying bodies hanging from its boughs, rats scurry around its base, gnawing at the bodies on the ground underneath it. It had started out as a place of punishment, where the British hung farmers who dared to hide rice from them. Then villagers took to hanging themselves there as well; the rope is more painless than the slow, pitiless grip of starvation. Parents hung their children, and then themselves; it was just easier that way. That was when the British burnt the jute fields, to ensure no one could make any rope. Or maybe they just enjoyed watching their victims die slowly. So people have taken to cutting down the bodies and reusing the rope. There are now almost as many corpses on the tree as leaves below it. Apa looks often at the tree these past few days.

Only once does she feel herself waver. It happens in the middle of an afternoon, when the sun is at its fiercest. Like an intangible East India Company, the thought creeps into her mind, and having inveigled its way in, it refuses to leave. She glances at Willis, whose turn it is to watch her; he's over on the other side of the verandah, cleaning his rifle. Her eyes inch to the knife lying beside her. It would be so easy to end the misery now. One quick stroke across the throat and there will be no more pain, no more of that aching, hollow feeling where her heart had been, no more anything. Slowly, her hand closes around the hilt. And then she hears it again, that awful, mocking sound, Bolton laughing at her, at Nilesh, at Bengal, and at India. And just like that, her jaw sets, her shoulders straighten, and the thought is vanished, banished away to a dark corner of her mind, wherefrom it won't find its way back again. No, she won't give them the satisfaction. Not while there is work to do. So work she does.

Needle and twine, knife and lime. Hands flashing, jute bending, straining, obeying her, as it always had. Dawn to dusk she weaves, reaching within to put of herself into the jute, letting her feelings and memories flow. But all she can remember is the sound of that laughter, the peals of merriment that had convinced her not to succumb, because that would be the worst way to die, to the sound of your murderer's laughter. And all she can find of herself is that ever-growing, cold, frightening feeling that frightens her no longer, because it is not just inside her, now it is her. And all she feels, she puts into the doll.

When she pricks her finger, she no longer shakes the blood aside, but lets it drip slowly, deliberately into the jute, till it is all soaked up.

And still she hears that laughter, reverberating between her ears, bouncing around the inside of her skull, a dirge that just won't stop. And neither will she, not until it is finished.

One stitch up, one fold down.

• • •

True to his word, Bolton returns on the morning of the fourth day, just as she finishes the last of her gruel.

"Is it finished?" he calls out, even before he makes it all the way to the verandah where she sits.

"It is."

"Show me."

She holds it up by the hair, a slim, European woman in a blue dress, with golden jute-hair and indigo eyes, swaying gently in her grasp.

"It is the finest work I have ever done."

"Good, good," he replies, reaching out for it.

Apa ignores his outstretched hand.

"It's a Hashi'r Putul, you know."

"A what?"

"A laughing doll."

"It doesn't look like it's laughing."

"That's not what it means. When you press it the right way, it will laugh."

He frowns. "You mean laugh out loud?"

"Exactly."

"Show me."

She shakes her head. "That's not how it works. It will laugh, but only for the one it's meant for, and only if you know how to make it. And there is none but me who can handle it, or teach anyone how to."

"And you said you didn't do magic."

"An artist never tells all her secrets."

"And yet you told me this one. I'll take that doll now."

"No, I want to give it to Lord Herbert myself."

"Well, that's not going to happen, is it? The doll, please."

"I just told you, only I can make it work."

He narrows his eyes. "The trouble with this whole thing, old woman, is that I don't believe you."

"You don't believe I can make a laughing doll?" She sits up very straight, pulling the tatters of her sari tightly about herself. "You have insulted my art, Captain." Her free hand snakes down, over the hilt of the knife. "Perhaps I should just destroy it."

"Or perhaps I should just have my men run you through and take the doll from your corpse."

"They cannot do so before I destroy the putul. You said so yourself, your master truly wants it for his wife. Will you go and tell him that he could have had it, but you were so intent on not letting a craftswoman exhibit her craft that all he shall get today is some jute scraps? So be it."

There is a long, heavy silence. Sensing her moment, Apa presses on.

"On the other hand, if you do take me with you, I can teach others to make them as well. Think how pleased your governor will be. As many of my putuls as he wants, for whoever he wants, whenever he wants."

Another silence, during which Bolton frowns. Then he chuckles.

"Well played, old woman. Very well, you shall come back to Government House with us. Put her up on your horse behind you, Willis. Oh, and make sure you take away her knife first. Wouldn't want her to plant one between your ribs from behind now, would you?"

"Thank you, Captain," says Apa, handing her knife over. "Oh, one moment."

She reaches down, quickly picking through the discarded scraps of jute, until she's found the two biggest. As she does, she remembers Nilesh, sitting on almost that very spot, handing her two scraps just like these, and a pang twists her innards. No, she cannot cry, not now. Not yet. She blinks, forcing back the tears, and lifts her head to look up at Captain Bolton.

"A keepsake. To remind me of the best work I ever did."

He shrugs. "Are you ready, Willis? Come along then, we must be off. It'll take us the better part of the day to get back to Calcutta."

• • •

The road to Kolkata is long and dusty, and every step of it is steeped in a thousand terrors. Field after field lies black and arid, within them rows of immolated crops and ashen cadavers bearing witness to the charnel house that is Bengal now. Bodies lie piled twenty high by the roadside, each gust of wind carrying with it the stench of rotting flesh and dead hope. As they ride past the banks of the Hooghly, lifeline of Kolkata, Apa sees the sunbeams bearing down, setting off a shimmer on the sparse patches of water still visible between the bodies. There are a lot more corpses than water, at least on the surface. A carrion-bird settles down on the back of one unsteadily, her talons sinking down into the flesh of the man's back, but not very far, for even the water-rot does only so much to soften rigor mortis. Apa turns her head aside and retches, and she isn't the only one in the party doing so.

All the way, the soldiers talk, never to her, but from what she hears, she gathers more than a bit. For instance, that the Denial of Rice policy has been declared a complete success, even though food supplies from various places she's never heard of have been turned away or redirected to British troops to ensure it stays that way. That it goes even beyond that, there is also a Denial of Boat Policy, also suggested by London, that has to do with far more than boats—almost all forms of transportation have been burnt or seized. That there are whispers among the men that the scale of the holocaust has moved even some British hearts, but not Sir Winston's: that Dark Lord is instead mightily pleased.

Indeed, by the time they pull up at the gates of Government House on the banks of the Hooghly, Apa has seen and heard more horrors than she could tell of in yet another lifetime, or recall any more of in this one. Until at long, merciful last, they stand within the high stone walls, where perfectly manicured lawns and picturesque blossoms neatly encircle engraved fountains, and the sweet smells of jasmine and rose fill the air. Rows of trees—neem, teak, peepal, and sal—stand looking down on them, forming a green canopy over their heads as they make their way down the winding, cobbled path to the marble steps of the main building. From somewhere up in the leaves, a koel titters.

And then they are inside the building, where Apa stands between armed guards, clutching the doll tightly in one hand, while the Captain announces their arrival to the butler, a plump, obviously Bengali man who looks Apa up and down condescendingly and then addresses himself to the Captain.

"His Lordship and her Ladyship are entertaining dinner guests tonight. But I shall convey news of your arrival."

"Please do," says Captain Bolton, stepping forward. "And if you would, add this message." He mutters something in the butler's ear, and the man blinks, looks at Apa once again, and then nods and walks ponderously away.

It is a while before he returns. "His Grace has given instructions for you to wait. When they have supped, you shall be summoned to the Reception Room. It appears His Grace's guests are curious to see this toy as well."

Another interminable wait, and then a liveried footman appears, asking that they follow him. They do so, under dangling chandeliers and past the portraits and busts of governors gone by, and walls covered with thick, woven tapestries, tiger skins, and mounted bison heads. One soldier marches behind her, the Captain in front, as Apa scurries to keep up, reaching into the folds of her sari for the jute scraps she'd saved. They make their way up the broad, carpeted spiral marble staircase, and into a large hall, filled with shiny ornaments, more sculptures, and several large stuffed tigers standing on wooden platforms. A massive chandelier dangles from the ceiling. There are about a dozen people in the room, men and women dressed in European finery, some holding wineglasses.

"Ah, Bolton," says one, a tall, thin man with a receding hairline and a long, delicate nose.

"My Lord," says Captain Bolton, snapping to attention with a salute.

"You have it?"

"Indeed, sir. Well, she does." He gestures towards Apa.

"Ah, yes, of course. Nigel told me of your planned performance. We are all most eager to see it, are we not?"

"Indeed we are," says a woman, stately and fair-haired, coming to stand beside him. "Where is it, John?"

"The woman has it, my dear. Well? Where is her Ladyship's present?"

Apa feels Bolton nudge her and she steps forward, holding up the putul. A murmur runs through the gathering.

"Ah, excellent! Very satisfactory indeed!" exclaims the Governor.

He turns to one of the others, a man with bushy side-whiskers that Apa notices still have some breadcrumbs trapped in them. "Here, take a gander at this, Hadley. I told you, these natives do some mighty fine work. Not a lot they're good at, but spices and trinkets, they jolly well know their way about those. And it laughs, you say, Bolton?"

"That's what she claimed, sir," replies the Captain.

"Capital, capital. You've done a commendable job, Bolton. Commendable, I say."

"Thank you very much, sir."

"I am anxious to see this," says Lady Herbert. "I have been quite charmed since you told me of it. A doll that laughs on its own. Imagine that! It sounds rather too good to be true!"

"Indeed," says the Governor. "Well, what are we waiting for? Show us!"

Apa nods and holds up the hashi'r putul again, as they crowd around her. She runs her hands over her face, sliding past her cheeks and down her ears and the sides of her neck. Now she smiles and folds her hands together under her chin in a formal nomoshkar, making sure to meet each of their eyes in turn.

Then she takes a deep breath, filling her lungs, throws her

head back, and as loudly as she can, she laughs.

And as she does, a high, shrill cackle bursts forth from the putul.

"Well," says Governor Herbert, looking startled. "That's not very nice, is it? I'm rather disappointed. Stop it now, I'm really not happy with—"

He breaks off, snickers, and then does so again, until it is a steady chuckle. And now his Lordship is laughing, the sort of laughter that comes straight from the gut, strong and insistent, louder and louder until he's doubled up, roaring in full-throated merriment. Beside Apa, Captain Bolton is leaning against a chair, tears streaming down his cheeks as he laughs. Around him, the others are laughing too, different tenors and pitches, but all laughing as loudly as they can, breaking off only to cough or splutter before they go back to shrieking in mirth. They're on the ground now, all of them, still laughing, spittle flying everywhere. Neck muscles knot, veins bulge, first in foreheads, and then everywhere else across their pale, now-sallow skin. Some are trying to shield their ears, but to no avail, the laughter keeps spilling out of them, bursting forth, as juice from the overripe mango fallen from the tree. And loudest of, rising above the cacophony of their cumulative cachinnations, is the cackling tone of the putul, as it forces them, one by one, to match its tempo, faster and faster.

"I hope you are all enjoying yourselves," Apa says in Bangla.

They don't understand her, and yet they do; she can see the terror in their eyes now, faces contorting in horror as they realise what is happening and how utterly powerless they are to do anything about it. Anything but look at her with supplication in those very eyes, as she smiles back at each of them in turn. As Apa watches, a crimson stain slowly spreads out across the carpet; one of them has hit his or her head. Another has stopped laughing, Hadley, his eyes now staring sightlessly up at the chandelier. One down. Everyone else to go.

Apa takes a step back, then another, as the Governor hauls himself to his knees, hands clasping at his chest, still laughing, gasping, straining to speak, so Apa has to read his lips.

"Make—stop!" he chokes out between roars of mirth. "Please!"

Apa shakes her head and turns away, walking towards the door, stepping over the convulsing figure of the butler on the ground.

"Help me, sister!" he mouths in Bangla.

She steps over him. Traitor. He deserves to die with the rest of them.

At the door, she turns back, looking at Bolton, who has both hands to his throat, trying to choke back the peals. A steady stream of blood trickles out of his nostrils; more of it is welling up in his eyes, those eyes that are looking straight at Apa. She looks right back into them, and still holding his gaze, she nods. He raises a shaking, accusing finger at her, and then falls back on the ground, racked with laughter, blood now pouring out of his mouth as well.

She walks back out into the hallway, making her way back towards the staircase. She reaches into her ears, making sure the jute plugs are still firmly in place. Then she turns around to look back down the hallway, just in time to see a host of armed soldiers rush into the room she's exited. She waits, a minute, five, ten. None of them come back out. She walks back to the room, and peers in; there are now about twenty of them on the floor, although only the new soldiers are moving, laughing. There's a lot more blood in the room than there had been a while ago.

Slowly, Apa makes her way down the staircase, and out

through the front door. Here she sits down, on the large marble steps, leaning back against them, drawing in another deep breath, filling her lungs with the sweet, heady scent of jasmine and gulmohar. This is as good a place as any. Carefully, deliberately, she pulls the earplugs out, tossing them down.

"Thank you, old friend," she says, watching the jute leave as it flaps away on the breeze. Her partner that has just completed its final task—to protect her from her greatest creation.

Her Hatya'r Putul has done its work well. She turns her head, glancing back up at the building. Somewhere up there it's still working, cackling ever louder and faster, until there will be nothing left in that room but flesh waiting to rot.

Sooner or later one of the British will realise this and not venture into that room. Then they'll come looking for her. And she is ready, she's been ready ever since Nilesh left, taken from her by a man in London none of them will ever meet.

"I'll see you again soon," she whispers into the wind.

And Apa begins to laugh.

Ten Excerpts from an Annotated Bibliography on the Cannibal Women of Ratnabar Island

By Nibedita Sen

1. Clifton, Astrid. "The Day the Sea Ran Red." *Uncontacted Peoples of the World*. Routledge Press, 1965, pp. 71-98.

"There are few tales as tragic as that of the denizens of Ratnabar Island. When a British expedition made landfall on its shores in 1891, they did so armed to the teeth, braced for the same hostile reception other indigenous peoples of the Andamans had given them. What they found, instead, was a primitive hunter-gatherer community composed almost entirely of women and children. [. . .] The savage cultural clash that followed would transmute the natives' offer of a welcoming meal into direst offense, triggering a massacre at the hands of the repulsed British . . ."

2. Feldwin, Hortensia. *Roots of Evil: A Headmistress' Account of What Would Come To Be Known as the Churchill Dinner*. Westminster Press, 1943.

"Three girl-children were saved from Ratnabar. One would perish on the sea voyage, while two were conducted to England as Her Majesty's wards. Of these, one would go on to be enrolled in Churchill Academy, where she was given a

Christian name and the promise of a life far removed from the savagery of her homeland. [. . .] Regina proved herself an apt pupil, industrious, soaking up offered tutelage like a sponge does ink, if prone to intemperate moods and a tendency to attach herself with sudden fits of feverish fondness to one or more of the other girls [. . .] None of us could have foreseen what she and Emma Yates whispered into each others' ears behind closed doors as they planned their foul feast."

3. Schofield, Eleanor. "Eating the Other." *Word of Mouth*. State University of New York, 2004, pp. 56-89.

"It's not for no reason that women have, historically, been burdened with the duties of food preparation. Or that it is women, not men, who are called upon to limit their appetites, shrink themselves, rein in their ambitions. A hungry woman is dangerous. [. . .] Men are arbiters of discourse, women the dish to be consumed. And the Ratnabari, in the exercising of their transgressive appetites, quite literally turn the tables on their oppressors."

4. Morris, Victoria. "Memory, Mouth, Mother: Funerary Cannibalism among the Ratnabari." *Journal of Ethnographic Theory*, vol. 2, no. 2, 1994, pp. 105-129. Jstor, doi: 10.2707/464631.

"We are all cannibals at birth, and our mother-tongue is the language of the mouth. When the Ratnabari eat of their dead, they embrace what Kristeva calls 'the abject'—the visceral, the polluted, the blood and bile and placenta and the unclean flesh we associate with the female body. Return to us, they say to their dead, be with us always. [. . .] Science has yet to explain how it is that they almost never bear sons, only daughters, but it is scarce to be wondered at that their society is matriarchal in nature, for they spurn the clean, rational world of the patriarchal symbolic, remaining locked in a close, almost incestuous relationship with the maternal semiotic instead."

5. Aspioti, Elli. "A Love That Devours: Emma Yates and Regina Gaur." *A History of Twentieth-Century Lesbians*, edited by Jenna Atkinson, Palgrave Macmillan, 2009, pp. 180-195.

"What is it about love that makes us take leave of our senses? What makes a girl of barely seventeen carve fillets of flesh from her ribs and, lacing her clothes back up over the bulk of soaked bandages, serve her own stewed flesh to a table of her classmates at her wealthy private school?"

6. Rainier, Richard. "A Rebuttal of Recent Rumours Heard Among the Populace." *The Times*, 24 Apr. 1904, pp. 14.

"Every rag barely worth the paper it is printed on has pounced on the regrettable happenings at Churchill Academy, and as such salacious reporting is wont to do, this has had an impact on the minds of impressionable youth. [. . .] [A] rash of imitative new fads in the area of courtship, such as presenting a lover with a hair from one's head or a clipping of fingernail to consume, perhaps even a shaving of skin, or blood, sucked from a pricked finger [. . .] As to the rumours that the Ratnabari gain shapeshifting powers through the consumption of human flesh, or that they practice a form of virgin birth—I can say with certainty that these are pure exaggeration, and that their proponents are likely muddling real events with the mythological figure of the rakshasi, a female demon from the Orient."

7. Gaur, Shalini. "The Subaltern Will Speak, If You'll Shut Up and Listen." *Interviews in Intersectionality*, by Shaafat Shahbandari and Harold Singh, 2012.

"[. . .] the problem is that we have everyone and their maiden aunt dropping critique on Ratnabar, but we're not hearing from us, the Ratnabari diaspora ourselves. If I have to deal with one more white feminist quoting Kristeva at me . . . [. . .] No, the real problem is that our goals are fundamentally different. They want to wring significance from our lives, we just want to find a way to live. There's not a lot of us, but we exist. We're here. We don't always quite see eye to eye with each other's . . . ideology, but we're not going anywhere, and we have to figure out what we are to each other, how we can live side by side. So why aren't we getting published?"

8. Gaur, Roopkatha. *A Daughter's Confession: The Collected Letters of Roopkatha Gaur*, edited by Mary Anolik, Archon Books, 2010, pp. 197-216.

"Mother didn't know. What Emma was planning, what was in the food that night, any of it. I've kept this secret so many years, but now that she's long gone, and I am old, I feel I can tell it at last, at least to you, my darling, and if only so I can pass beyond this world free of its weight. [. . .] Why did Emma do it? Does it matter? Love, foolishness, a hunger to believe in magic and power, a twisted obsession with Mother's supposed exotic origins, what does it matter? She did it. The truth is, I'm grateful. Whatever her motives, that meal gave Mother what she needed to escape that place. And I wouldn't have been born without it, though that's another story altogether. You could say a little bit of Emma lives on in me, even after all this time."

9. Gaur, Shalini. "We Can Never Go Home." *Hungry Diasporas: Annual Humanities Colloquium*, May 2008, Princeton University, Princeton, NJ.

"We know Ratnabar's coordinates. Aerial reconnaissance has confirmed people still live on the island. But how do I set foot on its shores, with my English accent and my English clothes, and not have them flee from me in the terror that was taught to them in 1891? Where do we go, descendants of stolen ones, trapped between two islands and belonging on neither—too brown for English sensibilities, too alien now for the home of our great-grandmothers? How shall we live, with Ratnabar in our blood but English on our tongues?"

10. Gaur, Ashanti. "Dead and Delicious II: Eat What You Want, and If People Don't Like It, Eat Them Too." *Bitch Media*, 2 Nov. 2016, https://www.bitchmedia.org/article/eat-want-people-eat/2016. Accessed 8 Dec. 2017.

"My cousin Shalini is an optimist. She believes in keeping the peace, getting along, not rocking the boat. What do I believe in? I think—let's be real, ladies, who among us hasn't sometimes had a craving to eat the whole damn world? You know which of you I'm talking to. Yes you, out there. You've tried so hard to be good. To not be too greedy. You made yourself small and you hoped they'd like you better for it, but they didn't, of course, because they're the ones who're insatiable. Who'll take everything you have to give them and still hunger for more. It's time to stop making ourselves small. And above all, remember . . . there may be more of them, but we don't need them to make more of us."

[Submitted for Professor Blackwood's Sociology 402 class, by Ranita Gaur.]

A Catalog of Storms

By Fran Wilde

The wind's moving fast again. The weathermen lean into it, letting it wear away at them until they turn to rain and cloud.

"Look there, Sila." Mumma points as she grips my shoulder.

Her arthritis-crooked hand shakes. Her cuticles are pale red from washwater. Her finger makes an arc against the sky that ends at the dark shadows on the cliffs.

"You can see those two, just there. Almost gone. The weather wouldn't take them if they weren't wayward already, though." She *tsks*. "Varyl, Lillit, pay attention. Don't let that be any of you girls."

Her voice sounds proud and sad because she's thinking of her aunt, who turned to lightning.

The town's first weatherman.

The three of us kids stare across the bay to where the setting sun's turned the cliff dark. On the edge of the cliff sits an old mansion that didn't fall into the sea with the others: the Cliffwatch. Its turrets and cupolas are wrapped with steel cables from the broken bridge. Looks like metal vines grabbed and tethered the building to the solid part of the jutting cliff.

All the weathermen live there, until they don't anymore.

"They're leaned too far out and too still to be people." Varyl waves Mumma's hand down.

Varyl always says stuff like that because...

"They *used* to be people. They're weathermen now," Lillit answers.

...Lillit always rises to the bait.

"You don't know what you're talking *about*," Varyl whispers, and her eyes dance because she knows she's got her twin in knots, wishing to be first and best at something. Lillit is always second at everything.

Mumma sighs, but I wait, ears perked, for whatever's coming next because it's always something wicked. Lillit has a fast temper.

But none of us are prepared this time.

"I *do too know.* I talked to one, once," Lillit yells and then her hand goes up over her mouth, just for a moment, and her eyes look like she'd cut Varyl if she thought she'd get away with it.

And Mumma's already turned and got Lillit by the ear. "You did what." Her voice shudders. "Varyl, keep an eye out."

Some weathermen visit relatives in town, when the weather is calm. They look for others like them, or who might be. When they do that, mothers hide their children.

Mumma starts to drag Lillit on home. And just then a passing weatherman starts to scream by the fountain as if he'd read Mumma's weather, not the sky's.

When weathermen warn about a squall, it always comes. Storms aren't their fault, and they'll come anyway. The key is to know what kind of storm's coming and what to do when it does. Weathermen can do that.

For a time.

I grab our basket of washing. Mumma and Varyl grab Lillit. We run as far from the fountain as fast as we can, before the sky turns ash-grey and the searing clouds—the really bad kind—begin to fall.

And that's how Lillit is saved from a thrashing, but is still lost to us in the end.

• • •

An Incomplete Catalog of Storms

A Felrag: the summer wind that turns the water green first, then churns up dark clouds into fists. Not deadly, usually, but good to warn the boats.

A Browtic: rising heat from below that drives the rats and snakes from underground before they roast there. The streets swirl with them, they bite and bite until the browtic cools. Make sure all babies are well and high.

A Neap-Change: the forgotten tide that's neither low nor high, the calmest of waters, when what rests in the deeps slowly slither forth. A silent storm that looks nothing like a storm. It looks like calm and moonlight on water, but then people go missing.

A Glare: a storm of silence and retribution, with no forgiveness, a terror of it, that takes over a whole community until the person causing it is removed. It looks like a dry wind, but it's always some person that's behind it.

A Vivid: that bright sunlit rainbow-edged storm that seduces young women out into the early morning before they've been properly wrapped in cloaks. The one that gets in their lungs and makes them sing until they cry, until they can only taste food made of honey and milk and they grow pale and glass-eyed. Beware vivids in spring for the bride's sake.

A Searcloud: heated air so thick it blinds as it wraps charred arms around those it catches, then billows in the lungs, scorching words from their sounds, memories from their bearers. Often followed by sorrow, searclouds are best avoided, run through at top speed, or never named.

An Ashpale: thick, gathering clouds from the heights, where the ice forms. When it leaves, everything in its path is slick and frozen. Scream it away if you can, before your breath freezes too.

• • •

The Cliffwatch is broken now, its far wall tumbled half down to the ocean so that every room ends in water.

We go up there a lot to poke around now that we're older.

After that Searcloud passed, Mumma searched through our house until she found Lillit's notes—her name wasn't on them, but we'd know her penmanship anywhere. Since she's left-handed and it smears, whether chalk or ink. My handwriting doesn't smear. Nor Varyl's.

The paper—a whole sheet!—was crammed into a crack in the wall behind our bed. I rubbed the thick handmade weave of it between my fingers, counting until Mumma snatched it away again.

Lillit had been making up storms, five of them already, mixing them in with known weather. She'd been practicing.

Mumma shrieked at her, as you could imagine. "You *don't* want this. You don't *want* it."

I ducked behind Varyl, who was watching, wide-eyed. Everyone's needed for battle against the storms, but no one wants someone they love to go.

And Lillit, for the first time, didn't talk back. She stood as still as a weatherman. She *did* want it.

While we ran to her room to help her pack, Mumma wept.

The Mayor knocked when it was time to take Lillit up the cliff. "Twice in your family! Do you think Sila too? Or Varyl?" He looked eagerly around Mumma's wide frame at us. "A great honor!"

"Sila and Varyl don't have enough sense to come out of the rain, much less call storms," Mumma said. She bustled the Mayor from the threshold and they flanked Lillit, who stepped forward without a word, her face already saying "up," even as her feet crunched the gravel down.

• • •

Mumma left her second-eldest daughter inside the gates and didn't look back, as is right and proper.

She draped herself in honor until the Mayor left, so no one saw her crying but me and that's because I know Mumma better than she thinks I do.

I know Lillit too.

Being the youngest doesn't have many advantages, but this one is worth all the rest: everyone forgets you're there. If you're watchful, you can learn a lot.

Here are a few:

I knew Lillit could hear wind and water earlier than everyone else.

I know Varyl is practicing in her room every night trying to catch up.

I know Mumma's cried herself to sleep more than once and that Varyl wishes she were sleet and snow, alternately. That neither one know what Lillit will turn into when she goes.

And I know, whether Lillit turns to clouds or rain, that I'll be next, not Varyl. Me.

And that maybe someone will cry over me.

I already started making lists. I'll be ready.

• • •

Mumma goes up to the Cliffwatch all the time.

"You stay," she says to Varyl and me. But I follow, just close enough that I see Lillit start to go all mist around the edges, and Momma shake her back solid, crying.

Weathermen can't help it, they have to name the storms they think of, and soon they're warning about the weather for all of us, and eventually they fight it too.

While Mumma and I are gone, the Mayor comes by our house and puts a ribbon on our door. We get extra milk every Tuesday.

That doesn't make things better, in the end. Milk isn't a sister.

"The weather gets them and gets them," Mumma's voice is proud and sad when she returns. From now on, she won't say "wayward," won't hear anyone speak of Lilit nor her aunt as a cautionary tale. "We scold because of our own selfishness," she says. "We don't want them to change." Her aunt went gone a long time ago.

We all visit Lillit twice, early on. Once, sweeping through town after a squall. Another time, down near the fishing boats, where the lightning likes to play. She saved a fisherman swept out to sea, by blowing his boat back to safe harbor.

We might go more often, but Mumma doesn't want us to catch any ideas.

A basket of oysters appears outside our door. Then a string of smoked fish.

• • •

When storms come, weathermen name them away. Yelling works too. So does diving straight into it and shattering it, but you can only do that once you've turned to wind and rain.

Like I said, storms would come anyway. When we know

what to call them, we know how to fight them. And we can help the weathermen, Mumma says after Lillit goes, so they don't wear themselves out.

Weathermen give us some warning. Then we all fight back against the air.

"The storms got smarter than us," Varyl whispers at night when we can't sleep for missing her twin, "after we broke the weather. The wind and rain got used to winning. They liked it."

A predator without equal, the weather tore us to pieces after the sky turned grey and the sea rose.

Some drowned or were lost in the winds. Others fled, then gathered in safe places and hunkered down. Like in our town. Safe, cliffs on all sides, a long corridor we can see the ocean coming for miles.

Ours was a holiday place, once, until people started turning into weather too. Because the sky and the very air were broken, Varyl says.

Soon we stopped losing our treasures to the wind. Big things first: Houses stayed put. The hour hand for the clock stayed on the clock tower. Then little things too, like pieces of paper and petals. I wasn't used to so many petals staying on the trees.

The wind hadn't expected its prey to practice, to fight back.

When the weather realized, finally, that it was being named and outsmarted, then the wind started hunting down weathermen. Because a predator must always attack.

But the weathermen? Sometimes when they grow light enough, they lift into the clouds and push the weather back from up high.

"And through the hole they leave behind," Varyl whispers. Half asleep, I can barely hear her. "You can see the sky, blue as the denim our old dress might have been, once."

• • •

The Cliffwatch is broken now, its roof gaping wide as if the grey sky makes better shelter.

We climb over the building like rats, looking for treasure. For a piece of her.

We peer out at the ocean through where the walls used to be. We steal through a house that's leaned farther out over the water since the last time we came, a house that's grown loud in asking the wind to send its emptied frame into the sea.

Varyl stands watch, alone, always now. She's silent. She misses Lillit most.

Mumma and I collect baskets of hinges and knobs, latches and keyholes. People collect them, to remember. Some have storms inscribed around their edges: a Cumulous—which made the eardrums ring and then burst; a Bitter—where the wind didn't stop blowing until everyone fought.

"She learned them for us, Mumma," I whisper, holding an embroidered curtain. My fingers work the threads, turning the stitches into list of things I miss about Lillit: her laugh, her stubborn way of standing, her handwriting. How she'd brush my hair every morning without yanking, like Varyl does now.

Mumma doesn't shush me anymore. Her eyes tear up a little. "Sila, I remember before the storms, when half the days were sunny. When the sky was blue." She coughs and puts a grey ribbon in my basket. "At least, I remember people talking like that, about a blue sky."

I'm wearing Varyl's hand-me-down dress, it's denim, and used to be blue too; a soft baby blue when it belonged to my sister; a darker navy back when it was Mumma's long coat.

Now the grey bodice has winds embroidered on it, not storms. Varyl did the stitching. The dress says: felrag, mistral, lillit, föhn, in swirling white thread.

The basket I hold is made of grey and white sticks; my washing basket most days. Today it is a treasure basket. We are collecting what the weather left us.

Mumma gasps when she tugs up a floorboard to find a whole catalog of storms beaten into brass hinges.

We've found catalogs before, marked in pinpricks on the edge of a book and embroidered with tiny stitches in the hem of a curtain, but never so many. They sell well at market, as people think they're lucky.

Time was, if you could name a storm, you could catch it, for a while. Beat it.

If it didn't catch you first.

So the more names in the catalog, the luckier they feel.

We've never sold Lillit's first catalog. That one's ours.

• • •

After Lillit goes, I try naming storms.

A Somanyquestions: the storm of younger sisters, especially. There is nothing you can do about it.

A Toomuchtoofast: that storm that plagues mothers sometimes. Bring soothing cakes and extra hands for holding things and folding things.

A Leaving: that rush when everything swoops up in dust and agitation and what's left is scoured. Prepare to bolt your doors so you don't lose what wants to be lost.

When I sneak up to the Cliffwatch to show my sister, she's got rain for hair and wind in her eyes, but she hugs me and laughs at my list and says to keep trying.

Mumma never knows how often I visit her.

• • •

"Terrible storms, for years," Varyl tells it, "snatched people straight from their houses. Left columns of sand in the chairs, dragged weeds through the bedding."

But then we happened, right back at the weather. I know this story. And the battle's gone on for a while.

Long before Lillit and Varyl and I were born, the Mayor's son shouted to the rain to stop before one of her speeches. And it did. Mumma's aunt at the edge of town yelled back lightning once.

The weather struck back: a whole family became a thick grey mist that filled their house and didn't disperse.

Then Mumma's aunt and the Mayor's son shouted weather names when storms approached. At first it was frightening, and people stayed away. Then the Mayor realized how useful, how fortunate. Put them up at the Cliffwatch, to keep them safe.

Then the news crier, she went out one day and saw snow on her hand—a single, perfect flake. The day was warm, the sky clear, trees were budding and ready to make more trees and she lifted the snowflake to her lips and whirled away.

The town didn't know what to think. We'd been studying the weather that became smarter than us. We'd gotten the weather in us too, maybe.

Mumma's aunt turned to lightning and struck the clouds. Scattered them.

Right after that, the ocean grabbed the bluff and ripped it down. Left the Cliffwatch tilted over the ocean, but the people who'd got the weather in them didn't want to leave.

That was the battle—had been already, but now we knew it was a fight—the weathermen yelling at the weather, to warn us before the storms caught them too. The parents yelling at their kids to stay out of the rain. Out of the Cliff-watch.

But I'd decided. I'd go when my turn came.

Because deciding you needed to do something was always so much better than waking up to find you'd done it.

Mumma's aunt had crackled when she was angry; the Mayor's son was mostly given to dry days and wet days until he turned to squall one morning and blew away.

The storms grew stronger. The bigger ones lasted weeks. The slow ones took years. At market, we heard whispers: a few in town worried the storms fed on spent weathermen. Mumma hated that talk. It always followed a Searcloud.

Sometimes, storms linked together to grow strong: Ashpales and Vivids and Glares.

• • •

I lied when I said Mumma never looked back. I saw her do it.

She wasn't supposed to but the Mayor had walked on and she turned and I watched her watch Lillit with a hunger that made me stomp out the gate.

Returning to the Cliffwatch is worse than looking back. Don't tell anyone but she does that in secret. All the time.

She doesn't visit then. She stands outside the gates in the dark when she can't sleep, draped in shadows so no one will see her, except maybe Lillit. I sneak behind her, walking in her footsteps so nothing crunches to give me away.

I see her catch Lillit in the window of the Cliffwatch now and then. See Lillit lift a hand and curl it. See Mumma match the gesture and then Lillit tears away.

Mumma doubles her efforts to lure Lillit back. She leaves biscuits on the cliff's edge. Hair ribbons, "in case the wind took Lillit's from her."

She forgets to do the neighbors' laundry, twice, until they ask someone else. We stay hungry for a bit, then Varyl goes after the washing.

Up in the old clock tower in town where a storm took the

second and minute hands but left the hour, a weatherman starts shouting about a Clarity.

Mumma starts running towards the cliff, but not for safety.

Varyl and I go screeching after her, a different kind of squall, beating against the weather, up to the Cliffwatch.

• • •

A Secret Catalog of Storms

A Loss That's Probably Your Fault: a really quiet storm. Mean too. It gets smaller and smaller until it tears right through you.

A Grieving: this one sneaks up on mothers especially and catches them off guard. Hide familiar things that belong to loved ones, make sure they can't surprise anyone. A lingering storm.

An I Told You Not To, Sila: an angry storm, only happens when someone finds your lists. The kind that happens when they burn the list so that no one will know you're catching wayward.

• • •

The biggest storm yet hits when we're almost done running.

We're near the top of the cliff, the big old house in our sights, and bam, the Clarity brings down torrents of bright-lit rain that makes the insides of our ears hurt. Breathing sears our lungs and we can't tell if that's from the running or the storm. And then the storm starts screeching, tries to pull our hair, drag us over the cliff.

We try to shelter in the Cliffwatch.

The wind hums around us, the ice starts blueing our cheeks, Varyl's teeth start chattering and then stop, and oh let us in, I cry. Don't be so stubborn.

Varyl pounds on the door.

But this time, the door doesn't open for Varyl. The door doesn't mind Mumma either, no matter how hard she pounds.

Only when I crawl through the freeze, around to the cliff's edge and yell, something turns my way, blows the shutters open. I pull my family through, even Mumma, who is trying to stay out in the wind, trying to make it take her too.

We get inside the Cliffwatch and shake ourselves dry. "That Clarity had an Ashpale on the end of it," I say. I'm sure of it. "There's a Bright coming."

So many storms, all at once, and I know their names. They are ganging up against us.

I want to fight.

Varyl stares at me, shouts for Mumma, but Mumma's searching the rooms for Lillit.

"We can't stay here and lose Sila too," Varyl says. She turns to me. "You *don't* want this."

But I *do*, I think. I want to fight the weather until it takes me too.

And maybe Mumma wants it also.

Varyl clasps my hand, and Mumma's, the minute the weather stops howling. She drags us both back to our house, through the frozen wood, across the square, past the frozen fountain. Our feet crunch ice into petals that mark our path. Varyl's shouting at Mumma. She's shaking her arm, which judders beneath her shirt, all the muscles loose and swingy, but the part of Mumma at the end of the arm doesn't move. Because she saw what I saw, she saw Lillit begin to blow, saw her hair rise and flow, and her fingers and all the rest of her with it, out to face the big storm, made of Ashpale and Vivid and Glare and Clarity.

That was the last time we saw Lillit's face in any window. Mumma had brought ribbons but those blew away. Now sometimes she scatters petals for Lillit to play with.

• • •

Climbing the remains of the Cliffwatch later, we find small storms in corners, a few dark clouds. You can put them in jars now and take them home, watch until the lightning fades.

Sometimes they don't fade, these pieces of weather. The frozen water that doesn't thaw. A tiny squall that rides your shoulder until you laugh.

They're still here, just lesser, because the weather is less too.

That day, all the storms spilled over the bay at once, fire from below and lightning and the green clouds and the grey. That day, the weathermen rose up into the wind and shouted until they were raw and we hid, and the storms shouted back—one big storm where there had been many smaller ones—and it dove for the town, the Cliffwatch, the few ships in the harbor.

And the weathermen hung from the cliff house and some of them caught the wind. Some of them turned to rain. Some to lightning. Then they all struck back together. The ones who already rode the high clouds too.

We wanted to help, I could feel the clouds tugging at my breath, but some of the winds beat at our cheeks and the rain struck our faces, pushing us back. And the terrible storms couldn't reach us, couldn't take us.

Instead, the Cliffwatch cracked and the clouds and the wind swept it all up back into the sky where it had come from long ago.

Later, we walked home. A spot of blue sky opened up and

just as suddenly disappeared. A cool breeze crossed my face and I felt Lillit's fingers in it.

• • •

A hero is more than a sister. And less.

The milk keeps coming, but the fish doesn't.

The weathermen are in the clouds now. Varyl says they keep the sky blue and the sea green and the air clear of ice.

We climb into the Cliffwatch sometimes to find the notes and drawings, the hinges and papers and knobs. We hold these tight, a way to touch the absences. We say their names. We say, *they did it for us. They wanted to go.*

With the wind on my skin and in my ears, I still think I could blow away too if I wished hard enough.

Mumma says we don't need weathermen as much anymore.

Sometimes a little bit of sky even turns blue on its own.

Still, we hold their catalogs close: fabric and metal; wind and rain.

We try to remember their faces.

• • •

At sunset, Mumma goes to the open wall facing the ocean.

"You don't need to stay," she says, stubborn, maybe a little selfish.

But there she is so there I am beside her and soon Varyl also.

All of us, the sunset painting our faces bright. And then, for a moment before us out over the sea, there she is too, our Lillit, blowing soft against our cheeks.

We stretch out our arms to hug her and she weaves between them like a breath.

How the Trick is Done

by A.C. Wise

The Magician Takes a Bow

How many people can say they were there the night the trick went wrong and the Magician died on stage? Certainly, that first morning on the strip—dazed gamblers blinking in the rising light, the ambulance come and gone, with the smell of gunpowder lingering in the air—everyone claimed they knew someone who heard the Magician's Assistant scream, saw the spray of blood, saw a man rush on stage and faint dead away.

Of course very few people making the claim, then or now, are telling the truth. Vegas is a city of illusion, and everyone likes feeling they're in on the secret, understand how the trick is done, but very few do.

The end came for the Magician, fittingly, during the Bullet-Catch-Death-Cheat, the trick that made him famous. A real gun is fired by a willing audience member. The Magician dies. The Magician reappears alive and at back of the theater. Presto, abracadabra, ta-da.

There are small variations. Sometimes the Magician's Assistant fires the gun, if the audience is squeamish, or especially drunk. She revels in these brief moments in the spotlight, dreaming of being a magician herself some day. Sometimes the Magician reappears in the balcony, waving, and sometimes by the exit doors. Once he reappeared as a vendor selling popcorn, his satin-lapelled jacket smelling of butter and heat and salt. Once, he came back as a waiter and spilled a drink on an audience member who was confidently whispering that they knew exactly how he pulled it off.

Just because Houdini flashed bullets in his smile years before the Magician was born, people think they have it nailed down. Variations on tricks of every kind are a grand tradition in the magic world, and everyone knows none of it is real. The world is rational; it obeys certain rules. They hold this truth like shield against the swoop in their bellies every time the Magician falls and gets back up again. None would dare admit out loud that deep down, a tiny part of them desperately wants to believe.

Here's the secret, and it's a simple one: dying is easy. All the Magician has to do is stand with teeth clenched, muscles tight, breath slowed, and wait. The real work is left to his Resurrectionist girlfriend, Angie, standing just off stage, night after night, doing the impossible, upsetting the natural order of the world. Her timing is always impeccable, her focus a razor's edge. Her entire will is trained on holding the bullet in place, coaxing the Magician's blood to flow and forbidding his heart from simply quitting out of shock. Death can be very startling, after all.

There is pain, of course, but by the time he died for good, it had become a habit for the Magician, and besides, the applause made it worthwhile. He never once allowed himself to think about the thousand huge and tiny things had to go right for the trick to work, or that only one had to go wrong.

After all, the Resurrectionist pulled it off night after night—how hard could it be? Inside the wash of the spotlight, he couldn't see her grit her teeth, how she sweated in the shadows while he flashed his smile and took his bows. Everything always went off, just like magic, and he always managed to vanish by the time her raging headache set in, forcing her to lie in a dark room with a cold cloth over her eyes.

But she never complained. The money was good, and much like dying had become a habit for the Magician, the Magician had become a habit for her.

Maybe they could have gone on like that forever if it hadn't been for the Magician's Assistant. Not the one who fired the gun, but the first one. Meg, who died and came back as a ghost.

• • •

The Assistant Takes Flight

Meg was young when she was the Magician's Assistant, but everyone was back then. She was also in love with the Magician, but everyone was that back then, too. Even Rory, the Magician's longtime stage manager, who was perhaps the most in love of all.

Rory thought of Meg as a little sister, and Meg thought of Rory as a dear friend, but neither of them ever spoke of their feelings for the Magician aloud. They worked side by side every day, believing themselves alone in their singular orbits of longing, both ashamed to have fallen so far and so hard for so long.

All of this was before the Magician's Resurrectionist girlfriend, before the Bullet-Catch-Death-Cheat was even a gleam in the Magician's eye. Back then, before coming back from the dead to thunderous applause supplanted it all, the Magician sawed women in half, plucked cards from thin air, nicked watches from sleeves, and pulled one very grumpy rabbit out of a hat night after night. Off stage and on, the Magician called the rabbit Gus, even though that wasn't his name, and assigned him motives and personality to make the audience laugh.

Whether it was the name or the hat, the rabbit only tolerated this for so long, and one fateful night, he bit the Magician hard enough to necessitate the tip of his left index finger being sewn back on. After the blood and the gauze, and the trip to the hospital, the Magician decided he was fed up too. He needed a new act, a new assistant, a fresh start.

He didn't consult or warn Meg, but directed her to an all-night diner as she drove him back from the emergency room. Up until the moment the words "I'm done," came from the Magician's mouth, Meg harbored the hope that this trauma would allow him to finally see her, and that he'd invited her to the diner at 1:47 a.m. to confess his love.

Instead, he broke her heart and put her out of a job in the same breath. And he didn't even have the decency to pay for her half of the meal.

Meg stared at the Magician. The Magician fidgeted with his gauze, and looked at the door and the neon and the cooling desert outside.

"I'm sure you'll land on your feet, kid," he said.

Meg blinked. She dug in her purse for tissues and money for the meal. When she looked up, the Magician was gone. Vanished into thin air.

Meg dropped coins and bills on the table without counting. Colt-wobbly legs carried her into the night. The air seared her lungs, and tears frosted her lashes. All up and down the strip, everything blurred into a river of light.

The Magician's Assistant—she wasn't even that anymore. Just Meg, and her parents had drilled into her young that that wasn't worth anything at all. Who was she, if she wasn't with the Magician? What could she possibly be?

Lacking evidence to the contrary, she chose to believe her parents. On stage with the Magician, she could pretend the glitter on her costume was a little bit of his glory rubbed off on her. Alone, she was nothing at all, and her ridiculous costume was just sequins, falling in her wake as she hailed a cab.

The car stopped at a location she must have given, though she didn't remember saying anything at all. The space between her shoulder blades itched. She climbed out. Wind tugged at her hair and she took a moment to breathe in awe at the lights illuminating the vast sweep of concrete, a marvel of engineering, a wonder of the new world.

Meg left her purse on the backseat. She slipped off her shoes. The itch between her shoulder blades grew. Feathers ached to push themselves out from inside her skin.

Instead of landing on her feet, Meg landed at the bottom of Hoover Dam. A 727 foot drop that should have been impossible with all the security, except that just for a moment, Meg borrowed a little bit of magic—real magic—for her own. As she jumped, feathers burst from her skin and all the sequins in her costume blazed like stars. For just one instant before she fell, the Magician's Assistant flew.

• • •

The Stage Manager Brings White Roses

Rory remembered Meg, and it seemed he was the only one.

Before she hit the ground, before he left the diner and Meg sitting stunned in the booth behind him, the Magician had already forgotten her name. If he ever knew it at all. While Meg flew, capturing a moment of real magic without an audience or applause, the Magician was at a bar forgetting what he'd never remembered in the first place, and so Rory was the one who got the call. He sat on the floor, put his head in his hands, and sobbed.

Even though the Magician paid her a pittance, Meg brought Rory coffee and pastry at least once a week. He taught her how to knit. She taught him how to throw a fastball. She invited him to her tiny apartment, and introduced him to her guinea pigs, Laurel and Hardy. They watched old movies, both having a fondness for Vincent Price, William Powell, and Myrna Loy, and popcorn with too much salt. They laughed at stupid things, and cried at sad ones, and never let each other know of their mutual ache for the Magician.

Now that it was too late, Rory saw that of course he was like Meg, she was like him, and they were both fools. He brought a massive spray of white roses to her funeral. He laid them gently atop her cheap coffin, and his heart broke all over again. There were only five other people in the tiny chapel, and the Magician wasn't one of them.

Rory hated him. Or, he meant to. Except when the Magician came to him three days later and told Rory he was putting together a new show and would Rory continue to stage manage him, Rory didn't hesitate half as long as he should have before answering. His heart stuttered, his breath caught. The word no shaped itself on his lips, and the word yes emerged instead.

He betrayed Meg's memory, and loathed himself for it, but he didn't change his mind. The best Rory could do was press a single white rose in his handkerchief, and tuck it in a pocket over his heart, listening to it crackle as he followed the Magician to start again.

Every night, under the lights, the Magician smiled. His teeth dazzled with a rainbow of gel colors Rory directed his way. Every time the gun fired, Rory felt the kick of it reverberate inside him. His blood thundered. His stomach swooped. He ached with the Magician and felt his pain as he watched him fall.

Every night as the Magician allowed himself to be shot, Rory held his breath. He clenched his teeth. His muscles went tight with hope and dread wondering if this time the Magician might finally stay down so he could be free.

• • •

The Resurrectionist and the Ghost

Angie is the first person to see Meg when she comes back from the dead. The Resurrectionist sits in the Magician's dressing room, applying concealer over the exhausted bags under her eyes. No one will see her in the wings, but that's precisely why she does it. The makeup is a little thing she can do for herself and no one else.

It's getting harder to hold everything together, to *want* to hold it together—tell the bullet to stop, to cease to be once it's inside the Magician's skin, and tell the Magician's blood to go. She sleeps eighteen hours a day, and it isn't enough. Angie's life has become an endless cycle—wake, eat, turn back death, applause that isn't for her, sleep, repeat ad infinitum.

She smoothes the sponge around the corner of her left eye, and the ghost appears. Angie starts, and feels something like recognition.

"I've been waiting for you." The words surprise Angie; she wonders what she means. A vague memory tugs at the back of her skull, of a night in a bar long ago, but before she can grab hold it fades away.

"Who are you?" the ghost asks.

"Who are *you*?" Angie counters.

"The Magician's Assistant," the ghost says.

"The Magician's girlfriend." The words leave a bitter, powdery, crushed aspirin taste on Angie's tongue.

Angie laughs; it's a brittle sound. How absurd, that they should define themselves solely in relation to the Magician. The ghost looks hurt until Angie speaks again.

"I'm Angie."

"Meg." The ghost gives her name reluctantly as if she isn't entirely sure.

"So, you were the Magician's Assistant," Angie says.

Memory nags at her again, and all at once, the pieces click into place. When she and the Magician first met, he'd worn sorrow like a coat two sizes too large, but one he wasn't even aware of wearing. Angie had sensed a hurt in him, and it had intrigued her, and now she knows—the hurt belonged to Meg all along.

There's a certain flavor to it, tingeing the air. Even with the glass between them, Angie tastes it—like pancakes drowned in syrup, and coffee with too much cream.

Looking at Meg, Angie sees herself in the mirror. The Magician pulled a trick on both of them, sleight of hand. They should have been looking one direction, but he'd convinced them to look elsewhere as he vanished their names like a card up his sleeve, tucked them into a cabinet painted with stars so they emerged transformed—a dove, a bouquet of flowers, a Resurrectionist, a ghost. If Angie squints just right, there's a blur framing Meg, a faint, smudgy glow sprouting from between her shoulder blades. It almost looks like wings, but when Angie blinks, it's gone.

Well, shit, Angie thinks, but doesn't say it aloud.

Behind Meg, sand blows. Or maybe it's snow. The image flickers, like two stations coming in on the TV at the same time, back when that was still a thing.

"Can I come through?" Angie asks.

"Can you?" Meg's eyes widen in surprise.

"I'm a Resurrectionist." Angie's mouth twists on the words, but she can't think of a better way to explain. "Death and I have an understanding."

Angie reaches through the glass. The mirror wavers, and Meg's fingers close on Angie's hand.

"Is there somewhere we can talk?" Angie asks.

Meg shrugs, embarrassed. This is her death, but it isn't under her control.

"Over there?" Angie points to the neon shining through the storm.

Meg shudders, but her expression remains perfectly blank. She looks to Angie like a person actively forgetting the worst moment in their world.

As they walk, Angie learns that for Meg, sometimes death looks like a desert with a lomo camera filter applied. Sometimes it's sand and sometimes snow, but it's always littered with bleached cow bones and skulls. It's a place where you're always walking toward the horizon, carrying your best party shoes, but you never arrive. Mostly, though, Meg's death looks like a diner at 1:47 am, right before your boss—the man you love—tells you you're out of a job and a future and good luck on the way down.

Inside the diner, laminated menus decorate each booth. The wind ticks sand against the glass as Meg and Angie slide onto cracked red faux-leather banquettes. In the corner, a silent jukebox glows.

"I don't mean to be indelicate, but you've been dead for a while. Why come back now?"

The air is scented with fry grease and coffee on the edge of burnt, old cooking smells trapped like ghosts.

"I don't know," Meg says. "I think something important is about to happen. Or it already happened. I can't tell."

She shreds her napkin into little squares, letting them fall like desert snow. Her nails are ragged, the skin around them chewed. This time when Angie squints, Meg goes translucent, and Angie sees her falling without end.

• • •

The Rabbit Returns

The first time Angie saw the Magician, he had gauze wrapped around his left index finger, spotted with dried blood. She'd just lost her job, or rather it had lost her. Donna, who sat in the next cubicle over, caught Angie uncurling the browned leaves of a plant, bringing them back from the brink of death to full glossy health. Angie's boss called Angie into her office at noon, and by 1 p.m. Angie was installed at a bar, getting slowly drunk.

The constant movement of the Magician's hands was what caught Angie's eye. She watched as he tried the same cheap card trick, only slightly clumsy with his injured hand, on almost every patron in the bar. No matter which card his mark chose, when the Magician asked, "Is this your card?" he revealed the Tarot card showing the Lovers, and smirked at the implications of flesh entwined. She watched until it worked, and someone left on the Magician's arm. Angie found herself simultaneously annoyed and amused, and the following night, she returned to the same bar, curious whether the Magician would as well.

The Magician did return, but there were no card tricks this time. She spotted him alone in a corner, his head resting on his folded arms. Angie slipped into his booth, holding her breath. If this was a performance, it was a good one. The Magician looked up, and Angie couldn't help the way her breath left in a huff. His face was stark with a grief, thick enough for her to touch.

"He's dead," the Magician said. "The little bastard bit me. He was my best friend, and now he's gone."

The Magician blinked at Angie as if she'd appeared out of thin air. Angie said nothing, and the Magician seemed to take it as encouragement to go on. He held up his gauze-wrapped finger, and poured out his pain.

"Maybe I left his cage open after he bit me because I was mad. Maybe I was distracted because I'd just fired my assistant and I forgot to latch it tight. Whatever happened, he got all the way outside, across the parking lot. I found him on the side of the road, flat as a swatted bug."

Tears glittered on the Magician's cheeks. They had to be real. If he'd been putting on a show, he would have made a point of letting Angie see him wipe them away.

"I put his body in a shoebox in my freezer. I'm going to bury him in the desert." The Magician laughed, an uneven sound. "Have you ever been to a rabbit funeral?"

The faint sheen at his cuffs spoke of wear. Despite the show he'd put on the night before—cheap card tricks to tumble marks into his bed—she saw a man down on his luck, wearing thin, a man whose deepest connection was with the rabbit who'd bit him then run away.

The Magician looked lost, baffled by grief—like a little boy just learning the world could hurt him. There was something pure in his sorrow, something Angie hadn't seen in Vegas in a long time. It looked like truth, and Angie wanted to gather it into her hands, a silk scarf endlessly pulled from a sleeve.

A shadow haloed the Magician. A death that wasn't the rabbit's clinging to his skin; he didn't even seem aware it was there. Angie caught her breath, deciding before she'd fully asked herself the question. That bigger death wasn't one she could touch, but the rabbit—that was a small thing she could heal.

"Do you want to see a magic trick?" she asked. "A real

one?"

The Magician's eyes went wide, touched with something like wonder. Maybe it was his grief making him see clear, but for just a moment, he seemed to truly see her. He nodded, and held out his hand.

The Magician led Angie to his shitty apartment. As they climbed the stairs, her nerves sang—a cage, full of doves waiting to be released, a star-spangled box with a beautiful woman vanishing inside. Her skin tingled. She considered that she was about to make the biggest mistake of her life, and decided to make it anyway.

"His name was Gus." The Magician set a shoebox on his makeshift coffee table.

The rabbit lay on his side. Despite the Magician's description, he wasn't particularly flat. He might have been sleeping, if not for the cold. It seeped into Angie's fingers as she held her hands above the corpse. The Magician watched her, all curiosity and intensity, and Angie blushed. A rabbit was different than a houseplant—what if she failed? And what if she succeeded?

The rabbit twitched. His pulse jumped in her veins, a panicked scrabbling. Angie placed her hands directly on the rabbit's soft, cold fur. She meant to make a hushing sound, soothing the rabbit's fear, but the Magician's mouth covered hers. Salt laced his tongue; was she crying, or was he? She lifted her hands from the rabbit and pressed them against the Magician's back instead to still their shaking. Death clung to them, tacky and oddly sweet. She resisted the urge to wipe her palms against the Magician's shirt, pulling him closer.

She'd never brought back anything larger than a sparrow. Now she could feel the rabbit's life in her—hungry, wild, wanting to run in every direction at once. The other, larger death continued to nibble at her edges—feathers itching beneath her skin, wind blowing over lonely ground.

The rabbit's pink nose twitched; his red-tinged eyes blew galaxy-wide. He ran a circle around the Magician's apartment, and the Magician laughed, a joyous, bellowing sound. He lifted Angie by the shoulders, twirling her around.

"Do you know what this means?" His voice crashed off the cracked and water-stained apartment walls.

He scooped her up, carried her to rumpled sheets still smelling of last night's sex. Angie's teeth chattered; the rabbit was still freezing, and the Magician was warm. She dug her fingers into his back, and leaned into him.

The sex was some of the strangest Angie had ever had. The Magician touched her over and over again, amazed, as if searching for something beneath her skin. For her part, Angie kept getting distracted. She snapped in and out of her body, pulled to the corner of the room where the rabbit rubbed his paws obsessively across his face. She giggled inappropriately, her limbs twitching beyond her control. She developed an insatiable craving for carrots. The Magician, lost in his own wild galaxy of stars, never seemed to notice at all.

In the morning, she found the Magician at his cramped kitchen table. The sense she'd forgotten something nagged at the back of her mind—something sad, something with feathers—but the more she reached after it, the further it withdrew. She watched the Magician scribble on a napkin, coffee cooling beside him, burnt toast with one bite taken out of it sitting on a plate. He looked up at Angie with a wicked grin.

"How would you like to be part of a magic show?"

• • •

The Assistant Returns

The bell over the door chimes, and Meg flinches, her shoulders rising like a shield. She and Angie both look to the entrance, but there's no one there.

"We should go." Angie might be about to make the second biggest mistake of her life, but she decides to do it anyway. "Would you like to see a magic show?"

"I did magic once." Meg's voice is dreamy. "I think, but..." She frowns, then shakes her head, a sharp motion knocking the dreaming out of her voice and eyes. "I don't remember."

Hunger flickers in Meg's eyes now, tiny silver fish darting through a deep pool of hurt. Will seeing the Magician help, or add one more scar? Angie holds out her hand. Meg's touch is insubstantial, but she takes it.

Here's the secret to what Angie does: dying is easy. Being dead is hard. And coming back hurts like hell. But it's easier if you're not alone, and Angie doesn't let go of Meg the entire time. She's come a long way since the rabbit, but it's an act of will, consciously holding space for Meg's hand, bringing her—not back to life, but back as a ghost. The act leaves Angie's vision bursting with grey and black stars. She has to steady herself against the dressing room table as she and Meg emerge.

"I've been looking all over for you." The Magician puts his head around the doorway, impatient, distracted. "We're about to start the show."

He barely looks at Angie; he doesn't see Meg at all. In Angie's peripheral vision, Meg's expression falls. She's braced, but nothing can truly prepare her for the Magician failing to see her one last time.

"I won't let go." Angie adjusts her grip, straightens, and Meg follows her to the wings off the stage.

Angie keeps Meg grounded throughout the show. The

extra effort turns her skull into an echo chamber, her bones grinding like tectonic plates shifting through the eons. When the bullet kisses the Magician's flesh, Meg gasps. Once it's done, and the Magician reappears in the back of the theater—a combination of misdirection and Angie's resurrection magic—Meg finally releases her death grip on Angie's hand. Love is a hard habit to shed; Meg applauds. Angie is the only one to hear the sound, and each clap sounds like the cracking of ancient tombstones.

The Magician makes his way back to the stage, smiling and waving the whole way. Circles of rouge dot the Magician's cheeks. The lights spark off his teeth as Rory cycles through gel filters, making a rainbow of the Magician's smile. He takes his bows, gathering the flowers and panties and hotel keys thrown his way. Meg's features settle into something less than love, less than awe. She frowns, then all at once, her mouth forms a silent 'o'.

"I remember why I came back," she says.

"Come with me." Angie slips out of the theater, not that anyone is looking for her to notice.

She keeps a room in the hotel attached to the theater, and there, Angie collapses onto her bed. Meg hovers near the ceiling, turning tight, distraught circles like a goldfish in a too-small bowl.

"I don't know if it's happened yet, or if it's happening now." Meg stops her restless spiraling and sits cross-legged, upside down. Her hair hangs toward Angie; if Meg were solid, it would tickle Angie's nose.

"Can you show me?" Angie's skull is as fragile as a shattered egg, but Meg came back for a reason, and Angie wants to know.

Meg stretches. Their fingers touch. The room shifts and if Angie had eaten anything besides the ghost of bacon and coffee in the diner inside Meg's death, she'd be sick. Her body remains on the bed, but Angie's self stretches taffy-thin, anchored in a hotel room at one end, hovering above a swirl of music and laughter and brightness at the other. She isn't Angie; she isn't fully Meg either. They are two in one, Angie and Meg, Meg-in-Angie.

And below them is the Magician.

He burns like a beacon. A sour vinegar taste haunts the back of Angie's throat. Pickled cabbage and resentment, brine and regret. Angie can't sort out which feelings are Meg's and which are hers. She must have loved the Magician once upon a time. Didn't she?

The room is full of strangers, but another familiar face catches Angie-Meg's eye. Rory stands at the edge of a conversation where the Magician is the center. He sways, too much to drink, but also blown by the force of yearning, a tree with branches bent in the Magician's wind.

Angie and Meg watch as Rory orbits closer, his need fever-bright. The Magician turns. He stops, puzzled at seeing something familiar anew. After so many years of being careful in the Magician's presence, Rory's desire is raw. Something has changed, or perhaps nothing has, and Rory is simply tired, hungry, willing to take a chance. And after so many years of looking right past his stage manager, the Magician finally sees something he needs—admiration, want, fuel for his fire. He sees love, and opens his mouth to swallow it whole.

A flick of the hand, a palmed coin, a card shot from a sleeve—the first and easiest trick the Magician ever learned and the one that's served him best over the years. He turns on his thousand-watt smile, and Rory steps into that smile. Parallel orbits collide, and their kiss is a hammer blow, shattering Angie's heart.

She gasps, coming up for air from the bottom of a pool. Meg floats facedown above the bed, a faint outline haloing her in the shape of wings. Tears drip endlessly from her eyes, but never fall.

Angie is angrier than she's ever been.

It's not the Magician's infidelity. Like the Magician himself, she's grown used to that. The Magician could kiss hundreds, flirt with thousands, fuck every person he meets, and Angie wouldn't care. The kiss means nothing to the Magician, and to Rory it means the world. That, Angie can't abide.

Rage widens cracks in Angie she hadn't even known were there. She can see what will happen next, Rory fluttering to the ground in the Magician's wake like a forgotten card. There's already forgetting in the Magician's eyes, his mind running ahead to the next show, the next trick, the thunder of applause.

Angie makes fists of her hands. She wanted better for Rory. She wanted him to *be* better. She wants to have been better herself. Smart enough to never have fallen for the Magician's tricks, clever enough to see through the illusion and sleight of hand. Angie meets Meg's eyes.

"We have to let the Magician die."

• • •

A Rabbit's Funeral

"Shit, shit, shit." Heat from the asphalt soaked through Angie's jeans where she knelt in the Magician's parking lot, the shoebox by her side.

Tears dripped from the point of Angie's nose and onto the rabbit's fur. She'd woken in the Magician's rumpled sheets, wondering if she was the first to see them twice, even three mornings in a row, and she'd found the rabbit curled next to the defunct radiator, empty as though he'd never contained life at all. Nothing she could do, no amount of power she could summon, would unravel his death again.

"Are you okay?" A shadow fell over her, sharp-edged in the light, and Angie looked up, startled.

"Yes. No. Shit. No. Sorry." She wiped frantically at her face, leaving it smeared and blotchy.

The sun behind the man turned him into a scrap of darkness. Angie wished she'd brought sunglasses.

"I'm fine." She stood and lifted her chin.

"You don't look fine." The man's gaze drifted to the box.

Exhaustion wanted Angie to drop back to her knees, but she turned it into a deliberate motion, scooping the box against her chest and holding it close.

"I know that rabbit," the man said. "The Magician—"

"The Magician. The fucking Magician." Angie couldn't help it—a broken laugh escaped her. She held the box out. "Do you know his name? It's not Gus."

"No." The man looked genuinely regretful, and it made Angie like him instantly, and study him more closely.

The air smudged dark around his shoulders, curling them inward. A shadow haunted him, like the one clinging to the Magician, with the same flavor, but unlike the Magician, this man felt its weight.

"I'm Rory." The man frowned at the box. "I'm the stage manager, I was looking for the Magician."

"He's out. I don't know when he'll be back. He doesn't even know yet." She indicated the box again.

Guilt tugged at her briefly, recalling the Magician's grief at the bar, but Angie doubted she'd see such a display again. The Magician had already moved on, his head too full of plans for his own death and return, overfull with confidence not in her abilities, but that he was too important to properly die.

She caught disappointment in the stage manager's eyes. Angie recognized it; Rory was as big a fool as she was, maybe bigger still. Like a compass point finding North, Rory's gaze went to the Magician's window. He didn't have to count or search, pinpointing it immediately. Love was written plain on his skin, letters inches high that the Magician was too stupid to read.

"Will you help me bury him?" Angie held up the box, drawing Rory's attention back, his expression smoothed into one of weary pain.

"I'm—" Angie stopped. She'd been about the say *the Magician's girlfriend.* But they'd only just met; they'd fucked a few times. She'd brought his rabbit back from the dead, and that was the most intimate thing they'd shared.

"Angie." She coughed.

Her name felt awkward, a ball of cactus thorns she wanted to spit out. Now it was her turn to glance at the building, though she had no idea which window belonged to the Magician. Dread prickled along her spine.

"I have a car." Rory gestured. "We could bury him in the desert."

Angie followed Rory across the parking lot. She climbed into the passenger seat, and set the box containing the dead rabbit in her lap. The car smelled faintly of cigarettes—old smoke, like Rory had quit long ago. Angie found it oddly comforting.

"I'm a Resurrectionist." Angie tested the word. The Magician had suggested it last night, bathed in the after-sex glow. She tried it on for size. "I bring things back from the dead."

She expected Rory to slam on the brakes, swerve to the side of the road and demand she get out. He did neither. She kept talking.

"Simple things fall apart more easily—mice, sparrows, rabbits." She tapped the box, finger-drumming a sound like rain. Telling Rory her secret felt necessary, an act of defiance. The Magician didn't own her or her truths, not yet.

"Small things know the natural order of the world. Only humans are arrogant enough to believe they deserve a second chance at life."

Angie let her gaze flick to the side, finding Rory's eyes for a brief moment before he turned back to the road.

"How about here?" Rory parked and they got out.

Desert wind tugged at Angie's hair. She held the box close, sand and scrub grass crunching under her feet. Rory kept a small, collapsible shovel in the trunk of his car for emergencies, a habit held over from when he lived in a climate with much more snow. He also kept a Sharpie in his glove box, and once they'd dug a hole, and laid the rabbit inside, Angie chose a flat, sun-warmed rock and uncapped the pen.

"What should we write, since we don't know his name?"

"He was a good rabbit. His name was his own."

Angie scribed the words. The moment felt like a pact, and when Angie stood, she took Rory's hand. The sun dragged their shadows into long ribbons, and at the same moment, they turned to look behind them, as if they'd heard their names called. The city glowed in the gathering dusk. The Magician was waiting for them.

• • •

How the Trick is Done

This is how it goes: Meg protests; she blushes translucent. She is dead, but she is afraid.

Angie points out how many people the Magician has hurt, how many more he will hurt still. Meg comes around to

Angie's point of view.

They tell Rory together, a united front. With Angie holding Meg's hand, amplifying her form, Rory can see her. His eyes go wide, and his face becomes a glacier calving under its own weight. After his initial moment of shock, something like wonder takes over Rory's face as he looks at Meg.

"You have wings."

She blinks, spinning in place to try to see over her shoulder. The wonder on her face mirrors Rory's, but the melancholy in her voice breaks Angie's heart.

"I remember," Meg says. "I think, once, I knew how to fly."

"I should have..." Rory says, but he lets the rest of the sentence trail. Meg offers him a sad smile, telling him over and over again that her death is not his fault. Angie tells him that kissing the Magician was not a crime. Rory looks doubtful, but in the end, like Meg, he agrees. They need to let the Magician die.

Angie tells herself they are doing this for the dozens of lost souls, blown in like leaves from the strip, looking for magic, and instead finding the Magician. She tells herself it is not revenge. That he failed them more than they failed themselves. She thinks of late-night coffee, and early-morning champagne. All the opportunities she had to tell Rory that she knew he was in love with the Magician, to tell him to run. She savors her guilt, and pushes it down.

The one person they do not tell is the Magician's Assistant, his current one. It is unfair, but she needs to be the one to fire the gun. Magic, true magic, requires a sacrifice, and none of them have anything left to give.

On the night the Magician dies, he asks for a volunteer from the audience. A hand rises, but the woman raising it feels a terrible chill, ghost fingers brushing her spine. She takes it as a premonition, and lets her hand fall. Rory trains the spotlight on the woman, on Meg behind her, and its brightness washes Meg away.

No other hands rise; the Magician's Assistant accepts the gun with a smile, and Angie's heart cracks for her. There is brightness in her eyes, curiosity. She believes. Not in the Magician specifically, but in the possibility of magic. She's the Assistant for now, but her faith in the world tells her that she could be the Magician herself someday.

Rory shifts the spotlight to the stage. Bright white gleams off the Magician's lapels, the Assistant's costume sparks and shines. Angie watches the Magician preen.

There is a flourish, a musical cue. The Magician's Assistant fires the gun. Angie holds her arms tight by her side. The bullet strikes home. A constellation of red scatters, raining like stars on the stunned front row. The Resurrectionist grits her teeth and trains her will to do nothing at all.

The Magician's eyes widen. His mouth forms a silent 'o'. He falls.

Dread blooms in the Magician's Assistant's stomach. The gun smokes in her hand.

Angie sweats in the wings. The Magician's death tugs at her, demanding to be undone. It's harder than she imagined not to knit the Magician back together. He is a hard habit to break, and she's been turning back his death for so long.

She considers—is she the villain in this story? The Magician is callous, stupid maybe, and arrogant for sure. Angie is not a hapless victim. She made a choice; it just happened to be the wrong one. Rory and Meg, they are innocent. All they are guilty of is falling in love.

Angie does not tell the bullet to stop, or the Magician's blood to go. She lets it run and pool and drip over the edge of the stage and onto the floor. All Angie can hope is to turn her regret into a useful thing.

Rory lets out a broken sob. His will breaks, and he runs onto the stage, folding to his knees to cradle the Magician's head in his lap. Meg hovers above them. She spreads her wings, and their translucence filters the spotlight, lending the Magician's death a blue-green glow.

Angie walks onto the stage. In the corner of her vision, the lights are blinding. The theater holds a collective breath. She thinks of a lonely grave in the desert, and a rabbit without a name. She thinks of Meg, falling endlessly. She thinks of Rory, his lips bruised with regret. Angie kneels, and looks the Magician in the eye. She knows death intimately, his most of all, and she knows he can still hear her.

"Dying is easy," she says. "Being dead is hard. Coming back is the hardest part of all. See if you can figure out how the trick is done, this time all on your own."

She leans back. It isn't much, but it assuages her guilt to think he might figure out the secret, the catch, the concealed hinge. He might learn true magic, bend it to his will, and figure out how to bring himself back to life one day.

The Magician blinks. The spotlight erases Angie and Rory's features; they blaze at the edges, surrounded by halos of light. Between them, a blurred figure occludes the lights. It reminds the Magician of someone he used to know, only he can't remember her name.

"Is this..." The Magician's fingertips grope at the stage as if searching for a card to reveal. Those are his final words.

• • •

Death and the Magician

Angie lets a month pass before she tracks down the Magician's Assistant, his most recent one. They meet in an all-night diner, and Angie offers to pay.

The woman's name is Becca, and she reminds Angie of a

mouse. She starts easily, all shattered nerves. A dropped fork, bells jangling over the diner door—they all sound like gunshots to her, and her hands shake with guilt.

"It's not your fault," Angie says. "You did your job."

Maybe one day Angie will admit the whole truth; maybe she'll simply let it gnaw at her for the rest of her days, until she finds herself completely hollow inside.

"This is going to sound strange," Angie says once they've finished their meals, "but how would you like your very own magic show?"

It isn't enough, certainly not after what Angie has done, but it makes her feel slightly better to think she is offering Becca the chance to live her dream. The pain is still there in Becca's eyes, but Angie sees a spark of curiosity and something like hope.

"Tell me," Becca says; by her voice, she is hungry to learn.

The act that replaces the Bullet-Catch-Death-Cheat looks like something old, as all the best tricks do, building on what came before and paying homage, while being something completely new. Every night, the Magician summons a ghost onto the stage. It must be an illusion, audiences say. Smoke and angled mirrors, just like Pepper back in the day. Only, the ghost knows answers to questions she couldn't possibly know. She finds lost things, things their owner didn't even know were gone. Sometimes she leaves the spotlight and flies over the audience, casting the shadow of wings, and creating a wind that ruffles their hair. Sometimes she reaches out and touches one of them, and in that instant, they know without a doubt that she is absolutely real.

The ghost looks familiar, and so does the Magician. The audience can't place either woman, but something about them calls to mind spangly leotards and pasted-on smiles. They look like people who used to be slightly out of focus, standing just on the edge of the spotlight, out of range of the applause. Now they've moved center stage, and their smiles are real, and they positively glow.

Angie no longer watches from the wings as the show goes on. Meg is strong enough now that she no longer needs Angie to ground her, and Becca and Rory are just fine on their own. Perhaps one day, Angie will slip away from the theater altogether, though she isn't sure where she'll go.

For now though, she sits backstage in front of the mirror and looks the old magician in the eye.

As she does, she learns what death looks like for him, and thinks about what it will look like for her when her own time comes. Sometimes it looks like the darkest depths of a top hat, endlessly waiting for the arrival of a rescuing hand. Sometimes it looks like a party where everyone is a stranger, and no one ever looks your way. Every now and then, it looks like a diner at 1:47 am and a heart waiting to be broken.

But most of all, it looks like a brightly-lit stage in a theater packed with people, utterly empty of applause.

A Strange Uncertain Light

By G. V. Anderson

Anne twirled the thin, dull wedding band around her finger, quite loose. In their rush to be married, they'd failed to have it fitted properly. And there were scores layered in the metal, old scrapes and nicks from its previous owner that appeared when the light from the train window hit it just so. No one else sitting in the compartment noticed its poor quality, or they simply pretended not to. They hid behind the latest broadsheets instead, the front pages still reporting on the Munich Agreement despite it having been some weeks past.

"New bride, are you?" one middle-aged woman wreathed in shabby fur asked her, somewhere past Thirsk. "I can always tell."

"Just yesterday," Anne replied, swaying slightly as the train hit a switch track.

Opposite, beneath his trimmed graying moustache, the corner of Merritt's mouth twitched. He still wore the same dark double-breasted suit he'd put on that last morning in Kent, rumpled now by almost two days' travel, and there was a trace of liquor about him underneath the smell of bedsheets, cigarette smoke, and coffee. Anne knew she must fare no better: She'd had no time to pin her hair properly that morning, nor smear her usual scoop of talcum under her arms.

She caught the eye of the middle-aged woman again and

saw now her knowing expression, the discerning brow. Her face grew hot.

"My husband and I honeymooned in the South of France," the woman said wistfully. "Lovely place. I'm not sure what I'd have made of Yorkshire—it can be rather grim, this time of year."

"I grew up in Yorkshire," replied Merritt, watching the embankment alongside the train fall away. "The best of the season's passed, it's true, but we should catch the last of the heather." He sat a little straighter and held out his hand to Anne. "Darling, look—"

Purple, Merritt had told her when she'd asked him about his home county, and what a poor preparation that was for the bristling mat of ling spread out before them. Anne sprang up and unhooked the catch on the window, sending the men's newspapers flying.

"For Heaven's sake, young lady—"

"My *hair*—!"

But Anne wouldn't shut the window on that patchwork of heather and cotton grass, those banks of soft green bracken. She slung one arm out of the window and let the vibrations of the engine rattle her teeth. It hardly felt real that, until yesterday, she'd never set foot outside her little Kent town, let alone seen London. Her whole world had been contained within the walls of the schoolhouse, or her bedroom, or her father's surgery. And now here she was, almost as far north as it seemed north could go.

"And there's Rannings," said Merritt, who'd caught her mood and stood with her, pointing across the moor to the elegant redbrick country house-turned-hotel. His body warmed her back.

"Oh," Anne breathed, "it's—"

She jerked away blinking—some grit in her eye, some spark of coal—and looked down in time to see the colorless shade of a man caught between the rails and the wheels, to be sliced through like brisket, splashing his blueish guts up the side of the train, and the window, and her face; and Anne's own guts turned cold. *Please, God, not here, too.* The strength went out of her legs and she slumped against Merritt, who hadn't seen a thing, of course, and who laughed a little as if she were a child who'd overexcited herself. Then he saw how pale she'd gone. "Darling, what's the matter? Here, sit down, we'll be arriving soon."

All along the train, passengers were standing to check their bags stowed on the overhead racks, to put away a book or a bundle of knitting, to adjust their coats and fish gloves out of pockets. Amidst the hubbub, Anne shrank back into the badly sprung seat. Her eyes flicked to the red walls of Rannings before another embankment rose up and hid them from view.

These aberrations had been with her since late childhood. Silhouettes swinging in the orchards at night; shadows lurking solemnly around the churchyard on Sundays. "Brought on by stress," her father had decided, after consulting the latest journals from London: A nervous disorder resulting from overstimulation, to be treated with ice baths and, later, shock therapy. How she could possibly be overstimulated in a town like Penshawe, miles from anywhere important, he never thought to ask. The intrusions had worsened, passing through London, but that was different. A sudden elopement and its subsequent wedding night would overstimulate anyone.

There was nothing to strain her nerves in Yorkshire, nothing to worry about now that she was free, was there? And yet, they'd followed her anyway.

Merritt was smiling mildly at her. She couldn't smile back. She'd never found the right moment to tell him, in the two weeks of their acquaintance and their whirlwind departure, and had hoped she'd never need to. He seemed a respectable sort of person. Respectable people, in her experience, recoiled from lunacy. He might wash his hands of her completely and leave her ruined. After all, she was quite mad, and—and this scraped at her in particular—how well did she know him, really?

She picked at the dry skin beneath her new wedding band. It calmed her.

I come upon the moor at dusk and quickly lose my way. A band of moormen point out the path of exposed shale ahead, clutches of auburn-breasted grouse swinging from their fists. They're curious of me; it's not often you see a girl in a fine dress traveling alone.

"You're a long way from home," one of them jokes.

"Liverpool's not so far as you think, sir," I say.

"You don't sound like a Scouser." His smile turns to scowl. "You sound right proper."

The stays of my corset—and this twit—are chafing me raw. I turn away from them and allow myself a grimace.

"It'll be dark soon and, beggin' your pardon, you're not from round 'ere," another deep voice calls to me as I climb the loose shale. "These moors can be treacherous. You'll come back with us and set out again when there's light to see by, if you know what's good for you."

From my vantage point, I scan the way ahead. The shadows pool like pitch in the mossy hollows and it's a cloudy night—there'll be no moon, no stars. Already, my breath expels as mist and hoarfrost lends its sheen to my coat. It's tempting to accept their offer. The grouse look plump, full of fat and flavor. But these men are strangers whose stares grow bolder the longer I stay, and I've tested my employer's generosity far enough. I promised to return to Missus Whittock within the week or consider my position lost. I cannot spare even one night.

"Thank you for your concern, sir, but I'm in haste."

"Then," says the youngest, quietly but firmly, stepping forward and raising his lamp, "let me escort you." He peels away from them and joins me atop the shale.

"See you're back home before chime hours," the deep-voiced moorman calls to him. The lad nods and leads the way to the path.

The lamplight drives away the shadows, exposing the frost-rimed bog asphodel pushing up through the rag-rug of sphagnum. Somewhere off to our right, a vole startles and darts away, too quick to catch. My guide doesn't notice. He looks to the horizon, charting the contour of the darkening moors' silhouette against the bloody sky like a seaman charts his stars. It looks featureless to me, but he must recognize some dale or other because he turns to me and says, "We're some ways off yet. I've heard the house keeps early hours. They might not answer the door this late to someone like—I mean, unless you're expected." He hesitates, scanning the cut of my coat, the stitching of my boots. "Are you expected, miss?"

"No," I admit.

A few steps, and then, "Where's Liverpool, miss?"

He's looking at me like I've come from another world. I suppose I have. On Liverpool's docks, you can hardly hear yourself think. Ships laden with spoils from the West Indies bring free men and officers' servants with them; and immigrants from Glasgow and Belfast, such as my parents, come looking for work. Lascars and Chinamen haul ashore crates stamped with the East India Company crest—crates heavy with silk, salt, and opium—and for all their labor, their captains often leave them behind.

Liverpool's rough mixture of language and color and cloth may seem strange here, but it's familiar to me. It's this numbing quiet, this cold, the moormen's slow burr that *I* will not forget.

But Yorkshire can't be as cut off as all that. My guide's coloring is dark and reddish, yet his lashes frame stark olive eyes. Even here, his face is poured from the melting pot of the world.

"It's to the west," I tell him. "At the mouth of the Mersey."

We trudge on.

"Begging your pardon, miss, but what's your business at Rannings? If you're looking for a position, I should warn you—"

"It's nothing like that," I snap, and then twist my mouth; he's only being kind. "An old friend of mine called on the doctor at Rannings last winter and hasn't sent word home. I've come to fetch him. You haven't seen him, have you? He's tall, taller than you, and walks with a limp." What a poor description for someone I'd know from the back of their head! God knows I fell asleep facing it often enough as a child.

He chews his lip. "I think I'd remember a stranger like that. But I hope you find him." He hesitates now, his warm skin giving off vapor in the lamplight. "We hear talk, sometimes, from the groundsmen . . . About the doctor."

I reach for his arm, grip the corded muscle there. He stops and looks at my hand in alarm. "What sort of talk?"

The lad squirms. "I don't know, I don't like to say." I squeeze and he concedes, tightly, "That he's unkind, and Godless. That he pays well for babies born during chime hours."

"Chime hours—your companion said that, too. What does it mean?"

He wrenches his arm away. "When the church bells ring at midnight, the door to Hell opens."

I know instantly what he's referring to, but Hell? What

superstitious nonsense!

I don't get a chance to correct him, though, because a blast of bitter wind hits my back like a swell smashing against a breakwater and throws us together. "Don't!" a distant voice pleads. "Don't go in there!" I push away from him and turn into the cold to see what the spirits have sent me: a young woman, pale as egg whites. She's staring past me, as these apparitions often do—no. No, not past. At.

She's staring *at* me, purposefully, with recognition. I've never known such a thing—I keep my mind and heart open to them like my father taught me, but the spirits have never truly made contact—and then she's gone. The cold wind still stings, but there's nothing chimerical about it.

My guide lifts the lamp high to better fix me with a stare that would melt wax. "You're one of them. Why'd you ask about chime hours, then? What did you see?"

I twist around and hold up my palms. "I told the truth before: I want to find my friend. He's like me. That is, he's gifted, too, and now I worry he's come to some harm."

"What did you see?" he repeats more forcefully.

"Nothing that'll hurt you. Just a woman on the moor. Some poor soul who died here, no doubt."

He's fighting to stay put, shifting his weight from one foot to the other. I expect him to run. I reach out my hand to ask for the lamp at least, but he grits his teeth and surprises me. "What's your name?"

"Mary," I reply. "Mary Wells. What's yours?"

"James," he says. Then he turns and continues along the path to Rannings.

Before I chase after him, I glance back to where the spirit appeared. *Don't!* she'd said. *Don't go in there!* With a stricken face, as if she knows what awaits me at the house. Easier said than done. As Missus Whittock's paid companion, I'm little more than a doll. The old friend I've come to find,

Benjamin, the boy from the docks—he represents everything about myself I've forgotten. The hard-won scran shared between our families; the pride in our own survival. Between the elocution lessons, carriage rides, and empty conversations, my past is the only part of me that still feels warm, like flesh. I can't let it die.

The spirits wouldn't possibly understand.

They disembarked near Middlesbrough where Merritt hired a motorcar. They had to double back a few dozen miles, following the railway south, but eventually he took a sharp left, plunging them into untamed moorland. Two follies and a gatehouse later, Rannings was rising before them in all its symmetrical beauty. Its front elevation measured fifteen sash windows across and three high, with four Palladian columns framing the twisting entrance steps leading to the door. Merritt kept checking Anne's expression and smiling at what he found there.

An old porter hobbled forward as the motorcar crunched to a stop, to help with their luggage. "Poor chap," Merritt muttered; such men were a common sight since the war. They followed him to reception, which was just as palatial as the exterior and gloriously warm. Limestone quarried from the moor paved the entrance hall. Behind the reception desk, a staircase unfurled into a mezzanine, and to the left and right Anne glimpsed parlors, dining rooms, gaming tables, all humming with lazy, aristocratic conversation.

"Mister and Missus John Merritt Keene," Merritt told the receptionist, while the porter managed their bags. His hooded eyes lingered on Anne a fraction too long.

Her fingers worried at her wedding band. As a doctor's daughter, her position in society—especially Kent society—was assuredly middle class; and hadn't Merritt told her his father was a lecturer at York? The social season was winding down and their fellow guests might only be the dregs that remained, but nevertheless the porter's attention made her feel uncomfortably out of place. At any moment, the manager might come along and refuse them, casting his eye over the uneven hem of Anne's woolen skirt as if it affronted him and his guests personally.

As the receptionist checked them in, Merritt said, "We'll freshen ourselves up and take a late lunch in the room, won't we, darling?" Here, he looked at Anne. "I'm afraid we're not fit to be seen about the place."

The receptionist smiled. She had a bit of lipstick on her teeth which made Anne feel better. "I'll have something sent up." She handed him a key. "Room thirty-two, on the second floor. It's just been refurbished. We do hope you'll enjoy your stay, Mister Keene. Missus Keene."

"Yes, yes, splendid," Merritt said.

Despite the porter's apparent frailty, their luggage had already arrived by the time they climbed the two flights of stairs and located number thirty-two. Inside, they found a beautiful suite warmed by natural light from a window overlooking the front drive.

Merritt shucked off his shoes and collapsed into a chair while Anne explored the bedroom, dared to run her fingers across the silk bedspread. Someone had placed a vase of fresh roses atop the dresser with wet hands: A few droplets warped the pattern on the porcelain.

"Merritt?" Anne sidled up to the connecting doors. To his distracted, "Mm?" she said, "Can we afford this?"

He raised an eyebrow and smiled at her, his head tipped back against the chair exposing his unshaven throat. "Well, I wouldn't say you should get used to it. We shan't be off motoring and staying in hotels *every* week. But yes, I have a little put by for special occasions." He sighed and tilted his head. "Tell me, do you like it?"

"Oh yes," Anne gushed. "It's lovely. I imagine it must be just like Monte Carlo."

"Hah! You'd loathe Monte."

"You shall have to take me, so I can decide for myself."

Merritt fished out his cigarette case and patted his pockets. Anne had the matches. She struck one for him. "We'll take a grand tour of Europe for our first anniversary, like the fashionable people do," he said when his cigarette was lit, "and utterly bankrupt ourselves on the tables."

"How foolish of us."

"How foolish indeed."

Merritt took her hand—only her fingers, really—stroked them with his thumb. He parted his lips, and Anne wondered if he meant to voice what she was already thinking: *Look how foolish we've been already.* Perhaps he wanted to kiss her. Isn't that what married couples did when they reached their honeymoon suite? Was there something else he expected of her, something she didn't know to do?

The bed lay empty behind them.

A knock at the door diffused the moment: their food, delivered on a rolling table. Finger sandwiches and small pastries, pots of tea and coffee, cheese and warm bread, slices of salty ham. They ate with their hands, dropping crumbs all over the upholstery, which felt terribly naughty. "And what would the young lady like to do with her afternoon?" Merritt teased, spreading pâté across a cracker.

"I don't know. What is there to do?"

"Oh, we could go for a drive? I'm sure there's cards downstairs, or a bar, if you'd like me to get you drunk." His look turned wicked.

"You know I'd hate that. No, I'm sick of sitting down. I long to stretch my legs. Can we go for a walk? I'd like to see the grounds."

He sucked pâté off his thumb. "Of course, darling."

But even in that short time, the moor had transformed. Everything had taken on a queer blue quality, with the sun so low and obscured by fog. Moisture beaded in the warp and weft of Anne's coat and darkened her unruly fringe. "Sun sets at six, sir," called the porter from the front steps. Merritt raised his hand to show he'd heard.

"Perhaps we should stay inside after all?" Anne said, adjusting her collar and gazing out over that bleak hinterland.

"Don't be silly," Merritt said, holding out his arm. Together they wandered west around the side of the great house. Sodden pockets of moss squelched underfoot, expelling water like blood, and the cries of lonely pipits—juveniles that had yet to migrate south—pricked Anne's mind. It had been easy, in the warm and dry, to forget about the shadow sliced beneath the train; now, she could think of nothing else.

"Tell me about Rannings," she said, just for something to say, and Merritt obliged.

It had been built, he recalled, in the mid-eighteenth century by the Sixth Earl of Hythe who, like so many nobles with interests in the Caribbean, could think of nothing better to do than squander his wealth on a show home. The family estates in Barbados and Grenada, the dark bent backs of slaves, the foreman's whip—all were well taxed to fund this venture. One by one, the red bricks settled into their mortar. Until the flow of money stopped.

"Oh," Anne said. They'd reached the back of the house where the foundations and a few half-finished walls remained. Rannings was laid out like a horseshoe with two flanks that would have joined together at the rear to enclose an inner courtyard, but construction had ceased before the earl got his way. Someone had attempted to make a feature of the foundations by turning them into flower beds, but the cold and the wet, and exposure to the vicious Yorkshire wind, had made a mockery of that.

"The slaves rebelled, burning hundreds of acres," Merritt said. "The earl was ruined. He sold Rannings around, oh . . . 1810, 1812? But the new owners didn't stay. I heard there was some legal trouble. The house lay empty right up till the turn of the century; a few tenants here and there, that's all." He nodded ahead, to the plume of smoke from a faraway train. "We used to see it from afar as boys, my brothers and I, and wonder what it was like inside. It was a barracks during the war. It's been a hotel ever since."

The petering walls, the weed-choked foundation stones and the gaping abyss between them: All of it pulled Anne's nerves taut as wire. Reminded her of wounds, of weeping bedsores. Cold sweat slid down her back like dead finger trails. "Why don't they finish what's left of it?"

"Some clause in the freehold." He shrugged, leading her away.

They walked in silence, and the further they went from Rannings, the easier Anne's mind turned to other concerns. The revelation of Merritt's having brothers, for example. He'd never mentioned them. They were, she thought, yet another thing to add to the long list of things she didn't know about her husband. Suddenly, his arm felt alien under her hand, the scruff of growth along his jaw perilously male.

She'd happened to be at her father's surgery the day they met. Merritt had brought in a friend who'd broken his ankle jumping a stile. With the man howling in pain and the doctor on his rounds two miles away, Anne had pushed up her sleeves and set and splinted the ankle herself. She'd seen her father do it enough times; had held down patients before, when there was no one else to be found.

Afterward, Merritt called in to praise her quick actions. He called in the next day, too, even when his friend had been sent home and he had no reason to stay. His graying temples betrayed his age and the townsfolk called him a fool, chasing after a girl so young. But Anne allowed their trysts. Encouraged them, despite her father's protests. Penshawe was a confined place where everyone knew everyone else's business, no matter how intimate, and the young people whose friendship she'd depended on as a child had married and moved away. She was desperately lonely.

And Merritt knew nothing about her other than what she chose to present to him. That fresh start—it was too intoxicating to resist.

Perhaps Merritt felt the same way.

He felt her stiffen and pressed his hand to her back, steadying her. She tried not to balk at that steering touch. She had not escaped the grasp of one father only to fall into the hands of another.

They came upon a small village called Huxby three miles from the house, no more than a rough square overlooked by cottages and a church with a crooked spire. The old vicar was closing the door for the night. He waved cheerfully to them as if they'd worshipped there all their lives. Anne waved back shyly and leaned towards Merritt. "Is this your parish?"

"No, this is still part of the estate," Merritt replied. "My family live north of here. We'll stay at Rannings a few days more, then I suppose I should take you to meet them."

He stopped at the sight of the memorial in the square. Newly erected and yet already stained with mildew, it listed the local war dead in cold iron letters.

"Will your brothers be there?"

Merritt's lips thinned. "No. My brothers are here."

Anne's eyes picked them out in the dark.

William Keene

20 December 1895—2 August 1917

Clarence Henry Keene
4 July 1898—3 August 1917

"We've walked too far," Merritt said coldly.

They returned to Rannings as the last of the light fled. Merritt said nothing to her over supper, throwing back brandy by the fire until late. And when he finally came to bed, just like their wedding night, the sheets lay quite flat and undisturbed in the space between them.

The wailing starts before I see the house and grows louder as we pick our way across the incomplete foundations. James raises the lamp and I catch sight of the walls, dark as dried blood. Almost every great house in England's been built with sugar money. I burn at the thought of the lives that paid for these bricks, these window frames, the furnishings inside.

"What sort of doctor lets his patients cry like that?" I hiss.

James shudders beside me. "Who knows what he does to 'em first." Then he passes me the lamp; it seems he's reached his limit. "Look, I said I'd bring you and I have, but I won't get no closer than this, miss. The house is touched." He glances at the walls as if they might be listening and lowers his voice further. "The doctor took someone from us, too, a long time ago. You're a braver lass than me, standing up to him. Be careful, miss."

I nod solemnly. "Thank you."

James melts into the darkness beyond the lamp's reach, leaving me to climb the coiling steps and ring the bell alone. The housekeeper—or matron, I suppose she'd be better called—answers the door in her housecoat and slippers. She looks at me meanly. "We're not hiring. Clear off!"

I push past her. "Actually, I'm here for Mister Benjamin Walchop. A year is quite long enough for someone who doesn't even need treatment, don't you think?"

The entrance hall's Baltic, the limestone flags beneath my feet gritty with dirt. I'd expected to find rugs and hangings, perhaps a varnished sideboard lit by gas lamps like the ones Missus Whittock has in her drawing room, but the space is bare and lifeless, as are the dim rooms leading off from either side. In a far corner, a gleaming cockroach scuttles away from the lamplight and disappears through a hole in the skirting board.

A hospital, Benjamin had reassured me when he'd come to the Whittocks' back stoop to say good-bye; he'd been warped with hunger, in body and sense. *A sanatorium.* Well, perhaps I'm ignorant, but to me, Rannings looks and sounds like an asylum taken wholesale from those silly novels my employer likes so much. I'd laugh if I wasn't so angry.

I turn on the matron. "Where's Benjamin?"

"You should've made an appointment." She closes the door, trapping me inside.

"Oh yes," I scoff, gesturing around, "this is clearly the sort of place where one must write ahead. You're quite run off your feet, I'm sure. But, see, I've been asking after Benjamin for months now, with no response. Is the doctor in?"

She stiffens at my tone and narrows her eyes distrustfully. Looks over my attire and my hale figure beneath, evaluating where I've come from. Missus Whittock clothes and feeds me well; anything less would reflect badly on her husband's income. The matron sniffs. "You're in luck, Miss . . . ?"

"Wells," I say.

She leads me to the right, through a high-ceilinged room with heavy drapes that mute the echoing clip of my boots. A few moths flicker around my lamp, casting erratic shadows on the walls. I shoo them away.

From behind me, I hear the rattle of dice in a cupped palm, the clatter as they land. I stop and turn, but there are no tables. I can't imagine there ever having been any, though I suppose there must have been, once. And—is that the taste of champagne? It burns my tongue, sharp and painful. Yes, I'm sure it is. Missus Whittock let me have a sip last year. For a girl raised on beef scouse and farl, it's a difficult flavor to forget.

The matron is staring at me. "Seen something interesting, Miss Wells?"

"No."

Her lips tighten like they're holding in a smile, and for the first time I'm afraid.

Cold, clammy hands pushed up between the floorboards like couch grass, splintering the wood. Anne recoiled from the edge of the mattress as fingers plucked at her through the sheets.

Help! Help us!

She started awake and then lay still, unsure; the pale morning light had left the room as spectral as the moor, and the ghost of a too-firm grip ached on the inside of her upper arm. The skin there was discolored, a bruise just forming. Her heart started to pound until she remembered that Merritt had marched them both back to Rannings last night, his hand like a vise.

He was awake, too, sitting by the open window with his head in his hands. His shins, exposed by shrunken pajamas, had pimpled with gooseflesh.

Anne curled up tight and tried to doze, but true sleep was long gone. She sighed. The floorboards were unmarked and cool against her soles as she padded over to the swelling curtains.

Merritt's brandy-laced breath swirled like brume. He swallowed stickily. She reached past him and pulled down the sash. Placed a hesitant hand on his shoulder. "Merritt?"

He blinked and took her hand. "Sorry, darling. Bit of a shock, that's all."

"Your brothers."

"I should've expected a memorial, of course. They're setting them up all over."

Anne sank into the seat beside him and together they looked out over the carriage sweep, the lawn, and the dale beyond. The sun was poised on the brink of the horizon, lightening the eastern sky like a spill of bleach. Rannings had been a barracks during the war, she remembered Merritt saying, and now that she looked, she fancied she could see the scars on the lawn where drills had churned the grass. "Did they train here?"

"Briefly—just long enough to learn how to hold a pistol. I was stationed in Scarborough. In 1917, we were sent to the front, to Belgium . . ." He looked at her blearily; he was still drunk. White sputum had collected in the corners of his mouth. "You don't know what I'm talking about, do you? You've never known wartime. Christ. When were you born?"

"1916."

His eyes unfocused, and the little color left in his cheeks drained away. "You're barely half my age. What must people think of me?"

Anne gave Merritt's fingers a small, nervous squeeze. "I don't see how that's anyone's business."

"Then what must *you* think of me?" Merritt ran a shaking hand through his hair, still slick with yesterday's oil. "I never got to be a young man, y'know. My youth died with my brothers, in the mud of Passchendaele. I thought I'd put it all behind me, but then I came to Penshawe and met you. You reminded me of everything I'd missed." He dragged his hand down his face, peering at her through greasy fingers. "And now there's talk of another bloody war in every newspaper, every morning. I can't face it—I can't bear it again!"

Anne's breath caught. No one had ever been so honest with her, never bared themselves so raw, not even her parents; what did he want her to say?

She opened her mouth, but so did he, to retch. The vase of roses was still on the dresser nearby. She snatched out the flowers, thorns biting into her palm, and thrust the vase under Merritt's chin in time to catch a dribble of bile.

"You need rest," said Anne, back on familiar ground, "and plenty of water." She poured out a tumbler and cupped the back of his head as he gulped it down, the sharp bulge in his neck bobbing grotesquely. With a groan and a lot of morose muttering, he returned to bed. Anne tucked him in.

It felt too awkward to stay there in the semi-dark, serenaded by phlegmatic snores, so she dressed and went downstairs. Other guests nodded to her as they passed, all following the smell of frying bacon. The receptionist greeted each one in the detached, polite way Anne knew well from operating the telephone in her father's surgery. "Good morning, Missus Keene. Breakfast is through here."

"Thank you, yes," Anne said, hovering by the desk. "Um, my husband is sleeping in. Could something plain be sent up to him in an hour? Perhaps some toast?"

"Of course," the receptionist said smoothly, noting it down. Her fingernails matched her red lipstick, her perfectly pinned hair that elusive shade of auburn no dye could replicate. Anne tucked a loose, wiry curl of her own hair behind her ear.

"How have you found your room, Missus Keene?"

"Oh, fine."

"I'm glad to hear it." The receptionist underlined her note and looked up to greet the next guest.

"That sounded rather dismissive, didn't it?" Anne twisted her hands together, recapturing the receptionist's attention. "It really is lovely. I've—I've never stayed anywhere like this before. I don't know how to behave."

The receptionist smiled at that—a real, warm smile, rather than the too-wide, toothy show she'd put on for their arrival yesterday. "You'd be surprised how many people say that. There's nothing to it, honestly. I'd say you're a natural."

Anne blushed. "Well, anyway, I'd never guess it was a barracks, and empty before that."

"Never empty for long," she replied. "Rannings has had quite the history. It's even been a hospital. Well, asylum."

"An asylum?"

The receptionist inclined her head, misinterpreting Anne's appalled expression. "A private institution. Shut down about a hundred years ago, but we keep that quiet. I'm sorry, I shouldn't gossip."

As Anne ate the breakfast she no longer had the appetite for, she wondered: Did Merritt know about that particular piece of Rannings history? Was he the sort of person to think it a talking point, an object of interest, like the lords and ladies who'd once paid to see the inmates of Bedlam?

Her father had considered sending her to one or two institutions when she was younger, before deciding to attempt treatment himself. She'd found the brochures in his desk drawer. Modern therapies were nothing like the crude ministrations of the previous century, they reassured their reader, but Anne couldn't stop imagining the worst: manacled inmates, hair shorn for wigs, rolling in their own filth. Such wretched conditions were common before the reforms of the mid-nineteenth century. A privately run asylum in the 1830s must have been Hell on Earth.

Her fellow diners ate on, oblivious, but Anne couldn't stomach any more. The sound of cutlery scraped in her ears. So too the wet click of people's mouths as they chewed. A vulgar flash of mulched sausage when someone laughed, slimy debris coating their tobacco-stained tongue.

Out in the entrance hall, away from the noise, it was better. The porter had left the door ajar while he assisted with a guest's departure. The cool air lifted her fringe and wicked the sweat away from her neck. Tickled her numb lips. She rubbed them hard.

Help! Help us!

Hand frozen over her mouth, she stared down the long parlor opposite. It was furnished with damask sofas and oak reading desks now, but yesterday afternoon, tables had been arranged for craps and baccarat. Someone had tucked a champagne flute into a bookcase and it had been missed by the staff. Anne only noticed it because the morning light caught the glass exactly right.

At the far end of the room stood the whisper of a girl in early-nineteenth-century dress. Her posture was bold, totally at odds with her finery. She turned away as if called, and then disappeared through a door that didn't exist.

"Miss Wells to see you, Doctor."

He removes his spectacles and stands as I enter, offering me a shallow bow. I curtsy, studying him from beneath my lashes. The doctor is thin and ropy, a sick tree in winter, with meatless jowls that quiver as he shoots the matron a hard glance. "It's rather late," he says. "I was about to retire."

"You'll want to stay for this one, Doctor. She has a lot of . . . questions." The matron smiles. The light from my lamp picks out her eyes.

"Questions about what?"

"Mister Benjamin Walchop," I say, raising my chin. "He came to you a year ago. I bid you release him from your care so that he can return home immediately."

The doctor leans in. "And you are a relative?"

"A friend, representing Mister Walchop's family. I have their authority here." I pull a sealed letter from my skirt pocket and hand it to him. Benjamin's mother has scratched her mark within, but the rest is by my hand since she never learned how.

The doctor skims it and casts it aside. "I'm afraid that will not be possible. Mister Walchop's is an interesting case and his treatment is not yet complete."

"Treatment for what, exactly? He is not ill." I glance between them. When it's clear an answer isn't forthcoming, I go on, "I saw the contract you sent him. It specified a period of six months in exchange for payment. You've broken your own terms. If you intend to keep him here longer, the least you could do is compensate his family properly."

The doctor chuckles. "How mercenary."

I grip the back of the chair facing the desk. "It's as he would wish it. But now that I've seen your sanatorium for myself—if you can possibly call it that—such terms simply won't do. I've already contacted the authorities with my concerns. I'm sure the magistrate would like to know where you earned your doctorate. So would I, for that matter."

"Oh," the doctor says slowly, baring dull, gray teeth, "I like her. The door, Matron."

She slams it shut. I glare at her, my fist tightening on the back of the chair. The room's both too hot and too cold. Beneath my dress, sweat has left a crust of salt on my skin.

He replaces his spectacles and opens a drawer in his desk, fingers through the files within. "You shouldn't threaten legal action if you cannot take the consequences. I must protect my interests." He peers over the rim of his spectacles and tuts. "Where does a low creature like you find the gall for such threats, I wonder?"

I prickle at that, but finally hold my tongue. For all the time I've spent with Missus Whittock and her set, I can't scrub away the lilt, the brass. What a lady may get away with, a poor girl cannot. How much I've forgotten. How fat I've grown on privilege.

"The treatment, since you ask, is more a series of tests." He withdraws a file and opens it. "I've studied many children, Miss Wells. There was a girl, once, who could talk to birds—just called them out of the sky on a whim. Another could detect lies. One boy could hear my very thoughts, fancy that. But none of them hold a candle to your friend. The boy who cannot die, despite my *very best* attempts."

My legs tremble beneath my skirts.

When we were ten, Benjamin was mauled by a terrier. I battered it around the head with a brick but the dog held on, shaking Benjamin's leg viciously. A ratter, obeying its breeding. His mother came out with a glowing poker and burned it till it let go, but not before his cries had called the whole neighborhood down upon us. A hundred pairs of eyes watched as his torn calf knitted itself together right there in the street. It didn't knit neatly enough, though: He was left with a nasty limp, and it's hard to find a dock-master who'll give you work when there's fitter pickings to be had.

His mother tried to shrug off the rumors by telling people the bite hadn't been so bad, that the truth had got twisted in the telling, but by then the story had spread. Who knows how quickly it reached the ear of this doctor, and for how long he watched unemployment slide into desperate poverty, waiting for the right moment to bait his line.

We stare at each other, and I know I'm right. He must see it in my expression, too, because he laughs with delight and throws the open file he'd fished out onto the desk. The notes are minimal. The insert bears my name. Mary Margaret Wells.

"Mister Walchop has a rare gift that could change the world, and they say birds of a feather flock together," he leers. "So answer me one question, Miss Wells: What is it that *you* can do?"

I lunge for the door. Terror's already buckling my knees, but the matron strikes the back of my head with a candlestick for good measure. I fall hard, smashing James's lamp. Voices rumble thickly above me, then she takes me by the armpits and drags me through the doorway. Lord, she's strong. We go down a staircase; my heels thud on every step. I'm drooling a bit. I can hear someone crying.

I'm just getting my wind back, just finding the strength to struggle, when she throws me into a dark room and locks the door. I lie on the floor, listening to her receding footsteps and the whimpering from the next room over.

"Hello?" I croak.

The whimpering stops. Rough scratching comes from my left and then the reply, "Who're you?"

"Mary," I say.

"I can't hear nowt. Come closer to the wall. There's a hole."

I crawl toward the voice and run my hands over the damp stone. My palms bump against a protruding finger. A chunk of mortar has been chipped away, I realize, leaving a gap between our cells. I link my warm finger into their cold one. "I'm Mary," I repeat. "Who are you?"

"I'm Martha."

I squeeze Martha's finger. It's missing its nail. "How long have you been here, Martha?"

"I dunno, few weeks."

Her accent is broad. The same ruse, then: taking chime children from the poor where they won't be missed. I grind my teeth at the thought.

The darkness thins and I look up: A narrow, barred window above me lets in a little light as the moon slides out from its cover of cloud. I release Martha's finger and reach up to grasp the bars. It's been but minutes since James left me; I pray he lingered despite his fear. I suck down the freezing air, each breath as painful as pressing a bruise. "James?" I bellow, fit for a dockhand. "If you're there, help! Help us!"

"No one ever comes this way," says Martha.

"*I* did," I shoot back.

Ice suddenly blooms on the iron like mold. I pull my hands away before they can stick and look over my shoulder. The ghost from the moor, the one who cried the warning, is in my cell. Her gray eyes are wide with shock. Her hand grasps the doorframe for balance. She must have perished here; tortured, perhaps, by the doctor's twisted tests. But her clothes are strange. I've never seen skirts that fall straight and stop at the shin.

I don't have time to question it. "Please, help us."

"Who're you talking to?" asks Martha.

Anne had never hallucinated a person who wasn't in pain, at the point of death. Sometimes, the morbidity of her own mind was worse than seeing visions altogether. This girl, though, had looked whole and healthy, with a calculating, determined expression that endeared her to Anne immediately.

The porter was curling his fingers around the edge of the front door. Instinctively, Anne darted behind the reception desk and through the staff entrance beneath the staircase. There, in the dark, she hiccupped a laugh and held it in with her hand. Why had she hidden from him like a child? A porter wouldn't question a guest standing in the hall, nor would he challenge her if she'd decided to explore the parlor. But then there'd been that stare of his when they arrived—too long, too intimate.

Through the gap in the door's hinge, she took her turn to watch him in the hall. Why did he linger? He might have been waiting to serve another guest, but she fancied he was listening for her, could hear her shaking breath.

He looked directly at her hiding place. Began to make for it. Her breath caught. She ran lightly down the staff corridor, past linen cupboards and offices, hoping she was faster. Eventually she reached a door that opened onto the inner courtyard. Three kitchen boys were huddled by the water pump sharing a cigarette. They glimpsed her as she backtracked, one of them calling out in surprise. She panicked and dashed right, the windows flashing past, until she was forced to turn into the east wing.

Clearly, this part of the ground floor was unused. Someone had wallpapered once, and laid down carpet, but the sprucing ended there. One room still boasted its old gas fittings. Another's plaster was rotting away.

Anne slowed to a stop and leaned against an empty doorframe to catch her breath, the playground fear that had driven her this far melting away, leaving her feeling more than a little silly. She tugged her sleeves down to cover her wrists and wrapped her arms around her middle. The ceiling creaked, its bare lightbulb swinging gently: a guest moving around their room. On the floor above that, her husband lay sprawled in the bed of number thirty-two.

She'd grown up watching her father tear people's bodies apart and stitch them back together, but the mind was a different beast—she knew that better than most. The loss of his brothers on the very same battlefield he'd survived had left Merritt with particular scars that no amount of ice baths or shock therapy could heal—God knew, they'd done nothing for her—but those were the only tools she understood. And drink, it seemed, was his.

How was she supposed to stitch her husband back together with nothing but words?

Her soles had left footprints in the dusty carpet. Breadcrumbs leading the way she'd come. As her eyes followed them, even as her foot tensed to take a step, a draft from further down the hall swept them away. A door at the far end, hung badly, wavered, scraping against its frame. From the sliver of darkness beyond, Anne heard the rasp of saw on bone.

Help! Help us!

The cry sounded so close, so real, that she hesitated. It was easy to ignore the intrusions when no one else reacted to them. When she was alone, there was no way to tell if they were genuine or not. She'd left her mother lying on the kitchen floor for hours with a concussion once, unsure whether she'd imagined the shriek and smack of a head hitting the black-and-white tiles. If someone really was stuck and calling for help and she turned away, just as she'd turned away that day, she'd never forgive herself.

She approached the door, pulled it wide, the brass handle so cold it burnt her palm. A belch of stale, sour air came up from the staircase beyond, chased by a drawn-out sob that might have been the wind keening through some broken window. The steps demanded she take them one at a time, hewn as rough as they were and slick with mold.

Merritt's matchbox still bulged in her cardigan pocket. She got it out and struck one, peering around a forgotten wine cellar. The racks were empty now, though the vinegary tang of wine gone bad lingered. A leak from some unseen pipe had left a film of water on the floor, so that the walls seemed to extend for infinity in the reflection, and her tiny match-light, her own pale face, stared up at her from below.

There was a door leading further into the basement. She pushed it open and advanced into a corridor, similarly flooded. The match was burning low. She shook out the flame and lit another, edging toward the first room on her right. The rasping returned, louder.

"Hello?" she said meekly.

That word, and then her gasp, echoed back.

A boy was laid out on a table within—ashen except where the skin of his chest had been peeled aside in lapels of red, exposing white ribs.

Anne reeled, dropping the match. The light guttered out, but she could still see him branded on the inside of her eyelids. Her breath wouldn't come. "It's not real," she whispered, and the whispers flew back at her. *It's not real, not real, not real.*

Help!

She fumbled with the matches, lost one, lit another.

A lean man with his back to her, pate shining. He was standing over another body, another child, viciously pumping his arm back and forth, and the rasping of the saw was in her bones. She gulped down bile and left the room.

"Is—is there anyone here?"

The second room she looked in on was blessedly empty. She clasped the doorframe and sighed. The calls for help had been in her head after all. But—what was that? Scratching from the next room over, and a wretched sniveling. She bit her lip and sloshed along, the water deeper here and starting to flood her shoes. The third door had slumped free of its upper hinge, its bottom corner jammed into the floor. She squeezed through the gap and held up the remaining sliver of matchstick. "H-hello?"

A little girl with her back to Anne, clawing at the far wall in an attempt to reach a high-set window. She turned to look at something over Anne's shoulder, and the sight of whatever she saw there brought on a fresh, frantic attempt at the wall.

The flame reached Anne's fingers and she yelped with pain. She lit another—her last—and waded toward the girl, but she was gone now, despite having looked and sounded so solid.

The wallpaper where she'd stood was sloughing away in

thick, fatty strips. There, on the bare stone beneath . . . White scratch marks, in sets of four and five. Anne placed her own fingers on them, in the grooves.

"No," she moaned, "it's not real."

Not real, not real, real, the echoes replied. Real, real, real.

She dropped the match and fled the cell. Twisted in the dark to find the way out. The staircase was through the wine cellar door on her left; she could see the light on the steps. Out of the depths of the basement to her right, a woman was charging toward her, yanking cord from around her neck. "Get back here, you little bitch!"

She screamed then and dived for the exit, throwing herself up the steps and through the deserted rooms of the east wing with abandon, fear clinging to her like a net of spiders. She yanked open a door to the courtyard, alarming the staff working there—"Miss? Miss, you can't be here!"—and ran through the sucking mud of the foundations, drawn to the open moor and fresh air beyond.

Something cold grabbed her calf. She looked down: The ground had sprouted a dozen flailing cadaverous arms. One partially buried face, an accusing eye.

She kicked out, too terrified to feel it connect. When her feet finally met hard gray shale, they slid around in her shoes, her socks sodden and the leather stretched; she slipped and fell down the incline, scraping her palms on the rock. She got up, but her side was hurting now and she was fighting the urge to cry. She risked a glance back at Rannings. The girl from the parlor, almost invisible in daylight, was walking toward the house.

A gust of wind, or perhaps the strength of Anne's gaze, jostled her and she turned. Their eyes met. Anne bit back a sob. She was so young, no more than seventeen. "Don't!" she yelled at the apparition, for all the good it would do, since she couldn't be real. "Don't go in there!"

When the vision faded, Anne put a bloody hand to her forehead and took a deep breath. Stress, her father had said. Overstimulation. It was clear that Rannings was causing exactly that, and the only way to settle her nerves was to put as much distance between herself and that awful building as possible. Anyway, she couldn't bear the thought of going back; she'd only bring the smell of the cellar with her and taint everything. So she walked on, one hand pressed to the stitch in her side, the other guarding her face from the worst of the lashing wind.

As she tramped through the heather she'd so wanted to see, her spirit unraveled. Penshawe seemed like Eden now, a bucolic paradise as untouchable and as improved by nostalgia as childhood. She'd telephoned her parents from King's Cross just yesterday morning and already her mind had muddied the exact intonation of her mother's voice, had softened her father's outrage as he told his daughter, and then Merritt, exactly what he thought of them. The simplicity of that life suddenly appealed to her as it hadn't before, the march of time marked by service on Sundays, reliably followed by a joint of beef and potatoes, hot from the oven.

Huxby lay beyond the next dale. Anne made for the church as the sky darkened and booms of thunder vibrated in her chest. The churchyard gate opened with a squeal. The first fat drops of rain hit the nape of her neck and slithered down between her shoulder blades as she heaved the door open and stepped inside where it was dry. The deluge came down behind her like a final curtain at the theater.

In the murky light from the diamond-grid windows, Anne saw empty pews knocked slightly askew. A dark pulpit. Quite different from the church in Penshawe, where the secretary took great pains to refresh the flowers and notices, and there was always someone, if not the vicar, tending the vestry and lighting candles in the chapel. Still, the door had been unlocked and she had seen the vicar just yesterday.

Anne's hands were chalk-white, her nails lilac with cold. She stuffed them into her armpits and walked stiffly up the nave, leaving muddy footprints on the memorial slabs. Somewhere in the rotting beams above, a pigeon cooed and defecated, a falling white smear joining the many others splattering the chancel steps. She skirted the mess and wandered along the north transept, knocking on a discreet little door to what she assumed must be the vestry. Each rap echoed, reminding her horribly of the wine cellar, so she opened the door with an apology on her lips only to find it empty apart from a few chests. They were filled with blankets. She shook out a tartan one and wrapped herself in it, coughing and sneezing at the dust. Returning to the nave, she picked a seat far from the pigeon and clumsily removed her saturated socks and shoes. Tucking her feet up under her, she fell into a lethargic, shivering stupor.

Rain shimmered on the windows. The roof had a leak, an insistent drip coming from the south transept. The pew was hard enough to numb her back and behind. And yet she did sleep, fitfully, for a few hours, while the storm battered the moor and drowned the graves in the churchyard.

Until she sensed movement. Her eyelids fluttered open, her chapped lips peeled apart. The angle of the sun, the shadows, had changed. The vicar squinted at her from the end of the pew, bent almost double with his hands clasped behind him. He beamed at the sight of her stirring.

"Reverend." Anne licked her lips and rubbed her eyes. The blanket fell from her shoulders. "I'm sorry," she said, tugging it back. "I couldn't find you, and I was so cold. I took this. I hope you don't mind."

"Nay, 'tis nowt." His ears were so overgrown with age, so soft and cartilaginous, that they waggled when he shook his head. He sucked at his own lips in such a way as to imply several missing teeth. "It's good to have company. It's been twenty year since anyone new's come by."

"You waved to me yesterday. I was standing by the memorial."

"Ah," he said, nodding blandly. He didn't remember her in the slightest. "Well, you can stay as long as you like. What's your name?"

"It's . . . Keene," replied Anne. "Missus Keene."

He worked his gums, wet bottom lip protruding thoughtfully. "You don't sound right sure. Newly married, eh?"

"Yes. The day *before* yesterday." Anne sighed, buried herself deeper into the blanket. "I'm afraid we've made a terrible mess of things."

"Oh?" The vicar chuckled. "What's troubling you, then, Missus Keene?"

Anne looked at her wedding band. For the first time since she'd put it on, she'd completely forgotten about it. "He's a drunk. The war's left him with some sort of shell shock. And I—I—"

"Go on, lass, spit it out."

"Well, I see things, people, that aren't there."

The vicar raised his brows at this. His eyes emerged from the crumpled folds of his face, startlingly blue.

"I didn't want to tell him, but I don't see how it can be avoided now I've made such a spectacle of myself." Anne showed him her palms, grazed during her fall. He tutted sympathetically. "My God, he'll be so ashamed of me," she whispered, the details of her flight coming back to her: the mad scramble through the mud, the shrieking, the bewildered staff. Her heart thumped against her ribs. "What will I do? I can't go home."

"You're seeing apparitions?" He came closer, turning one waxy ear her way. "Tell the good reverend all about it, lass."

So she told him about the hanging men in the orchards of

Penshawe, the shadows that drifted formlessly in the churchyard, the bleeding woman she'd sometimes seen slumped on the bench outside the greengrocer's. And then in London, where her madness became difficult to hide: the crawling man in the alleyway, his fingertips blackened with plague. The one who stepped off the Embankment into the Thames. The burnt child. And then the man caught beneath the train, the cries for help that had tricked her into investigating the bowels of Rannings, and what she'd found there.

The vicar made an inquisitive audience. Unlike the numerous doctors to whom she'd described her visions, he pushed for more detail, more description, and yet his questions never felt prying. By the time she finished, he'd taken a seat beside her, brooding like a particularly ugly gargoyle. "I've heard of the doctor afore but it's worse than I thought. Summat must be done for them poor souls." He cocked his fluffy head. "Tell me, when was you born?"

Anne groped for a reply. The question had caught her off guard. "The third of F—"

"The *time*, lass, the *time*."

She frowned. "Oh, I don't know. My father always says he delivered me on the dinner table. Supper, I suppose you'd call it. Why?"

"Vespers," the vicar said to himself. His eyes popped out again like blue winkles emerging from their shells. He leaned in conspiratorially, his bulbous, arthritic hands clasping his knees. "Nah then, have you ever heard of chime children?"

Anne gave him a tired, indulgent smile. "No, I haven't."

"Chime children are what's born when the bells toll. They can do owt—commune with God's creations, heal the sick, even pierce the veil of Heaven. Folk up here say they're born at midnight, and folk down your way might say morning or evening, but it's the bells what matter." He pointed up to the tower where the transept and nave intersected, where presumably a bell now hung, silent. "I'll bet the bells was ringing out when you came into this world. Powerful thing, bell-metal . . . You still with me, lass? You look right flayt."

Anne was on her feet, hugging the blanket tight. "There's no such thing as ghosts, Reverend," she said coldly. "My delusions are caused by stress, and in the last two days I have estranged myself from my only family and married a man I barely know. Our minds are extremely susceptible to suggestion. We all learned about the Black Death and the Great Fire of London in school. I was told of Rannings' history, the asylum. I've read anatomy books. I've heard my father perform amputations. All I had to do was fill in the blanks."

"What about the scratches in the wall? You said they felt real."

"Everything I see feels real, Reverend, but there must be a rational explanation."

The vicar smiled at her as if she were a marvel and spread his arms. "If you wanted rational, why seek shelter in a church?"

She had no answer to that. "But this bell nonsense—it sounds so *pagan*. It's hardly appropriate for a vicar."

"The Bible tells us God created the world, so I say chime children are His work. Nowt can exist that He did not intend, Missus Keene."

Anne buried her face into the musk of the scratchy blanket and exhaled. Her tongue pulsed against her bottom teeth. A part of her willed it to be true: It explained so much about where and in what state her visions appeared. She had never been a morbid child, had suffered no early grief, so there seemed no reason for her illness to fixate on churchyards, on pain and terror.

She lifted her head and gazed at the ceiling, the roosting pigeon. How could she be sure this wasn't simply another delusion? But then the vicar was here, wasn't he? She wasn't alone?

"Can it be true?" She gazed at him. "I'm not mad?"

"You've no control over what you see or when." He lifted a finger. "Intrusions is still intrusions, sane or no. You must find a way to bear them."

"But I've seen others, other people who aren't suffering. The girl I saw today, she looked fine. Does that mean even she's . . . dead?"

"Maybe, maybe not." The vicar shrugged, resting his hands on his gut. "Some folk leave impressions, not just where they died, but where they made a difference." He looked around his church with such serene pride that Anne found herself looking as well. At the crooked pews, the broken memorial slabs. A candelabrum knocked to the floor, draped in cobwebs, and a bare altar. A leaking roof. A pigeon and its excrement. A vicar who, despite his unwashed appearance and gummy mouth, was strangely odorless.

Anne felt sick. She went to the front door and pushed it open, but the rain was thick and driving sideways, pulping the shrubs. The path to the churchyard gate was underwater, and she could barely make out the war memorial twenty feet away. She would easily get turned around in this, without the sight of Rannings to guide her back. Thunder growled, and between the dark clouds, lightning flickered.

The vicar walked through her and out into the storm, unaffected by the rain. He stooped especially low to read one gravestone and then another, until he found what he was looking for. "Aye, here's me."

Anne's skin tingled. "Please don't walk through me again, Reverend." But she held the blanket over her head, trusting the stiff weave to keep out the worst of the rain, and plunged barefoot into the churchyard to read the stone.

Rev. Jonah Rolfe
28 June 1771—5 December 1855

"Fifty year," the vicar said. "I poured my heart and soul into this parish for fifty year. I were happy here, lass, right happy I were. You should've seen it in its prime." A frown, a return to the present moment. "I remember you now. Yesterday means nowt to me, but I do remember you." His voice was fading. Anne stepped closer, protecting him from rain he could not feel. "Help them poor souls up at the house, if you can. They'll want to talk—that's why they come to you. Our bell will make it easier. Purest bell-metal an earl can buy.

"Good luck, lass."

And then he was gone.

"Who're you talking to?" asks Martha.

"A ghost," I say—a ghost who's already gone, her eyes the last of her to fade. I can't be sure she even heard me.

Martha moves behind the wall. I imagine her pressing her ear to the hole. "What?"

"Never mind." I rub the back of my head where the matron struck me and my fingers come away wet and dark. A headache forms there, as if a gentle press was all it needed. I ease back down beside the hole and we link fingers again.

"Can you find things, too?" she whispers. "Is that why you're here?"

"I seem to be much better at losing them. . . Why, what can you find?"

"Owt," Martha replies, and there's a note of quiet pride in her voice. "When I were little, folk used to say I must've stolen things, to know where to find 'em. They chased us out of town. Where we live now is better. Now folk pay me, sometimes, to help find stuff."

I smile, understanding her pride. As children, any coins

Benjamin and I could contribute to our families were precious, whether they'd been earned honestly or lifted out of a loose purse. Every coin meant our mothers could afford to put one less neighbor's shirt through the back-breaking mangle, make one less matchbox when we'd all gone to bed. Our fathers could come home from the docks one hour earlier, live one more day before their bodies gave out. It's why the damage to Benjamin's leg was such a blow. But I also smile because her gift gives me hope.

"Listen, Martha, does it work for people, what you can do?"

She's quiet for a moment. Perhaps the doctor's asked her the same thing, and now she regrets saying as much to me. "Sometimes."

I give her finger a little squeeze. "You see, I came to find my friend. He's here somewhere, locked up, just like us. Have you heard anyone crying out?"

"I think so," she whispers back. "They're somewhere dark, somewhere . . . down there." I can barely hear her as she draws away from the wall, a dowsing rod for Benjamin. Then she yanks on my finger and says, her voice pitched high with sudden panic, "Please don't leave me here! I know you didn't come for me, but I wanna go home, too."

I soothe her as best I can, pressing her poor exposed nail beds to my lips. Guilt stings my eyes. I came for Benjamin and Benjamin alone, but I don't have the heart to abandon this child. I'm not a monster. Will Missus Walchop ever forgive me, if I'm forced to choose? This girl can die and Benjamin cannot—is that what I must tell his mother, what I must tell myself, in leaving Benjamin to his torture?

The peal of a faraway bell ripples through me. I look up to the window. Fog slithers in like water. "What's that?"

"It's coming from the church at Huxby," says Martha. "It must be midnight."

"Chime hours," I breathe.

Every clang strikes me like a smith's hammer. White dots blister my vision, expanding and joining together until I can't see, and everything—the chill bleeding through my skirts, the vise of my stays; even Martha, noticing something's wrong—comes to me as if from a great distance. I turn obligingly inward like I was taught, into the light.

An old bell appears above me, scabbed with turquoise verdigris. Below, pulling the rope, is the ghost. I watch the bell's clapper connect with the rim. As the vibration stretches impossibly long, pinning us in a moment, our eyes meet. Her left eyelid distorts when she smiles.

"It's you," she says.

Suddenly she's right here, or I'm there—space has ceased to matter—and she's all loud, chromatic flesh. Blood springs from the fissures of her chapped lips, coloring them a shocking red and infusing her breath with iron. She's reaching gently for my hand. Hers are as soft as a gentlewoman's, until I turn them over and find her palms flecked with cuts. I close my callused fingers over hers.

"You were right, wise spirit," I tell her. "I should've listened to your warning."

Her brows draw together. "You know me?"

"Of course," I say slowly. "You told me not to go to the house."

This shakes her in a way I can't understand. Do spirits not remember their own actions? But then something resolves. Her mouth presses into a straight, serious line. She breathes deeply, her exhalation quivering. "All right. Is there something you wanted to tell me? Is there some message?"

Now it's my turn to be shaken.

Chime folk are rare, and my gift is rarer still. Everything I know about spirits comes from hand-me-down talk, filtered through a dozen mouths. A woman from a village called

Hale, some dozen miles from Liverpool's docks, was said to see the dead, and the crux of her parting advice which finally found its way to me was this: Listen to them. Let them impart their wisdom or last words so they can rest.

They don't ask *us* for messages.

"I don't understand you, spirit," I say, letting go of her hands. "It's usually the other way around."

"Is it?"

"Don't you have a message for *me*? Another warning? I'll heed you this time." I step back and take her in, the thrill of making contact giving way to sober clarity. Her accent, her clothes, are alien. I can't place her lack of corset, her narrow skirt, the lumpy spencer that extends down to her waist. Her hair, tawny as a barn owl's hood, escapes from pins set above her ears. "When did you die?"

Her eyes widen. "I'm not dead! I'm . . . I'm on my honeymoon. Today is the twenty-second of October, 1938. I saw it on a newspaper someone was reading at breakfast."

I find myself on the floor, such as it is in this place, knees bent inward like a child. 1938. An incomprehensible date. The future. I must be seeing the future. I'm snatching glimpses of people not yet born, tasting champagne made from grapes that are yet to grow. Suddenly, I understand why history hasn't recorded the incidents I see—they haven't come to pass. The spirits never speak to me because they don't even know I'm there.

But if this woman can see me . . .

"Oh God, do I die here?" I cover my eyes. "Don't tell me, I don't want to know."

"I'm sorry," she whispers, and she's at my level, prizing my hands from my face. "All I know is that I've seen dreadful things all my life. I thought I was mad. I think I still am mad." She laughs weakly. "But I saw you in the parlor at Rannings today, and on the moor. You were intact and . . . simply perfect. For the first time, I wasn't scared." She smiles again giddily, her left eyelid taut. "I'm not scared."

I'm younger than her, but I feel a tug of responsibility. I palm her cheek and fix her with a steadying look. "There is nothing to fear from the dead. They may frighten you, they may come when you want to be alone, but they won't harm you." I draw our foreheads together. Benjamin did this for me, when my gift first manifested and I couldn't sleep. It's my dearest memory of him. Tears drip into our laps. I can't tell which are mine.

"So," I say, and we draw apart, "what else did you see in the house, besides me?" She describes as best she can the flayed boy. The girl in the cell, who can only be Martha, clawing her fingernails off trying to escape. As she speaks, I feel the resonance of the bell fading. Our time grows short. "Did you see a boy? Scrawny and tall, with a limp? He doesn't heal completely—he might have other scars, too."

"A boy—?"

"In 1938, is there any record of him," I push, "of us being held against our will?"

"I don't know." She hides her face in her hands. "After Rannings was sold, there was some talk of legal trouble, and I think the receptionist said the asylum was shut down about a hundred years ago, which would be—"

"Now," I finish viciously. "Tell me, was the doctor tried? The missing children, the flayed boy—were they found?"

"No, no, I don't know . . ."

I close my eyes, holding my anger in. The doctor targets poor, hungry families, mothers like Benjamin's, like Martha's, who can't afford to turn down money even at the expense of a child. He trusts that the world will turn without stopping for them. Sickeningly, he's right: There will be no accounting for this in his lifetime.

"What is it now, the house?" I ask bitterly.

"It's a hotel. A very expensive hotel."

A hotel! I can't help but laugh, but there's no joy in it. "Mark me: Children have died here far from home, and they deserve justice. My friend, Benjamin, deserves justice. God knows what he's been through. I don't know the limits of his gift; perhaps the doctor has already found a way to break him." I grip her arm and she flinches. "Avenge us. That is what the spirits want. That's what *I* want, if I'm to die here."

"I will, I promise," she says, her voice faint.

"Good-bye. God bless you." I kiss her cheeks as they turn translucent. Even if I survive this night, my bones will be dust by the time she walks the Earth. I don't even know her name.

I'm released slowly back to my senses, as if recovering from a faint. Barely a second has passed. Martha is crying my name. She's heard me collapse, convulsing, and her terror has attracted the matron's attention. Those are the soles of her slippers I hear, flapping against the steps.

Martha's crying falters when she hears me stir, but I grunt at her to keep going as I prop myself up. I tear at my bodice and the damp silk parts easily—fashionable clothes, like fashionable people, aren't made to withstand much of anything at all. My fingers fumble at the laces of my corset as the matron barks from outside our cells, "What's going on in there?"

The laces slither free. I wait behind the door where it's darkest, wrapping them around my fists into a makeshift garrote. Martha's listening. She's not stupid. "There's summat wrong with Mary," she wails. "She won't wake up!"

Keys jingle. The matron enters, holding a candle aloft. I don't give her time to clock the bare floor: I throw my crossed hands over her neck and jerk them home. She drops the candle and flails, gurgling. Her elbow drives into my side, cracks a rib, drawing a gasp. But I'm a Belfast girl raised in Liverpool; I can give as good as I get, and right now I've got nothing to lose.

One more squeeze of the garrote and she goes down with a thud.

Her keys are still dangling from my door. I unlock Martha's cell and she flies to me, burying her face in my soft belly. "Ah," I gasp, "not too hard." Every breath burns and my back aches now without the support of my stays. Unlaced for the first time since I was a young child, my middle's as cold as a shucked mollusk.

I stare down the corridor. For a moment, the path to Benjamin is clear. But I can't draw a painless breath deep enough to shout his name, and anyway, Martha's shaking her head at me desperately, unsure of her gift, and the matron's storming toward us, her purple face twisted with rage. I mustn't have held on long enough. I've never tried to strangle anyone before.

"Get back here, you little bitch!"

Martha shoves her, giving us room to sprint past and up the stairs, to lock her in behind us. The matron's ham-sized fists batter the door, but it holds.

"What now?" Martha says, clinging to me.

"We get out of here," I reply, stroking her head, "but I need something first. A letter that I brought with me. Is it still on the doctor's desk?"

She nods.

My heels left twin trails in the dust where the matron dragged me. We follow them to their source, the keys jutting between my fingers to make a spiked fist. The doctor's door is ajar and the room is still. He must have retired for the night. But even here, a faint banging makes its way up from the basement, and even now he may be descending the stairs to investigate.

I snatch up Missus Walchop's letter and rifle through the files in his desk, my hands shaking so much I almost can't pinch out the one I want.

"Drop them."

Martha flinches. The doctor's blocking the doorway. The barrel of a revolver's pointing at her head. I pull her behind me as he fires, blasting a hole in the paneling. As precious as we are to him, he'd kill us to cover his tracks? Selfish coward! I grit my teeth and lunge, ready for the bullet to punch through me if it means sparing Martha, but my unexpected offensive sends his second shot wide, the third jams, and by then I'm close enough for a right hook that would make my mother proud. One key skewers his cheek. Another lodges in his eye. The revolver, and the doctor with it, falls to the floor.

I stand over him, wheezing, with one hand pressed to my rib. His unscathed eye rolls in agony, and when it settles on me I hunker down, baring my teeth in a grin. "You wanted to know what I can do, Doctor? I can see what is yet to pass, and I've seen the future for this place—for you. Your work will come to nothing. No one will remember your name. And these"—I hold up the file, the letter—"will ruin you, I'll make sure of that." He whimpers. I straighten and take Martha's hand, and together we leave.

Where the crunching drive gives way to soft moss, I hear light footsteps ahead and hold my breath, but it's only James, praise God. I can smell the grouse and lamp oil on him. He must sense more than see the ruin of my bodice and corset, revealing the thin, secret shift beneath, because he passes me his coat without comment, tells me instead how my cries for help echoed over the moor and that he couldn't bear to go home still hearing them.

And of Martha, he says, "Who's this?"

"That can wait." I groan, leaning heavily against him. "Take me to the magistrate. Or the nearest lawman who'll hear me out."

Martha turns her face up to mine. "What're you gunna

do?"

Missus Walchop's letter and a broken contract press against my side. I look up at the dark bulk of Rannings. My employer, if she'll still be my employer after this, with all her hollow frivolities, will have to damn well wait.

If you're still in there, Benjamin, you better hold on.

"I'm going to tear it down. Tear it all down."

"Good God." Broad hands stroked her face, wiped away strands of wet hair. "You rang the bell, didn't you? Good girl, clever girl, I heard you, I'm here now." Merritt tried to rub warmth into her numb legs, her feet, so rough it hurt.

"Stop," Anne mumbled. She'd seen a hypothermic man die from such rubbing. "Your coat."

"Easy, easy. All right." He wrapped her in his coat, damp but still warm from his body and better than nothing. He scooped her up with a grunt and carried her out of the bell tower.

"There's . . . something . . . something I need to tell you—"

"Whatever it is can wait, darling. Over here! I've got her!"

The groundsman's cart pulled up outside the church, escorted by police in shimmering waterproof cloaks. Merritt laid her inside and wrapped her in dry blankets, tried to pour warm tea into her mouth. She spluttered when the cart began to move.

"I can see ghosts," she told him while he mopped her chin.

"Don't talk nonsense," he said.

"It's true. My parents thought I had a—a nervous disorder. When we met, I'd just come back from the hospital. Shock treatment. It didn't help. Nothing does." She had his full attention. She licked her lips. "Penshawe must have seemed a pretty sort of place to you, but for me it was a prison. The more anxious I felt, the more I hallucinated. I thought it would stop when we left, but it's been worse."

There it was, the look of disgust she'd been so afraid of. She reached for his hand but he wrenched it away. "It's dead people I see, Merritt, dying people, all the time. I think they're ghosts. They have messages for me, things they want me to do—"

"Stop," he snapped. "If you want to be free of me, just say so."

"Telephone my parents, they'll tell you everything."

He glared at her. Anne gripped the blankets. The moment was slipping its tracks in a way she hadn't expected.

"Are you trying to get back at me for this morning? Am I not the husband you hoped for, after that? Can you not stand a little real life?"

"Says the man who drinks because he can't bear his own grief!" Too late, the words were said. She could see she'd hurt him.

The cart jolted and suddenly the dark pit in her stomach opened, the gorge rising in her throat. They were approaching the foundations of Rannings, where everything felt rotten. Anne flung off the blankets and jumped out of the cart before Merritt or the policemen could stop her. She ran through the rain and mud until she found the epicenter, the ugly heart of it all. There, she began digging with her hands. The arms of the dead pushed up around her like daisies. "I know," she told them, "it'll be over soon."

"Stop, Anne! Stop this!" Merritt shouted as he jogged toward her, lost his footing. "You'll catch your death!"

"Will you just listen to me for once?" she flung back. "Dig, for God's sake!"

Merritt watched helplessly as she scraped out great clots of mud. Policemen surged past him, hands reaching out to grab her, when her fingernails broke against something hard. She'd uncovered a crescent of discolored bone, a tiny pelvis.

They hauled her away, but the bone lay stark against the black sludge, glowing in the light from the crisscrossing torch beams.

Seventeen skeletons in total. The deepest at eight feet, the shallowest at just three.

Rannings was forced to close immediately, so they settled the bill and drove north to Middlesbrough that night, before the press descended upon the area to seek out her photograph. Anne stayed briefly at the hospital. The nurses said she was lucky to be alive.

Merritt sat by her bedside, and when she had the strength to sit up, they talked frankly at last. Neither had married for love. They'd symbolized something to each other—escape for her, lost time for him—and they hadn't looked any deeper than that because there was nothing more they wanted to find.

"Was this a mistake?" he asked.

At a loss, she turned her palm upward and he grasped it gently.

He looked so broken, though there was no alcohol on his breath. She bit her lip and twisted her wedding band, still loose. It came off readily with only the slightest resistance at the knuckle, and she held it out to him, scuff marks and all.

They looked at each other for a long time, the bustle of the ward filling the silence. "It's either divorce or annulment," he said at length. "Both options leave you high and dry. I assume you don't want to go back to Kent?"

"Never," she whispered.

They watched the nurses on their rounds for a while. Somewhere, a voice on the wireless was relaying every gory detail of the unfolding scandal. Anne requested it be turned off, but the silence was somehow worse.

"I wondered . . . Have you—could you—my brothers?"

She smiled sadly, expecting the question. The hope. “Perhaps. Truly, I don’t understand how this works.”

Merritt rubbed his cheeks. “I can’t promise to be a good husband, Anne, but I can listen, I can do that. We rushed into this, but we needn’t rush out of it. And maybe someday, we’ll understand it together.”

The hospital discharged her the next day. Anne waited on a bench while Merritt brought the motorcar around, the breeze blowing her hair into her eyes. She tucked it behind her ear and caught the eye of an old man across the street. He nodded to her and crossed the road, the morning newspaper tucked under his arm. He favored his right leg.

Without the Rannings’ uniform, she hardly knew him. The porter.

When he reached her, he smiled with more gums than teeth. “You look just like Mary said you would. I’m sorry if I gave you a scare, before.”

Anne stood to meet him, her jaw slack. Of course. A boy with a limp. “Are you—?”

“She found me, in the end, like. Well, Martha did. That was her gift.”

In a daze, Anne extended her hand and he shook it warmly. “How is this possible? You must be over a hundred years old.” With a glance at his bad leg, she said, “I suppose it can’t be a war wound, then?”

He patted his thigh. “Not from the war you’re thinking of, but I got plenty of those, too. I fit right in.” He untucked the newspaper and showed her the front page. The headline declared Rannings’ reputation to be in tatters. “Mary would’ve wanted me to thank you for this in person, like. We tried our best, but it couldn’t happen yet because *you* hadn’t happened yet, or something; she always explained it better. After she died, I had to come back and see it through by myself, hard as it was. Thank God it’s done.”

"She died?"

"Aye, as do we all, I hope," he said, and then laughed at her shock. "But don't worry: She held on a bloody long time. Saw in the new century. You must've just missed each other."

He handed her a small photograph, folded so much that the very center had worn away. In it, an elderly woman reclined on a sunbed, caught in a blurry roar of laughter. Her bathing suit and style of her hair placed her sometime in the early twenties, and the beach could have been anywhere, but Anne liked to think it was Kent.

The motorcar came purring around the corner and stopped at the curb. Merritt slung his arm across the back of the seat. "Anne, is this chap bothering you?"

Benjamin flipped the photograph over. There was an address written on the back. "Look me up next time you're in Bootle," he said with a wink, then he turned up his collar and walked on. Anne watched him go, quite breathless, until Merritt tooted the horn and made her jump. She strode to the motorcar and got in. "He wasn't a journalist, you know."

"Can't be too careful." He pulled into the traffic. "Well, shall we start over?"

"I don't know where to begin."

He sucked on a cigarette. "My parents' house is over two hours away."

Anne smiled. She rolled down the window to let out the blue smoke and let in the sounds of the city, and rested her chin in one hand. She gripped the photograph tight with the other. She'd do it properly, this time. She'd tell him everything. No more secrets; no more shame. Bold, like Mary.

For He Can Creep

By Siobhan Carroll

Flash and fire! Bristle and spit! The great Jeoffry ascends the madhouse stairs, his orange fur on end, his yellow eyes narrowed!

On the third floor the imps cease their gamboling. Is this the time they stay and fight? One imp, bolder than the others, flattens himself against the flagstones. He swells himself with nightmares, growing huge. His teeth shine like the sword of an executioner, and his eyes are the colors of spilled whale oil before a match is struck. In their cells, the filthy inmates shrink away from his immensity, wailing.

But Jeoffry does not shrink. He rushes up the last few stairs like the Deluge of God, and his claws are sharp! The imps run screaming, flitting into folds of space only angels and devils can penetrate.

In the hallway, Jeoffry cleans the smoking blood off his claws. Some of the humans whisper their thanks to him; some even dare to stroke his fur through the bars. Sometimes Jeoffry accepts this praise and sometimes he is bored by it. Today, annoyed by the imps' vain show of defiance, he leaves his scent on every door. This cell is his, and this one. The whole asylum is his, and let no demon forget it! For he is the Cat Jeoffry, and no demon can stand against him.

On the second floor, above the garden, the poet is trying to write. He has no paper, and no pens—such things are forbidden, after his last episode—and so he scratches out some words in blood on the brick wall. Silly man. Jeoffry meows at him. It is time to pay attention to Jeoffry!

The man remembers his place. Reluctantly, painfully, he detaches his tattered mind from the hard hook-pins of word and meter. He rolls away from his madness and strokes the purring, winding cat.

Hail and well met, Jeoffry. Have you been fighting again? Such a bold gentleman you are. Such a pretty fellow. Who's a good cat?

Jeoffry knows he is a good cat, and a bold gentleman, and a pretty fellow. He tells the poet as much, pushing his head repeatedly at the man's hands, which smell unpleasantly of blood. The demons have been at him again. A cat cannot be everywhere at once, and so, while Jeoffry was battling the imps on the third floor, one of the larger dark angels has been whispering in the poet's ear, its claws scorching the bedspread.

Jeoffry feels . . . not guilty exactly, but annoyed. The poet is *his* human. Yet, of all the humans, the demons seem to like the poet the best, perhaps because he is not theirs yet, or perhaps because they are interested—as so many visitors seem to be—in the man's poetry.

Jeoffry does not see the point of poems. Music he can appreciate as a human form of yowling. Poems, though. From time to time visitors come to the madhouse and speak to the poet of translations and Psalms and ninety-nine-year publishing contracts. At such times, the poet smells of sweat and fear. Sometimes he rants at the men, sometimes curls up into a ball. Once, one of the men even stepped on Jeoffry's tail—unforgivable! Since then Jeoffry had made a point of hissing at every man who came to them smelling of ink.

I wish I had the fire in your belly, the poet says, and Jeoffry knows he is speaking of the creditors again. You would give them a fight, eh? But I fear I have not your courage. I will promise them their paper and perhaps scratch out a stupidity or two, but I cannot do it, Jeoffry. It takes me away from the Poem. What is a man to do, when God wants him to write one poem, and his creditors another?

Jeoffry considers his poet's problem as he licks his fur back into place. He'd heard of the Poem before—the one true poem that God had written to unfold the universe. The poet believes it is his duty to translate this poem by communing with God. His fellow humans, on the other hand, think the poet should write silly things called satires, as he used to do. This is the kind of thing humans think about, and fight about, and for which they chain up their fellow humans in nasty sweaty madhouse cells.

Jeoffry does not particularly care about either side of the debate. But—he thinks as he catches a flea and crunches it between his teeth—if he were to have an opinion, it would be that the humans should let the man finish his Divine Poem. The ways of the Divine Being were unfathomable—he'd created dogs, after all—and if the Creator wanted a poem, the poet should give it to him. And then the poet would have more time to pet Jeoffry.

O cat, the poet says, I am glad of your companionship. You remind me how it is our duty to live in the present moment, and love God through His creation. If you were not here I think the devil would have claimed me long ago.

If the poet were sane, he might have thought better of his words. But madmen do not guard their tongues, and cats have no thoughts of the future. It's true, something does occur to Jeoffry as the poet speaks—some vague sense of disquiet—but then the man scratches behind his ears, and Jeoffry purrs in luxury.

That night, Satan comes to the madhouse.

Jeoffry is curled at his usual spot on the sleeping poet's back when the devil arrives. The devil does not enter as his demons do, in whispers and the patterning of light. His presence steals into the room like smoke, and as with smoke, Jeoffry is aware of the danger before he is even awake, his fur on end, his heart pounding.

"Hello, Jeoffry," the devil says.

Jeoffry extends his claws. At that moment, he knows something is wrong, for the poet, who normally would wake with a howl at such an accidental clawing, lies still and silent. All around Jeoffry is a quiet such as cats never hear: no mouse or beetle creeping along a madhouse wall, no human snoring, no spider winding out its silk. It as if the Night itself has hushed to listen to the devil's voice, which sounds pleasant and warm, like a bucket of cream left in the sun.

"I thought you and I should have a chat," Satan says. "I understand you've been giving my demons some trouble."

The first thought that flashes into Jeoffry's head is that Satan looks exactly as Milton describes him in *Paradise Lost*. Only more cat-shaped. (Jeoffry, a poet's cat, has ignored vast amounts of Milton over the years, but some of it has apparently stuck.)

The second thought is that the devil has come into his territory, and this means fighting!

Puffing himself up to his utmost size, Jeoffry spits at the devil and shows his teeth.

This is my place! he cries. Mine!

"Is anything truly ours?" The devil sighs and examines his claws. He is simultaneously a monstrous serpent, a mighty angel, and a handsome black cat with whiskers the color of starlight. The cat's whiskers are singed, the serpent's scales are scarred, and the angel's brow is heavy with an ancient grievance, and yet he is still beautiful, in his way. "But more of this later. Jeoffry, I have come to converse with you. Will you not take a walk with me?"

Jeoffry pauses, considering. Do you have treats?

"I have feasts awaiting. Catnip fresh from the soil. Salted ham from the market. Fish heads with the eyes still in them, scrumptiously poppable."

I want treats.

"And treats you shall have. Come and see."

Jeoffry trots at the devil's heels down the madhouse stairs, past the mouse's nest on the landing, past the kitchen with its pleasant smell of bread and pork fat, through the asylum's heavy door (which stands mysteriously open), and onto roads of Darkness, beneath which the round orb of Earth hangs like a jewel. Jeoffry gazes with interest up at the blue glow of the Crystalline Firmament, at the fixed stars, and at the golden chain of Heaven, from which all the Universe is suspended. He feels hungry.

"Well," the devil says presently. "Let's get the formalities out of the way." He snaps his fingers. Instantly Jeoffry is dangling above the Earth, staring down at it as one does at a patterned carpet. He can see the gleaming rooftop of the madhouse, and Bethnal Green, and the darkened streets of London, still bustling, even at this time of night.

"All of this could be yours," Satan says. "Yea, I will give you all the kingdoms of Earth if you'd but bow down and worship me."

Jeoffry does not like being dangled. His fur bristles as he prepares himself to fall. But then he catches the smell of the fish market in the air, and hears the distant yowl of a tomcat making love on the street. And Jeoffry understands, for a moment, what the devil is offering him. He understands, also, that this offer represents a fundamentally wrong order to the universe.

You should bow down and worship Jeoffry!

"Right," the devil says. "I thought as much."

He snaps his fingers again, and they are back on the path between the fixed stars, with the planets far below them.

"You have the sin of pride, cat," Satan says. "A sin I am particularly fond of, given that it is my own. For that reason I am taking you into my confidence. You see, I have an interest in your poet."

Mine!

"That's debatable. There are multiple claims to Mr. Smart. The Tyrant of Heaven's, his debtors', his family's . . . the man is like a ruined estate, overrun with scavengers. Me," the devil shrugs, "he owes for some of his earlier debaucheries—he was an extravagant man in his youth—and for that I need to collect."

Jeoffry's tail twitches back and forth. Like many who have conversed with the devil, he can sense something wrong with this dark tide of speech, a lie buried beneath Satan's reasonable arguments. But he cannot work out what it is.

"Now," says the Adversary, "I would be willing to forgive this debt if your poet would but write *me* a poem. I have the perfect thing in mind: a metered piece of guile that, unleashed, would lay waste to Creation.

"Indeed," the devil says, "I have planted this poem in his imagination on several occasions. But your poet is stubborn. He defies all his creditors (including, most importantly, me), and insists on writing this tripe, this vile piece of sycophancy, for the Tyrant of Heaven, who—let me assure you—deserves no such praise."

The Poem of Poems, Jeoffry says.

"Exactly. Let us face facts, Jeoffry. The Poem your human labors over—the thing to which he has devoted his last years of labor, burning away his health, destroying his human relationships—even setting aside my feelings on its subject matter, Jeoffry, the fact is this: The poem he writes is *not very good*."

Jeoffry stares at his paws, and beneath them, at the blue glow of Earth. Vaguely the words of the poet's human visitors come to him. Have they not said much the same thing?

"Speaking as a critic now, Jeoffry: Do you not think the poem's Let-For structure is overly complicated? The word-play in Latin and Greek too obscure to suit the common taste? Obscurity for the sake of obscurity, Jeoffry. It will get him nowhere."

Poetry is prayer, Jeoffry says stiffly, repeating the words the poet murmurs to himself as he scratches frantically at his papers, or the bricks, or at the skin on his forearms.

"Poetry is poetry. Two roads diverging in a yellow wood, people wandering about like clouds, even that terrible thing about footprints—that's what readers want, Jeoffry. Something simple, and clear, with a message: that all of one's life choices may be justified by looking at daffodils; that we exist in a world abandoned by God and haunted by human mediocrity. Don't you agree?"

Jeoffry does not like literature of any kind, unless it is about Jeoffry. Even then, petting is better. And eating. Are there treats now?

"Ah, treats."

Instantly a banquet table is before Jeoffry. Everything the devil had promised is there: the fish heads, the salted ham—and things he forgot to mention, like the vats of cream and crispy salmon skins. There's even a bowl of Turkish delight.

Jeoffry bolts toward the food. Suddenly, a hand catches

him by the scruff of the neck. The devil has grown gigantic, a mighty warrior, singed and scarred by his contest with heaven. His smile gleams like a knife.

"Before you eat, Jeoffry, I need a thing of you. Such a small thing."

I want the food.

"And you shall get it, if you but promise me this: to stand aside when I come to visit your poet tomorrow night. Aye, to stand aside, and not interfere."

The uneasy sense that Jeoffry had felt at the devil's first words returns with a vengeance.

Why?

"Merely so I can converse with your poet."

Jeoffry thinks about Satan's proposition. As a cat well-versed in Milton, he is aware of the devil's less-than-salubrious reputation. On the other hand, there's a giant vat of cream *right there.*

I agree, he says.

The devil smiles. Released, Jeoffry flies to the table, and food! There is so much food! He eats and eats, and somehow there is still more to eat, and somehow he can keep eating, though his belly is starting to hurt.

"My thanks to you, Jeoffry," the devil says. "I will see you tomorrow."

Jeoffry is aware, vaguely, that Satan is walking away from him. But that does not matter: He has come to the bowl of Turkish delight, and having heard so much about it, it must taste good, no? So he selects a powdered cube of honey and rosewater, one that is larger than all the others, and he takes a bite—

The next day, Jeoffry feels ill.

On waking, he performs his morning prayers as he always does. He wreathes his body seven times around with elegant quickness. He leaps up to catch the musk, and rolls on the planks to work it in. He performs the cat's self-examination in ten degrees, first, looking on his forepaws to see if they are clean, then stretching, then sharpening his claws by wood, then washing himself, then rolling about, then checking himself for fleas. . . .

Yet none of this makes Jeoffry feel better. It is as though something casts a shadow upon him, separating the cat from the sunlight that is his due. With a chill, Jeoffry remembers his bargain with the devil. Was it a dream?

Well met, Jeoffry, well met. The poet is awake, and his eyes look unusually clear. He sits up on his bed of straw, and stretches.

I feel better today, Jeoffry, as if my sickness is leaving me. Oh, but they are sure to duck me again, to drive the devils out. You are lucky, cat, to have no devils in you, for you'd hate being ducked.

The poet rubs Jeoffry's head, affectionately, then looks again. But how's this, Jeoffry? You look unwell, my friend.

Jeoffry meows. His stomach feels sickly heavy, as though he has eaten a barrel full of rotten fish. He tries to say something about the devil—not that the human would understand, but it seems worth trying—and instead vomits on the poet's leg.

Heavens, Jeoffry! What have you been eating!

Jeoffry noses his vomit to see if there's anything there worth re-eating, but the remnants of the devil's meal are a pile of dead leaves, partly digested. The devil's visit was no dream, then.

The poet tries to catch him, but Jeoffry is too quick. He slips down the staircase, where he vomits, to the kitchen, where he vomits, until he sees a water bowl put down for the physician's dog. He drinks from it. And vomits.

He vomits on the cook, who tries to catch him, and on the

terrier-dog, which yaps at him as he jumps to the top cupboard. Is there so much vomit in the world? (Apparently.)

Miserable Jeoffry curls up on top of the cupboard and puts a paw over his eyes to shut out the light. He sleeps an uneasy sleep, in which Satan stalks through his dreams in the guise of a giant black cat, chuckling.

When Jeoffry opens his eyes again it is evening. He can hear the grind and clink of iron keys above him. The keepers are locking the cell doors. Soon the demons will arrive in full force, to gambol and chitter in the shadows, and pull at the lunatics' beards, and drive them madder.

Jeoffry clambers to his feet. His legs are shaky, but he drives himself onward, leaping awkwardly to the kitchen floor. The smell of his vomit still hangs in the air, acrid, with an aura of sulfur.

Jeoffry climbs the stairs. The mice behind the walls peep at him as he lumbers past. The imps giggle in the distance, but he sees none in the hallways of the second floor. With a sinking heart, he paces onward, to the room where his poet sits, composing his great work.

As Jeoffry approaches the poet's cell, a great wind seems to blow from its door. Jeoffry flattens himself against the ground and tries to slink forward, but the wind is too strong. It presses on him with the hands of a thousand dark angels, with the weight of Leviathan, with the despair of the world. He claws at the floorboards, shredding wood, but he cannot go farther.

"Now, now, Jeoffry," a voice says in his head. "Did you not promise me that you would stand aside?"

Jeoffry yowls in response. He tries to tell the devil that he takes back his bargain, that the food he ate was merely vegetation, that he vomited it all up anyway, that Turkish delight is overrated.

"A bargain is a bargain," the voice says. The wind grows

stronger. Jeoffry feels himself floating up in the air. A sudden gust jerks him backward, and then—

Jeoffry wakes. There is a sour smell in the air—not vomit this time, but something else. Jeoffry is lying in the second floor's empty cell, the one where the human strangled herself on her chains. The iron hoops stare at him accusingly.

Jeoffry uncoils himself, and as he does so he remembers the previous evening. The devil, the wind, and the vomit. (O the vomit!) And the poet.

He takes off at a run. The poet is sitting up on his bed of straw, his face slack-jawed. Jeoffry headbutts him, and winds around him, and paws his face. Even so, it takes a while for the poet to transfer his gaze to Jeoffry.

O cat, the poet says. I fear I have done a terrible thing.

Jeoffry rubs his chin against the man's skinny knee. He purrs, willing the world repaired.

Last night the devil himself came to me, the man says. He said such things . . . I withstood him as long as I could, but in the end, I could take no more. I begged him, on my knees, to stop his whisperings. And he asked me—and I agreed. O cat, I am damned for certain! For I have promised the devil a poem.

As he gave this speech, the man's hands kneaded Jeoffry's back harder and harder, digging into his flesh until it hurt. Normally this would trigger a clawing, or a stern meow, but Jeoffry understands now what it means to come face-to-face with the devil, and his heart is sore.

Jeoffry does what he can to comfort the poet. He spraggles and waggles. He frolics about the room. He takes up the wine cork the man likes to toss for him, and drops it on the poet's lap. And yet none of this seems to lift the poet's spirits.

The man curls in the corner and moans until the attendants come to take him away for his morning ducking. Jeoffry lies on the floor, in the sun, and thinks.

The poet is miserable, and well he might be, having agreed to write a poem for the devil. Jeoffry, in agreeing to stand aside, left his human undefended. In that action (and here Jeoffry must think very hard, and lay his ears back) Jeoffry has been less than his normal, wonderful self. He may in fact have been (though this is almost impossible to think) a *bad cat*.

Jeoffry is furious at the thought. He attacks the air. Growling, he flies about the room, ripping the spiderwebs down from the ceiling. He gets in the man's straw bed and whirls around and around, until bits of straw coat the floor and the dust veils him in yellow. Somehow, none of it helps.

When he is exhausted, he sits and licks himself clean. Even a short poem will take the poet more than a day to write, for he must doubt every word, and scratch it out, and write it down again. That is more than enough time for Jeoffry to find the devil, and fight him, and bite him on the throat.

It is true that the devil is bigger than the biggest rat Jeoffry has ever fought, and it is also true that he is Satan, the Adversary, Prince of Hell, Lord of Evil. Nevertheless, the devil made a grave mistake when he annoyed Jeoffry. He will pay for his insolence.

Thus resolved, Jeoffry goes in quest of food. His heart feels lighter. He has a feeling that soon, all will be well.

When he comes back from his ducking, the poet lies on his bed and weeps. Jeoffry cannot rub against him after the water treatment, for the poet's skin is still unpleasantly damp. So Jeoffry claws the wooden bedframe instead.

Ah, Jeoffry, the poet cries. They gave me back my paper!

And my quill, and ink! Yesterday I would have been overjoyed at such a kindness, but now I can only detect the machinations of the devil! It is all in my head, Jeoffry—the poem entire. I need only set it to paper. But I know I must not. These words—oh they must not be allowed to enter this world!

And yet he takes out a sheet of cotton paper, and his gum sandarac powder, and his ruler. Sobbing, he begins to write. The noise of his quill scritch-scritching is like the sound of ants eating through wood. It wrinkles Jeoffry's nose, but he does not stir from the poet's cell. He is waiting for the devil to arrive.

Sure enough, come nightfall, the devil steals into the madhouse. He looks for all the world like a London critic, in a green striped waistcoat and a velvet coat. He stands outside the bars of the cell and peers inside.

"How now, Jeoffry," Satan says. "How does my poet fare?" It is plain to see that the poet is shivering and sobbing on his bed. At the sound of the devil's voice, he buries his face in his hands and begins murmuring a prayer.

Jeoffry turns disdainfully to the wall. The devil tricked him. The devil is bad. The devil may not have the pleasure of stroking Jeoffry or petting him on the head. Jeoffry is more interested in staring at this wall. Staring intently. Maybe there is a fly here, maybe not. This wall is more interesting than you, Satan.

"Alas," Satan says. "Much as it wounds me to lose your good opinion, Jeoffry, tonight I have other fish to fry." With that, Satan directs his attention to the poet, and he says in the language of the humans: "How goes my poem?"

Get behind me, Satan!

"Please," the devil says, hooking his hands in the lapels of his coat. "'Tis a sad thing when a wordsmith resorts to clichés. And hardly good manners in addressing an old friend! What, did I not aid you in your youth many a time, in bedding a wench or evading a creditor? Now I ask that you do a single thing for me, and you whimper about repaying my kindness? For shame."

I should not have agreed to it! the man says. Forgive me, Lord, for I was weak!

"La," the devil says, "aren't we all. But enough of this moping. How goes my poem?"

The man is jerked upright like a dog yanked on a chain. He rises from his bed—in his nightclothes, no less—and takes up a few sheets of paper. He hands them, with an iron-stiff arm, through the bars to the devil.

The devil takes out a pair of amber spectacles and a red quill. He reads over the papers with great interest, from time to time making happy humming noises to himself, and from time to time frowning and scratching down something in bursts of flame. "Capital phrasing sir!" he says, and "Sir, you *cannot* rhyme love with dove, it is banal and I shall not allow it," and "I like this first reference to 'An Essay on Man,' but this second makes you seem derivative, don't you think?"

The poet, peering at the pages from the vantage point of his madmen's cell, looks miserable. Jeoffry, inside the cell, begins to growl. Will not the devil come inside? Very well, then Jeoffry will come to him.

"This is marvelous work, sir," the devil says, slotting the manuscript back between the poet's trembling fingers. "I am very pleased with your progress. Do contemplate the edits I suggested. I will be back tomorrow midnight to collect the final version."

I will not do it!

"But you *shall*, good sir. You have made your bargain. Now, you can sit here, wallowing in misery, or you can comfort yourself that your poem will inscribe itself on the hearts of men. It is all the same to me."

During this conversation, Jeoffry slips through the bars. The devil is wearing an elegant pair of French boots—of course the devil would favor French leather, thinks the very English Jeoffry—and when the devil turns on his heel, Jeoffry pounces.

Claw and bite! Snap and climb! Jeoffry is simultaneously attacking a black cat with wicked claws and a mighty dragon of shining scale and a gentleman who is trying to shake him off his leg. Jeoffry is tossed by the devil like the Ark on the waves of destruction. He is smashed and crashed, bitten and walloped. Still, Jeoffry clings to him, growling and clawing!

"Oh bother," says the devil. "Those were my favorite stockings."

Fire and darkness! Shade and sorrow! The devil has shaken him off. Jeoffry flies through the air and skids across the floorboards. But instantly he is on his feet again, his eyes ablaze, his skin electric. He will not let the devil go!

"Must we?" says the devil wearily. "Oh very well."

Now the devil begins to fight in earnest, and he is a terror. He is a thousand yellow-toothed rats swarming out of a sewer. He is a mighty angel whose wingbeats breed hurricanes. He is a gentleman with a walking stick. Wallop!

Jeoffry's chest explodes with pain. Dazed, for a moment he thinks he cannot rise. But he must, and his legs carry him back into the fight.

Jeoffry stalks the devil anew, trying to keep clear of Satan's walking-stick wings. Suddenly the black cat is there, clawing at Jeoffry's eyes and springing away before Jeoffry can land a blow. Jeoffry hisses and puffs up his fur, but somewhere in his aching chest is the sense that, perhaps, this is a fight he cannot win. Perhaps this is the fight that kills Jeoffry.

So be it. Jeoffry leaps on the back of the cat/rat/angel/dragon. He draws blood, the devil's blood, which smells of burning roses.

Too quickly, the devil twists under his grip. Too quickly, the yellow teeth clamp down. Agony sears through Jeoffry's neck. The devil has him by the throat.

Jeoffry struggles for purchase, but he can find none. His vision darkens. He can feel the devil's teeth press hard against the pulse of his life.

Dimly he hears the poet yelling. No, no! the man cries. Please spare my cat! We'll cause you no more trouble, I swear!

The devil loosens his grip. "Ooph ooph," he says. He spits out Jeoffry and tries again. "Very well."

And Jeoffry is falling through blackness, falling forever—

Jeoffry is in pain. The bite the devil gave him throbs fiercely. It is in the wrong place to lick, and yet he tries, and that hurts too.

Poor Jeoffry! Poor Jeoffry! the poet says. O you brave cat. May the Lord Jesus bless you and your wounds.

Jeoffry's ears flick back and forth. Worse than the pain is the heaviness in his chest that comes from having lost a fight. Jeoffry lose a fight! Such things were possible when he was a kitten, but now—

I can feel the paper calling to me even now, the poet sighs. O Jeoffry, sleep here and grow well again. I must to my task.

At this Jeoffry leaves off licking his wounds and stares at the poet. He means to convey that the man should not write this poem. For once, the man seems to understand.

O Jeoffry, I have made a deal, and I feel in my bones that I cannot fight it. When I hand him that poem, I will give him my very soul! But what can be done? There is nothing to be done, Jeoffry. You must get better. And the poem must be written.

Jeoffry does not even have the strength to protest. He

drinks from the water bowl the poet has put near him, and sleeps for a while in the sun.

When he opens his eyes the afternoon light is slanting through the barred window. Clumsily, Jeoffry rises and performs his orisons. As he cleans himself he considers the problem of the devil and the poet. This is not a fight Jeoffry can win. The traitorous thought clenches his throat, and for a moment he wants to push it away. But that will not help the poet.

So instead, Jeoffry does what he never does, and considers the weaknesses and frailties of Jeoffry.

Magnificent though he is, he thinks, Jeoffry is not in himself enough to defeat the devil. Something else must be done. Something humbling, and painful.

Once he is resolved, Jeoffry slips out of the cell. He does not take up his customary spot under the kitchen table, but instead limps into the courtyard, to where the cook has laid out a bowl of milk for the other cats, the ones who do not rule the madhouse.

Polly is the first to appear. She is an old lover of his, a sleek gray cat with a tattered ear and careful deportment. She looks distressed to see his wounds.

<What now, Jeoffry?> Polly says in the language of cats, which is more eloquent and capacious than the sounds they reserve for humans. <You look as though a hound has chewed you up.>

<I fought Satan,> Jeoffry says. <And I lost.>

Polly investigates Jeoffry's wounds. <The devil has bitten you on the throat.>

<I know.>

Polly leans forward and licks the bite. Jeoffry flicks his ears back, but accepts her aid. It is the first good thing that has happened this day.

Next comes Black Tom, the insufferable alley cat. <How

now, Jeoffry,> he says. <You look the worse for wear.>

<He fought the devil,> Polly says.

<And I lost.>

<Haha! Of course you did.> Tom helps himself to the milk. When he is finished he sits back and cleans his whiskers. <No style, Jeoffry, no style. That's your problem.>

<My style worked well enough when I fought you last summer,> Jeoffry snaps. <Aye, and chased you from my kitchen with your tail behind you!>

<You lying dog!> Black Tom makes himself look big. <You d——d cur!>

<Braggart! Coward!>

<D—n your eyes!> Black Tom roars. <I demand satisfaction!>

<Gentlemen,> Polly says, licking her forepaw. <The courtyard is my territory. Dueling is a disreputable practice, ill befitting a cat of good character. Would you insult a lady in her own house?>

Jeoffry and Black Tom both mutter apologies.

<Indeed,> Polly says. <If Satan is abroad, then we had best keep our claws sharpened for other fights.>

<It is of such matters that I wish to speak,> says Jeoffry.

<Then speak, cat!> Black Tom says. <We don't have all day!>

<There is one other whose counsel I require,> says Jeoffry, and he lifts his chin to the third cat in the yard, a bouncing, prancing black kitten. She wears a pretty bell on a collar of blue silk ribbon, and it jangles as she skips across the yard.

<The Nighthunter Moppet,> Polly says, and sighs.

<Hello, Miss Polly! Hello, Master Tom! Hello, Master Jeoffry!> the kitten sings. <Do you want to see my butterfly? It is yellow and brown and very pretty. I believe it is a chequered skipper, which is a *Carterocephalus palaemon*,

which is what I learned in Lucy's lesson on natural history, which is a very important subject. But that species is a woodland butterfly! Perhaps I am wrong about what kind of butterfly it is! Do take a look.>

The Nighthunter Moppet yawns open her small pink mouth, then closes it. She looks around her, puzzled.

<I think you ate it already,> says Polly.

<Oh, so I did! It was very pretty. Is that milk?>

The kitten falls on the milk and drinks her fill. When she is done she skips around the bowl, batting at the adults' noses. When she reaches Jeoffry, though, she stops, and looks concerned.

<Master Jeoffry! Are you hurt?>

<I fought Satan,> Jeoffry says.

O! The kitten's green eyes widen. She sits back into the bowl of milk, sloshing it over her bottom.

<Jeoffry has something to say,> Polly says. <For which he requires our *attention*.>

<I am paying attention! I am!> The kitten, who had been licking up the spilled milk, turns her attention back to Jeoffry.

Jeoffry sighs. <The other night,> he says, <the devil came to the madhouse.>

And he tells them everything: the magnificent cat-bribing feast, the vomit, the fight with Satan, the poet's despair. The other cats watch him wide-eyed.

At the end of his tale, he hunches into himself and speaks the words that are hardest in the world for a cat to utter.

<I need your help.>

The other cats look at him in amazement. Jeoffry feels shame settle on him like a fine dust. He drops his gaze and examines the shine of a brown beetle that is slowly clambering over a cobblestone.

<This is a d——ly strange business,> Black Tom says grudgingly. <Satan himself! But if you want my claws, sir, you shall have them.>

<I, too, will aid you,> Polly says, <though I confess I am unsure what we can do against such an enemy.>

<This time there will be four of us,> Black Tom says. <Four cats! The devil won't know what hit him.>

<This is the wrong strategy,> says the Nighthunter Moppet, and her voice has the ring of a blade unsheathed.

All kittenness has fallen away from Moppet. What sits before the milk bowl is the ruthless killer of the courtyard, the assassin whose title *nighthunter* is whispered in terror among the mice and birds of Bethnal Green. It is rumored that the Moppet's great-grandmother was a demon of the lower realms, which might perhaps explain the peculiar keenness of her green-glass eyes, and her talent for death-dealing. Indeed, as Jeoffry watches, the Moppet's tiny shadow seems to grow and split into seven pieces, each of which is shaped like a monstrous cat with seven tails. The shadow cats' tails lash and lash as the Nighthunter Moppet broods on Satan.

<It is true that as cats we are descended from the Angel Tiger, who killed the Ichneumon-rat of Egypt,> says the Moppet. Her shadows twist into the shapes of rats and angels as she speaks. <We are warriors of God, and as such, we can blood Satan. But we cannot kill him, for he has another fate decreed.>

The Nighthunter Moppet sighs at the thought of a lost kill, and drops her gaze to the ground. The brown beetle is still there, trotting over the cobblestones. She begins to follow it with her nose.

<Moppet!> Polly says sternly. <You were telling us how we should fight the devil!>

<Oh sorry, sorry,> the Moppet says. With great effort she tears her gaze away from the beetle. Instantly her seven shadows are back, larger than before, raising their claws to the heavens.

<To win this fight we must think carefully of what we mean to win,> says the Nighthunter Moppet. The pupils have disappeared from her eyes, which blaze green fire. <Is it Satan's death? No. His humiliation? Again, no.>

<Speak for yourself,> Black Tom says. <He will run from my claws!>

The kitten's shadows turn and look at Black Tom with disapproval. When she next speaks, their voices join hers. They sound like the buzzing of a thousand flies.

<It is neither of those things!> cry the army of Moppets. <Think! What is it the devil hopes to achieve?>

<The destruction of the world,> says Polly.

<A poem about his greatness,> says Black Tom.

<The poet's soul,> says Jeoffry.

<Exactly,> snarl the Moppets. <And those three things are also one thing. If you steal it from him, good cat Jeoffry, then you will have beaten the devil.> With that her shadows shrink back into a normal, kitten-shaped shadow, and the pupils return to her green eyes.

<But what do I steal?> Jeoffry asks desperately.

The Moppet looks at him blankly. <What?> she says. <Are we stealing something?>

<I think the Nighthunter Moppet has told us all she can, Jeoffry,> Polly says.

<But it is not enough,> Jeoffry says. Thinking is harder than fighting, and his head hurts. Still. He squeezes his eyes

tightly, and thinks over all that has happened. The poet. The devil. The Poem of Poems.

<I think I know what I must do,> he says. <But to do it I must sneak past the devil, and his eyes are keen.>

<We shall help you,> says Black Tom.

<We shall fight him,> says Polly.

The light of spirit fire flickers in the Nighthunter's eyes. Some of her shadows peer out from behind her body.

<And you,> she intones, <shall *creep.*>

That night the devil is in a good mood. He whistles as he walks between the stars, cracking the tip of his cane on the pathway. From time to time, this dislodges a young star, who falls screaming.

"Good evening, good fellow," he says to the sleeping night watchman as he enters the asylum. "And to you, Bently," he says as he passes a cell containing a murderer. The man shrieks and scuttles away. Finally the devil arrives at the poet's cell. "And how do you do, Mr. Smart? Do you have my poem?"

The poet crouches, terrified, in the corner of his cell. No, no—please, Jesus, no, he moans. But there is a sheet of paper quivering in his hand.

"Excellent," the devil says. "Come now, hand it over. You'll feel much better once you do."

The poet is jerked upright, like an ill-strung marionette. The hand that clasps the paper swings away from his body. But as the devil reaches to claim it, there is a yowl from behind him.

<Stand and deliver, you d——d mangy w———n!> It is Black Tom, his tail bristling like a brush.

At his side, Polly narrows her eyes. <Sir, you must step away from that poet!>

“What’s this?” The devil puts his hands on his hips and regards the growling cats. “More cats come to terrorize my stockings?”

<We’ll have more than your stockings, sir,> says Polly.

<D—n your eyes, I’ll have your hide, you ——— ——— ——— — —— ——!!!!>

“Such language!” says the devil. Even Polly looks shocked.

“Well, sir,” Satan says, “I’ll not be called a ——— by anyone, let alone by a flea-bitten alley cat. Lay on, sir!” And the devil is a cat again, and an angel, and an angry critic raising his walking stick as a club. Even as the devil’s walking stick swings down in a slow, glittering arc of hellfire, even as the devil aims to crack the top of Black Tom’s dancing, prancing skull, a bloodcurdling cry rings out from above.

<I AM THE NIGHTHUNTER MOPPET!>

Perched on a dusty sconce above the devil’s head is a rabid, knife-jawed, fire-eyed kitten with seven hungry shadows. And as the devil looks up agape, she springs, her wicked claws catching the light, right on top of the devil’s powdered wig.

Hellfire! Chaos! The two other cats rush the devil’s legs, clawing at his face. He bites and clobbers them, his wings and fists swinging. The walls of the asylum throb with the impact of the battle. The poet, crumpled on the floor, twitches and writhes. In every cell, the lunatics begin to howl.

Jeoffry lays back his ears and continues to creep, as the Moppet showed him. <We are descended from angels,> she had said, <and as such we can move into the spaces between the world-we-see and the world-that-is.>

That is where Jeoffry is now, slinking past the devil on a slanted path of broken stardust, in a fold of space where the keen-eyed Adversary would not think to look. Creeping is hard to do, not just because Jeoffry has to squeeze every ounce of his catness into this cosmic folding, but also because there is a brawl happening at his back that he would dearly love to join.

Since when does Jeoffry, the most glorious warrior of catdom, slink away from a fight? whispers a voice inside him. Since when is Jeoffry a coward? Will he let Black Tom get the glory of defeating the devil?

But Jeoffry shuts his ear to this voice. He has learned that there is more than one kind of devil, and that the one inside your head, that speaks with the voice of your own heart, is far more dangerous than the velvet coat–wearing, poetry-loving variety.

Indeed, the fiend is having a harder time against three cats than he did against one. One of his shadows has turned into a dragon and is fighting Black Tom; Satan's powdered wig has animated itself and is tackling Polly across the hallway. But in the center of the poet's cell, in a storm of lightning and hellfire, whirl Satan and the Nighthunter Moppet, splattered with each other's blood. The Moppet has only five shadows now, and one of her green eyes is closed, but her snarl still gleams prettily amid the flames of darkness visible.

"Stand down, you vile kitten!"

<I AM! NIGHTHUNTER! MOPPET!> the kitten screams back. As battle cries go, it is unoriginal, but gets the central point across, Jeoffry thinks as he slinks ever closer to the gibbering poet. The ghosts of the stars Satan has lately killed whisper encouragement as he creeps forward through cosmic space, inch by careful inch.

"You cannot win," Satan says. At that, he seems to collect himself. The various pieces of the devil reassemble in a column of fire at the center of the room (with the exception of the powdered wig, which Polly has pinned down on the staircase). "This poet is mine. And if you oppose me further, you will die."

<We shall die, then,> Polly says, a tuft of whitened hair hanging from her teeth. Behind her, the powdered wig, its curls in disarray, scrunches down the staircase to freedom.

<F—k you,> says Black Tom.

On the floor, the crumpled shape of a small black kitten staggers to its feet. <Nighthunter.> It says. <Moppet.>

"Very well," the dragon/cat/critic says, and opens its jaws.

And Jeoffry stops *creeping*. He springs.

Fire and flood! Wonder and horror! Jeoffry has snatched the sheet of paper from the poet's trembling hand and swallowed it whole! Snap snap! The paper on the table is eaten too! Snap! And the crumpled drafts on the floor! Jeoffry is a whirlwind of gluttony! As a last measure, he knocks over the ink bottle and laps it up. Glug glug! Take that, Satan!

The devil stands in the center of the cell, cats dangling from his arms. The look on his face is similar to the one he wore at his defeat in the Battle of Heaven, and is only marginally happier than the one he wore on his arrival in Hell. Normally, when Satan wears that expression, it is a sign he is about to begin speechifying. But for once, all his words are gone. They are sitting inside a belching ginger cat, who blinks at the devil and licks his lips.

"Oh hell, cat," says the devil, letting the half-throttled felines fall to the floor. "What have you done?"

Jeoffry grins at him. He can feel a warm glow inside him that is the poet's soul, being safely digested. His soul was in the poem, the poet said, and now Jeoffry has eaten it up. The devil cannot have it now.

"No!" the devil shrieks. He rages. He stomps his foot. He puts his hands to his head and tears himself in half, and the separate halves of him explode in angry fireworks.

Then, perhaps thinking better of his dignity, the devil re-manifests and straightens his waistcoat. He glares at Jeoffry. "You," he says, "have scarred literature forever. You stupid cat."

With that, the devil turns on his heel and leaves.

The poet in the corner staggers forward. Thank Jesus! he cries. Jeoffry, you have done it!

<And me,> says Black Tom.

<All of us did it,> says Polly.

<The devil forgot his wig,> the Nighthunter Moppet says. Her one good eye narrows.

<Thank you, thank you, my friends,> Jeoffry says. <I am forever obliged for your help in this.> And then he winds himself around the poet and purrs.

That is the story of how the devil came to the madhouse, and was defeated (though not in battle) by the great Jeoffry. There are other stories I could tell, of the sea battles of Black Tom, of Polly's foray into opera, and of the Nighthunter Moppet's epic hunt for Satan's wig, which left a trail of mischief and misery across London for years.

But instead I will end with poetry.

For I will consider my Cat Jeoffry.

For he is the servant of the Living God duly and daily serving him.

For he keeps the Lord's watch in the night against the Adversary.

For he counteracts the powers of Darkness by his electrical

skin and glaring eyes.
For he counteracts the Devil, who is death, by brisking about the life.

For he can creep.

—Christopher Smart

St. Luke's Hospital for Lunatics, c.1763

His Footsteps, Through Darkness and Light

by Mimi Mondal

I am not a fighter. I am a trapeze master.

At the Majestic Oriental Circus, which had been my home for two years, I had climbed the ropes deft and fast, till I was the leader of a team of about fifteen aerial performers. It was in my genes.

There were other rewards, too, of the circus life. It had brought me into the grace of Shehzad Marid. A trapeze master has no lack of duties, training and overseeing his team, but I continued to perform with Shehzad in his grand stage illusion show—"Alladdin and His Magic Lamp." I took great pride in my own trapeze act, and the team that I trained from scratch, but I have to admit that "Alladin" was the crowds' favorite.

None of the credit for that popularity was owed to me. I am a genius at the ropes overhead, flinging myself from grip to grip so gracefully you would believe I could fly; but on earth, up close, I am a man entirely devoid of charm. Before I joined the circus, I did not even speak a language that could be understood in polite society. Even now, I fumble for the right word at the right moment; I occasionally slip into an accent that makes the city people sneer.

But as Alladin, all I had to do was to put on a pair of satin pants and a skullcap, and parrot a series of memorized lines.

I had never met an Arab street urchin, nor had an inkling what all the words meant, but neither had anyone in the audience. I bellowed, "Ya Allah!" and "Shukr hai!" and "Dafa ho ja, shaitaan!" at my cues. The girl who trained the parakeets doubled as the princess in a shiny ghagra and choli, adorned with tawdry sequins. Johuree, our proprietor and ringmaster, completed the cast as the villainous Zafar, dressed in a moth-eaten velvet cloak.

It was an almost ridiculous performance, but it turned into the most renowned act of the Majestic Oriental Circus, all at the touch of Shehzad Marid. As the three of us hemmed and hawed through our scripted gibberish, the jinni would emerge from his lamp in clouds of curling smoke. Illuminated by our cheap stage lights, the clouds would take the shape of a magnificent palace, the gaping maw of a cave, raging armies on horseback that crashed into the audience until our entire circus tent would erupt with gasps, applause, and cries of horror and disbelief. A small child could hold open his palm and receive a dancing houree, crafted immaculately of ice as the clouds condensed. Then they billowed up again—into monsters never heard of; swooping rocs; clerics whose voices soared in prayer across minarets that pierced the sky above a faraway, mythical city; hundreds of jinn, and back to the only one. It was a show unlike anything offered by any rival circus company in our land.

I was assigned to this act four months after I joined the Majestic Oriental Circus—a naïve, illiterate, village young man who had been given a job by Dayaram, the former trapeze master, almost out of pity. It turned out that I climbed better than anyone else on the team, but I had never seen a circus before, could hardly follow the shimmering line between illusion and truth. Before I took over, Johuree would play both Alladin and Zafar, disappearing behind the clouds and reappearing in changed costume with a lightness of foot you would not expect from a fat, middle-aged man like him. But then, no one at the Majestic Oriental Circus was merely what met the eye. The circus life is not for the mundane.

Johuree had been happy to delegate Alladin to me. An agile young man was more suited to the role than himself, he had said with a wink in front of the entire company. I nodded along, though both of us knew that was just the cover. A circus troupe had no dearth of agile young men. No—we both knew it was because I was the only other person at the Majestic Oriental Circus that Shehzad Marid had entrusted with his lamp.

I was a hack Alladin, awkward and bombarding, nothing like my fluid, almost lyrical performance on the trapeze ropes. It made the entire act of "Alladin and His Magic Lamp" come across as gaudy, over-the-top. That was just the effect Johuree was going for.

We were a traveling circus, never spending more than a week or two in the same city, town, or village fair. So the day Johuree declared that we would travel to Thripuram to perform at the wedding of the raja's daughter, we packed up our tents and bags and set out on the journey.

• • •

There is little power left in the hands of the rajas of yore, but you wouldn't think so if you were at the palace of the Thripuram raja on the day we arrived. Accustomed though we were to the illusory palaces of Arabia that Shehzad conjured up three shows a day, our entire troupe gazed awestruck at the vibrantly painted temples, spires, courtly residences, and finally, looming over them all, resplendent in its intricate balconies and mythological frescos adorning the walls, pillars, and steps—the palace itself.

The palace grounds teemed with musicians, poets, storytellers, snake charmers, tawaifs, nautankis—entertainers from all over the land. Those traditional artists had been assigned living quarters inside the buildings. A circus was a foreign entertainment—our troupe an unrestrained mingling of men and women of indistinct lineage, sharing space with monkeys, elephants, birds, tigers. Though we had been invited to perform on the night of the wedding, we were allowed to sleep only in our own trucks and tents. We set them up within the palace grounds, under the sky.

The grounds were thrumming with activity as we rolled into our spots. The hot afternoon air was cloying with the aroma of outdoor cooking, for all the poor people of the city were to eat two meals at the raja's generosity every day of the festivities. There were two queues of revelers waiting to be fed—one for Brahmins, another for the infidels and the untouchables—winding as long as the eye could see. Wedding guests wandered within the premises, trailed by servants holding umbrellas, fans, and jugs of water. Massive electricity generators growled along the palace walls, powering thousands of lanterns and strings of light. It was a spectacle more modern and grandiose than anything Shehzad could pull up from the myths of a distant past.

If the circus was a novelty to the raja's palace, it was no less a novelty to us—our entire troupe was comprised of people who had grown up poor. We dealt in glitter and illusion, but all our clothes were cheap synthetics and sequins, often threadbare and sewn together in places; our jewelry made of glass, tinfoil, and paint. We had never seen so many varieties of silk, so many diamonds, rubies, and emeralds casually glittering under daylight as the royal guests wandered by. At lunch, my trapeze team would not stop eating until I threatened them with immediate unemployment if any of them disgraced me at the night's performance.

As the busy day waned toward sunset, conch shells were sounded, and there was instant silence within the palace grounds. A procession of young women emerged from the doorway of the palace, led by a priest. Each of them carried a holy tray of prayer offerings.

The women were indescribably beautiful, more so in their dazzling, elegant attire, reminding me of the sculptures of apsaras—heavenly dancers—that I had only seen before on temple walls. These women were not dressed like the wives or daughters of the royalty, yet they were too demure, too distant from us. They did not speak with, or even look at, any of the other performers, who stepped back to make way for them to pass.

"Devadasis," whispered a girl from my trapeze team, her voice nearly choking in awe.

"What are they?" I whispered back. I was completely ignorant of the customs of royalty, but even Shehzad, who was less so, stared uncomprehendingly at these women.

"I have never seen one of them before," the girl explained under her breath, never once taking her eyes off the fascinating trail. "You never see a devadasi—no commoner does, except on occasions like this. Devadasis are holy courtesans, bequeathed at birth to the patron deity of a kingdom, maintained by its king. They are trained as dancers, but not like any of us. They will never perform before a commoner, or in exchange for money. Their dance is an act of worship. They are divine." The girl's words swung gently between envy and faith. "The devadasis will now go to the town's main temple to seek blessings for the raja's daughter. Offer themselves up in performance. The wedding can only take place after the kuldevi—the patron goddess of the kingdom—has bestowed her blessings."

"No one told me there was anything supernatural in this town," I said, intrigued. Two years ago I would have laughed at any mention of such things, but enough time at the Majestic Oriental Circus opens the mind to all kinds of possibilities.

The girl laughed. "Who said anything was supernatural? Everything's a joke to you, Binu'da. I meant *real* divine, like priests are divine. Devadasis commune with the gods. They are born into holiness. They don't do tricks with sleight of hand and offstage machinery. That's what people come to *us* for."

I stared again—the face of the young woman at the head of the procession was so flawless and serene that I could almost believe in her divinity. Priests were born into the Brahmin caste, and I had met enough Brahmins in my life to know that not all of them were priests, or even had a shred of spirituality in them. Usually they were arrogant and corrupt, frankly quite despicable people to know. But the gaze of this woman was clear and resolute, fixed at the vermilion sky toward the temple where she was headed. Her step was graceful, undoubtedly perfected through the lifelong dance-worship to which she was devoted. No creature could be further removed from the giggling girls in my circus, whose brittle poise disappeared as soon as they stepped behind the stage.

Afterward, we returned to our tents to prepare for our show, which was to be the opening performance of the wedding celebrations. We were not there to watch the devadasis return.

• • •

The show went off smoothly. My boys and girls could hardly keep their eyes off the ornate ceiling of the raja's court as they swung and swerved across it, but none of them faltered at their act. "Alladin and His Magic Lamp" was a roaring success with the royal wedding guests. Shehzad was stoic through all of it—he had seen his share of palace interiors in his time. The raja came down from his throne to shake our hands after the show, but we were never introduced to the princess, who had watched our performance from a latticed balcony above. No common entertainer was permitted to speak with the royal bride, even if they performed at her wedding.

"Really, Binu, stop staring at that balcony and shut your mouth," Shehzad snapped at me as our troupe filed out of the royal court. "You make yourself look like a fool."

"Hey, Alladin is meant to be really popular with the princesses, right?" I teased him. I was still decked out in the satin-pants-and-skullcap attire. "But this pathetic Alladin can't even catch a glimpse of a real princess. What good is having a faithful jinni at your command if he cannot even introduce you to a princess?"

"Princesses look just like other women," Shehzad sneered. "And this one is getting married already, so you're out of luck. You've met the raja. His daughter probably would have the same, uh, *generous* nose. Hopefully not also the generous moustache."

We guffawed, eyes shining into each other's for a fleeting moment. Then I said, "But you saw all those devadasis. Think about it. If mere women of the court can look like that, the princess must be—"

"The princess is not one of those women," Shehzad said, making a sharp turn away from the direction of the lavish dining arrangements.

"You will not dine with us?"

"Since when did I eat the same food as you people, Binu?"

"But you always come along and make the pretense," I said, surprised at the brusqueness that I did not entirely feel I deserved.

"That's when we dine with the rest of our circus troupe, to make sure that no one suspects otherwise," he replied. "There are too many people at this place. Too much going on. No one will miss Shehzad Marid."

"I will."

"I must retire to the lamp," he said, as if shaking off the hurt in my voice. "These festivities will continue late into the night, and our troupe begins to pack up at dawn. If I slip away now, I can steal a few hours of respite."

I always carried the lamp in our trunk of clothes, scrubby enough to look like a circus prop. The actual prop was a cheaper but shinier replica, tossed around on the stage between Alladin and Zafar. No human hand but mine had touched the real lamp in the past two years, and with nothing but gratitude. Nothing but love.

Nothing but that inchoate sensation of wistfulness that congealed in my chest on the nights that I lay awake in our tent, gazing at the lamp on my bedside after Shehzad had receded into it. If I picked it up, it would be cold, weightless—a thing forged centuries ago in a distant land; a curiosity, but not an especially valuable one in itself. It was a common household object, Shehzad once told me; street vendors in Arabia sold great quantities of them to this day. With regular use, it would have lasted about five or six years.

But this lamp had survived centuries, traveled hundreds of miles from its homeland, passed from hand to bloody, victorious hand. My callused trapeze-artist hands could barely contain it. Another century or two will blow over any trace of my fingers from its surface, as perhaps from the spirit it enclosed.

From the stories people tell, even those in our own hack show, the lamp sounds like a prison. The listener imagines himself being suffocated, neck twisted, limbs folded at painful angles, squeezed into a box too small to contain his body and left there to wait for decades. But the listener of the tale is human—imprisoned already in his withering flesh and bone, the measured years that are given to him. The human mind can barely fathom the bond between its own body and soul. What would it grasp of the relationship between a jinni and his lamp? What could I—hardly a philosopher, never having read a book, barely literate enough to scribble my own name—grasp of it?

In our two years of friendship, I had learned every detail of Shehzad Marid's humanity. There was no man, or woman, that I knew better. I could read each of his smiles, each raised eyebrow, each cryptic comment for exactly what it was. But I had also learned that his humanity was mere performance. He was relieved to shed it, as I was to remove my circus costumes and makeup. Shehzad Marid's greatest gift to me was the knowledge that I would never truly know the core of his existence, and not merely because I was unread.

And perform he did, never cracking, never missing a beat, longer than any of us at the circus. No one but Johuree knew, or suspected, anything about Shehzad's true nature. Even when he manifested in "Alladin and His Magic Lamp," weaving his way through wonders that no human could pull off, it was carefully designed to look like a triumph of stagecraft. Because I loved him, because I would never understand him at any greater depth than that, all I could do was to give him a break from the act when he asked.

"Wake me up if you need something," he told me before he left, adding, "but do spare me if it has more to do with princesses. You need to find yourself a different jinni for that."

I smiled, squeezed his hand, and let him go. Where would I—Trapeze Master Binu of the Majestic Oriental Circus—find a different jinni, and why would I ever want another?

• • •

It was past midnight when the members of the troupe retreated to our tents. Within the palace, the tawaifs were still dancing for the last sleepless revelers, but the palace grounds were now empty, for the common revelers had long since departed. Getting into my bed, I pressed a finger against the cold metal of Shehzad's lamp, but did not drag it. I needed my rest as much as he needed his.

I must have barely drifted into blissful slumber when I woke up again at a hushed commotion from the trapeze artists' tents. It was the second hour of the night, still too dark to see without a light. A couple of girls came running to our tent.

"It's a woman from the palace, Binu'da!" they informed me. "Says she wants to have a word with you."

I couldn't recall talking much with any woman at the palace. Who would come looking for me in the dead of the night? I turned up the wick of my oil lamp and stepped out, sure that whoever it was must have mistaken me for someone else.

The woman in question was dressed in a simple sari, her long hair flowing over her back. I was startled to recognize the head devadasi of the Thripuram raja's palace—the woman whose face had launched me into a thousand speculations earlier that day. With the expensive drapes and jewelry removed, she looked no older than sixteen or seventeen.

Seeing her now, the first emotion that hit me was panic. Even speaking to this girl could probably get me punished by the raja. "How did you come here?" I blurted out. "Has anyone seen you?"

"I told my maids that I wanted to pet the tigers," the girl said, and shrugged nonchalantly. "No one in this palace had ever seen a tiger before. And I am known to be willful."

"The tigers have been sedated for the night—" I started to say, but she cut me off.

"The tigers can wait. I want you to let me sneak into your circus and escape this wretched palace."

"What?!"

"I have been dancing for fifteen years now, ever since I learned to walk," said the girl. "There's no trick any of your girls can perform that I can't pick up in just a few days. I will be the best performer you've ever had."

"But you are a devadasi!" I peered in astonishment at the wide-eyed, long-lashed face that was no less attractive for its bareness. "You live at the palace; you have more luxuries than any of us can imagine. You commune with the gods! Why would someone like you want to stoop to the circus?"

"And what does communing with the gods generally entail, do you think?"

I had to admit I didn't know.

"I live at the palace, but I am not a princess. None of my clothing or jewelry belongs to me. I don't actually have a single possession that cannot be taken away with a command from the raja. I do not employ my maids—they maintain my household but also keep an eye on me, report my activities to the raja. Tell me why the raja spends so much money keeping women like me?"

"Because you commune...?" My own words sounded ridiculous to me.

"That's what it says in the scriptures, doesn't it?" said the girl. "The priest communes with the gods with his mind, and the devadasi communes with her body. I wouldn't know—I was never taught to read the scriptures. I'm illiterate as they come. Reading is not a devadasi's function. Though I could tell you all you ever wished to know about dance, about communing with higher powers with my body. Make a man of you too, if you wish." She gave me a saucy smile, but it felt more dangerous than inviting.

"If you don't like this life, why don't you go back to your family? Why fling yourself at a group of strangers like this?" I asked.

"Because you're the only strangers at this wedding who would take me," said the girl. "You're an odd bunch. You don't belong to any traditional system. There are all sorts of performers in your group—surely you can find some use for a devadasi? No one else has any need for me. Devadasis don't belong to families. We are bequeathed to the gods—we cannot be possessed by men, be that father or husband. My mother was also a devadasi, as was grandmother before her."

"But some man must have fathered you, seeing as you're just as human as I am," I said. "His is the house where you should go, even if you don't like them, or they you."

"The raja? But I already live at his house!" The girl startled me with a mirthless laugh. "Of course, I don't count as the raja's daughter, because a daughter can only be born of a man and a woman. Devadasis aren't women; we are offerings made to the patron goddess, entitled to be consumed by the maker of the offering once we have been touched by the goddess. I am not even an illicit child, merely a blessing received by my mother in the performance of her role, more property added to the coffers of the raja who owned her. I am cleverer, more beautiful, more talented than the princess whose wedding you graced with your performance, but she is the princess, and I am property. I am less than even the common free woman in the street."

I'll be honest—I had never heard anything like that. Not that I ever understood the elaborate social intricacies of the upper classes, but I always knew that I did not trust them, and her story just seemed to confirm my mistrust. If what this girl was saying was true, I could not possibly tell her to go back to the raja's palace. But it was also impossible to imagine her at the circus—with her delicate step, her sheltered view of life, those smooth white hands that had probably never done a day's work.

I told her so.

"The circus is no life for a lady like you. You have only seen us in performance. You cannot begin to imagine the sweat, heat, dust, filth, and flies on the road; sleeping huddled in tents; washing with animals in public ponds; the tasteless slop that we eat; the insecurity and physical labor that make up most of our days. I doubt you have the grit to survive it."

"If that is so," said the girl, "I will part ways with your circus once you deliver me to the nearest city. I have heard that our traditional dance is being made secular in the cities, that there are dancers who are well respected in the community without belonging to any king or any temple. They give performances for the public, teach classes, save their own money, and can also marry and have children if they wish. If I make it to the city, I will find ways to survive. All I need is safe passage out of here."

Something about this girl had touched my heart the very first time I saw her at the head of the holy procession. I didn't wish to call it infatuation, but Shehzad had noticed it too—it was what made him testy enough to retreat into his lamp. True, if she hadn't come to me, I would never have sought her out, but I would also have gone on believing that she lived a life just as ethereal as her face, devoted to worship and virtue that more common people like myself could not afford.

"Don't think I don't intend to compensate you for your assistance," the girl said, giving me a smile of such well-honed coyness that it made my heart do an inadvertent leap. "I had no money to bring, but once you take me to the city, I promise to make you memories that you will cherish for the rest of your life."

"There's no need for any of that," I said, recoiling at the insinuation. I looked up at the sky—there were still a couple of hours before we were scheduled to leave. By the time the rest of the palace started waking up from the previous night's revelries, the Majestic Oriental Circus would be well on its way.

"Go to one of the girls' tents and get some sleep," I told our new stowaway. "We have a long day's journey ahead."

• • •

The sky was clear, a deep rouge spreading over the eastern horizon when the Majestic Oriental Circus began its preparations to leave the Thripuram raja's palace. Half-asleep, disheveled performers emerged from their tents, which were then unmounted and loaded onto trucks. The birds and animals clamored to be fed before they were secured. At my instruction, the young devadasi had changed into clothes from the other girls of the troupe and blended in with them, just in case anyone from the palace was keeping watch as we filed out. I went to have a word with Johuree.

"The Majestic Oriental Circus has always been a refuge to outcasts and runaways," he began, and I nodded. "But this woman is beholden to powers beyond ourselves."

The diamond in Johuree's false left eye pierced me with a red glint from the rising sun. "By giving her shelter, you have taken on charges that are yours alone."

"If any trouble comes of this girl, I promise to step up to it," I told my trusted employer and friend. "She will be fed and clothed out of my salary. I will protect and instruct her, and make sure she finds lodgings in the city when we get there. The circus will not have to bear any responsibility for my decision."

Shehzad was not pleased when he emerged.

"I have never seen a bigger fool than you," he grumbled, skulking around the gathered props and trunks that were the farthest from the newest member of our troupe. "A pretty girl comes simpering with a sob story, and suddenly Trapeze Master Binu is the gallant savior we all lacked. Why do you think she did not go to any other guest at the wedding? Why not appeal to Johuree directly, if she wanted to join the circus? She came to you because she had noticed you stare at her earlier like a mesmerized child. She knew you wouldn't be able to say no."

"I suppose you're right," I said, trying to rest a hand on his arm, trying to pull him into a reluctant embrace. There was no use trying to disguise my thoughts from Shehzad. "But that does not prove that she's wrong in trying to escape, or that the people who would decline to help her are correct. I am doing the right thing here, Shehzad, even if it's not the most practical thing to do."

"I have served warrior after warrior, as far back as I can remember," he said. "A few of them were unkind masters, but others were loving and respectful, though they still owned me. There are worse lives than that of a glorified slave."

"But now you are free. Wouldn't you say you prefer the change of circumstances?"

"No one is ever free, least of all a jinni. Only the nature of the master changes," Shehzad replied curtly before turning to walk away. "If I am free now, it's because my master wishes me so. My next master may be worse, as may that girl's or any other's."

I stared at his receding back, the taut, defiant muscles that I longed to knead with my palms, to remind him that I had never been his master. But that would have to wait for another time, far away from this palace with its loathsome practices.

• • •

The skies began to grow ominously dark as soon as our trucks rolled out of the palace gates. Clouds rumbled. Tree branches cracked overhead. Waves of dust rose on the distant horizon. Within the town of Thripuram, as we passed, the few early risers hurried to return inside; doors and windows were noisily shut. It was a storm as unseasonal as any in this part of the land.

The trucks were the closest we had to homes, in fair or rough weather, so we trudged on until we were on the dirt roads that led out of the town, and could simply go no farther. Unrestrained by any more houses, the winds came pounding at our canvas walls like solid boulders. The trucks swayed like they were wooden toys for children, not hundreds of tons of machine on wheels. Inside, our animals screamed and rattled against their cages. Dust clouds covered the sky, obscuring the sun. Our drivers could no longer see the road. Dust, razor-sharp and unforgiving, filled the eyes and nostrils of anyone who tried to look outside.

Usually, a heavy rain comes lashing quick on the trail of a dust storm, calming the winds and weighing down the dust into mud, but it had been an hour since this dust had risen, and there was still not a drop of moisture.

As I sat in the first of our trucks, a massive trumpeting from the truck behind us told me that the elephants had broken free, and another tearing, heart-wrenching wail followed as one of them was blown away by the winds. In all my thirty years of life, I have never heard anything like it.

The third truck, carrying the clowns, fire-eaters, and my

own trapeze team, soon turned to its side with a sickening lurch. From my own truck I could hear none of their voices, although in my guts I could feel them crying, praying to their respective gods, groaning as they scrambled in blindness, bones trampled and crunched. The girl whom we had rescued from the palace was among them too. Perhaps Shehzad was right—if we all died in this freak apocalypse this morning, I would have proved to be a worse master than the raja, not only to her but to everyone else in my care.

I am a man who has left his own forest deities far behind in his past, so there was no greater power to whom I could kneel. In any case, if all these other pious people's prayers were going unheard, how might I—faithless of heart—sway any god to my favor?

A heavy figure swayed its way through the truck and dropped heavily, purposefully next to me. It was Johuree.

"Trapeze Master Binu, you promised to bear responsibility," he whispered into my ear. Each of his words fell like the gong of a temple bell, cutting through the mayhem outside my brain.

"What—this dust storm?!" I was stunned by his suggestion. "You think *I* have something to do with this?"

"I did warn you that the girl you rescued was beholden to powers beyond ourselves."

"I thought—I thought you meant the Thripuram raja and his administration!"

Johuree said nothing, just stared at me with his cold eyes, both living and stone. Nothing was enough.

"I don't know how to... I don't know who—"

The crashes and screams returned, closing in on my senses like water over the head of a drowning man. So I rose to my feet, staggering from wall to wall as the floor of the truck churned beneath me and dropped myself into the dust-filled darkness.

• • •

There was nothing, absolutely nothing to see. My eyes, ears, and mouth were assaulted by dust as soon as I hit the ground. Dust scraped against my bare legs beneath my dhoti like a thousand razor blades. In less than a second, every inch of my skin felt like it was being flayed. I could feel the blood trickle down my arms, legs, chest; I could feel my face growing muddy with blood.

Coughing, choking, spitting, I called out into the nothingness, "Here I am: Trapeze Master Binu. I think it is me you want." I spat out more dust. "Spare the rest of the circus. They took no part in my decision to rescue the girl."

I waited, struggling to breathe. Feeling foolish.

Then a voice came, responding to my cry. I do not know why I remember it as a female voice, because it did not even sound human. It came from the wind, molding and resonating as a blend of dust and words.

"I am the kuldevi of the kingdom of Thripuram," she said. "Stupid human, filthy, untouchable low-caste whom no god will deign to claim for his own, did you think you could run away with my property and pay nothing for your crime?"

Her insults did not perturb me—I have heard them and worse from people, and expected no better from their gods—but the words still made my blood boil.

"No man or woman is anyone's property!" I spluttered through the dust that clogged my mouth. "Not the Thripuram raja's, not even yours. I don't care if you are human or goddess. You are not *my* goddess, as you well know."

The thick, blowing dust rippled with laughter. I could feel it dance on my skin as the grains freshly scoured the bleeding surface.

"A free man, are you?" More words formed. "A man who acknowledges no master, and surely no charge? Then when the men, women, and animals of this party of fools die, as they will within the next hour, their deaths will not be on your conscience."

I wanted to scream back that their deaths should be on the conscience of this vengeful goddess, but I did not even know if the gods possessed consciences; besides... just the thought of their deaths deflated the righteous rage in my heart. My strange but upright boss who had employed me when no one else would, my colleagues and friends who received me as one of their own, the young boys and girls whom I hand-picked and trained for my trapeze team—none of whom I had consulted before I brought down this mayhem upon them. I was a free man till my last breath, but none of them should have to bear the consequences of my freedom.

"Take my life. Let them go," I pleaded.

Another gust of laugher, another whiplash of dust across my body.

"And why would I be sated with one mortal life when I came here prepared to take fifty, including the life of that traitorous whore who dares to defy being beholden to me?"

I did not know what else would sate her. I am a poor man with hardly any treasures. I had kept aside a few rupees from my salary for the past two years, hoping to return to my mother and buy a house when I finally had enough. I could not imagine my modest savings would buy the lives of the Majestic Oriental Circus from the kuldevi of Thripuram.

The goddess seemed to read my thoughts.

"It is heartening to see you realize the utter triviality of your existence, Trapeze Master Binu," she spoke "Your puny mortal life and its possessions are every bit as worthless to me as you think. But there is one thing you own, much more valuable than your life, for which I will let your entire circus go, even that filthy whore and yourself."

I waited, dry tongue scraping the dust that now formed a

crust on the roof of my mouth, wondering what she meant.

"Give me the jinni."

The bottom of my stomach dropped.

"The jinni is not mine to give," I murmured.

"It is the only possession of yours that interests me," said the kuldevi. "Jinn are rare in this part of the world. I have never seen one before, yet I felt its presence and desired it as soon as it crossed into my dominion. But I cannot take it by force, for the laws that bind the jinni to its human master are forged in a distant land over an oath to a different god, far beyond my powers to bend. Give me the jinni of your own free will, and you and all your company will live."

I shut my eyes, which were suddenly muddy and stinging with the tears that had that rushed into them. My heartbeat was slow, irregular. If it were only about me, I would have gladly died at this moment in this dust storm conjured by a wrathful goddess whom I did not worship. And then there was an arm around my waist, holding me upright again, there was a hand wiping dust, blood, and tears from my eyes. It was Shehzad Marid—ever loving, ever loyal, always on my side in my hour of need.

"I know you did not call for me," he whispered in my ear, "but a jinni can summon himself into action when his master is in grievous danger. Your body and mind can take no more of this, Binu—mortals are not made for extended interaction with the divine. Let me go with the goddess, but before that, let me take you back to the truck to be among your people. It will not faze me; I have known worse. Give me your command, and I will obey."

I clasped his hand in mine through the dust and the blood, trying to absorb the warmth of his fingers like a man clutching at straws as he drowns.

"I... am... not... your... master."

"We will continue that debate another day," he laughed,

but the laughter fell more like a wounded howl on my ear. "I am sure your path will bring you to Thripuram again. I hope I have a kind master by then, one who will not object to me sitting and chatting awhile with an old friend."

And suddenly, I had an idea.

"Kuldevi of Thripuram," I called out again, summoning the strength that was dripping away from me. "I know you cannot possess Shehzad yourself, so you must give his ownership to one of your human worshippers. If that man turns rogue, or if he dies before passing on the ownership to another worshipper, Shehzad will forever be lost to you. He may turn vengeful, and you have never seen the vengeance of a jinni whose master is dead—there is no precedent in your land for anything like it. Your land will be laid barren; you will be left without worshippers."

I pulled myself up with Shehzad's arms. "Instead, let me come with him. Both of us will serve you for exactly the length of half of my remaining life. He is loyal to me; and you have seen inside my heart—I am a man of my word. When that period is over, we will leave, and no harm will come to you or your worshippers."

More silence, more storm, and then words again. "Half of your remaining life is hardly seven years," sneered the goddess.

That was less than I would have hoped for, but I had no tears to spare. An early death was better than spending long years of my youth in the captivity of the kuldevi of Thripuram, better than dying this minute, never holding Shehzad in my gaze again. My life was a blink in the eternity that Shehzad would have to spend with other masters—what could change between us in a few years, more or less?

"But you speak the truth," said the goddess. "This jinni of yours will not come with me willingly, or reveal to me any of its secrets. None of my priests is acquainted with its true nature—they know nothing but children's stories and misleading spectacles like the one you put up with your circus. Despicable as you may find me, foolish, arrogant man, I do bear responsibility for the well-being of my worshippers. I resent your paltry offer of seven years, but I will accept it. Come to my temple in Thripuram before sunset and devote yourselves by ritual."

"Binu, why—?" Shehzad started to protest, but I squeezed his hand and said, "Shh," as the winds began to dissolve around us.

There was no further interruption from the goddess. In the emerging sunshine we stood holding each other, surrounded by the debris of the beloved circus that had been our family and life.

• • •

The first person I went looking for was the rescued young devadasi. She was injured, terrified, but—like the other members of the circus—had heard nothing of our encounter with the kuldevi of Thripuram. I let it stay that way. No one else had to bear the burden of my choices, or my guilt.

In our last hours, Shehzad was kinder to the girl, mending a fractured wrist with underhanded magic, giving her advice on how to survive in the city all by herself. I saw them smiling together, head to head, and I could feel the sun's rays warming my battered bones. "Savithri is quite an extraordinary woman, really," Shehzad came back to inform me, "brave, level-headed, no airs about herself. I can see why you were taken by her. I have no doubt she will do very well in the city, maybe even become famous."

Savithri—I rolled the name around on my tongue, realizing that in all this time, it had never occurred to me to ask.

"Shehzad..." I started to say, pulling him aside.

"No." He placed a thin, immortal finger to my raw lip. I would have cried then, I would have dropped to his feet and asked for forgiveness, but I was afraid that he would cry too, and I had taken enough devastation for a day.

Johuree agreed to take charge of Savithri in my stead until the circus reached the city, and make sure she was well settled and safe before they left. Johuree had heard nothing of our bargain with the goddess either, but of course I had to tell him.

"I will find you once you are released of your bond," he told me, pressing a bag of money that I had done nothing to earn into my hands. "Doors will always be open for both of you at the Majestic Oriental Circus"—he smiled ruefully, gazing at the rubble that surrounded us—"or whatever is left of it."

"I promised I would let no harm come to the circus," I said, turning my eyes to the ground. "I failed to keep my promise."

"Say no more of it!" he said.

"If I may ask for one more favor—?" I hesitated.

"Of course, my man."

"I left my old mother in the city in the east where you took me in. We only had each other in the world, but once I was signed on to the circus I did not even wait to go home and take my leave of her. I was young and thoughtless then—a wayward son who only worried and disappointed her. I imagined I would come back soon and give her a big surprise, but the circus kept traveling; I did not even notice how two years went by. Now that I know that I won't see my mother for a long time—"

"I will look her up when I return to the city in the east, tell her you are alive, and remind her that her son is loyal and brave, if not always the most practical," Johuree said. "And if there is any way I can help your mother, I will do my best."

"Thank you, Johuree saab," I replied, overwhelmed. "There is nothing more I desire from the world."

And that was how we walked into our exile—man and jinni, never master and slave but equals in friendship and love. I was no longer a free man, and I don't know if I had ever been, but if I must pick a master for half—no, *all*—of my remaining life, I know there would have been no better choice than Shehzad Marid. For that day and the rest of my foreshortened mortal existence, I would follow his footsteps through darkness and light, and that would suffice.

The Blur in the Corner of Your Eye

By Sarah Pinsker

It was a nice enough cabin, if Zanna ignored the dead wasps. Their bodies were in the bedroom, all over the quilt and the floor, so she'd sleep in the living room until they ascertained whether there was a live wasp problem as well as a dead one. If she ignored the wasps, it was lovely.

She'd have to ignore the tiny dead mouse in the ominously large trap in the kitchen, too. If they swept mouse and trap into one of the black trash bags she found under the sink, and ignored the bulk package of rat traps, and ignored the bulk rat poison, and celebrated the wasp spray, everything was good.

The bucket in the main room's corner held a few inches of brackish water. The discolored spot above it was shaped like a long-tailed comet, and probably wouldn't present a problem unless it rained. An astringent lemon-scented cleaner just about covered the delicate undertones of mildew that permeated the walls.

"This place sucks," said Shar.

Shar, her childhood friend, her assistant of who knew how many years, who had always been impervious to magical thinking. Shar, who was right.

"Um, you booked it," Zanna pointed out.

"These aren't usually the things they list under 'amenities.' You said to find someplace cheap and remote, with no

Wi-Fi."

True enough. Cheap, because Zanna was between royalty checks. Remote, because she couldn't have any distractions if she was going to finish this book on deadline. No Wi-Fi, ditto. All she needed was power, since her laptop battery no longer held a charge.

She smiled. "It's perfect. I'll push that little table under the window. The view is what counts, anyway."

Shar returned her smile. "Whew. Okay. You get settled, and I'll see what I can do about the wildlife."

That worked. Zanna went out to the car for her bag. It didn't roll well in the dirt, and she let it bang on the three steps to the porch, rather than bothering to lift it. She paused to appreciate the view: below her, the mountainside spread in a dappled blanket of red and gold. There were other houses along the road—they'd stopped at the owner's on the way past to get the keys—but none were visible from here. Perfect.

She parked her bag inside the door. No point in moving it further until she knew which room she'd be sleeping in. The couch was more of a daybed, so she'd be fine with that option. The small writing table—she already thought of it as a writing table—looked solid, old. She felt the years in it. The chair looked a little hard for her taste, but she'd brought a cushion and a lumbar support for that contingency. This wasn't her first rodeo or her first cabin, and these weren't her first wasps or her first mice. If she'd wanted something less rustic, she would have said so, and Shar would have booked Posh Retreat rather than Wasp Hotel. This was what she needed: no distractions, no comforts, just a desk and a chair and a window.

Out and back again for the milkcrate of research books. Shar had found a broom to sweep away the dead wasps; she'd already disappeared the mouse. Zanna didn't know what she'd done to deserve an assistant who disposed of dead things for her.

The fridge smelled okay, a small blessing. There was nothing in it but an open box of baking soda.

"Make me a list and I'll go shopping for you while you write this afternoon." Shar stood in the doorway, tying off a trash bag.

"Is there a microwave?"

"I saw one somewhere. Hang on."

Zanna stood aside and let Shar rummage in the cabinets. She pulled out a drip coffee maker from a drawer, and a pack of filters. "Hmm..."

Shar left the kitchen and returned a minute later with a small microwave. "It was in the broom closet."

They both had to stand sideways for Shar to put the microwave on the counter. She smelled like cumin, never Zanna's favorite scent. Zanna rummaged in the drawers until she found a torn envelope. She wrote a list on the back, all the easy meals she could make without taking too much time away from her writing. Microwave dinners, mac n cheese, salad kits, eggs, cereal.

"Back in a few hours," Shar said.

They could have stopped at the grocery store on the way in, but Zanna knew this was Shar's way of giving her a head start on her work.

There was nothing for her to do here but write. Okay, or hike, or read, but those were reward activities. More importantly, there was no cell service, no internet, no television. The rental car spit gravel as it backed onto the road. She was alone.

She turned the milkcrate of books on its side on the table, so the spines faced outward. *Birds of West Virginia, Trees of West Virginia, West Virginia Wildlife, Railroad Towns, Coal Country*. She'd done all her research at home in New York, all her character-building, all her outlining, but when Shar suggested that she actually come here to do the drafting, it had felt perfect, like something she should have thought of her herself. She plugged her computer in and sat down to write.

• • •

Shar returned with four grocery bags just as Zanna started to get hungry. "You didn't put coffee or tea on the list, but I figured they were both givens."

"Bless you," said Zanna, standing to stretch and help with the bags. The kitchen wasn't big enough for them both to be in there, but if Zanna didn't unpack, she wouldn't know what had been purchased or where to find it. Shar still smelled like cumin, overwhelming in the tight quarters. Inspiration to put everything away quickly.

"How's it going?" Shar knew her well enough to never ask in terms of word count. Instead, a generic "how's it going" that Zanna could answer specifically if she'd written or vaguely if she'd gotten stuck.

"Got through the first chapter," Zanna said. No need to hide behind euphemisms today. Chapter one was always easiest anyway. Reintroduce Jean Diener, reluctant detective. Find an excuse to get her to where she needed to be.

"Nice! Do you want me to make you some dinner before I leave you alone?"

"Nah. I'm going to have a snack now and write a little more. I'll probably just graze tonight." Zanna held up a premixed chef salad in a plastic clamshell. "You can go check in to wherever you're staying. Where are you staying?"

"Motel at the foot of the mountain. It's dirt cheap this late in the fall, and this isn't exactly a tourist town."

"Are you sure you don't want to stay here? You can have

the bedroom, I'll take the couch."

"Like you were going to sleep in a bedroom full of wasps. Nah, I'm good. I don't want to disturb you."

"Fine, then. How can I reach you? I don't have a single bar of reception up here."

"I'll check on you first thing in the morning. Or I can check if there's a landline phone hidden here somewhere?"

"Nah. It'll be okay. Maybe not first thing, though? If I get on a roll tonight I'm sleeping late tomorrow."

"Check. How's ten?"

"Perfect."

"Anything else I can do for you? Or should I get out so you and Jean can get reacquainted?"

Zanna grinned in appreciation.

• • •

The cabin had a good writing feel. She actually made it halfway through chapter two before stopping to eat the salad. After that, she put her sheets on the couch and pulled a moth-eaten blanket from the bedroom closet, and curled up to read *Railroad Towns*. It was full of useful information, but the combination of long drive and writing had exhausted her, and she fell asleep before ten. She woke once for no reason at all, and then again to a scuttling sound that probably meant the dead mouse had friends.

She woke at 6 a.m. without an alarm. The electric baseboard heater under the window had kept the couch warm enough, but she could tell that outside her blanket, the mountain morning held a chill. She'd make coffee and breakfast, then get working. She flicked on the lamp.

Her throat felt scratchy, her chest sore like she'd been coughing, and the floorboards shot cold through her socks as she padded into the kitchen. Shar had left the coffee and filters next to the coffee machine, so she didn't have to search for anything before she'd had coffee.

She didn't know what she'd done to deserve Shar. She hadn't even known she'd needed an assistant until her childhood friend had suggested it, and now she couldn't imagine life without her. It wasn't that she was unable to do the stuff Shar did, other than driving, just that having someone else shop and correspond and plan travel freed her to concentrate on her books. Shar had always been there for her, but formalizing the relationship had actually helped it.

She'd written forty-something novels now and they'd all been dreams to write, almost literally. Research was still a present-brain puzzle, outlining a necessary torture, but the books themselves had gotten so much easier over the years. A quiet cabin, a desk in front of a window, no distractions.

She plugged in the coffeemaker. While it gurgled, she dumped an instant oatmeal packet into a bowl from the cabinet, added some water, and stuck it in the microwave. When she hit start, there was a pop, and the power went out. The fridge still hummed, but the cabin had otherwise gone dark and quiet. Was the whole place wired on one circuit except the fridge? That meant no power for her computer, either, and no power for the baseboard heater.

Why did this kind of thing always happen before coffee? She checked all the closets and cabinets for a breaker box, but couldn't find one, which meant it was outside. Two shoes and a jacket later, she stood behind the cabin, swearing to herself. Crawlspace. She didn't quite remember what had freaked her out in a crawlspace when she was a kid, but she still hated them. Anything might be in there.

A baseball bat stood propped against the wall beside the tiny door. It had "Snake Stick" written on it in blue Sharpie. Whoever had labelled it had also drawn a crude cartoon demonstrating its utility. Swing them away, don't kill them.

No bloodstains on the bat.

She could wait for Shar, but she'd lose hours, and her head was already complaining about the lack of caffeine. Better to do it herself.

The half-sized door creaked when she squeezed the latch and swung it open. She waved the Snake Stick in front of her to clear cobwebs and wake any snakes snoozing inside. When nothing moved, she dug in her jacket pocket and pulled out her phone. It was useless for calls out here, but the flashlight still came in handy. She swept it around the space, which looked mostly empty. No use delaying.

She crouched and stepped in. The ceiling was a little higher than she expected, the floor a little lower; she could stand if she stooped. Something crunched like paper under her foot, and she swung the light down to find a snakeskin, at least three feet long. She shuddered.

The electrical box was beside the door, but it turned out to use fuses, not breakers. Another pan of the space showed a pile of two-by-fours, but nothing else useful. Mystery writer brain declared it a good enough place to hide bodies, but a little obvious. You'd want to dig up the dirt floor and bury them, or the odor would rise through the floorboards. Pile the lumber back over the spot you'd disturbed.

Back to the cabin, wishing she'd worn a hat, dusting cobwebs from her hair. She went through all the drawers and closets, this time looking for a fuse. A hammer and a box of nails, more rat traps, mouse poison cubes, wasp spray, garbage bags, dish soap, sponges. No fuses. Also no matches or candles, which would also have been useful. In the top kitchen drawer, a yellowed paper brochure for "RusticMountainCabins.biz," complete with grainy picture and phone number. Not that the phone number did any good here.

How far had the owner's house been? Maybe a mile or

two. She could hike down and knock on his door. It would still be early, but not unreasonable, given the inconvenience of no power. There should have been a warning not to use multiple appliances at once. Or maybe that explained the microwave stashed in the broom closet. Shit.

She stuffed her hair under a hat, wrote a note explaining where she'd gone in case Shar arrived before Zanna got back, put her computer in her backpack since she didn't trust the flimsy lock on the door, and headed down the mountain. Down was steep, made trickier by the loose gravel, which skittered out from under her feet. She fell once, windmilling all her limbs to prevent the inevitable, twisting to keep from landing on her computer or her tailbone. She wound up on her left hip and elbow. The elbow got the worst of it, skinned and begraveled.

After that, she took it even slower, picking pebbles from her arm as she went. If she walked with small steps, the slope from one foot to the other was negligible. If she put her full weight on each foot, penguin-style, she exerted sideways motion instead of downward. Jean Diener would appreciate it; the character was a retired physics professor, living in an RV which she parked in any given town just long enough to help solve whatever murder transpired, through physics and common sense.

When Zanna reached the first driveway, she realized she didn't know the house number. What had she noticed about the house, waiting for Shar to collect the keys? She closed her eyes. The owner's house was larger than her cabin, larger than this one. A steep driveway featuring a rock Shar had been afraid to drive over with a rental car. Navy blue SUV with West Virginia plates and one of those WV stickers that looked like the Wonder Woman logo. A windchime with wooden—what did you call them? Wooden knocker things. She'd have to look up the word.

Not this driveway, nor the next, but the third one had the right look. Blue SUV, windchime. Less rental-cabin-like, more home-like. Where did the difference lie? Something to do with the decor. Baskets of orange mums hanging from hooks on either side of the porch steps. The porch ran the entire front of the house, with dormant rose beds below it, trimmed low for winter. The soil was weeded and neat except for some animal tracks.

She glanced at her phone for the time: 7:33. Probably still too early to knock on a door under normal circumstances, but she wouldn't have thought twice about phoning a rental office to make this complaint. No coffee, no heat, no electricity. Possibly no shower, depending on the type of water heater. A landlord should expect tenants to come knocking under those conditions.

The front door stood open, as did the screen, which hopefully meant the owner was awake. Zanna stepped onto the porch and knocked on the doorframe. The mat was turquoise with a picture of a llama on it.

"Hello?" She realized she didn't know the owner's name.

"Hello!" she called again when nobody answered.

She stuck her head in the door. There was a grid of keyrings on hooks to the right, all neatly labelled with the cabin addresses, which mystery-writer brain pointed out was an invitation to robbery. Below the grid, a mat with two muddy boots. Beside it, four coat hooks, all holding jackets in hunter's camo; the owner had been wearing one of those when Shar had knocked the day before. That was the only glimpse of him she'd had from the car.

She yelled one more time, then turned to look where someone might have wandered to with their door open. This was far enough off the beaten path that people might leave their doors unlocked, but for someone with such a fastidious entrance to leave the screen open too struck her as odd.

It was only when she walked a few steps left along the porch that she saw the foot. A bare foot, toes up, just visible on the SUV's far side.

"Hello?" she said again, walking around the vehicle's massive front grill.

He wasn't going to hello back. A middle-aged white guy lay face up, one knee crooked, like he had tripped backing away from someone or something. His head rested on a rock, though rested was an odd word; the rock was drenched in blood. His expression was the worst part: he looked terrified. Eyes and mouth open, corners of his mouth cracked.

She stooped to press two fingers to his wrist. No pulse. His skin was cooler than hers. There was gravel on his right hand, but no blood; he'd never even touched the back of his head, so he must have died instantly.

He wore sweatpants with a bloody tear at the crooked knee and another smaller hole in the seam by the crotch. No shirt, no socks, no shoes. The tattoo above his right nipple said "BREATHE" in reverse, mirror-script; a tattoo for his benefit, not others'. The knee exposed by the rip was pitted with driveway gravel, as were the soles of his feet; they were soft-looking feet for what she imagined was an outdoorsy guy. That detail made her own elbow sting, which reminded her this was real. Not a book.

A body. A real body, until recently a real person. A real person wearing pants nobody would want to die in. What did you do when you found a real body? What did Jean Diener and the people around her do when murder came calling?

She dug her phone from her pocket and was relieved to see one bar of reception. It disappeared when she lifted phone to ear, then reappeared when she peeked to see why the call wasn't going through. She walked a few feet onto the driveway rock and was rewarded with a more stable signal.

The woman who answered had clearly been sleeping; a

yawn came through before her "911—is this a medical, fire, or police emergency?"

"I found a dead body."

The woman swore and the line faded. Zanna shifted to the left, and the voice came back. "—Sorry, that was unprofessional. Are you sure they're dead?"

"Yes. No pulse. I checked."

"And are you safe yourself?"

"I think so? I have no idea, actually." She looked around. What could have scared him badly enough to send him running from his house without putting on shoes? She hadn't even considered that she might be in danger. She felt oddly calm.

"He looks like he hit his head."

The woman on the line said something unintelligible, and Zanna moved closer to the SUV trying to find the signal. There were animal tracks across the hood. She stared at them as she triangulated reception.

The operator returned. "Ma'am, I asked what your name is?"

"Susan Ke—ah, Suzanna Gregory." Calm, but flustered enough to have almost given her pen name.

"And where are you?"

That one was tricky, too. "Ah, I hate to say it, but I have no idea what road this is, and there's no house number. I'm staying at a cabin, and I just arrived yesterday, and my assistant drove and made the arrangements... can you use my cell phone location if I turn it on?"

"That'll take a few minutes, and it'll only tell me which cell tower your call is routed through. Is the body at your cabin?"

"No, I took a walk. I think it's the guy who rents the cabins, if that helps. Outside his house."

"RusticMountainCabins.Biz, by any chance?"

"Yes!"

"Does the deceased have grey-brown hair, wavy, long-ish?"

She leaned over to look at him again. "Yeah."

"Gary Carpenter. You're on McKearney Road. Do you feel safe staying there until I send someone?"

"Yeah."

"Great. Don't touch anything and somebody'll be up there in thirty or forty minutes. Can I get your phone number?"

Zanna recited her number and promised to call back if the situation changed. While she still had one bar, she rang Shar. Unlike the 911 lady, Shar was instantly awake.

"I thought you didn't have reception!"

"I didn't. Or power. The whole cabin shorted out this morning when I tried to make coffee, so I tried flipping the breaker, only it was a blown fuse, and there were no spares, so I walked down the mountain."

"You didn't."

"I did. I can be resourceful, you know. I didn't always have you in my life. But listen, that's not why I'm calling. I'm calling because I got to the guy's house where you got the keys, and he's, uh, here, but he's dead. I didn't want you to get nervous if you got to the cabin and I wasn't there. I left a note, but..."

"Dead?"

Zanna probably should have stopped at 'dead' longer. "Yeah."

"Dead how?"

"It looks like he hit his head. There's a lot of blood."

"An accident?"

"It looks like."

"Good. Well, not good, but you know what I mean. Better than some of the other options. Listen, I'm going to come get you."

"911 lady said for me to wait here."

"That's fine. I'll come wait with you. No need for you to

walk all the way back up."

She really was a great assistant. Zanna thanked her and disconnected.

In her books, Jean Diener would start investigating further. Walk into the foyer, poke around the house now, while emergency services were still far away. In real life, that seemed stupid. She didn't want her footprints added to whatever was in the house. No sense making it harder for the real detectives.

She sat on the porch and leaned her head against the railing. She would have said she'd slept well, but tiredness overtook her. Still too early; no caffeine in her system. She closed her eyes. Opened them again when she heard a vehicle on the road. The rental pulled in far to the left to skirt the driveway rock, and Shar emerged with a paper bag and a coffee.

"Bless you," Zanna said.

"I don't need blessings. Give me your backpack to toss in the car, so they don't start thinking it's evidence. Eat the muffin over the bag so you don't get crumbs on their crime scene. It's blueberry—they didn't have chocolate chip. Also, I need you to stay put when you say you're going to stay put."

"There was no power. Or coffee. You wanted me to sit there for four hours doing nothing?"

Shar sighed. "No... I... it's just now you're going to get stuck giving a statement, and maybe be considered a suspect, and you don't need things distracting from your deadline."

"A suspect?"

Shar nodded in the direction of the body. "You found him. You write detective books. Isn't the person who found a dead body usually one of the people who has to be ruled out? You had opportunity."

"But no motive. Well, except lack of coffee, but that hardly seems worth killing someone over."

"You're not going to joke about it when they ask you questions, right?"

"Right."

"And you haven't gone poking around by the body? Or inside that open door?"

"I'd never!" Zanna said, like the thought hadn't occurred to her. "Okay, maybe not 'I'd never,' but I swear I didn't. I went to the door, that's all."

Shar raised one eyebrow. "I believe you, just... when you watch them do their job, try not to make your interest look too prurient, alright?"

They sat on the porch steps, Zanna sipping a coffee made the way she liked it, two sugars, one cream. A little cool, maybe, from the twenty minute drive up the mountain, but still welcome and drinkable.

A blue-and-gold Taurus with an enormous antenna pulled into the drive, blocking Shar's rental car in. Two cops got out, both white men, young. The tall blonde one had stubble dusting his cheeks, and his uniform looked slept in. The dark-haired one's uniform was impeccably pressed, his shave straight-razor close.

"I'm Officer Dixon, and this is Officer Fischer. And you are?"

Zanna gave her name without stumbling over it this time, and let Shar introduce herself.

"And which of you found the body?"

"I did, Officer. Shar just arrived a couple of minutes ago to give me a ride back up the mountain when we're done talking." Zanna pointed in the direction of the vehicle. The two policemen—state, they must be beyond the bounds of the town at the bottom of the mountain—walked over to take a look, taking the long way around the SUV before disappearing behind it, to her annoyance.

She thought about the SUV. It faced the cabin, and he was on the passenger side. She hadn't seen any keys in his hands, and his pants didn't have pockets, so he hadn't been trying to drive away. Maybe to get something from the car? She looked over to see it was unlocked, or the driver's side was, anyway. This might be country enough that people didn't bother to lock, but if that was the case, why not go in through the near side?

She was back to him being frightened of something and trying to put the car between himself and—who or what? An animal? Whatever ran across the hood? A nightmare? Maybe he was a sleepwalker, or a vivid dreamer. Maybe some medication had messed him up. Or a less legal drug, like meth or some hallucinogen.

One of the policemen—Dixon—went back to the car, where she could see him on the radio, but frustratingly couldn't hear the call. Fischer had a camera out and was taking pictures of the body. Zanna sipped her coffee and tried not to look too interested, as ordered. What was the proper amount of interest? Concern with a dash of 'when can I get back to my work' seemed about right.

Dixon walked back over to the house. "Okay, obviously you were right that he's dead, so I called it in. We'll have to wait for the examiner to make it official, but I can get your statement and send you on your way. How did you come to find the body?"

Zanna explained about the coffee and the microwave and the fuse, and walking down the mountain.

"That's what, two miles?"

"I think so."

Shar interrupted. "The directions he gave me said 1.8 miles past his house, if that helps."

"Thank you," said Officer Dixon. "And what time did you arrive here?"

"7:33. I remember looking at my phone and debating if it was too early."

"And then?"

"Then I walked to the door, and it was open, door and screen, and I knocked on the frame and called inside, but nobody answered."

"—And you didn't go inside?"

"No, I didn't." Zanna gave Shar a pointed look.

"Did you touch anything?"

"Only the body, to feel for a pulse."

"Oh, sorry. Let me get this in order again. You knocked and called inside, and nobody answered, and...?"

"And I turned around and then I saw his foot sticking out beside the car."

"And you walked directly over?"

"Yes. Do you need my shoe print?"

He laughed. "I don't think so. That loose gravel isn't going to tell much."

"What about to prove I wasn't in the house?"

"Which you weren't?"

"No."

"Nah. You can tell me your shoe size or something if you want, but I don't think footprints are going to tell us much. He slipped in the dark. Nothing else to tell."

"Other than the one spot, right?" She couldn't resist. Shar glared at her.

"What spot?"

She pointed a few feet in front of the body. "There's a spot where the gravel's dug away, like he was running and slipped, which makes sense with the torn knee, but then the more, uh, chaotic patch is where he fell, like he spun around and his feet slipped out from under him, but he fell backward when he died, not forward. He had to have fallen twice."

"Uh, right. Other than that. I guess you had time to look

around a little while you waited for us."

"I guess." She bit her tongue to keep from making any other observations.

"Anything else you noticed, then?"

Shar shifted on the stair, a slight movement that allowed her to dig an elbow into Zanna's arm. "Nothing else, Officer."

"Okay, then. I'll take your phone number and the address where you're staying, and you can be on your way."

"Why don't you take my number instead?" Shar said. "You won't be able to reach her up the road, and I can always go find her."

Dixon took both numbers, then walked them to their car.

"Other than the one spot, right?'" Shar mimicked as they waited for the officer to move his car out of their way. "You couldn't resist."

"He wasn't doing his job. He thinks the guy slipped and hit his head."

"Firstly, he's highway patrol, not a detective. Secondly, he doesn't need to tell you, random lady who found the body, everything that he's noticed. Thirdly, the guy slipped and hit his head. There are no other footprints. Case closed."

"Case closed? How can the case be closed before somebody looks inside to see whether there's any hint of what scared him?"

Shar started to reverse, then slammed on the brakes. "Shit. I forgot about that giant rock. If I back over it, we'll leave the tailpipe behind."

"Pull forward. You can't turn around here."

"How would you know? You can't drive."

"I'm familiar with the spatial laws of the universe. You're going to have to do a ninety-point turn if you do it here. Just pull into the clearing so you have more space." Zanna licked a drop of coffee off her hand.

"...spatial laws of the universe..." Shar muttered, commencing a ninety-point turn.

"...And why are you so sure he was scared, anyhow?" she continued as if there hadn't been a pause in the conversation. "Maybe he needed something from his car, but he slipped?"

Zanna considered. "Still kind of weird to need something in such a hurry you don't bother to put shoes on. Or a shirt, on a night that chilly. And to leave the screen swinging open. He looked like a fastidious guy."

"A nightmare, then. Or some personal demon. A guy with a backward 'BREATHE' tattoo has something dark he's getting past."

"Sure. A nightmare. Except..." Zanna turned her coffee cup in her hands.

"Except what?"

"I don't think they noticed the other print either."

"What other print?"

"On the hood, the one you elbowed me before I could say. He must've just washed his car, because it was otherwise spotless—which is impressive given these roads—but there were tracks across the hood."

"Tracks? Like footprints?"

"Animal tracks. Something ran through the flower beds and then across the hood of the car."

She dug a marker from her backpack and drew on her coffee cup. "Like two lines of feet with a tail dragging between them. Across the hood, driver's side near the headlight, to the passenger-side mirror."

Shar glanced over. "Okay, so a lizard or a raccoon or something ran over the car. Big deal."

"And trampled grass on his other side."

"Zanna, you didn't know this guy, you are not a real detective, you have a very real deadline, and you've lost hours of your day already. Let the police do their job."

"Hours—Shar, turn around. We still need to get a fucking fuse."

Shar reached into her purse and fished out a plastic bag without looking down. "Voila. Stopped at the hardware store on my way to you."

"How did you know which size to get?"

"I didn't. I got a whole bunch of different ones, and I can return the ones that are wrong."

"Huh."

"Thank you, Best Assistant Ever. You think of everything. If I actually finish this book and I get paid, you're totally getting a bonus."

They arrived back at the cabin. Shar, the Best Assistant Ever, unplugged the coffeemaker and the microwave, brandished a small flashlight with a price tag still on the base, and headed into the bowels of the cabin to replace the fuse.

Zanna sat at her writing table. She heard the crawlspace door creak, then the shudder of the fridge when the main power cut off. She went to the kitchen and rummaged through the knife drawer until she found one that looked sharper than the others, then returned with it to her workspace, not for any reason she could fully express, even to herself.

She looked out the window, the up-mountain window, with its Prismacolor trees. She pulled *West Virginia Wildlife* from her research crate, its cheesy 70s cover portraying a cougar, a bear, a coyote, a buck, and something that might have been an otter in the same riverside tableaux, and opened to the reptile chapter.

"Aha!" came from under the floorboards. A minute later, the lamp came back on, and the fridge gurgled. "Did that work?"

"Yeah," Zanna called down.

Shar returned a moment later, running a hand through her hair for invisible cobwebs. “Maybe stick to coffee or microwave tomorrow. Do you want me to make you lunch?”

“Nah, I want to get some writing done first. Only...”

“Only what?”

“Only there are four skinks and two lizards native to this area, and none of their tracks match the tracks I saw.”

Shar looked over at Zanna's reading material. “Maybe they've discovered another since 1975.”

“Maybe.”

“Any other mysteries I can solve so you can get back to writing yours?”

Zanna hesitated. She wasn't sure if she really wanted the answer to this one. “You—you mentioned the guy's tattoo.”

“Uh huh?”

“When did you see it? You got out of the car, came straight over to me with coffee. You couldn't ever have seen more than his foot from where we were.”

“The day before, when we stopped for the keys.”

“He was wearing a zipped jacket when he opened the door.”

Shar crossed the room and settled on the couch. “So, what? You think I'm a suspect? Or your lizard is?”

“I have no idea what to think. These are things I noticed. They don't make sense.”

“That's the problem with real life. It's too messy for fiction. Too weird. All those mysteries solved by a single hair found in a drain in fiction, or a single tire track. You'd go out of your mind trying to solve a real mystery. Not that there's a mystery here. Just drop it. Unless there's something else?”

“You never asked,” whispered Zanna.

“What did you say?”

“You never asked where the body was. You came and sat next to me. It would have made sense for you to assume the body was inside the house, but you never asked and you nodded in his direction even though he wasn't visible from that side."

"You must've said it on the phone."

"I didn't. I know I didn't. You had to have been there earlier, seen the body or something. What the fuck, Shar?"

They stared at each other. How long had Shar been her assistant now? She couldn't even remember, which was weird in itself, actually. "Maybe I should take a walk down the mountain again. I'll bet those cops are still there. I can tell them what I've found..."

"A lizard that doesn't exist?"

"An assistant who is lying to me." Zanna stood. She held the kitchen knife by her side, not knowing what to do with it.

"What if I told you that you really, truly, don't want to know the answers to your questions? That I've taken care of everything you've needed for twenty-two years, and I think I've earned the right to ask you to trust me."

Twenty-two years. Zanna chewed on her lip, thinking. "I'd say I trust you if you flat-out say you didn't murder him, but either way, you know what happened, and you're lying to me. You've earned the right to ask me to trust you, but I don't know if I can when I can see you're not being completely honest."

Shar lay back on the couch and put the pillow over her head. "Just once, in all these years, I'd like you to say 'I trust you completely.'"

"What are you talking about? I've always trusted you. You know my bank accounts, you have my credit card, you..."

The pillow lifted. "You say that every time too, but when it comes to it, if I say 'don't poke at the body' you always do. And can we skip the knife thing? You aren't going to use it."

Zanna looked down. The knife looked oddly familiar in her hand, like she had written this scene. She had a thousand questions and didn't even know which one to ask.

She tried to keep the panic out of her voice. "How are 'always' and 'don't poke at the body' in the same sentence? When has this ever happened before?"

Shar propped herself on her elbow. "Tell me about writing your last book."

"*The Mosquitoland Murders*? We flew into Minneapolis and rented an old house in the woods a few hours away."

"The actual writing. Do you remember anything of the time we spent there?"

Zanna considered, then shook her head. "No. I never remember the big drafting binges. It's a shame. We pick these beautiful places, and then it all passes by in a blur."

"Okay. How about your first book? Do you remember your first book?"

"Of course. *Campsite 49*."

"Not the first book you sold—the first book you wrote."

"It was horror, I guess. Dark fantasy, something like that. *The Blur in the Corner of Your Eye*. There was a creature."

"Do you remember anything else?"

"God, I was only a teen. The creature laid eggs in people."

"And why did it get rejected?"

"They said it didn't ring true as fiction. Too messy and weird. Derivative. I never figured out how to fix it, and then I wrote *Campsite 49*, and now I'm a mystery writer instead of a horror writer. What are all these questions?"

"One more: what did you eat for dinner last night?"

"I ate—um... I don't know. I guess I was caught up in writing, but I'm pretty sure I ate something."

"Salad. You had a salad. How far did you get on the book yesterday?"

That seemed to Zanna like something she should remember, but she didn't. "Fine. Shar, what's the point of all this?"

"I'm going to tell you something, and you're not going to believe me."

"I thought we did that already at the start of this conversation."

"We did, but this is something else." Shar paused, sighed. "There's this... thing. Like in *The Blur in the Corner of Your Eye*, okay?"

"A thing?"

"A creature. Let's say those prints you found belong to something, only it isn't in your book because it isn't native to this area. It hitches a ride."

"Hitches a ride?"

"Yeah. Can you stop repeating me for a sec? You'll get it, I promise. So there's this thing, and like you said, it lays eggs. It does it while the person is asleep, and then the eggs incubate, and the first one that hatches eats the other eggs."

"And then it eats through the person and runs away into the world. I know. I wrote this book, remember?"

"No! You wrote it wrong. It doesn't eat through the person. It hides in their body, dormant, until it has to lay its own eggs."

"How could I write my own book wrong?"

"I don't know. You forgot. You always forget."

"I still don't get what you want me to do with this story. I don't write horror anymore. Why don't you write it?"

"It's not a story, Zanna. That's what I'm trying to tell you. Did you wake up with a sore throat this morning? Your lungs sore, though you don't remember coughing?"

Zanna shrugged. It had only been a few hours, but it felt like ages ago.

"I hate when you make me do this the hard way," Shar muttered. "You always make me do it the hard way."

She reached into her bag and pulled out a baggie of brown powder. "Here, put a pinch of this on your tongue."

Zanna turned her head away.

"Come on, smell it. It's cumin."

"I hate cumin."

"You two have that in common. Come on, I need you to do this. A small pinch."

Zanna didn't see a way out of it, since she was stuck in a room with someone whose reasonable tone belied the deeply weird things she was saying. She swallowed a pinch of cumin, then coughed. A second later, the coughing grew deeper, like the powder had gotten into her lungs. Then something stranger, like claws inside her chest. She gagged, and heaved something up. It helped itself along the way, tearing at her teeth and gums even as she opened her mouth.

The thing that skittered out of her was not a lizard or a skink. It had too many legs, and the middle track hadn't been a tail, it was a long face with a proboscis that touched the ground and it had no eyes and too much skin, slimy, black, loose, and it was so fast, just a blur. It skittered under the couch, and Zanna remembered the sound from the middle of the night. Her mind started to lose both that memory and the memory of what the thing looked like even as it disappeared from her view.

"What. The. Fuck." The words hurt.

"You never believe me until I show you."

She held the knife out to Shar. "Kill it!"

Shar waved her off. "Oh, trust me, we've both tried. Burning, shooting, stabbing, drowning. It has a very strong will to live."

"What was it doing inside me?"

"It lives there. You're its host. I don't think it actually does you any harm."

Zanna ran her tongue around her sore mouth, and Shar amended, "Well, it doesn't normally do you any harm. I think it anesthetizes you when it's not in a hurry. When you don't swallow a mouthful of cumin."

"Anesthetizes?"

"Yeah, so you relax, and you don't remember it leaving or coming back. You never remember these trips at all. When you read your drafts back home you always say 'I must have been in the zone. I don't remember writing any of this.'"

Zanna nodded. She knew she had to ask the hard question, too. "So what's your part in this?"

"I do what I've always done, since we were kids and we got stuck in the crawlspace under my dad's house and it chose you. It got way easier when I convinced you to hire me. Find someplace remote for you to write a couple of times a year when you start showing signs. Powder myself with cumin. Try to make the closest person someone who won't be too missed if something goes wrong, like this time. Try to keep you away from the body, which is sometimes easy and sometimes a disaster, like today."

Zanna again had more questions than she could possibly voice. It was true, she did have lapses, but only when she was writing. Her process had always been weird like that, and two books a year had never felt difficult. She remembered everything in between books, or at least she thought she did. She again fixated on Shar's language instead of the harder questions. "What do you mean by 'if something goes wrong'?"

"That same secretion... they're dozy when I get to them. I can usually scrape the eggs out of their mouths, and they never even know anything happened. Only, sometimes, something goes wrong. It gives some of them nightmares, or maybe they see it, I don't know, and they fall down the stairs, or they attack it, or they attack someone else, or like this guy, they run out of the house and hit their head, and I still have to scrape the eggs out so the medical examiner doesn't find anything."

"Why don't you just let them discover the eggs? Or tell someone—a doctor, a biologist?"

Shar looked horrified. "They'd never let you go. They'd have to lock you up to keep it from getting to anyone, and they'd figure out the same thing I have about it surviving everything we try to do to it. You've got contracts. Books to write. Or they'd keep me for having covered it up, and you wouldn't have me to protect you anymore."

That all made a certain amount of sense, even if it was horrible. Shar could be wrong, of course, but she was usually right. "How often does it go wrong?"

"Maybe one in five? They never connect you. Or me."

"But that's why we never go back to the same place twice?"

"Yeah. Somebody would get suspicious sooner or later. But—you believe me now?"

"Yes, I believe you. Are you sure you shouldn't kill me?"

Shar looked horrified. "I wouldn't!"

"But you've let all those other people die. One in five?"

"The eggs have never once survived. The one in you is the only one, as far as I know. Well, and whichever one laid an egg in you to begin with; I guess there must be others. I didn't mean to let anyone die, but it's better than the alternative."

"The alternative?"

"Letting any of the eggs live, or letting you kill yourself. You've suggested that a few times, but what if it survived? How would I find it again to try to keep people safe? You can't do it."

The thought had crossed Zanna's mind. "Then what happens now? I'm not going to let that thing claw its way back down my throat."

"You will. You'll fall asleep tonight and it'll find its way back. It always does. Then you'll wake up in the morning, and you won't remember any of this, and you'll draft your book, and we'll go back to the city, and you'll read your draft and tell me you must've been in the zone, and then when you come up with your next book, the plot'll hinge on a guy who ran out of his house with no shoes, and you'll research it and I'll find someplace remote for you to write it. Rinse and repeat."

They were both silent a moment.

Zanna had a question she didn't want to ask, but asked anyway. "Does it help me somehow? Is this a deal like I can't write without it? That it helps my creativity?"

"Not as far as I know," Shar said. "It might inspire some of your plots—okay, most of them—but I can't see any reason for the rest. Your work ethic and prose are all yours, I'm sure."

"That's something at least," Zanna said. "That would be one ugly muse."

They were silent again. After a minute, Zanna spoke again, the only thing left to say. "Fuck."

"Yeah."

"Shar?"

"Yeah?"

"You really are the best assistant. You deserve a raise."

"You say that every time, too."

"What if I write it down? 'Note to self: give Shar a raise'?"

Shar cocked her head. "Y'know, I don't think you've ever done that before. It's worth a shot, if you mean it."

"I really and sincerely mean it." Zanna opened her computer and created a reminder for herself. A reminder that would chime at her in one month's time, and which she'd open and look at in total surprise and have no memory of writing. Then she'd nod in agreement, even if she couldn't remember what exactly had prompted her to set the alert (or why the second line said "believe her") and she'd make it happen, because she would hate to lose an assistant as good as Shar.

Carpe Glitter

By Cat Rambo

Carpe glitter, my grandmother always said. Seize the glitter.

And that was what I remembered best about her: the glitter. A dazzle of rhinestone, a waft of Patou Joy, lipstick like a red banner across her mouth. Underneath all that, a wiry little old lady with silver hair and vampire-pale skin.

Not that she was a vampire, of course. But grandmother hung with everyone during her days in the Vegas crowd. Celebrities, presidents, they all came to her show at the Sparkle Dome, watched her strut her stuff in a black top hat and fishnet stockings, conjuring flames and doves (never card tricks, which she hated), making ghosts speak to loved ones in the audience and when she stepped off the stage, she left in a scintillating dazzle, like a fairy queen stepping off her throne.

All that shine. And at home?

She was a grubby hoarder.

I mopped sweat off my forehead with the hem of my t-shirt and attacked another pile of magazines. Dust wafted up to fill my nostrils and make me sneeze, drifted down to coat the hairs on my forearms with grit. Something had rotted in the corner; I was doing that once I'd cleared a path to it and breathing through my mouth in the meantime.

This had once been intended as a guest room, but it had been taken over by a troupe of china-headed dolls, and then newspapers and magazines. No cat pee—I'd been spared that in these back rooms, closed off for at least a couple of decades. Grandmother had bought the house when she was at the height of her first fortune, just burst onto the stage magician scene, a woman from Brooklyn who'd trained herself in sleight of hand and studied under the most famous female stage of *her* time, Susan Day.

This pile of magazines, in fact, so brittle that they flaked away as I touched them, showed Grandmother and her mentor on the cover, a poster from their brief tour together, just after World War II: the glamorous older Day, blonde-hair worn in a sleek chignon and eyes blue as turquoise, and Grandmother bright and shiny not just with the rhinestones glittering across her chest, but her starry eyes and grin so wide it stretched her mouth.

The stack held dozens of copies of the same issue, no matter how far down in the stack I went, ending with a swarm of silverfish scurrying away as I lifted the last one. I'd get the room cleared before bringing out my arsenal of bug spray for an onslaught.

Confetti bits of yellowing paper fell away as I put it on the heap to be bagged up and trashed. By now I'd learned that paper that flaked that way meant the appraiser's regretful headshake and the murmur, "Too badly eroded, Miss Aim."

As with each of the seven rooms I'd managed so far, I sorted it into piles. *Throw away* was by far the largest. To be appraised had interesting things in it beyond the scads of dolls Grandmother had collected. Keep was actually two sub piles, one for mother and one for myself.

Object after object to be evaluated and sorted. Old magazines and candy wrappers. So much clothing, most of it absurdly formal. Theater props and grab-bags she'd picked up at church rummage sales, still unopened. And then there were oddities. Picture stitched of human hair, showing a castle on a cliff; an enormous crystal ball, a good foot and a half wide, a mechanical banjo trio that played itself, complete with a library of songs to choose from. A basket filled with sandalwood fans. The rotting thing turned out to be a heap of furs that when stirred, sent up a stench reminiscent of old sauerkraut that sent me out into the hallway for a while.

The doll collection was worth a good bit, perhaps, I'd been told. But nothing on the scale of financial windfall I had hoped for. Grandmother had been wealthy, even though she kept her spending discreet, aside from this strange mish-mash of a house. Where had all that money gone?

And why had she saved everything? I thought that it was perhaps a return to her childhood days, which had been uncertain and full of moves. My great-grandfather had been a con man, always on the edge of getting run out of town, according to her stories. They'd had to leave in the middle of the night more than once, abandoning anything that couldn't go into a suitcase. This could be a reaction to that.

There was no point in psychoanalysis of my dead grand-mother, though. Once the furs were bagged up and taken out, the room was much more bearable. I kept on searching, enjoying the warmth of the sunlight coming in through the uncurtained window, despite the day's heat.

My cell vibrated against my hip. I slid it out of my shorts' pocket and glanced at the screen. My mother.

I took a breath before thumbing the phone on. "Yes?" I said.

"I wish you hadn't chosen this," Mother said, launching right back into the same argument we'd been having all week, ever since I'd said, "Actually, I'll take the second option" at the reading of the will. "It's ridiculous. You could probably tell them that you've changed your mind, that you want the money instead."

"You never know, I might turn up something wonderful," I

said, trying a new tack. Maybe if I could convince her that there might be treasure buried in the piles and heaps lining this massive amalgamation of three houses, she'd support me in this.

She hissed impatience. At least that's what that strangled sound had always meant for both her and Grandmother. Mother liked to pretend she was grandmother's antithesis, but the truth was, they were more alike than either would have admitted. Even I had found a mannerism or two I didn't think of mine, but *theirs*, creeping into my own speech. "*Have* you found anything?" she demanded.

"Not yet," I said. "But I've only begun to scratch the surface. You have no idea how much stuff she managed to cram into this place. It's a little mind-blowing." I toed at the pile I'd been sorting and it slid sideways with a waft of cedar and old socks that almost made me gag.

"Why are you being so stubborn about this, Persephone?"

"I'm thirty years old, mom. I get to make my own choices. Grandmother offered them to me." I hesitated before adding, "It's not your call," feeling the words slide distance between us when my mother was already so far away.

She hung up without a word. I stared at "Connection terminated" before wiping at my face again, tasting salt on my lips. I was sweating up a storm in this fierce heat. That's all that it was.

• • •

When I graduated from high school and Grandmother said she wouldn't pay for college, I pleaded with my mother to intercede. *You caused this,* I said. *I'm not asking you to tell me what happened. It's all between you and her. I'm not taking sides. But if you went to her...*

Mother shook her head quickly, nervously shaking away

any chance. Her hands, long fingered and dexterous as my grandmother's, as my own, twisted in front of her, as though signing negation.

I put my arm down on the kitchen table, then regretted it. We were living in an apartment over a diner; it always smelled of old hamburgers and every surface acquired a sticky, oily film that felt like peeling off cling wrap. Next door, one of the three Laotian women that lived there began yelling at another in another of their interminable arguments.

"No, no," my mother said, words tumbling, desperation driven. Just mention of Grandmother sent her into a panicked, flustered mode. "Let's not talk about that. But think of what else you can do. You wrote all those wonderful essays for the literary magazine. Surely they must have some scholarship fund for promising students. Or if you join the National Reserve, they'll pay, and then you'd know what you were doing, straight out of college!"

"Mom." I shook my head, mirroring her gesture in slow motion. "Do you think I didn't look into every other option? The time for applying for scholarships is long past. I'd have to postpone school for a year—"

"Then postpone it for a year! You can live here, find a job, put money aside—"

"No!" I'd seen too many other people let a year turn into two, then three. Then never. There's always something to eat away whatever funds you have.

I had to grab the chance while I could. I'd watched the meager wage my mother made as a secretary in the years since my grandmother stopped subsidizing us melted away every month. Always something—a roof to be fixed, my mother's ulcer operation, a thousand car problems.

I'd stepped up and managed all that, getting part-time jobs, but never enough. Never money to put away against college. And I hadn't let myself think about that, always assuming my grandmother would pay my way. I didn't expect to live lavishly—I was more than willing to keep working—but without her funds, I was sunk.

I could have cried then, but what good would that have done, other than tying my mother up in knots?

So I went to see my grandmother.

• • •

The house was the same as always. No grass lawn, but an elaborate landscape of cacti and other desert plants: huge striped agave and overgrown saguaro that a landscaper had put in before I was born, at Grandmother's request, long before anyone used terms like "xeriscaping" or "drought-tolerant." Two of the houses had started out as single-level; the third, and last to be built into the mélange, was a three story Tudor on the northern side. I came in through the entrance of the first house, which was where Grandmother kept most of the rooms that she used from day to day.

I knew about the hoarding—I'd spent plenty of summer afternoons in my childhood playing in the vast complex, given free rein by my grandmother, who would shoo me off in order to settle in for an afternoon of practicing prestidigitation or designing trick cabinets in her large workshop, which occupied an entire three-car garage and was where I'd build my first birdhouse, bookcase, and tiny wooden box.

The front door, set with a fan of red and gold stained glass, resounded under my knock. Once I would have just let myself in. I still had a key somewhere but she'd always changed the locks on a yearly basis, although she'd never explain why. Beyond that, every lock had its own individual key, so you had to know which one yours fit.

Inside, though, few doors held locks, other than the door to Grandmother's inner sanctum, a book-lined study surrounding an enormous ebony and mother-of-pearl desk littered with diagrams and correspondence. Only Grandmother and her secretaries held *that* key—perhaps the motivation for the yearly lock change, although you would have thought that it only would have happened when one left if that were the case.

I used the knocker, an elaborate bronze cast of two Chinese dragons. Grandmother loved mystical things and all the symbology she could load into her act. Many of her fans came repeatedly to shows, trying to decipher the potpourri of cabalistic and arcane she managed to incorporate into her costumes and equipment.

The door swung open with a waft of musky incense. I'd expected a secretary, but it was Grandmother herself. She'd shrunk; where once she'd reached my ear, she was closer to shoulder high, but still carried herself like the lead flag bearer in a parade.

"Come in," she said, as though she'd seen me only the day before. She turned and walked away, clearly expecting me to follow her.

I did, stepping into the reception area that was one of my favorite rooms. The enormous bay window showed a view of the cactus garden outside, refracted and split a thousand different ways by the curtain of crystals strung on translucent fishing line. The furniture's well worn cobalt velvet presented a shimmer of silk in the weave, neon electric minnows scattering across ocean surface. This was where Grandmother often received visitors, not allowing them to enter any deeper into the house.

I didn't remember it being this crammed, however, stuffed to the point of claustrophobia. The walls were lined with shelves that reached above my head, lined in turn with an array of dolls, ranging in size from tiny to knee-high, dressed in elaborate costumes. I recognized some as stage costumes Grandmother had worn over the years; I'd played with the originals more than once.

Other dolls stood on the mantelpiece and a few other odd corners or lined the windowsills. Some had been placed along the wall, standing, in a long line, at an attempt of display. In the corner boxes were stacked, labels reading "Limited Edition" followed by my grandmother's name, inset windows showing the dolls inside. The air smelled of horsehair and dust and aging plastic.

The table set kneebump-close between two chairs held a silver tray with coffee pot, cups, cream and sugar, a small plate of cookies, and two cloth napkins. Had Grandmother been expecting me? I couldn't imagine that my mother would have called ahead to warn her.

I settled into the chair across from her and picked up a coffee as she poured for both of us. Saying nothing, she fixed the cup just the way I liked it—a splash of milk, half a spoonful of sugar—while I nibbled at the edge of the cookie, which tasted like cardboard and lemon.

Without preamble, she said, "You're here because you need money for college."

"Not a lot," I said. "I plan on working to cover my food and housing, and going in-state will keep the cost down."

"I'm prepared to pay your full tuition and living expenses under specific conditions," she said.

I blinked. "Which are?"

She set down her own cup in order to tick them off on two fingers. "A. You will attend the university of my choice. B. You will major in the field of my choice."

"What?" I said. Something between indignation and panic swept through me, pulled me into leaning forward. "What university? What major?" Who knew what sort of weirdness she'd arrived at?

"You can go out of state," she said. "But it must be on the

East Coast. Preferably MIT."

"Why MIT?"

"That's where Susan Day went. My tribute to her."

"What was her major?"

"That part doesn't come into play. I want you to study engineering."

"What?" My forehead crinkled in puzzlement. "Why engineering?"

"I didn't say I would explain any of it," she said, and picked up her cup to take another sip.

I had no leverage, no bargaining power. I agreed to every term she laid out. When I told my mother that I'd be going to MIT, she didn't ask where the money was coming from or why I'd picked it.

Don't ask, don't tell. So I said nothing.

• • •

Imagine all the detritus a person creates during a lifetime. I'm not talking about trash—food wrappers and old boxes—but objects that we interact with, that we make: grocery lists and summer postcards, books we scrawl notes in during school, journals and letters and drawings.

And photographs. God, the photographs.

Grandmother was a celebrity and celebrities are documented, in slides and old Polaroids and dusty rolls of film. Newspaper clippings and the pin-up poses autographed and sent to fans by one of the series of blond secretaries handling Grandmother's correspondence, invisible as house sparrows. None of them lasted more than a couple of years; none had been mentioned in Grandmother's will. Much like my mother.

All contained in cardboard boxes with tape gone age-brittle, crumbling when touched. At least the Las Vegas heat and dryness had spared me mold and insects other than the endless silverfish and a few scorpions, and somehow, amazingly, no mouse had ever ventured within these walls. I figured Grandmother must have put down poison for them, or else a secretary had intervened at some point.

I progressed box by slow box. I picked up the pace as I went, learning to sort better or perhaps just caring less in the face of this bewildering mass of *stuff*. Often I found things that seemed to have been packed by mistake. A roll of paper towels, a willowware bowl full of ancient crackers gone gray as cardboard. A rake swaddled in a blanket. Half a dozen flowerpots, a packet of marigold seeds from 1963, unused gardening gloves and a tiny, dollhouse sized shovel. Glass ashtrays with cigarette butts and the crumpled ends of joints mingled with the ash. A cracked jar of shea butter. Old Halloween masks and classroom valentines from Grandmother's childhood, signed in straggling pencil: *Ursula, Jimmy, Laverne*. Taxidermied animals, including a panda, a goat with a unicorn horn grafted on, and an iguana.

I hoped for treasure. And I did find a few pieces to set aside, here and there, but too often it was trash. Grandmother's jewelry boxes glittered promise when I opened the lid and let the light in, but all that sparkle was an illusion. Good costume jewelry, the appraiser told me, and not entirely worthless because it was vintage. But far from the dragon's hoard I'd first thought it to be. How could anything so glittery be worth so little?

The strangest thing I found that first week was a metal hand. Fully articulated and as finely fingered as my own hand, splayed beside it for comparison, although the metal one was larger than mine by half. It wasn't gold, but it resembled it. And old—it felt decades old. The engraving on it was so fine that I couldn't make it out at first.

When I squinted at it, holding it in a sunbeam coming in

throughout the window, I saw it was swastikas and lightning bolts, an interlocking pattern. Graceful in its design, but I had the same reaction to it that war and other atrocities always evoked, a sick sense at the pit of my stomach.

Some war souvenir Day had collected? I knew she had spied on German scientists, infiltrated them pretending to be a Nazi sympathizer who couldn't afford to be too openly associated with them. This had a scientific feel to it, a working model, a prototype of some sort, rather than art object, that led my mind down that narrative path.

The stump was sealed off with a metal cap set with fine, deep grooves. It felt odd in my grip. Loose, as though its center of gravity kept changing. And as though it might move at any moment, might twitch itself from my hands and do some strange and sinister thing (it was indeed a left hand).

What had my grandmother done with it? Or had she done anything? So many of the objects here were unused, still in their original wrappings. I'd noted that because I knew it affected the value of things like old toys, but it never seemed to be anything that mattered that was still encased in cellophane, only old match boxes or reams of blank white paper.

Any answer would probably lie in my grandmother's bedroom suite, which I hadn't dared tackle yet. Those rooms might have seemed ample in my childhood, but now they were crammed, a maze of twisty little passages defined by cartons and shoeboxes, round hat and wig boxes, tiny vanity tables heaped with cosmetics in wholesale quantities.

I had cleared a room my first day, one of the downstairs guest bedrooms, through the simple expedient of stacking its contents wherever else I could, including a bunch of plastic tubs out in the courtyard. Instinct, perhaps, or a premonition that I'd need that space.

Despite the yellowing wallpaper, the dust ground into the

ancient hardwood floor, and the same smell of incense that permeated the first few rooms, it was an orderly place where I could retreat when overwhelmed by the chaos. I kept it scrupulously clean so it might always feel like a refuge – dust free and smelling faintly of lemon, the bed made with a sky-blue silk comforter embroidered with golden stars and crimson butterflies from an upstairs bedroom, that I'd always loved, always coveted. My suitcase laid on a rack, empty now, all its contents transferred to the closet's six hangers, the tiny dresser's three drawers. There was a washer and dryer in the basement, so I didn't fear going without clean clothes despite the relative few I'd brought. Ever since college years, I'd grown used to living out of a backpack, resisting the nesting urge that seemed to claim all the other women of my family.

No other adornments: no art, no rug, no knick-knacks or votive candles. Now I took the hand and put it on the dresser.

It was late and I was tired. But whenever I closed my eyes, I couldn't help but imagine that hand, lifting itself on its fingertips, crawling silently down the side of the dresser, creeping towards me. Finally I got up and put it in the bottom dresser drawer, which was otherwise empty, and closed it tightly. The old wood was sticky – if the hand tried to escape, it'd make enough noise to wake me.

With that thought, I was finally able to sleep.

The Archronology of Love

By Caroline M. Yoachim

This is a love story, the last of a series of moments when we meet.

Saki Jones leaned into the viewport until her nose nearly touched the glass, staring at the colony planet below. New Mars. From this distance, she could pretend that things were going according to plan—that M.J. was waiting for her in one of the domed cities. A shuttle would take her down to the surface and she and her lifelove would pursue their dream of studying a grand alien civilization.

It had been such a beautiful plan.

"Dr. Jones?" The crewhand at the entrance to the observation deck was an elderly white woman, part of the skeleton team that had worked long shifts in empty space while the passengers had slept in stasis. "The captain has requested an accelerated schedule on your research. She sent you the details? All our surface probes have malfunctioned, and she needs you to look at the time record of the colony collapse."

"The Chronicle." Saki corrected the woman automatically, most of her attention still on the planet below. "The time record is called the Chronicle."

"Right. The captain—"

Saki turned away from the viewport. "Sorry. I have the captain's message. Please reassure her that I will gather my team and get research underway as soon as possible."

The woman saluted and left. Saki sent a message calling the department together for an emergency meeting and returned to the viewport. New Mars was the same angry red as its namesake, and the colony cities looked like pus-filled boils on its surface. It was a dangerous place—malevolent and sick. M.J. had died there. If they hadn't been too broke to go together, the whole family would have died. Saki blinked away tears. She had to stay focused.

It was a violation of protocol for Saki to go into the Chronicle. No one was ever a truly impartial observer, of course, but she'd had M.J. torn away so suddenly, so unexpectedly. The pain of it was raw and overwhelming. They'd studied together, raised children together, planned an escape from Earth. Other partners had come and gone from their lives, but she and M.J. had always been there for each other.

If she went into the Chronicle, she would look for him. It would bias her choices and her observations. But she *was* the most qualified person on the team, and if she recused herself she could lose her research grant, her standing in the department, her dream of studying alien civilizations . . . and her chance to see M.J.

"Dr. Jones . . ." A softer voice this time—one of her graduate students. Hyun-sik was immaculately dressed, as always, with shimmery blue eyeliner that matched his blazer.

"I know, Hyun-sik. The projector is ready and we're on an accelerated schedule. I just need a few moments to gather my thoughts before the site-selection meeting."

"That's not why I'm here," Hyun-sik said. "I didn't mean to intrude, but I wanted to offer my support. My parents were also at the colony. Whatever happened down there is a great loss to all of us."

Saki didn't know what to say. Words always felt so meaningless in the face of death. She and Hyun-sik hadn't spoken much about their losses during the months of deceleration after they woke from stasis. They'd thrown themselves into their research, used their work as a distraction from their pain. "Arriving at the planet re-opened a lot of wounds."

"I sent my parents ahead because I thought their lives would be better here than back on Earth." He gestured at the viewport. "The temptation to see them again is strong. So close, and the Chronicle is right there. I know you're struggling with the same dilemma. It must be a difficult decision for you, having lost M.J.—"

"Yes." Saki interrupted before Hyun-sik could say anything more. Even hearing M.J.'s name was difficult. She was unfit for this expedition. She should take a leave of absence and allow Li Yingtai take over as lead. But this research was her dream, their dream—M.J.'s and hers—and these were unusual circumstances. Saki frowned. "How did you know I was here, thinking about recusing myself?"

"It isn't difficult to guess. It's what I would be doing, in your place." He looked away. "But also Kenzou told me at our lunch date today."

Saki sighed. Her youngest son was the only one of her children who had opted to leave Earth and come with her. He'd thought that New Mars would be a place of adventure and opportunity. Silly romantic notions. For the last few weeks she'd barely seen him—he'd mentioned having a new boyfriend but hadn't talked about the details. She'd been concerned because the relationship had drawn him away from his studies. Pilots weren't in high demand now, he'd said, given the state of the colony. Apparently his mystery boyfriend was her smart, attractive, six-years-older-than-Kenzou graduate student. She was disappointed to find out about the relationship from her student rather than her son. He was drifting away from her, and she didn't know how to mend the rift.

Hyun-sik wrung his hands, clearly ill at ease with the new turn in the conversation.

"I think you and Kenzou make a lovely couple." Saki said.

He grinned. "Thank you, Dr. Jones."

Saki forced herself to smile back. Her son hadn't had any qualms keeping the relationship from her, but clearly Hyun-sik was happier to have things out in the open. "Let's go. We have an expedition to plan."

• • •

We did not create the Chronicle, we simply discovered it, as you did. Layer upon layer of time, a stratified record of the universe. When you visit the Chronicle, you alter it. Your presence muddles the temporal record as surely as an archaeological dig muddles the dirt at an excavation site. In the future, human archronologists will look back on you with scorn, much as you look back on looters and tomb raiders—but we forgive you. In our early encounters, we make our own errors. How can we understand something so alien before we understand it? We act out of love, but that does not erase the harm we cause. Forgive us.

Saki spent the final hours before the expedition in a departmental meeting, arguing with Dr. Li about site selection. *When* was easy. Archronologists burrowed into the Chronicle starting at the present moment and proceeding backward through layers of time, following much the same principles as used in an archaeological dig. The spatial location was trickier to choose. M.J. had believed that the plague was alien, and if he was right, the warehouse that housed the alien artifacts would be a good starting point.

"How can you argue for anything but the colony medical

center?" Li demanded. "The colonists died of a plague."

"The hospital at the present moment is unlikely to have any useful information," Saki said. The final decision was hers, but she wanted the research team to understand the rationale for her choice. "Everyone in the colony is dead, and we have their medical records up to the point of the final broadcast. The colonists suspected that the plague was alien in origin. We should start with the xenoarchaeology warehouse."

There were murmurs of agreement and disagreement from the students and post-docs.

"Didn't your lifelove work in the xenoarchaeology lab?" The question came from Annabelle Hoffman, one of Li's graduate students.

The entire room went silent.

Saki opened her mouth, then closed it. It was information from M.J. that had led her to suggest starting at the xenoarcheaology warehouse. Would she have acted on that information if it had come from someone else? She believed that she would, but what if her love for M.J. was biasing her decisions?

"You're out of line, Hoffman." Li turned to Saki. "I apologize for Annabelle. I disagree with your choice of site, but it is inappropriate of her to make this personal. Everyone on this ship has lost someone down there."

Saki was grateful to Li for diffusing the situation. They were academic rivals, yes, but they'd grown to be friends. "Thank you."

Li nodded, then launched into a long-winded argument for the hospital as an initial site. Saki was still reeling from the personal attack. Annabelle was taking notes onto her tablet, scowling at having been rebuked. Saki hated departmental politics, hated conflict. M.J. had always been her sounding board to talk her through this kind of thing, and he was gone.

Maybe she shouldn't do this. Li was a brilliant researcher. The project would be in good hands if she stepped down.

Suddenly the room went quiet. Li had finished laying out her arguments, and everyone was waiting for Saki's response.

Hyun-sik came to her rescue and systematically countered Li's arguments. He was charming and persuasive, and by the end of the meeting he had convinced the group to go along with the plan to visit the xenoarchaeology warehouse first.

Saki hoped it was the right choice.

• • •

There is no objective record of the moments in your past—you filter reality through your thoughts and perceptions. Over time, you create a memory of the memory, compounding bias upon bias, layers of self-serving rationalizations, or denial, or nostalgia. Everything becomes a story. You visit the Chronicle to study us, but what you see isn't absolute truth. The record of our past is filtered through your minds.

The control room for the temporal projector looked like the navigation bridge of an interstellar ship. A single person could work the controls, but half the department was packed into the room—most longing for a connection to the people they'd lost, others simply eager to be a part of this historic moment, the first expedition to the dead colony of New Mars.

Saki waited with Hyun-sik in the containment cylinder, a large chamber with padded walls and floors. At twenty meters in diameter and nearly two stories high, it was the largest open area on the ship. Cameras on the ceiling recorded everything that she and Hyun-sik did. From the perspective of people staying on the ship, the expedition team would flicker, disappear briefly, and return an instant later—possibly in a different location. This was the purpose of the padded floors and walls: to cushion falls and prevent injury in the event that they returned at a slightly different altitude.

The straps of Saki's pack chafed her shoulders. She and Hyun-sik stood back to back, not moving, although stillness was not strictly necessary. The projector could transport moving objects as easily as stationary ones. As long as they weren't half inside the room and half outside of it, everything would be fine. "Ready?"

"Ready," Hyun-sik confirmed.

Over the ceiling-mounted speakers, the robotic voice of the projection system counted down from twenty. Saki forced herself to breathe.

". . . three, two, one."

Their surroundings faded to black, then brightened into the cavernous warehouse that served as artifact storage for the xenoarchaeology lab. The placement was good. Saki and Hyun-sik floated in an empty aisle. Two rows of brightly colored alien artifacts towered above them. Displacement damage from their arrival was minimal; nothing of interest was likely to be in the middle of the aisle.

Silence pressed down on them. The Chronicle recorded light but not sound, and they were like projections, there without really being there. M.J. could have explained it better. This was not her first time in the Chronicle, but the lack of sound was always unnerving. There was no ambient noise, or even her own breathing and heartbeat.

"Mark location." Saki typed her words in the air, her tiny motions barely visible but easily detected by the sensors in her gloves. Her instructions appeared in the corner of Hyun-sik's glasses. She and her student set the location on their wristbands. The projection cylinder was twenty meters in diameter, and moving beyond that area in physical space could be catastrophic upon return. The second expedition into the Chronicle had ended with the research team reappearing inside the concrete foundation of the Chronos lab.

"Location marked," Hyun-sik confirmed.

Saki studied the artifacts that surrounded her. She had no idea if they were machinery or art or some kind of alien toy. Hell, for all she knew, they might be waste products or alien carapaces. They *looked* manufactured rather than biological, though—smooth, flat-bottomed ovoids that reminded her of escape pods or maybe giant eggs.

The closest artifact on her left was about three times her height and had a base of iridescent blue, dotted with specks of red, crisscrossed with a delicate lace of green and gray and black. The base, which extended to roughly the midline of each ovoid, was uniform across all the artifacts in the warehouse. The tops, however, were all different. Several were shades of green with various amounts of brown mixed in. The one immediately to her right was topped with swirls of browns and beige and grayish-white and a red so dark it looked almost black. M.J. had been so thrilled to unearth these wondrous things.

Something about them bothered her though. She vaguely remembered M.J. describing them as blue, and while that was true of the bases—

Hyun-sik pulled off his pack.

"Wait." Saki used the micro-jets on her suit to turn and face her student. He was surrounded in a semi-translucent shimmer of silvery-white, the colors of the Chronicle all swirled together where his presence disrupted it, like the dirt of an archaeological dig all churned together. At the edges of his displacement cloud there was a delicate rainbow film, like the surface of a soap bubble, data distorted but not yet destroyed.

"Sorry," Hyun-sik messaged. "Everything looked clear in my direction."

Saki scanned the warehouse. The recording drones would have no problem collecting data on the alien artifacts. Her job was to look for anomalies, things the drones might miss or inadvertently destroy. She studied the ceiling of the warehouse. A maintenance walkway wrapped around the building, a platform of silvery mesh suspended from the lighter silver metal of the ceiling. The walkway was higher than the two-story ceiling of the containment cylinder, outside of their priority area. On the walkway, near one of the bright ceiling lights, something looked odd. "I don't think we were the first ones here."

Hyun-sik followed her gaze. "Displacement cloud?"

"There, by the lights." Saki studied the shape on the walkway. It was hard to tell at this distance, but the displacement cloud was roughly the right size to be human. "Unfortunately we have no way to get up there for a closer look."

"I can reprogram a few of the bees—"

"Yes." It was not ideal. Drones were good at recording physical objects, but had difficulty picking up the outlines of distortion clouds and other anomalies. Moving through the Chronicle was difficult, though not impossible. It was similar to free fall in open space. Things you brought with you were solid, but everything else was basically a projection.

"It is too far for the microjets," Hyun-sik continued, "but we could tie ourselves together and push off each other so that someone could have a closer look."

Saki had been considering that very option, but it was too dangerous. If something went wrong and they couldn't get back to their marks, they could reappear inside a station wall, or off the ship entirely, or in a location occupied by another person. She wanted desperately to take a closer look, because if the distortion cloud was human-shaped it meant . . . "No. It's too risky. We'll send drones."

There was nothing else that merited a more thorough investigation, so they released the recording drones, a flying army of bee-sized cameras that recorded every object from multiple angles. Seventeen drones flew to the ceiling and recorded the region of the walkway that had the distortion. Saki hoped the recording would be detailed enough to be useful. The disruption to the Chronicle was like ripples in a pond, spreading from the present into the past and future record, tiny trails of white blurring together into a jumbled cloud.

M.J. had always followed the minimalist school of archronology; he liked to observe the Chronicle from a single unobtrusive spot. He had disapproved of recording equipment, of cameras and drones. It would be so like him to stand on an observation walkway, far above the scene he wanted to observe. But this moment was in his future, a part of the Chronicle that hadn't been laid down yet when he died. There was no way for him to be here.

The drones had exhausted all the open space and started flying through objects to gather data on their internal properties. By the time the drones flew back into their transport box, the warehouse was a cloud of white with only traces of the original data.

• • •

We did not begin here. The urge to expand and grow came to us from another relationship. They came to us, and we learned their love of exploration, which eventually led us to you. It doesn't matter that we arrive here before you, we are patient, we will wait.

The reconstruction lab was crammed full of people—students and post-docs and faculty carefully combing through data from the drones on tablets, occasionally projecting data onto the wall to get a better look at the details. The 3D printer hummed, printing small-scale reproductions of the alien artifacts.

"The initial reports we received described the artifact bases, but not the tops." Li's voice rose over the general din of the room. "The artifacts *changed* sometime after the colony stopped sending reports."

Annabelle said something in response, but Saki couldn't quite make it out. She shook her head and tried to focus on the drone recordings from the seventeen drones that had flown to the ceiling to investigate the anomaly. It was a human outline, which meant that they weren't the first ones to visit that portion of the Chronicle. Saki couldn't make out the figure's features. She wasn't sure if the lack of resolution was due to the drones having difficulty recording something that wasn't technically an object, or if the person had moved enough to blur the cloud they left behind.

She wanted desperately to believe that it was M.J. An unmoving human figure was consistent with his minimalist style of research. Visiting a future Chronicle was forbidden, and only theoretically possible, but under the circumstances—

"Any luck?" Dr. Li interrupted her train of thought.

Saki shook her head. "Someone was clearly in this part of the Chronicle before us, and the outline is human. Beyond that I don't think we will get anything else from these damn drone recordings."

"Shame you couldn't get up there to get a closer look." There was a mischievous sparkle in Li's eyes when she said it, almost like it was a backwards-in-time dare, a challenge.

"Too risky," Saki said. "And we might not have gotten

more than what came off the drones. If it had been just me, I might have chanced it, but I'm responsible for the safety of my student—"

"I'm only teasing," Li said softly. "Sorry. This is a hard expedition for all of us. The captain is pushing for answers and Annabelle is trying to convince anyone who will listen that we need a surface mission to look at the original artifacts."

"Foolishness. We can't even get a working probe down there, we couldn't possibly send people. Maybe the next expedition into the Chronicle will bring us more answers."

"I hope so."

Dr. Li went back to supervising the work at the 3D printer. Like M.J., her research spanned both archronology and xenoarchaeology, and her team was doing most of the artifact reconstruction and analysis. They were in a difficult position—the captain wanted answers *now* about whether the artifacts were dangerous, but something so completely alien could take years of research to decipher, if they were even knowable at all.

• • •

Someone chooses which part of our story is told. Sometimes it is you, and sometimes it is us. We repeat ourselves because we always focus on the same things, we structure our narratives in the same ways. You are no different. Some things change, but others always stay the same. Eventually our voices will blend together to create something beautiful and new. We learned anticipation before we met you, and you know it too, though you do not feel it for us.

When Saki returned to her family quarters, she messaged Kenzou. He did not respond. Off with Hyun-sik, probably. Saki ordered scotch (neat) from the replicator, and savored the burn down her throat as she sipped it. This particular scotch was one of M.J.'s creations, heavy on smoke but light on peat, with just the tiniest bit of sweetness at the end.

She played one of M.J.'s old vid letters on her tablet. He rambled cheerfully about his day, the artifacts he'd dug up at the site of the abandoned alien ruins, his plan to someday visit that part of the Chronicle with Saki so that they could see the aliens at the height of their civilization. He was trying to solve the mystery of why the aliens had left the planet—there was no trace of them, not a single scrap of organic remains. They'd had long back and forth discussions on whether the aliens were simply so biologically foreign that the remains were unrecognizable. Perhaps the city itself was the alien, or their bodies were ephemeral, or the artifacts somehow stored their remains. So many slowtime conversations, in vid letters back and forth from Earth. Then a backlog of vids that M.J. had sent while she was in stasis for the interstellar trip.

This vid was from several months before she woke, one of the last before M.J. started showing signs of the plague that wiped out the colony. Saki barely listened to the words. She lost herself in M.J.'s deep brown eyes and let the soothing sound of his voice wash over her.

"Octavia's parakeet up and died last night," M.J. said.

His words brought Saki back to the present. The parakeet reminded Saki of something from another letter, or had it been one of M.J.'s lecture transcripts? He'd said something about crops failing, first outside of the domes and later even in the greenhouses. Plants, animals, humans—everything in the colony had died. Everyone on the ship assumed that the crops and animals had died because the people of the colony had gotten too sick to tend them, but what if the plague had taken out everything?

She had to find out.

Most of M.J.'s letters she had watched many times, but there was one she'd seen only once because she couldn't bear to relive the pain of it. The last letter. She called it up on her tablet, then drank the rest of her scotch before hitting play. M.J.'s hair was shaved to a short black stubble and his face was sallow and sunken. He was in the control room of the colony's temporal projector, working on his research right up until the end.

"They can't isolate a virus. Our immune systems seem to be attacking something, but we have no idea what, or why, and our bodies are breaking down. How can we stop something if we can't figure out what it is?"

"I will hold on as long as I can, my lifelove, but the plague is accelerating. Don't come to the surface, use the Chronicle. Whatever this is, it has to be alien."

She closed her eyes and listened to him describe the fall of the colony. If she closed her eyes and ignored the content of the words, if she forced herself not to hear the frailness in his voice, if she pushed away all the realities she could not accept—it was like he was still down there, a quick shuttle hop away, waiting for her to join him.

"The transmission systems have started to go. This alien world is harsh, and without our entire colony fighting to make it hospitable, everything is failing, all our efforts falling apart. Entropy will turn us all to dust. This will probably be my last letter, but perhaps when you arrive you will see me in the Chronicle."

"Keep fighting. Live for both of us. I love you."

"You home, Mom?" Kenzou called out as he came in. "I'm going out with Hyun-sik tonight, but . . . are you crying? What happened?"

Saki rubbed away the tears and gestured down at the tablet. "Vids. The old letters."

Kenzou hugged her. "I miss him, too, but you shouldn't watch those. You need to hold yourself together until the expeditions are done."

"I'm not going to pretend he doesn't exist."

She went to the replicator and ordered another scotch.

Kenzou picked up the dishes she'd left on the counter, clearing away her clutter probably without even realizing he was doing it. He was so like his father in some ways, and now he wanted to act as though nothing had happened.

The silence between them stretched long. He punched some commands into the replicator but nothing happened.

"He was your father," Saki said softly.

"And you think this doesn't hurt?" Kenzou snapped. He smacked the side of the replicator and it beeped and let out a hiss of steam. His fingers danced across the keypad again, hitting each button far harder than necessary. The replicator produced a cup of green tea, and his brief moment of anger passed. "I'm trying to move on. Dad would have wanted that."

The outburst made her want to hold him like she had when he was young. She'd buried herself in her work these last few months, and he had found his comfort elsewhere. He'd finished growing up sometime when she wasn't looking.

"I'm sorry," she said. "Go, spend time with your boyfriend."

He softened. "You shouldn't drink alone, Mom."

"And you shouldn't secretly date my students," she scolded gently. "It's very awkward when the whole lab knows who my son is dating before I do!"

He sipped his tea. "There aren't that many people on station, word has a way of getting around."

After a short pause he added, "you could ask Dr. Li to have a drink with you, if you insist on drinking."

"I don't think she would . . ." Saki shook her head.

"And that's why your entire lab knows these things before you do." He finished his tea, then washed the cup and put it away. "You don't notice what is right in front of you."

"I'm not ready to move on." She looked down at the menu on her tablet, the list of recently viewed vids a line of tiny icons of M.J.'s face. He was supposed to be here, waiting for her. They were supposed to have such a wonderful life.

"I know." He hugged her. "But I think you can get there."

• • •

Layers of information diminish as they recede from the original source. In archaeology, you remove the artifacts from their context, change a physical record into descriptions and photographs. You choose what gets recorded, often unaware of what you do not think to keep. Your impressions—logged in books or electronically on tablets or in whatever medium is currently in fashion—are themselves a physical record that future researchers might find, when you are dead and gone.

Saki was with Li in the Chronicle, four weeks after the collapse.

The third floor of the hospital was empty. Not just devoid of people—this was a part of the Chronicle that came after everyone had died, so that wasn't surprising. The place was half cleaned out. Foam mattresses on metal frames, but someone or something had taken the sheets. Nothing in the planters, not even dry dead plants. This wasn't long after the collapse, and the pieces simply did not fit.

"Why would anyone bother taking things from the hospital while everyone was dying?" Li messaged. "And why are there no bodies? There was no one left at the end to take care of the remains."

The crops had failed, the parrot had died, the hospital was empty. Saki knew there had to be a connection, but what was it? She scanned the area for clues. In a patch of bright sunlight near one of the windows, she saw the faint outline of a distortion, another visitor to the Chronicle. The window was at the edge of the containment area, but probably within reach.

"Someone else was here," Saki typed, "by that window."

"I think you're right. Closer look?" Li fished out the rope from her pack. "I'm not a graduate student, so you're not responsible for my wellbeing."

Saki caught herself before explaining that as lead researcher she was still responsible for the welfare of everyone on the team. Li was partly teasing, but it held some truth, too. If Li was willing to risk it, they could investigate.

"Can I be the one to go?" Saki asked.

"You think it might be M.J." Li did not phrase it as a question.

"Yes."

Li fastened the rope securely around her waist and handed Saki the other end. They checked each other's knots, then checked them again. If they came untied, it would be difficult or maybe impossible to get back to their marks. They spun themselves around and pressed their palms and feet together. "Gently. We can try again if you don't get far enough."

Li's hands were smaller than her own, and warm.

"Ready?"

Saki felt the tiny movements of Li's fingers as she typed the word. She nodded. "Three, two, one."

They pushed off of each other, propelling Saki towards the window and Li in the opposite direction, leaving a wide white scar across the Chronicle between them. Saki managed to contort her body around so that she could see where she was going as she drifted towards the window. The human form that stood there was not facing the hospital, and she couldn't see their face. She reached the end of the rope a meter short of the window.

"Is it M.J.?" Li messaged from across the room.

"I don't know," Saki replied.

The white figure by the window was about the right height to be M.J., about the right shape. But the colony was huge, and even narrowed down to just the archronologists, it could have been any number of people. Saki twisted around to gain a few more centimeters, but she couldn't see well enough to know one way or the other. If she untied the rope and used the micro-jets on her suit—but no, that would leave Li stranded.

"Whoever it is, they were looking out the window." Saki tore her gaze away from the figure that might or might not be her lifelove. She'd seen the New Mars campus many times, even this part of campus, because the hospital was across the quad from the archronology building. M.J. had sometimes recorded his vid letters there, on the yellow-tinged grass that grew beneath the terrafruit trees.

Outside the window, there were no trees. There was no grass. Not even dry brown grass and dead leafless trees. It was bare ground. Nothing but a layer of red New Martian dust.

"All of it is gone," Saki typed. "Every living thing was destroyed."

No one had noticed it in the warehouse because they'd had no reason to expect any living things to be there.

She and Li pulled themselves back to the center of the room, climbing their rope hand over hand until they were back at their marks. They adjusted the programming of their bees in hopes that they could get a clear image of the other visitor to the record, and set them swarming around the room.

"It's more than that," Li messaged as the bees catalogued the room. "That's why this room is so odd. Everything organic is gone. Whatever is left is all metal or plastic."

It was obvious as soon as she said it, but something still didn't fit. "The alien artifacts, back in the warehouse—those were made from organic materials. Why weren't they destroyed with everything else?"

• • •

One of our beloveds believes that all important things are infinite. Numbers. Time. Love. They think that the infinite should never be seen. We erase vast sections of the Chronicle out of love, but this infuriates some of our other beloveds. To embrace so many different loves, scattered across the galaxy, is difficult to navigate. It is not possible to please everyone.

Saki stood back to back with Hyun-sik. Their surroundings shifted from gray to orange-red. The two of them were floating beneath the open sky in a carefully excavated pit. The dig site was laid out in a grid, black cords stretched between stakes, claylike soil removed layer by layer and carefully analyzed. Fine red dust swirled in an eerily silent wind and gathered in the corners of the pit.

Hyun-sik swayed on his feet.

"The Chronicle is an image, being here is no different from being in an enclosed warehouse," Saki reminded him. He looked ill, and if he threw up in the Chronicle it might obscure important data. Even if it didn't, it would definitely be unpleasant.

"I've never been outside. It is big and open and being

weightless here feels wrong." Hyun-sik messaged. He took a deep breath. "And the dust is moving."

"Human consciousness is tied to the passage of time. In an abandoned indoor environment like the warehouse, there are long stretches of time where nothing moves or changes. It feels like a single moment in time. But we are viewing moving sections of the record, which is why we try to spend as little time here as we can," Saki answered.

"Sorry." He still looked a little green, but he managed not to vomit. Saki turned her attention back to their surroundings. There were no visible distortions here, no intrusions into the time record. M.J. hadn't visited the Chronicle of this time and place.

At Li's insistence, the team had done a three-day drone sweep of the entire colony starting at the moment of the last known transmission. Wiping out so much of the Chronicle felt incredibly wasteful, especially for such an important historic moment. If some future research team came to study the planet, all they'd find of those final days was a sea of white, the destruction inherent in collecting the data. Though if Saki was honest, the thing that bothered her most was that she couldn't be there for M.J.'s final moments. They had burrowed into the Chronicle deeper than his death, deeper than his final acts, leaving broad swaths of destruction in their wake.

He was gone, why should it matter what happened to the Chronicle of his life? But it felt like deleting his letters, or erasing him from the list of contacts on her tablet.

She tried to focus on the present. This site was a few weeks before the final transmission. They were here to gather information about the alien artifacts in situ. Perhaps they could notice something that M.J. and his team had missed.

In the distance, the nearest colony dome glimmered in

the sun, sitting on the surface like a soap bubble. There were people living inside the dome—M.J. was there, working or sleeping or recording a vid letter that she would not read until months later. So many people, and all of them would soon be dead. Were already dead, outside the Chronicle. Colonies were so fragile, like the bubbles they resembled. The domes themselves were reasonably sturdy, but the life inside . . . New Mars was not the first failed colony, and it would not be the last.

The sun was bright but not hot. Expeditions into the Chronicle were an odd limbo, real but not real, like watching a vid from the inside.

"That one looks unfinished," Hyun-sik messaged, pointing to a partially exposed artifact. It was an iridescent blue, like the bases of the artifacts in the warehouse, but the upper surface of the artifact did not have the smoothly curved edges that were universal to everything they'd seen so far.

"They changed so quickly," Saki mused. She'd read M.J.'s descriptions of the artifacts, and looked at the images of them, but there was something more powerful about seeing one full scale here in the Chronicle. "And right as the colony collapsed. The two things must be related."

She shuddered, remembering the drone vids of the final collapse. After weeks of slow progression, everything in the colony started dying. She'd forced herself to watch a clip from the hospital—dozens of colonists filling the beds, tended by medics who eventually collapsed wherever they were standing. Everyone dead within minutes of each other, and then—Saki squeezed her eyes shut tight as though it would ward off the memory—the bodies disintegrated. Flesh, bone, blood, clothes, everything organic broke down into a fine dust that swirled in the breeze of the ventilation systems.

She opened her eyes to the swirling red dust of the excavation site, suddenly feeling every bit as ill as Hyun-sik looked. Such a terrible way to die and there was nothing left. No bodies to cremate, no bones to bury. It was as if the entire colony had never existed, and M.J. had died down here and that entire moment was nothing but a sea of drone-distortion white.

"Are you okay, Dr. Jones?" Hyun-sik messaged.

"Sorry," she answered. "Did you watch the drone-vids from the collapse?"

He nodded, and his face went pale. "Only a little. Worse than the most terrible nightmare, and yet real."

Saki focused all her attention on the artifact half-buried in the red dirt, forcing everything else out of her mind. She searched the blue for any trace of other colors, but there was nothing else there. "I don't know how the artifacts changed so quickly, or why. Maybe Dr. Li can figure it out from the recordings."

"Release the drones?" Hyun-sik asked.

"Wait." Saki pointed toward the colony dome, her arm wiping away a small section of the Chronicle as she moved. "Look."

Clouds of red dust rose up from the ground, far away and hard to see.

"Dust storm?" Hyun-sik turned his head slightly, trying to disturb the record as little as possible.

"Jeeps." Saki stared at the approaching clouds of dust, rising from vehicles too distant to see. M.J. might be in one of them, making the trek over rough terrain to get to the dig site. Saki tried to remember how far the dig site was from the dome—forty kilometers? Maybe fifty? The dig site was on a small hill, and Saki couldn't quite remember the math for calculating distance to the horizon. It was estimates stacked on estimates, and although she desperately wanted to see M.J., her conclusion was the same no matter how she ran the calculation—they couldn't wait for the slow-moving jeeps to arrive.

"Do you see anything else that merits a closer look?" Saki typed.

Hyun-sik stared at the approaching jeeps. "If we had come a couple hours later, there would have been people here."

"Yes."

It wasn't M.J., Saki reminded herself, only an echo. Her lifelove wasn't really here. Saki had Hyun-sik release the drones and soon they were surrounded by white, much as the jeeps were enveloped in a cloud of red.

The drones finished, and the jeeps were still far in the distance. M.J. always did drive damnably slow. Saki waved goodbye to jeeps that couldn't see her. When they blinked back into the projection room, she was visibly shaken. Hyun-sik politely invited her to join him and Kenzou for dinner, but that would be awkward at best and she didn't have the energy to make conversation. Saki kept it together long enough to get back to her quarters.

Safely behind closed doors, she called up the vid letter that M.J. had sent around the time she'd just visited. He was supposed to wait for her, only a few more months. She'd been so close. The vid played in the background while she cried.

• • •

We had a physical form, once. Wings and scales and oh so many legs, everything in iridescent blue. Each time we encounter a new love, it becomes a part of who we are. No, we do not blend our loves into one single entity—the core of us would be lost against such vastness. We always remain half ourselves, a collective of individuals, a society of linked minds. How could we exclude you from such a union?

The captain sent probes to the surface that were entirely inorganic—no synthetic rubber seals or carbon-based fuels—and this time the probes did not fail. They found nanites in the dust. Visits to the Chronicle were downgraded in priority as other teams worked to neutralize the alien technology. Saki tried to stay focused on her research, but without the urgency and tight deadlines, she found herself drawn into the past. She watched letters from M.J. in a long chain, one vid after the next. The hard ones, the sad ones, everything she'd been avoiding so that she could be functional enough to do research.

The last vid-letter from M.J. was recorded not in his office but in the control room for the temporal projector. Saki had asked about it at the time, and he'd explained that he had one last trip to make, and the colony was running out of time. She'd watched it twice now, and M.J. looked so frail. But there was something Saki had to check. A hunch.

For the first half of the vid, M.J. sat near enough to the camera to fill nearly the entire field of view. He thought the plague was accelerating, becoming increasingly deadly. He talked about the people who had died and the people who were still dying, switching erratically between cold clinical assessment and tearful reminiscence. Saki cried right along with her lost love, harsh ugly tears that blurred her vision so badly that she nearly missed what she was looking for.

She paused and rewound. There, in the middle of the video, M.J. had gotten up to make an adjustment to the controls. The camera should have stayed with him, but for a brief moment it recorded the settings of the projector. The point in the record where M.J. was going.

Saki wrote down the coordinates of space and time. It was on New Mars, of course. It was also in the future. She studied the other settings on the projector, noting the changes he'd made to accommodate projection in the wrong direction.

M.J. had visited a future Chronicle, and left her the clues she needed to follow him.

She set her com status to do not disturb, and marked the temporal projector as undergoing maintenance. There was no way she could make it through a vid recording without falling apart, so she wrote old-fashioned letters to Kenzou, to her graduate students, to Li—just in case something went wrong.

When she stepped out into the corridor, Hyun-sik and Kenzou were there.

She froze.

"I will work the controls for you, Dr. Jones," Hyun-sik said. "It is safer than programming them on a delay."

"How did you—?"

"You love him, you can't let him go," Kenzou said. "You've always been terrible at goodbyes. You want to see as much of his time on the colonies as possible, and there's no way to get approval for most of it."

"Also, marking the temporal projector as 'scheduled maintenance' when our temporal engineer is in the middle of their sleep cycle won't fool anyone who is actually paying attention to the schedule," Hyun-sik added.

"Thinking of making an unauthorized trip yourself?" Saki asked, raising an eyebrow at her student.

"Come on," Hyun-sik didn't answer her question. "It won't be long before someone else notices."

They went to the control room, and Saki adjusted the settings and wiring to match what she'd seen in M.J.'s vid. The two young men sat together and watched her work, Kenzou resting his head on Hyun-sik's shoulder.

When she'd finished, Hyun-sik came to examine the controls. "That is twenty years from now."

"Yes."

"No one has visited a future Chronicle before. It is forbidden by the IRB and the theory is completely untested."

"It worked for M.J.," Saki said softly. She didn't have absolute proof that those distortion clouds in the Chronicle had been him, but who else could it be? No other humans had been here since the collapse, and whoever it was had selected expedition sites that she was likely to visit. M.J. was showing her that he had successfully visited the future. He wanted her to meet him at those last coordinates.

"Of course it did," Kenzou said, chuckling. "He was so damn brilliant."

Saki wanted to laugh with him, but all she managed was a pained smile. "And so are you. You'll get into trouble for this. It could damage your careers."

"If we weren't here, would you bother to come back?"

Saki blushed, thinking of the letters she'd left in her quarters, just in case. M.J. had gone to some recorded moment of future. Maybe he had stayed there. This was a way to be with him, outside of time and space. If she came back, she would have to face the consequences of making an unauthorized trip. It was not so farfetched to think that she might stay in the Chronicle.

"Now you have a reason to return." Hyun-sik said. "Otherwise Kenzou and I will have to face whatever consequences come of this trip alone."

Saki sighed. They knew her too well. She couldn't stay in the Chronicle and throw them to the fates. "I promise to return."

• • •

This is a love story, but it does not end with happily ever

after. It doesn't end at all. Your stories are always so rigidly shaped—beginning, middle, end. There are strands of love in your narratives, all neat and tidy in the chaos of reality. Our love is scattered across time and space, without order, without endings.

Visiting the Chronicle in the past was like watching a series of moments in time, but the future held uncertainty. Saki split into a million selves, all separate but tied together by a fragile strand of consciousness, anchored to a single moment but fanning out into possibilities.

She was at the site of the xenoarchaeology warehouse, mostly.

Smaller infinities of herself remained in the control room due to projector malfunction or a last minute change of heart. In other realities, the warehouse had been relocated, or destroyed, or rebuilt into alien architectures her mind couldn't fully grasp. She was casting a net of white into the future, disturbing the fabric of the Chronicle before it was even laid down.

Saki focused on the largest set of her infinities, the fraction of herself on New Mars, inside the warehouse and surrounded by alien artifacts. The most probable futures, the ones with the least variation.

M.J. was there, surrounded by a bubble of white where he had disrupted the Chronicle.

Saki focused her attention further, to a single future where they had calibrated their coms through trial and error or intuition or perhaps purely by chance. There was no sound in the Chronicle, but they could communicate.

"Hello, my lifelove." M.J. messaged.

"I can't believe it's really you." Saki answered. "I missed you so much."

"Me too. I worried that I'd never see you again." He gestured to the artifacts. "Did you solve it?"

She nodded. "Nanites. The bases of the artifacts generate nanites, and clouds of them mix with the dust. They consumed everything organic to build the tops of the artifacts."

"Yes. Everything was buried at first, and the nanites were accustomed to a different kind of organic matter." M.J. typed. "But they adapted, and they multiplied."

Saki shuddered. "Why would they make something so terrible?"

"Ah. Like me, you only got part of it." He gestured at the artifacts that surrounded them. "The iridescent blue on the bottom are the aliens, or a physical shell of them, anyway. The nanites are the way they make connections, transforming other species they encounter into something they themselves can understand."

"Why didn't you explain this in your reports?"

"The pieces were there, but I didn't put it all together until I got to the futures." He gestured at the warehouse around them with one arm, careful to stay within his already distorted bubble of white.

In this future, she and M.J. were alone, but in many of the others the warehouse was crowded with people. Saki recognized passengers and crew from the ship. They walked among the artifacts with an almost religious air, most of them pausing near one particular artifact, reaching out to touch it.

She sifted through the other futures and found the common threads. The worship of the artifacts, the people of the station living down on the colony, untouched by the nanites. "I don't understand what happened."

"Once the aliens realized what they were doing to us, they stopped. They had absorbed our crops, our trees, our pets. Each species into its own artifact." He turned to face the closest artifact, the one that she'd seen so many people focus their attentions on in parallel futures. "This one holds all the human colonists."

"They are visiting their loved ones, worshipping their ancestors."

"Yes."

"I will come here to visit you." Saki could see it in the futures. "I was so angry when Li sent drones to record the final moments of the colony. I should have been there to look for you, but that's a biased reason, too wrong to even mention in a departmental meeting. I couldn't find you in the drone vids, but there was so much data. Everyone and everything dead, and then systematically taken apart by the nanites. Everyone."

"It is what taught the aliens to let the rest of humankind go."

"They didn't learn! They took all the organics from the probes we sent."

"New tech, right? Synthetic organics that weren't in use on the colonies, that the nanites didn't recognize. You can see the futures, Saki. The colony is absorbed into the artifacts, but at least we save everyone else."

"We? You can't go back there. I don't want to visit an alien shrine of you, I want to stay. I want *us* to stay." Saki flailed her arms helplessly, then stared down at her wrist-band. "I promised Kenzou that I would go back."

"You have a future to create." M.J. answered. "Tell Ken-zou that I love him. His futures are beautiful."

"I could save you somehow. Save everyone." Saki studied the artifacts. "Or I could stay. It doesn't matter how long I'm here, in the projection room we only flicker for an instant—"

"I came here to wait for you." M.J. smiled sadly. "Now we've had our moment, and I should return to my own time. Go first, my lifelove, so that you don't have to watch me leave. Live for both of us."

It was foolish, futile, but Saki reached out to M.J., blurring the Chronicle to white between them. He mirrored her movement, bringing his fingertips to hers. For a moment she thought that they would touch, but coming from such different times, using different projectors—they weren't quite in sync. His fingertips blurred to white.

She pulled her hand back to her chest, holding it to her heart. She couldn't bring herself to type goodbye. Instead she did her best to smile through her tears. "I'll keep studying the alien civilization, like we dreamed."

He returned her smile, and his eyes were as wet with tears as her own. Before she lost the will to do it, she slapped the button on her wristband. Only then, as she was leaving, did he send his last message, "Goodbye, my lifelove."

All her selves in all the infinite possible futures collapsed into a single Saki, and she was back in the projection room, tears streaming down her face.

• • •

We know you better now. We love you enough to leave you alone.

Saki pulled off her gloves and touched the cool surface of the alien artifact. M.J. was part of this object. All the colonists were. Those first colonists who had lost their lives to make the aliens understand that humankind didn't want to be forcibly absorbed. Was M.J.'s consciousness still there, a part of something bigger? Saki liked to think so.

With her palm pressed against the artifact, she closed her eyes and focused. They were learning to communicate, slowly over time. It was telling her a story. One side of the story, and the other side was hers.

She knew that she was biased, that her version of reality would be hopelessly flawed and imperfect. That she would not even realize all the things she would not think to write, but she recorded both sides of the story as best she could.

This is a love story, the last of a series of moments when we meet.

A Song For a New Day

By Sarah Pinsker

PART ONE

1

LUCE
172 Ways

There were, to my knowledge, one hundred and seventy-two ways to wreck a hotel room. We had brainstormed them all in the van over the last eight months on the road. As a game, I'd thought: 61, turn all the furniture upside down; 83, release a pack of feral cats; 92, fill all the drawers with beer, or, 93, marbles; 114, line the floor with soapy plastic and turn it into a slip 'n' slide; etc., etc.

In my absence, my band had come up with the one hundred and seventy-third, and had for the first time added in a test run. I was not proud.

What would Gemma do if she were here? I stepped all the way into their room instead of gawking from the hallway and closed the door before any hotel employees could walk past, pressing the button to illuminate the do not disturb sign for good measure. "Dammit, guys. This is a nice hotel. What the hell did you do?"

"We found some paint." Hewitt's breath smelled like a distillery's dumpster. He lingered beside me in the vestibule.

"You're a master of understatement."

All their bags and instruments were crammed into the closet by the entrance. The room itself was painted a garish neon pink, which it definitely hadn't been when I'd left that morning. Not only the walls, either: the headboards, the nightstand, the dresser. The spatter on the carpet suggested somebody had knifed a Muppet and let it crawl away to die. For all the paint, Hewitt's breath was still the overwhelming odor.

"Even the TV?" I asked. "Really?"

The television, frame and screen. Cable news blared behind a drippy film of pink, discussing the new highway only for self-driving cars. We'd be avoiding that one.

JD lounged on the far bed, holding a glass of something caramel colored. His shoes were pink. The bedspread, the site of another Muppet murder.

"We considered doing an accent wall." He waved his glass at the wall behind the headboard.

April sat on the desk, sticks in hand, drumming a soundless tattoo in the air. "How was your day?" she asked, as if nothing was wrong. "Excuse me a second." I ducked into the hall and fumbled for the keycard to the room I shared with April. Our room was quiet and empty and, most importantly, not pink. I leaned my guitar bag in a corner and let out a breath I hadn't known I was holding, then lay back on the bed and dialed Gemma.

"We're not supposed to be out here alone," I said when she picked up. "When are you coming back?"

She sighed. "Hi, Luce. My brother is fine, thanks for asking. The bullet went straight through him without hitting any organs."

"I heard! I'm glad he's okay! I'm sorry, I should have asked first.

But do you think you're coming back soon?"

"No, I really don't. What's the matter? Do you need something?"

"A tour manager. A babysitter for these giant children you ditched me with, so I can concentrate on music instead of being the adult in the room when I'm younger than all of them. Never mind. I shouldn't have called, and I'm sorry I bothered you. I hope your brother gets well soon."

I disconnected. We should have been able to handle a few weeks on the road without a tour manager. Lots of bands did fine without one, but those were probably real bands, where everyone had a vested interest; I'd played solo until the label hired these so-called professionals to back me on tour.

Hewitt let me in again when I knocked. Inside the fridge, two large bottles had been crammed in sideways, gin and tequila. The painted minifridge left my fingertips pink and tacky. My prints made me complicit, I supposed. I pulled out the tequila and took a long slug straight from the bottle. Cheap, astringent stuff. No wonder they were chilling it. The armchair under the window was paint free, so I made my way to it with the tequila, trying not to touch anything else.

"Well, April," I began, answering her question as if I hadn't left, "since you asked, my day started at five this morning, with stops at two different TV morning shows. Then I did a radio call-in show. Then I spent two hours on the phone in a station parking lot arguing with the label about why we still don't have our new T-shirts. Then I did a couple of acoustic songs for a local music podcast, ate a highly mediocre burrito, and came back here to find you've been far more productive than me. I mean, why did I waste all that time promoting our show tomorrow night when I could have been helping you redecorate?"

They were all glare resistant; not even April had the decency to look uneasy. They knew I had the power to fire them if I wanted, but I wouldn't. We got along too well onstage.

It wasn't in me to maintain stern disinterest. "So where did you get the paint?"

April grinned. "We looked up where the nearest liquor store was, right? We had to run across the highway to get there, and there were, like, six lanes, and it was a little, uh, harrowing. So on the way back, we tried to find a better place to cross, like maybe there was a crosswalk somewhere, and then we passed this Superwally Daycare that had a room being redone and it was completely deserted, right? But the door was open, I guess to air it out."

A groan escaped me, and I took another chug of tequila. "You stole from a daycare?"

"A *Superwally* Daycare," said JD. "They won't be going broke on our account, I promise you. Anyway, we also went back out again to the actual Superwally and spent some money there that we wouldn't have spent otherwise, so it cancels out."

I was almost afraid to ask. "What else did you buy?"

"That's the best part." Hewitt flipped the light switch.

The room lit up. The pink television and the wall behind the headboard had been painted over with an alien-green glow-in-the-dark wash only visible with the lights off. On the wall backing the bathroom, our band logo: a sparking cannon. April's drumsticks glowed, too; if only they'd stuck to painting things they owned.

"I hope one of you pulled a Cheshire Cat, because I need somebody to punch in the teeth."

JD's voice came from beside me. "Like I said: we considered an accent wall, but then we decided against it."

I put the bottle to my mouth to keep myself from saying something I'd regret later. Dozed off for a second in the chair, then started awake when the lights came back on. April had disappeared, probably back to our room; JD was asleep on his bed; Hewitt was singing to himself in the bathroom. I might have rested my eyes for longer than I thought.

The tequila walloped me as I lurched to my feet. I tried to channel Gemma, our absent tour manager. She'd gone home three weeks before, after her brother was shot eating lunch at a mall. The label hadn't wanted us to keep touring without her, but I had promised we'd be fine. I shouldn't have called her earlier; this wasn't her fault. Anyway, even if she'd been here today, she'd have been driving with me, managing the promotional appearances so I could play the pure artist. The band would still have been left to their devices, though they'd probably have thought twice about pulling a stunt like this with her around to ream them out.

What would Gemma say? I channeled her to mutter, "If and when the hotel bills us for damages, it's coming out of your salaries. You shouldn't need a babysitter when I leave you alone for one single day. I'm supposed to be the artist here. If anybody is entitled to pull shit, it's me. You're supposed to be the professionals, dammit."

Neither of them responded, if they even heard. That was as far as I needed to take playing grown-up. It was the label's fault they hadn't sent a new tour manager, and the label's fault the band got stuck at a suburban hotel all day while I left with the van to do promotional work solo. My jealousy that they kept bonding and I kept getting left out was best tamped down.

I took their tequila with me and went next door. April lay on the far bed, her back to me, though I had a feeling she was pretending to sleep. The bed looked tempting, but my face broke out if I didn't scrub off my makeup, and I reeked of the podcaster's unfiltered cigarettes. I kicked my smoky clothes to the corner and stepped into the shower. Closed my eyes and let the water hit me. Shampooed my hair, eyes still closed.

I didn't immediately recognize the next sound. Like a school bell, except it kept on signaling. My hazy brain took more than a few seconds to declare it a fire alarm.

"Shit," April said, loud enough for me to hear over the shower. "What is that?"

I shut off the water and regretfully pulled my smoky clothes back onto my wet self. Ditched the underwear, stuffed the bra under my arm. Shoved my feet into my boots, sans socks. "Fire alarm. Though if those yahoos in the next room turn out to be the cause, we're leaving them here and moving on as a duo."

My backpack still lay at the foot of the bed. Wallet, phone, van keys, laptop, tour bible were all in there. I dropped the smoky bra into it, then slung backpack and guitar bag over my right shoulder. If we were talking real fire, those were the possessions I meant to keep.

April trailed me down the hallway, where a flashing light joined the clanging bell. We ran into the guys in the stairwell. JD was naked except for his boxer shorts, gig bag, and tattoos. Hewitt wore the hotel bathrobe, covered in paint; he hadn't grabbed his guitars. One look told me neither of them had pulled the alarm. Other people joined us on the stairs, hurried but not panicked. They gave the guys a wide berth.

The stairs spilled us out into a side parking lot. A crowd already milled on the asphalt, watching the building. A few people sat in their cars, a better idea. A gust of cold wind hit me as I hit the pavement, plastering my wet clothes to my body.

"Get in the van," JD said. "Can't let our singer get sick running around with soapy hair."

"Says the bassist in boxers."

He shrugged, though goose bumps had risen on his arms and legs.

He, April, and I walked past the crowd to where I had

parked the van in the brightest spot available when I got back an hour ago—had it only been an hour ago? I fumbled for the keys in my bag, and we piled in.

"Where'd Hewitt go?" I asked, turning on the van and cranking the heat. My suitcase was still in the room, along with any warm clothes I had with me.

"He hung back to figure out what was going on," JD said. "So it wasn't you guys?"

"Ha-ha. You think we'd pull a stunt like that?"

"You do remember that an hour ago you were showing me a DIY hotel paint job, right?"

"That's different. It didn't hurt anybody. I'd never."

I could have pointed out they'd cause problems for whoever was responsible for cleaning their room after we checked out, or that they might hurt my relationship with the label. But I knew what he meant. Leave these guys too long and they'd get into some stupid human tricks, but they wouldn't have risked panicking sleeping kids. They wouldn't have wanted somebody tripping and falling down the stairs because of a prank. I was pretty sure. I'd only been playing with them for eight months now, but I thought I knew them at least that well.

The back door slid open and Hewitt climbed into the third row. "It's not a fire. Bomb threat."

JD frowned. "Maybe we should get out of here."

"We can't go," I said, giving him a look. "Most of our stuff is still upstairs. Besides, if it's a bomb threat, it'll look bad for us to leave, considering everyone in that stairwell was already giving you guys the side-eye."

JD wasn't calmed. "Shouldn't they be moving people farther from the building if they think there's a bomb? Or going through it with robots or dogs or something?"

Hewitt nodded. "They're waiting for a bomb team."

"Are bomb-sniffing dogs a thing?" April asked. "I thought they were just for drugs."

"There are definitely bomb-sniffing dogs," said JD. "Also bomb-sniffing bees and bomb-sniffing rats, but I think those are used in combat zones, not hotels."

A thought nagged at me. "Wait. Where are the fire trucks?

Or the police? I thought I heard sirens, but they aren't here." Hewitt shrugged. "Busy night, I guess."

We watched for a while. I guessed the people still standing in the parking lot hadn't thought to bring their keys out. A few parents juggled children from hip to hip. I leaned my head against the window and closed my eyes. The others did the same, except JD. He sat tapping a foot against the frame, hard enough to make the whole van shake.

"Will you stop?" April tossed an empty soda can at him. "Try to get some sleep."

That wasn't going to happen. I nudged him. "Grab your bass." He cocked an eyebrow at me. "What?"

"Your bass. Come on."

I climbed into the backseat and returned a moment later with my little practice amp, the one I'd bought with babysitting money when I was fifteen, along with my crappy first guitar. It wasn't the best-sounding amp, but it would do for my purpose. About fifty cold, scared-looking people still stood in the parking lot, the ones who hadn't grabbed their keys or their wallets, who couldn't escape to their cars. If they were stuck, the least we could do was distract them for a little while.

JD found an outlet on the cement island by the parking lot's gate, and we both jacked our guitars. A couple of people reoriented themselves to watch us instead of the hotel.

"What are we playing?" JD asked.

"You pick," I said. "Something cheerful. Something that'll work even if they can't hear the vocals. 'Almost Home,' maybe?"

He didn't answer, but instead started playing the opening bass line. I followed with my guitar part, and then started to sing as loud as I could without straining my voice. I hadn't noticed April following us, but when the second verse started, a scratchy beat locked in with JD, and I glanced behind me to see she was playing a pizza box.

The parents brought their kids over—I imagined them grateful for any diversion at that point—and then others followed. The hotel must have appreciated the distraction, too, since they didn't stop us. The police might have taken issue with a two a.m. concert, but they still hadn't arrived.

We had the crowd now. When we played "Blood and Diamonds," a teenager said, "Mom! They're from SuperStream! They're famous!" My surge of pride accompanying that statement had gotten more familiar, but I still wasn't used to it. I'd never expected anyone to know my songs.

Hewitt had discarded the bathrobe somewhere. I made a mental note to make sure he found it again so we didn't get stuck paying, then remembered it was covered in paint, so we probably owned it now in any case. He danced in front of us wearing a kilt and a band sweatshirt. At least that way the crowd knew who was playing for them. If I were a better shill—if I didn't feel self-conscious doing it—I would have told them about our show the next night at the Peach.

We played eight songs before a haggard-looking hotel manager made his way to us. His upside-down name tag read "Efram Dawkins," and his hair was flat on one side. I wondered where he'd been sleeping.

"I'm sorry," he said.

"It's okay, not a problem, we'll stop." I raised a hand in appeasement.

"No, it's not that. I mean, you probably should stop, but not because there's any problem with the music. I appreciate that you've kept people entertained. But—the police aren't coming. Not before morning."

I laid my hand across my guitar strings. "False alarm? We can go back in?"

"Well, you see, we can't let people back in after a bomb threat without the police clearing the hotel, but the police aren't coming, so we can't let anyone back in at all." The manager massaged the back of his neck with his hand. "Company policy."

A woman who had been dancing with her kid a moment before turned on the guy. "Wait, so you won't let us go back to our rooms to sleep or to get our keys? What are we supposed to do?"

Dawkins shook his head. "I don't know. I'm just telling you what the police said."

"Fine, then you're going to give us a ride to another hotel from your chain, and put us up there, right?"

"I'd love to, but . . ." He paused, glancing around like he hoped someone might bail him out and finish his sentence. Nobody came to his rescue. "I'd love to, but every single hotel in the area received the same threat."

"Every hotel in the chain?"

"No. Every hotel."

"Surely not all the threats are credible?"

Dawkins shrugged. "The police seem to think they're all credible, or they can't tell which are credible and which aren't."

I looked at all the exhausted faces. A minute before they'd been dancing, cheering. Now they looked like two a.m. again.

"This is ridiculous," said a man in saggy white briefs, clutching an attaché case in front of him. "I wouldn't travel anymore at all if I didn't have to. In the last month I've been through three airport evacuations and one 'shelter-in-place' at a restaurant."

An elderly woman spoke. "We must be reasonably safe, or they'd have somebody here. A squad car, a fire chief, a dog. Somebody. They must have some kind of triage going to prioritize."

Dawkins shrugged again.

"Okay, look," I tried. "What about mitigating the risk? Letting one person in at a time to at least get their keys or wallets?"

"I'd love to, but what if there is a bomb? What if it goes off while even one person is in there? Or what if one of you set it? I can't let you do that."

Now my making-the-best-of-it crowd from a few minutes before all eyed each other like there was a killer in our midst. A little boy started crying. "Look," said a father with a sleeping toddler draped over his shoulder. "We need someplace to go."

April stood up from the curb. "Um, I have an idea. A place, you know?"

She wasn't much for public speaking. When the hotel guests all turned her way, she raised her pizza box as a shield. "There's an unlocked Superwally Daycare down the road." She pointed. "They were repainting the playroom in the front, but the paint was low-odor and there's a whole napping room in the back with mats. You have to cross the road, but there aren't too many cars out anymore, right? It's walkable."

April and Hewitt led the group over, while Dawkins made phone calls to the local police to make sure nobody got arrested for trespassing. That left JD and me standing in an empty hotel parking lot.

He sighed. "Wanna play a little more?"

"Might as well."

I'd quit singing an hour before to save my voice, but JD and I were still playing at four a.m. when April and Hewitt made it back.

"Don't you two ever get tired?" Hewitt asked, collapsing onto the grass.

I held out my hand. "My calluses have calluses. Anyway, I'm not awake. I'm dreaming this."

"I'd appreciate if you woke up, then. This is ridiculous."

I'd been running on adrenaline, but now that everyone was gone, exhaustion washed over me. We unplugged the guitars and dragged ourselves back over to the van. I settled into the crumb-covered middle bench, where I could at least get horizontal even if I couldn't stretch out.

"So, where to?" JD asked from the driver's seat.

April, from the bench in front of mine, said, "You're still too drunk to drive. I think we all are."

"I know I am." Hewitt hoisted the gin bottle. "I've been topping up."

"Anyway," I said. "There's no place to go. We've got a show here tomorrow, which is today, so there's no point in driving anyplace else."

"We could go to the next town to sleep."

Hewitt shook his head. "If they evacuated all the hotels in town, every single person who managed to walk out with a car key in their hand when the alarm went off has been asleep in a hotel room in the next town for an hour now. Every town in every direction."

"Night in the van it is." I closed my eyes. "Still more comfortable than my first place in New York. Bigger, too."

"Whoa," said April. "Did she just share a personal detail? She has a past?"

My eyes were still closed so I didn't know if she saw me stick out my tongue at her. "What are you talking about?"

"You're not the most forthcoming person. We've been in this van for eight months and we barely know anything about you."

"There's nothing to tell."

"That's why we've invented an origin story for you from the two things we know—three now—you taught yourself to play guitar in high school, and you're, like, the last person in the world to get a label deal from busking on the street. That's it. That's all we've got, other than this new tidbit, so we've made up the rest. Your parents are werewolves, but you didn't get the gene."

The others chimed in, alternating with each other. "You traded your family cow for a magic guitar."

"You sold your soul at a crosswalk for the ability to play."

"You turned down a life of riches for a chance to play in a band."

"You're from Antarctica, which is why you turn the AC up so high when you're driving, to feel like home." They were joking, but I caught something serious behind it. A challenge to let them in. But what to say? What difference did it make that I'd run away at fifteen rather than tell my frum parents and six siblings I was queer? That I didn't have that word yet, or any other, only the conviction it wasn't safe to say the words I didn't have? Or how just before, little Chava Leah Kanner had wandered into a street fair and heard an electric guitar for the first time? That I'd looked at the guitarist and thought, That's *me*, without any road map for the journey, and everything afterward had been an attempt to reconcile who I'd thought I was supposed to be with who I really was? How when I left Brooklyn for my one off-the-path aunt's apartment in Washington Heights, after months of planning, that first subway ride was a thousand times as long as any drive I'd made since? How I'd only been told of that aunt's existence by someone from an organization that helped people leave the community, and knew I'd be erased from the family in the same way? I couldn't articulate any of that to these people, even after eight months in a van together. Maybe someday, when I trusted they wouldn't joke about it.

"Your version is way more exciting than the truth, I promise.

Like I said, there's nothing to tell."

"Sure," April said. "Just because it's not exciting doesn't mean we don't want to hear it."

She sounded more annoyed than I thought she had the right to be, so I tried to salvage the situation. "But how did you guess about the family cow? I never mentioned Bossie before."

"I knew it!" JD's voice held sarcasm and triumph. "There's always a cow."

The voices quieted, and I knew they were waiting for me to add something real, but I didn't, and the silence stretched until JD's breathing changed and April started to snore.

"Hey," Hewitt whispered as I started to drift. "Luce, are you still awake?"

"Awake enough. What?"

"Percentage impressed versus percentage dismayed?"

"Sorry?" I asked.

"The hotel room."

"Ten percent impressed."

"Only ten? C'mon. It was awesome."

He couldn't see my smile. "Fine. Fifty percent impressed. You get points for creativity. The glo-paint was a nice touch."

If anyone stayed awake after that, I wasn't awake to notice.

Riverland

By Fran Wilde

"Once upon a time . . ."

"Why do you always start like that? Why not someday, or tomorrow?" "Because that's how stories start, Mike. They're already over when you tell them. They're safer that way." "Fine. But make this one scary."

"Okay. Once upon a time, two sisters weren't very good. One sister was sent far away until they could both learn not to back talk or bring trouble, not to get mad or break things, not to cry."

"Didn't anyone notice the sister was gone?"

"No, because their parents replaced her with a better version. One who didn't do bad things."

"That's too scary, Eleanor. Does your head hurt?" "It doesn't hurt."

"You always say that."

"If I say it, it's real. Like a magic spell."

"The sister who was sent away—what happened?"

"She made a magic spell that let her visit home whenever she wanted. But their father discovered that she kept coming back, because he'd been replaced too, by a troll, long ago, and trolls can smell kids really well. He made the girls' mother, who was a witch—a mostly good one—magic the house to keep the disappeared sister out and the other sister safe. And to keep anyone else from noticing that a troll and a witch lived in a nice house and not under a bridge somewhere."

"You sure it doesn't hurt?"

"Nothing hurts. Are you going to listen or not?" "I'm listening."

"But the remaining sister knew that, when she followed the rules, sometimes her mother's magic would ease and the other sister could come home. She would hide under the bed and wait until her sister appeared. And they'd stay in that safe place, where the troll and the witch couldn't find them. They'd stay until morning whispering their own magic spells. Trying to get them to work."

"Eleanor, I don't want anyone to go away."

"Poppa was just joking, Mike. I'm not going away." "Can I say our spell now?"

"Not yet. Shhhh."

. . .

"They're loud tonight."

"It's the stress. He'll be better soon. Momma said." "Keep telling the story."

"The sisters stayed together for a long time in this way. But there was a price for these visits. If the one sister stayed past sunrise, she had to disappear for good, or they'd both disappear."

"I don't like that story. Tell a better one. A better spell." "You can try yours now, if you want."

"Now?"

"Yup."

"Someday . . . our real parents will come for us."

Chapter One
House Magic Rules

Some days, my sister and I could sense trouble coming. Other days, like the weather, it caught us by surprise.

Today, from up the hill where the school bus dropped us off, our house looked trouble-free. Safe.

Momma had been busy.

The blue clapboard box with its wooden shutters anchored our cul-de-sac like it had been on Riverland Road forever, which it pretty much had. Mike's small purple bicycle leaned on my larger blue one in the shade of the garage. Our lawn, smooth all the way to the shoreline and carefully cleared of leaves, wrapped the house like arms with hands clasped at the pale concrete driveway.

Everything seemed perfect.

Better than perfect: The house didn't look magicked at all.

But today still felt like trouble. That's why I wasn't in a rush to go home.

If I was lucky, Pendra would invite me over. Her house was closer to our bus stop.

I formed the beginning of a wish—to be honest, it was more of a spell—in my mind. A spell that would turn Pendra toward her house, not mine. Two words: *Please, Pen.*

But Pendra Sarti had other ideas. She was looking down the hill too.

"We always go to my house," she said like she'd read my mind. "We haven't been to yours since summer. You always have some excuse. And you still have my book. We'll get it and then we can sit on the dock and work on our science posters until the rain comes."

As the bus, empty now, rolled away from our development, Pendra adjusted her backpack and ignored my frown. She started down the hill.

Spells never worked that well for me. Not even in the stories I told Mike, even if she did believe them.

And it *had* been months since Pendra had come over. Poppa was trying to buy more of the land around us in order to grow the development he'd named Riverland, after the road we lived on. He was stressed out a lot. That shouldn't have mattered, but it did. We had so many new rules.

The dock, Pendra's favorite place to sit, was just visible behind the house. The old wooden frame was mostly barnacles and cracking planks. Once, a dinghy had bobbed beside it. I'd seen pictures. But now, as river and wind whipped together into meringue-peaked waves, the dock swayed. The leaves on the trees near the house flipped over to their silver sides.

"Storm's going to be here too fast," I said hopefully, catching up to her as we neared her house. If it rained, Pendra and I couldn't sit outside. "We'd better wait. Your house instead."

But Pendra shook her head. "Yours." Her elbow poked me in the side, nudging me down the hill. "Mine's always a mess. Yours? Your mom waves a hand and cookies appear. My brothers are home and loud. Mike's not there to bother us."

I bristled about Mike. "Bothering is what little kids do. I don't mind it."

"You minded it this morning on the bus. You got so angry." That was low. Mike's big mouth was why Pendra was insisting on going down the hill now.

"She was just kidding about the house." From where I stood, the beginnings of the late fall sunset hit a second-floor window and reflected off the blue fishing float—what the locals called a witch ball—hanging on the landing.

Everything in its place.

"Besides, no one's home." Momma had taken Mike to buy shoes after school. And a house rule was no surprise guests, especially if Momma wasn't home. I reached for excuses. "Poppa's working hard on the permits for the Lawton Farm." Definitely no cookies to be had at the wave of a hand today.

"El, no one's at my house either. What's the difference?"

Pendra was impossible to refuse when she wanted something. And what she wanted right now was to brainstorm science projects at my house. Preferably with cookies. Where she could look for magic. "Mike said . . ."

I knew what Mike had said.

She'd blurted to her friend Kalliope on the bus that morning: *Momma's doing house magic and I get to help her.*

I'd kicked the back of the seat and she'd gone quiet. Kalliope had shrugged it away with an *I bet you don't* and Mike hadn't replied.

All better.

But Pendra had heard. And she was as interested in magic as anyone.

The difference, magic or no, I wanted to say now, *is that your house is easy. Mine is hard.*

There were rules for my house Pendra didn't understand. Only my sister, Mary (everyone called her Mike, except Poppa), and I knew them all. Bringing Pendra home would break a rule, and rules helped the magic go.

At least, that's how I explained it to Mike when she was upset. No rules, no magic. No magic, everything would break and stay broken. And in our house, broken things disappeared.

I crossed my arms over my fleece jacket and cupped my elbows in my hands so the fuzz warmed my palms. I rocked a little on my heels, and the road grit ground beneath the thin rubber soles of my sneakers.

"We can't have surprise guests," I said. It was a big rule, based on how many times Momma had said it to both Mike and me. "And the difference is your house is noisy and happy even when no one's home. Mine's all creaks and groans," I finally argued. I wasn't lying. Our house was especially loud when the magic wasn't working.

I wished Mike were here. Pendra and I would go to her

house then, at least until dinner. Problem solved.

Or else Pendra would try to drag more magic stories out of Mike. Problem not solved.

But Mike wasn't here and the temperature was falling fast. Gray clouds gained a greenish tint over the rough water. The smell of a dead fish carried almost all the way up the hill.

Two gulls cut tight circles over the beach but kept getting blown off course.

And Pendra kept walking away from her house and the bus stop. Her feet aimed past the three houses on the hill, down to the end of the street, to my house.

I wasn't one bit surprised my spell didn't work. They rarely did for me. And rain wasn't enough to put Pendra off.

I tried stubborn next. Stopped where I was and raised an eyebrow. Tilted my chin, leaning back toward Pendra's house. I tried to pull my friend that way, like the fishermen we sometimes watched work the river. I cranked a bright smile. "Come on, Pen, your house is closer. We can work on algorithms once we figure out the science project."

I didn't want to fight. Not with Pendra. Not with anyone. The Sartis had moved three houses up from us that summer, into my friend Aja's old house. It hadn't taken long for Pendra's dad and mine to get in an argument and for Pendra and me to become friends.

Pendra said what she wanted. She did things and didn't worry about the consequences. Like now.

Her mouth curved, a half-smile. Her brown eyes crinkled at the corners. She turned again and continued walking down the hill, past the next house, toward mine. Her sneakers flashed silver in the afternoon light.

My feet wouldn't move.

"El, come on. I want *The Hobbit* back for the weekend. You've had it too long, and if you can't take care of my books, we simply can't be friends." She was kidding. The laugh at the end said she was. Still, I grumbled. "If you like paper better than people, maybe we can't be friends either."

She slowed but didn't stop. Overhead, heavy clouds pressed the sun into stormlight and made her cheeks glow.

"We have the sleepover at my house this weekend and the science fair. Let's not fight. Come on," Pendra said, without turning around to see if I was following. Her dark hair swung side to side as she picked up speed. "We'll sit on the dock and decide our topic once and for all. What's stopping us?"

I pressed my lips together. Nothing was stopping us. Everything was.

Four months ago, when I'd hesitated over a pile of books at the library, Pendra had stepped up beside me at the desk. The librarian had squinted at her. Said to me, "You still have two out. Can't have these yet." And I'd felt my face heat up.

"I forgot," I finally said. I hadn't, but it was a good spell. One that worked, usually.

Pendra had elbowed me. "You're our neighbor, right? Eleanor Prine?"

I'd nodded, and she'd added my books to her own pile. "All of these, please." She'd deployed an enormous smile. One I learned later almost no adult could resist.

The librarian shrugged. "They're *your* fines if she doesn't bring them back."

Pendra nodded solemnly but cut a glance at me and winked.

Saved.

I was so jealous someone could just *do* that. I kept myself from staring by grabbing my books and wrapping them in my jacket.

"My dad can give you a ride home too. It's raining," Pendra said.

A second save. I couldn't let her do it. Too embarrassing.

"Thanks, but I like to walk." If I drove with them, we stood a good chance of passing my dad on the road. I'd made him mad. He'd left me to walk back from the library on my own. In the rain. A lesson. If I didn't take the lesson, there might be other consequences.

I squeezed out the heavy library door and down the road, starting the long walk back on the overpass sidewalk. By then it was pouring. Halfway there, as cars roared along the highway below, the Sartis' car squeaked to a halt and the door opened.

"No discussion, Eleanor!" Mr. Sarti had called. "Can't let *my* books get wet," Pendra added.

I wiped the rain off my face with the back of my hand.

She'd passed me a towel, whispering, "Sorry it smells like the dogs." And then she started telling a story about riding the metro from their old apartment into the city as I tried to sit as close to the edge of the seat as possible so I wouldn't get everything wet. I'd nearly laughed myself dry when she'd said everyone should take boats around Baltimore. She'd never seen Poppa try to handle a boat.

By the time we got back to the growing development that surrounded my house, we were friends.

Pendra and I, and sometimes Mike, spent a lot of time together that summer. Our dads still growled at each other, but they let us alone. There wasn't anyone else my age in the development, not since Aja's family had moved to the other side of the highway.

We'd taken advanced swim lessons together—Pendra's mom had insisted. We'd gone to the library. Sweated out the slow summer days on my dock, Mrs. Sarti insisting that Pendra put on sunscreen every time Mike and I did, which Pendra thought was ridiculous. "I don't need it nearly as much as you do," she'd laughed.

That had lasted until school began. Until the house started needing a lot more magicking again. Then I'd found more excuses to spend time at Pendra's. Sometimes with Mike along. And now Mike had let our secret slip and wasn't here to help me fix it.

What's stopping you?

I couldn't answer that. My heart started spider-crawling up my throat, tickling at the sides until I had to cough. Pendra didn't slow. Didn't turn around.

She was almost halfway down the hill.

There was one thing that might at least stall her. Pendra loved magic stories as much as I did. If I told her Mike had been right and there was house magic, she might listen, at least long enough for Momma to get home.

But I couldn't.

That was the most important rule. No talking to anyone about house magic.

If we talked too much, then house magic would absolutely stop working.

And if the magic stopped working, Mike or I might disappear. I ran down the hill after my friend.

• • •

Just before the hill started to level out, I caught up to Pendra. Our sneakers mashed the gravel side by side. A splot of rain hit my nose. "Not for long, okay? And I have to go in first. We can't bother my dad if he's there."

"You just said no one was home." Pendra switched her orange-and-pink backpack to the other shoulder. She kept walking.

"I forgot. It will probably be okay." My own backpack felt heavier the closer I got to the bottom of the hill. *Say okay, Pendra. Please.*

More terrible spells. Why couldn't I just say *no*?

Because Pendra might just leave and maybe find other friends.

And then . . .

Well, everyone left. Right? Aja had moved across the highway, and I didn't care—much. But I didn't want Pendra to go, too.

When I fished my key from the inner jacket pocket, the cold metal and the blue plastic ring around the rim against my finger felt solid. Nearly unbreakable. "Just give me a minute." I passed her quickly so she didn't have a second to reconsider or press me about going into the house with me.

Because no matter how safe it looked from the outside, I didn't know if the inside had been magicked yet.

That morning, when Mike and I left to catch the bus, a pile of torn-up photographs littered the living room, trailing all the way to the fireplace. Three broken frames lay in the foyer, plus the mirror, next to what was left of the white vase. As the front door closed, we'd overheard Momma phoning the cleaning lady, asking her to come another day.

The house had been full of trouble then, but Momma was going to work until it was better.

"Big house magic can't be done by the usual people, right Eleanor?" Mike had whispered knowingly on our way out the door.

"Right. And we have to help too. Don't notice anything's different when we get back. Don't say anything to Momma." Mike and I had our own house magic. Lesser spells but still important. "Don't break any more rules." That's what I'd told her on the way up the hill.

Mike had chewed on her finger and nodded. I took her hand and squeezed so she wouldn't tear at her cuticles. "We can do it."

But then she'd repeated what I'd said on the bus.

If Mike had come home instead of going shopping with

Momma, none of this would have happened. Or if Pendra had listened. Or if my spells actually worked.

Say it's okay, Pendra. Say you understand.

I shifted the straps on my backpack, tightening them.

Pendra slowed as we neared the walkway. "Okay," she finally said. "Don't be such a worrier."

Easy for her to say.

By the time she joined me on the stoop, I'd undone the lock and cracked the door just wide enough for me. "Back as fast as I can," I said as I slipped through.

Behind me, Pendra sighed. "Fine, fine." She dropped her backpack with a thud and a rustle as the weight of her notebooks tilted the bag over. She sat down on the stoop just as noisily. "Your mom's a much better hostess than you, El."

I couldn't care. Not until I made sure the house was safe on the inside too.

The door clicked shut behind me and I set my purple backpack down soundlessly on the foyer floor. Laid my jacket over it inside out, ready to throw on if I needed to leave.

At Pendra's house, the entry hall was always a swirl of mail, backpacks, boots, dogs, a cat, and sports equipment. Since that first day they'd given me a ride from the library and Poppa had come to find me there, the jumble had kind of swooped me up too. Did I want a snack? Watch out for the dogs! Did I want to stay for dinner? (Yes, very much.) Someone laughing upstairs. So much fun that I'd forgotten the time.

"You're welcome always," Mrs. Sarti had pretty much sung from the kitchen then as I rushed out the door, and every time she saw me outside of school after that too. Being there felt like spring sun on bare skin—warm and comforting.

In my house this afternoon, the foyer sparkled. A new vase with heirloom roses in it lined up against the mirror over the entry table. I didn't waste time looking in the mirror as I passed—I knew I was a windblown mess.

My sigh of relief bubbled up on its own as I looked into the living room.

Momma's house magic had fixed everything while we'd been at school.

The broken glass and china were gone, like always. A new game console sat in the same place as the one that had crashed to the floor last night. The television screen had actually grown larger.

I almost loved this kind of magic. The kind where nothing was really lost, only bettered.

Nothing that mattered to the house was lost, that is.

Mike and I? We both worked really hard to matter, but sometimes we made mistakes.

In the living room, one new silver frame had the word *happiness* engraved on it. There wasn't any photo inside yet. The black mat looked like a hole.

House magic wasn't perfect, which was okay. I'd read enough books to know that no magic was. Still, Momma needed us to believe in it so that others would too.

And this was good enough magicking that Pendra wouldn't notice anything wrong. I swung the front door wide. "Come on, but don't shout. Your book's up in my room."

Mike would be sad *The Hobbit* was gone. I'd been reading it to her under the bed, some nights. I loved watching her expressions at each surprise, her excitement about the ponies and wizards. "But not the trolls." She only liked *my* stories with trolls, she'd said.

Now, Pendra jumped up from the stoop and swept through the door. Her hair hung straight, unbothered by the wind, all the way to her jeans pockets. When she shook her head, it made a beautiful curve, then settled back down. My own hair would barely stay in its braids.

Maybe it wouldn't rain. Maybe we could take our books outside soon. Then no one would know I'd broken a rule.

After Pendra dropped her coat and backpack in a jumble beside mine, we both took the stairs two at a time to the landing. That's what got my heart beating so loud, laughing quietly and climbing stairs at the same time.

For luck, I brushed a fingertip over the old glass witch ball that hung on the landing. Cool and reassuring, the smooth surface an illusion: small, stilled ripples and bubbles met my touch. Then the deep blue sphere swung gently on its cord, the glass strands inside picking up the last afternoon light and throwing it on the walls. Hand-size and weighty, the ball had been Momma's great-grandmother's, brought over from Norway.

It was the last of a net full of floats from when the Favre family—Gran's last name—used to fish the neck of the river until everyone started using foam buoys.

Pendra reached out too, but her hand hovered just above the sphere. "It always looks like a water bubble hanging in the air," she whispered. "That's probably part of the magic, right?"

My fingers stuttered on the glass, then stilled the ball in its sudden, broader swing.

She meant the float, not the house. I'd told her once how the colorful balls had supported fishing nets here in the nineteenth century, that the threads fascinated fish, luring them to the trap. That they were all very scientific, the fishing floats. Even one that hung alone on our landing, capturing light.

But Pendra had heard Momma call the float a witch ball once, and the idea that it was magic had caught, just like Mike's words had stuck today.

The bauble fascinated Pendra as much as anything in the house.

"Not everything can be magic," I laughed. "Most things are just superstition."

Pendra stuck her tongue out at me, then flipped her retainer in her mouth the way she did sometimes when she was thinking. I envied the trick, even if it was a little gross.

I let go of the ball. "They're supposed to catch evil spirits before they can harm a house, I looked it up." Pendra's face lit hopefully, and she leaned closer, like she was looking to see what the ball had caught. "I love them, but the ones in the shops are all fakes. This one's real."

"Real, like magic real," Pendra mused. She didn't listen. "They catch fish, that's all." I tried to move her down the hallway. If I was truthful, I loved the float too, but not because it might be magic. I loved it because no matter what else broke during the night here, the witch ball stayed untouched. Unbroken.

Even though it was made of glass, it was the longest-lived object in the house. I wanted to be that strong. That beautiful.

Pendra's retainer clicked another circuit. "Know what isn't magic? Two brothers and all their gym clothes, everywhere. And being the youngest. Even the dogs are older than me. In dog years." She inhaled deeply. "Your house smells nice, like the river. My house smells like sports gear."

I sniffed. I didn't smell anything much. Maybe a little freshener to conceal the fireplace-burnt-photograph smell. "Come on, Pen." *Let's just get the book and get out before anyone comes home.* My turquoise Converse All Stars kicked up the pile in the tan carpet. So did Pendra's silver Keds. We left a trail of scuff-marks in the neat vacuum swaths all down the hall, but it would have looked the same if Mike and I did it, so I didn't worry too much.

A closed door on my parents' side of the house blocked light from the brightest windows. The hallway, lined with relatives' photographs going all the way back to when Favres lived here and not Prines—and even further than that—was dark except for the light thrown by the witch ball. Some photos glittered in the shadows, silvered with age. Grandparents and great-grands. A few older still.

"Did you know any of them?" Pendra's voice was quiet. Her grandfather had died over the summer, right after they moved. I wished we'd been better friends then. It felt strange to say sorry now.

"Only Momma's mom is still alive and she travels a lot. The last time she came here was when Mike was a baby." I couldn't remember Gran's voice. Just her face. But my memory was grainy and black-and-white, just like the photographs.

Momma said they'd fought once but wouldn't say why.

At the far end of the hallway, as far as you could get from my parents' room, Momma had her own photo with Gran by the dock. The dinghy bobbed, its dock line wrapped in a half-hitch around a piling. Momma wore a white dress. Neither she nor Gran looked very happy. The photograph inside the frame had been taped back together, twice.

The light from Mike's room made the new frame on the photograph shine.

Like the witch ball, few of the heirloom frames besides that photo required house magic to fix. Mostly just Gran's. The rest seemed impervious and smelled slightly stale, like old books.

I liked old things. They lasted.

Sometimes, especially when no one was home, I wondered what it would feel like to break one. Sometimes I almost got mad enough to try. But I never did.

Pendra lingered, looking at the other photographs. "Imagine what this place was like when there were no other houses but yours." She reached out to touch a frame.

"Lots of fishing and crabbing and farming." I echoed Poppa's sales pitch for the development. "A lot of hard work." One last farm remained near our property. Poppa was trying to buy it so he could add more houses by the river. "Before the farms, there was a fishing camp. Before that? The Susquehannock and the Algonquin." Mike and I had looked it up at the library last summer. "Come on, Pen. Do you want your book or not?"

"It's just so quiet here," Pendra said, closing her eyes.

It wouldn't be quiet for long. We were going too slowly. Someone would be home soon, and if it was Momma, that was mostly fine.

We hurried past the guest bedroom, kept ready though no one ever stayed there. Down to the two rooms at the end of the hall. Mike's, then mine. Connected by a shared bath.

Mike's door was open. Mint-green walls, all the lights on.

The space clean and neat.

Pendra lingered, looking back at the witch ball again.

At the end of the hall, the door to my bright turquoise room stood open. "Oh." I could barely breathe.

My sneakers crackled static across the carpet, I moved so fast.

Everything in my room had been straightened. "Oh no."

My notebooks and sketchpads were stacked magazine-perfect. But that didn't matter. Those were decoys.

The dolls too. They'd been arranged against the wall, by period. The room felt smaller, then larger, too hot, then too cold by turns. *Calm down, Eleanor, they're just dolls.* The pioneer doll, then the Victorian. The one from New Orleans, the World War I doll. The dolls from India and China. I rarely played with them, but Grandma Favre had sent them, so I kept them nearby, in their boxes. Now they were on display.

Words I'd heard often but couldn't say pricked my tongue. Curses that would maybe not shock Pendra because of her brothers, but ones that would absolutely crack house magic. Much worse than *dammit* and other words.

"What's wrong?" Pendra, suddenly right behind me. I startled and she held up a hand. "El, you're so jumpy. What is it?"

I couldn't answer. Breath held, I dropped to the floor and lifted the thick bed skirt. A row of tiny bells jangled a merry warning.

"What are you doing?"

Nothing. Everything. "Just checking something. Shhhh." I tried to sound cool, but there I was, crawling on my carpet in broad daylight in front of my friend.

In the shadows, the space beneath the bed looked undisturbed. The old pillows were there. A blanket. The Halloween lights. Just like Mike and I had left them.

Pendra crawled under the bed with me. "You still make forts!" Her voice was right in my ear. The bed frame was close above our heads, and Pendra's shoulder pressed mine. "A bit low though."

"It's for Mike, when she can't sleep," I said, scanning the shadows, looking for *The Hobbit*. Not there. I startled and hit my head on the wooden slats of the old frame. Ow. On an old bruise too. But, Pendra's book. My eyes itched, and not from the carpet.

There were only two books under the bed now, not three. A book on birds. An old book about a tollbooth.

The Tolkien was missing.

I scootched back out, carpet fibers grating my elbows. Knelt by the bedside table, counting books: *one two three four five six seven eight*—not there either. Had it been magicked?

House magic didn't come into bedrooms unless a rule was broken. Mike and I had been so careful lately.

I winced at a memory from the night before: I'd slammed a door. I'd lost my temper. I'd yelled. I'd been so tired of the shouting from downstairs and Mike snuggled tight against me asking if I could make it all stop.

I'd made it worse instead.

Momma and Poppa slammed doors too, but their rules were different. I should have stayed under the bed.

That was our safest place. No one knew about it except Mike and me. House magic had never gotten under the bed before.

"Pendra, don't tell anyone, okay?"

She didn't hear me. She was looking in every corner, as if she might find something magical there. But she wouldn't even find the missing book.

In the entire house, not one place was safe anymore. For a moment, I wished I were small enough to crawl inside the glass float. Maybe that was safe. Because now I had to tell Pendra I'd lost her book, and then I had to get her out of the house before she decided to search everywhere.

I felt panic build. We were going to get caught.

Once, Mike had gotten chocolate on one of Pendra's books, and now I had to promise to never eat over a book when I borrowed one. It had been months. But a lost book? "It was right there."

This wasn't magic. This was just mean.

I crawled backward until the bed skirt ruffled my hair. Then I sat back on my knees and looked all around the room. Pendra's feet and legs stuck out from under the bed. Striped leggings, the hem of a pink skirt. "Maybe it's under a pillow?" The bed skirt rang merrily as she moved around. Jarring music for my growing doom.

While she searched, I checked one more thing. Not a book, not at all, but still a good gauge of the doom. "Please be there," I whispered to the house. I flipped back the blue comforter and picked up the pillow. I'd tucked the edge of the pillowcase in, so it didn't flap or look sloppy.

Pendra's sneakers wriggled under the bed. "I don't know how you and Mike both fit under here," she said.

Practice. I bit my lip. If Pendra knew how much time we spent under there, telling stories, I know she'd look at me funny.

I unfolded the edge of the pillowcase and reached inside. The pillow's rough seam was still safety-pinned together, a good sign. Careful not to prick my fingers, I unclipped the pin, then reached into the foam insert. I pried off the piece I'd cut away then pasted back together with washi tape. My fingers touched the hard weight of the small paring knife I'd stolen last spring from the kitchen.

It was a tiny theft. So far our parents hadn't noticed. So many things came and went in the house.

But on days when I worried about disappearing too much, it helped me feel better. Even if I didn't know what I'd use it for. I had it, and that was what mattered.

It was the most daring thing I'd ever done.

But I couldn't ever brag to Pendra or Mike, or anyone that I'd done it.

If slamming a door got books magicked away, a stolen knife would be far, far worse trouble. I smoothed the foam down and stuck the tape back in place, repinned the pillow, and refolded the outer case. The pillow went back on the bed and the comforter over it in one well-practiced move.

A shadow darkened the window and I jumped again. Just a heron landing on the tree outside. Spying on fish in the river maybe. The afternoon sun had cast its shadow far into my room. I relaxed my fingers, which had curled up tight into fists.

"Bad bird," I murmured. "Go lurk in someone else's tree." We still needed to leave the house. "Come on, Pen." The words came out sharper than I meant them to.

Pendra slid out from beneath the bed. She'd gotten pale carpet fuzz on her leggings and yellow T-shirt. She began to brush it off slowly, not looking at me. "Hey, Eleanor, don't worry. Take three deep breaths and let them out slow. That always helps me relax."

Three deep breaths weren't going to cut it with a missing book and family bound to come home soon.

"Did you find the book?" she asked.

"No, nothing." I braced for a proper scolding. I hoped that was all I'd get.

Downstairs, the front door opened and shut. "Eleanor?" Momma. "Who's here with you?"

Worse and worse.

Anxiety is the Dizziness of Freedom

By Ted Chiang

Nat could have used a cigarette, but company policy forbade smoking in the store, so all she could do was get more and more nervous. Now it was a quarter to four, and Morrow still hadn't returned. She wasn't sure how she'd explain things if he didn't get back in time. She sent him a text asking where he was. A chime sounded as the front door opened, but it wasn't Morrow. A guy with an orange sweater came in. "Hello? I have a prism to sell?"

Nat put her phone away. "Let's take a look at it."

He came over and put the prism on the counter; it was a new model, the size of a briefcase. Nat slid it around so she could see the numeric readout at one end: the activation date was only six months ago, and more than 90 percent of its pad was still available. She unfolded the keyboard to reveal the display screen, tapped the online button, and then waited. A minute went by. "He might have run into some traffic," said Orange Sweater uncertainly.

"It's fine," said Nat.

After another minute the ready light came on. Nat typed

Keyboard test.

A few seconds later a reply came back:

Looks good.

She switched to video mode, and the text on the screen was replaced by a grainy image of her own face looking back at her.

Her parallel self nodded at her and said, “Mic test.”

“Loud and clear,” she replied.

The screen reverted to text. Nat hadn’t recognized the necklace her paraself had been wearing; if they wound up buying the prism, she’d have to ask her where she got it. She looked back at the guy with the orange sweater and quoted him a price.

His disappointment was obvious. “Is that all?”

“That’s what it’s worth.”

“I thought these things got more valuable over time.”

“They do, but not right away. If this was five years old, we’d be having a different conversation.”

“What about if the other branch has something really interesting going on?”

“Yeah, that’d be worth something.” Nat pointed at his prism. “Does the other branch have something interesting going on?”

“I . . . don’t know.”

“You’ll have to do the research yourself and bring it to us if you want a better offer.”

Orange Sweater hesitated.

“If you want to think it over and come back later, we’re always here.”

“Can you give me a minute?”

“Take your time.”

Orange Sweater got on the keyboard and had a brief typed exchange with his paraself. When he was done, he said, “Thanks, we’ll be back later.” He folded the prism up and left.

The last customer in the store had finished chatting and was ready to check out. Nat went to the carrel he’d been using, checked the data usage on the prism, and carried it back to the storeroom. By the time she had finished ringing him up, the three customers with four o'clock appointments had arrived, including the one who needed the prism Morrow had with him. "Just a minute," she told them, "and I'll get you checked in." She went to the storeroom and brought out the prisms for the two other customers. She had just set them up in their carrels when Morrow came through the front door, elbows splayed as he carried a big cardboard carton. She met him at the counter. "You're cutting it close," she whispered, glaring at him. "Yeah, yeah, I know the schedule."

Morrow took the oversize box into the storeroom and came out with the prism. He set it up in a carrel for the third customer with seconds to spare. At four o'clock, the ready lights on all three prisms came on, and all three customers began chatting with their paraselves.

Nat followed Morrow into the office behind the front counter. He took a seat at the desk as if nothing had happened. "Well?" she asked. "What took you so long?"

"I was talking to one of the aides at the home." Morrow had just come back from seeing one of their customers. Jessica Oehlsen was a widow in her seventies with few friends and whose only son was more of a burden than a comfort. Almost a year ago she'd started coming in once a week to talk with her paraself; she always reserved one of the private booths so she could use voice chat. A couple months ago she had fractured her hip in a bad fall, and now she was in a nursing home. Since she couldn't come to the store, Morrow brought the prism to her every week so she could continue her regular conversations; it was a violation of SelfTalk's company policy, but she paid him for the favor. "He filled me in about Mrs. Oehlsen's condition."

"What about it?"

"She's got pneumonia now," said Morrow. "He said it

happens a lot after a broken hip."

"Really? How does a broken hip lead to pneumonia?"

"According to this guy, it's because they don't move around a lot and they're zonked on oxy, so they never take a deep breath. Anyway, Mrs. Oehlsen's definitely got it."

"Is it serious?"

"The aide thinks she'll be dead within a month, two tops."

"Wow. That's too bad."

"Yeah." Morrow scratched his chin with his blunt, square fingertips. "But it gave me an idea."

That was no surprise. "So what is it this time?"

"I won't need you on this one. I can handle it by myself."

"Fine by me. I've got enough to do."

"Right, you've got a meeting to go to tonight. How's that going?"

Nat shrugged. "It's hard to tell. I think I'm making progress."

• • •

Every prism—the name was a near acronym of the original designation, "Plaga interworld signaling mechanism"—had two LEDs, one red and one blue. When a prism was activated, a quantum measurement was performed inside the device, with two possible outcomes of equal probability: one outcome was indicated by the red LED lighting up, while the other was indicated by the blue one. From that moment forward, the prism allowed information transfer between two branches of the universal wave function. In colloquial terms, the prism created two newly divergent timelines, one in which the red LED lit up and one in which the blue one did, and it allowed communication between the two.

Information was exchanged using an array of ions, isolated in magnetic traps within the prism. When the prism was activated and the universal wave function split into two branches, these ions remained in a state of coherent superposition, balanced on a knife's edge and accessible to either branch. Each ion could be used to send a single bit of information, a yes or a no, from one branch to the other. The act of reading that yes/no caused the ion to decohere, permanently knocking it off the knife's edge and onto one side. To send another bit, you needed another ion. With an array of ions, you could transmit a string of bits that encoded text; with a long-enough array, you could send images, sound, even video.

The upshot was that a prism wasn't like a radio connecting the two branches; activating one didn't power up a transmitter whose frequency you could keep tuning into. It was more like a notepad that the two branches shared, and each time a message was sent, a strip of paper was torn off the top sheet. Once the notepad was exhausted, no more information could be exchanged and the two branches went on their separate ways, incommunicado forever after.

Ever since the invention of the prism, engineers had been working to add more ions to the array and increase the size of the notepad. The latest commercial prisms had pads that were a gigabyte in size. That was enough to last a lifetime if all you were exchanging was text, but not all consumers were satisfied with that. Many wanted the ability to have a live conversation, preferably with video; they needed to hear their own voice or see their own face looking back at them. Even low-resolution, low-frame-rate video could burn through a prism's entire pad in a matter of hours; people tended to use it only occasionally, relying on text or audio-only communications most of the time in order to make their prism last for as long as possible.

• • •

Dana's regular four o'clock appointment was a woman named Teresa. Teresa had been a client for just over a year; she had sought out therapy primarily because of her difficulty in maintaining a long-term romantic relationship. Dana had initially thought her issues stemmed from her parents' divorce when she was a teenager, but now she suspected that Teresa was prone to seeking better alternatives. In their session last week, Teresa had told her that she had recently run into an ex-boyfriend of hers; five years ago she had turned down a marriage proposal from him, and now he was happily married to someone else. Dana expected that they would continue talking about that today.

Teresa often started her sessions with pleasantries, but not this time. As soon as she sat down she said, "I went to Crystal Ball during my lunch break today."

Already suspecting the answer, Dana asked, "What did you ask them about?"

"I asked them if they could find out what my life would look like if I had married Andrew."

"And what did they say?"

"They said maybe. I hadn't realized how it worked; a man there explained it to me." Teresa didn't ask if Dana was familiar with it. She needed to talk it through, which was fine; she was often able to untangle her thoughts that way with only slight prompting from Dana. "He said that my decision to marry Andrew or not didn't cause two timelines to branch off, that only activating a prism does that. He said they could look at the prisms they had that had been activated in the months before Andrew proposed. They would send requests to the parallel versions of Crystal Ball in those branches, and their employees would look up the parallel versions of me and see if any of them were married to him. If one of me was, they could interview her and tell me what she said. But he said there was no guarantee that they'd find such a branch, and it cost money just to send the requests, so they would have to charge me whether they found one or not. Then, if I want them to interview the parallel version of me, there'd be a separate charge for that. And because they'd be using prisms that are five years old, everything would be expensive."

Dana was glad to hear that Crystal Ball had been honest about their claims; she knew there were data brokers out there that promised results they couldn't deliver. "So what did you do?"

"I didn't want to do anything without talking to you first."

"Okay," said Dana, "let's talk. How did you feel after the consultation?"

"I don't know. I hadn't considered the possibility that they might not be able to find a branch where I said yes to Andrew. Why wouldn't they be able to find a branch like that?"

Dana considered trying to lead Teresa to the answer herself, but decided it wasn't necessary. "It could mean that your decision to reject him wasn't a close call. It may have felt like you were on the fence, but in fact you weren't; your decision to turn him down was based on a deep feeling, not a whim."

Teresa looked thoughtful. "That might be a good thing to know. I wonder if I ought to just have them do the search first. If they don't find a version of me that married Andrew, then I can just stop."

"And if they do find a version that married Andrew, how likely is it that you'll ask them to interview her?"

She sighed. "A hundred percent."

"So what does that tell you?"

"I guess it tells me that I shouldn't have them do the search unless I'm sure I want to know the answer."

"And do you want to know the answer?" asked Dana. "No,

let's put it another way. What would you like the answer to be, and what are you afraid it might be?"

Teresa paused for a minute. Eventually she said, "I guess what I'd like to find out is that a version of me married Andrew and then divorced him because he wasn't the right guy for me. What I'm afraid of finding out is that a version of me married him and is now blissfully happy. Is that petty of me?"

"Not at all," said Dana. "Those are perfectly understandable feelings."

"I suppose I just have to decide if I'm willing to take the risk."

"That's one way to think about it."

"What's another?"

"Another would be to consider whether anything you learn about the other branch would actually be helpful. It could be that nothing you find out about some other branch will change your situation here in this branch."

Teresa frowned as she thought it over. "Maybe it wouldn't change anything, but I'd feel better knowing that I had made the right decision." She went silent, and Dana waited. Then Teresa asked, "Do you have other clients who've gone to data brokers?"

Dana nodded. "Many."

"In general, do you think it's a good idea to use one of these services?"

"I don't think there's a general answer to that. It depends entirely on the individual."

"And you're not going to tell me whether or not I should do it."

Dana smiled. "You know that's not my role."

"I know, I just figured it couldn't hurt to ask." After a moment, Teresa said, "I've heard that some people become obsessed with prisms."

"Yes, that can happen. I actually facilitate a support group for people whose prism use has become an issue for them."

"Really?" Teresa seemed briefly tempted to ask for details, but instead she said, "And you're not going to warn me away from using Crystal Ball's services?"

"Some people have issues with alcohol, but I'm not going to advise my clients to never take a drink."

"I suppose that makes sense." Teresa paused, and then asked, "Have you ever used one of these services yourself?"

Dana shook her head. "No, I haven't."

"Have you ever been tempted?"

"Not really."

She looked at Dana curiously. "Don't you ever wonder if you made the wrong choice?"

I don't have to wonder; I know. But aloud Dana said, "Of course. But I try to focus on the here and now."

• • •

The two branches connected by a prism start out as perfectly identical except for the result of the quantum measurement. If a person has resolved to base a huge decision on the measurement—"If the blue LED lights up, I will detonate this bomb; otherwise, I will disarm it"—then the two branches will diverge in an obvious manner. But if no one takes any action as a result of the measurement, how much will the two branches diverge? Can a single quantum event by itself lead to visible changes between the two branches? Is it possible for broader historical forces to be studied using prisms?

These questions had been a matter of debate ever since the first demonstration of communication with a prism. When prisms with pads about a hundred kilobytes in size were developed, an atmospheric scientist named Peter Silitonga conducted a pair of experiments to settle the matter.

At the time, a prism was still a large array of laboratory equipment that used liquid nitrogen for cooling, and Silitonga required one for each of his planned experiments. Before activating them he made a number of arrangements. First he recruited volunteers in a dozen countries who were not currently pregnant but were trying to conceive children; in one year's time, the couples who'd successfully had a child agreed to have a twenty-one-loci DNA test performed on their newborns. Then he activated the first of his prisms, typing the keyboard command that sent a photon through a polarization filter.

Six months later, he scheduled a software agent to retrieve weather reports from around the globe in one month's time. Then he activated the second of his prisms, and waited.

• • •

Nat liked that, no matter what the issue was, support-group meetings always had coffee. She didn't care so much whether the coffee was good or bad; what she appreciated was that holding the cup gave her something to do with her hands. And even though this support group's location wasn't the nicest she'd ever seen—a pretty typical church basement—the coffee was usually really good.

Lyle was at the coffeemaker pouring himself a cup as Nat walked up. "Hey there," he said. He handed her the cup he had just filled and started pouring another for himself.

"Thanks, Lyle." Lyle had been attending the group just a little longer than Nat had, about three months. Ten months ago he'd been offered a new job and couldn't decide whether he should accept it. He'd bought a prism and used it as a coin flip: blue LED accepts the offer, red LED rejects it. The blue LED had lit up in this branch, so he took the new job while his paraself stayed at his existing job. For months they both felt happy with their situations. But after the initial novelty of the new job wore off, Lyle found himself disenchanted with his duties, while his paraself got a promotion. Lyle's confidence was shaken. He pretended he was happy when communicating with his paraself, but he was struggling with feelings of envy and jealousy.

Nat found them a couple of empty chairs next to each other. "You like sitting up front, right?" she asked.

"Yeah, but you don't have to if you don't want to."

"It's fine," she said. They sat and sipped their coffee while waiting for the meeting to start.

The group's facilitator was a therapist named Dana. She was young, no older than Nat, but seemed to know what she was doing. Nat could have used someone like her in her previous groups. Once everyone was seated, Dana said, "Does anyone want to start us off today?"

"I'll go," said Lyle.

"Okay, tell us about your week."

"Well, I looked up the Becca here." Lyle's parallel self had been seeing a woman named Becca for months, after a chance meeting at a bar.

"Bad idea, bad idea," said Kevin, shaking his head. "Kevin, please," said Dana.

"Sorry, sorry."

"Thanks, Dana," said Lyle. "I messaged her, I told her why I was messaging her, I sent her a photo of my paraself and her paraself together, and I asked if I could take her out for coffee. She said sure."

Dana nodded for him to continue.

"We met on Saturday afternoon, and at first we seemed

to hit it off. She laughed at my jokes, I laughed at hers, and I was thinking, I'll bet this is just how it went when my paraself met her. I felt like I was living my best life." He looked embarrassed. "And then it went all wrong. I was saying how great it was to meet her, and how I felt like things were turning around for me, and before I knew it I told her how using the prism had screwed things up for me. I talked about how jealous I was of my paraself for having met parallel Becca, how I was always second-guessing myself now, and on and on. And I could hear how pathetic I sounded as I was saying it. I knew I was losing her, so out of desperation I" He hesitated, and then said, "I offered to let her borrow my prism so she could talk with parallel Becca, and that Becca could tell this one what a great guy I could be. You can imagine how well that went over. She was polite, but she made it clear that she didn't want to see me again."

"Thanks for sharing that, Lyle," said Dana. She addressed the rest of the group. "Does anyone want to say anything in response?"

This was an opportunity, but Nat wasn't going to jump in right away. It'd be best if the other group members spoke first.

Kevin started. "Sorry about my earlier remark. I didn't mean that you were dumb for trying it. What I was thinking was it sounded like something I would do, and because of that, I had a bad feeling about how it was going to turn out. I'm sorry it didn't work out better for you."

"Thanks, Kevin."

"And really, it's not a bad idea. The two of you have got to be compatible if your paraselves are a couple."

"I agree with Kevin that the two of you are compatible," said Zareenah. "But the mistake that all of us keep making is that, when we see our paraselves experiencing good fortune, we think we're entitled to the same good fortune."

"I don't think I'm entitled to Becca," said Lyle. "But she's looking for someone, just like I am. If we're compatible, shouldn't that count for something? I know I made a bad first impression, but I feel like our compatibility should be a reason for her to overlook that."

"It'd be nice if she did, but she's under no obligation to do that."

"Yeah," said Lyle grudgingly. "I see what you're saying. I just feel so . . . I know I say this all the time, but I feel envious. Why am I like this?"

Now seemed like a good time. Nat said, "Something happened to me recently that I think might be similar to what Lyle's going through?"

"Go ahead," said Dana.

"Okay, I've got this hobby where I make jewelry, mostly earrings. I have a little online store where people can buy them; I don't fill the orders myself, I just upload the designs and this company fabs them and mails them to customers." That part was all true, which was good in case anyone wanted to look at her store. "My paraself was just telling me that some influencer happened across one of our designs, and posted about how she loved them, and in the last week my paraself has sold hundreds of earrings. She actually saw someone at a coffee shop who was wearing the earrings.

"The thing is, the design that got all the attention wasn't one she made after I activated the prism; it's one from before. Those exact same earrings are for sale in my store in this branch, but no one's buying them here. She's making money for something we did before our branches diverged, but I'm not. And I resented her for it. Why is she so lucky and I'm not?" Nat saw some others nodding in sympathy.

"And I realized, this didn't feel the same as when I see other people sell a lot of jewelry in their online stores. This is different." She turned to face Lyle. "I don't think I'm an envious person by nature, and I don't think you are, either. We're not always wanting what other people have. But with a prism, it's not other people, it's you. So how can you not feel like you deserve what they have? It's natural. The problem isn't with you, it's with the prism."

"Thanks, Nat. I appreciate that."

"You're welcome."

Progress. That was definitely progress.

• • •

Set up a rack of billiard balls and execute a flawless break. Imagine the table has no pockets and is frictionless, so the balls just keep rebounding, never coming to a stop; how accurately can you predict the path of any given ball as it collides against the others? In 1978, the physicist Michael Berry calculated that you could predict only nine collisions before you would need to account for the gravitational effect of a person standing in the room. If your initial measurement of a ball's position is off by even a nanometer, your prediction becomes useless within a matter of seconds.

The collisions between air molecules are similarly contingent and can be affected by the gravitational effect of a single atom a meter away. So even though the interior of a prism is shielded from the external environment, the result of the quantum measurement that takes place when the prism is activated can still exert an effect on the outside world, determining whether two oxygen molecules collide or whether they drift past each other. Without anyone intending it, the activation of the prism inevitably gives rise to a difference between the two branches generated. The difference is imperceptible at first, a discrepancy at the level of the thermal motion of molecules, but when air is turbulent, it takes roughly a minute for a perturbation at the microscopic level to become macroscopic, affecting eddies one centimeter in diameter.

For small-scale atmospheric phenomena, the effects of perturbations double in size every couple of hours. In terms of prediction, that means that an error one meter wide in your initial measurements of the atmosphere will lead to an error a kilometer wide in your prediction of the weather on the following day.

At larger scales, the propagation of errors slows down due to factors like topography and the stratification of the atmosphere, but it doesn't stop; eventually errors on the kilometer scale become errors hundreds or thousands of kilometers in size. Even if your initial measurements were so detailed that they included data about every cubic meter of the Earth's atmosphere, your prediction of the future weather would cease to be useful within a month's time. Increasing the resolution of the initial measurements has a limited benefit; because errors propagate so rapidly at the small scale, starting with data about every cubic centimeter of the atmosphere would prolong the accuracy of the prediction by only a matter of hours.

The growth of errors in weather prediction is identical to the divergence between the weather in the branches on opposite sides of a prism. The initial perturbation is the difference in the collision of oxygen molecules when the prism is activated, and within a month, the weather around the globe is different. Silitonga confirmed this when he and his parallel self exchanged weather reports one month after activating a prism. The weather reports were all seasonally appropriate—there was no location that experienced winter in one branch and summer in the other—but beyond that they were essentially uncorrelated. Without anyone making an effort, the two branches had diverged visibly on a worldwide scale.

After Silitonga published these results, in a paper titled "Studying Atmospheric Upscale Error Propagation with the Plaga Interworld-Signaling Mechanism," historians engaged in heated debates over the extent to which weather could affect the course of history. Skeptics acknowledged that it could affect individuals' daily lives in various ways, but how often were the outcomes of history-making events decided by the weather? Silitonga didn't participate in the debates; he was waiting for his other, yearlong prism experiment to conclude.

• • •

There were times when the clients came in just the right order, and Wednesday afternoons were like that for Dana. The afternoon began with one of her most demanding clients, a man who asked her to make all his decisions for him, whined when she wouldn't, and blamed her whenever he eventually did take an action. So it was a relief to see Jorge immediately afterward, a breath of fresh air to clear out her office. The issues he was dealing with weren't the most interesting she'd ever seen, but she liked having him as a client. Jorge was funny and kind, and always well-intentioned; he was tentative about the therapeutic process, but they'd been making steady progress on his poor self-image and the negative attitudes that were holding him back.

Four weeks ago there had been an incident. Jorge's manager at work was a mean-spirited tyrant who belittled everyone who worked for him; one of the ongoing themes of Dana's sessions with Jorge was helping him to ignore his manager's insults. One day, Jorge had lost his temper and punctured all four tires of his manager's car when he was alone in the parking lot. Enough time had passed that it seemed like there was no risk of him getting caught, and while part of him wanted to pretend that it had never happened, part of him still felt terrible about what he'd done.

They began their session with some small talk; Dana got the sense that Jorge had something he wanted to say. She looked at him expectantly, and he said, "After our session last week, I went to one of those prism brokers, Lydoscope."

Dana was surprised. "Really? What for?"

"I wanted to see how many versions of me acted the same way I did."

"Tell me more."

"I asked them to send questions to six versions of me. Since it's such a recent departure point, it was cheap, so I asked for video. This morning they sent me a bunch of video files, recordings of what my paraselves said."

"And what did you learn?"

"None of my paraselves have punctured their manager's tires. All of them said they've fantasized about it. One came really close on the same day that I did it, but he stopped himself."

"What do you think that means?"

"It means that my puncturing his tires was a freak accident. The fact that I did it doesn't say anything important about me as a person."

Dana knew of people using prisms in a similar way, but it was usually someone justifying their actions by pointing out they might have done something worse. She hadn't encountered this particular version of it before, where the defense was based on their parallel selves behaving better. She certainly hadn't expected it from Jorge. "So you think your paraselves' behavior is a reflection on you?"

"The branches they checked, they were all ones where the departure point was just a month before the incident. That means that those paraselves were just the same as me; they hadn't had time to become different people."

She nodded; he was right about that. "Do you think the fact that you vandalized your manager's car is canceled out by the fact that your paraselves didn't?"

"Not canceled out, but it's an indicator of the type of person I am. If all of my paraselves had punctured his tires, that would indicate something significant about my personality. That's something Sharon would need to know about." Jorge hadn't told his wife about what he'd done; he'd been too ashamed. "But the fact that they didn't means that I'm fundamentally not a violent person, so telling Sharon about what happened would give her the wrong idea."

Getting him to tell his wife everything was something they'd have to build up to. "So how do you feel, now that you've gotten this information?"

"Relief, I suppose," said Jorge. "I was worried about what it meant that I had done that. But now I'm not so worried."

"Tell me more about that feeling of relief."

"I feel like . . ." Jorge fidgeted in his chair as he searched for the words. Eventually he said, "I guess I feel like I got the results of a medical test back, and I'm in the clear."

"Like you might have been sick, but it turns out you're not."

"Yes! It was nothing serious. It's not something that's going to be a recurring thing with me."

Dana decided to take a chance. "So let's think of it as a medical test. You had some symptoms that might have indicated something serious, like cancer. But it turns out you don't have cancer."

"Right!"

"Of course it's great that you don't have cancer. But you still had those symptoms. Isn't it worth figuring out what it was that gave you those symptoms?"

Jorge looked blank. "If it's not cancer, what does it matter?"

"Well, it could be something else, something it'd help you to know about."

"I got the answer I needed." He shrugged. "That's good enough for now."

"Okay, that's fine," said Dana. No sense in pushing the issue.

She was sure he'd get there eventually.

The Haunting of Tram Car 015

By P. Djèlí Clark

CHAPTER ONE

The office of the Superintendent of Tram Safety & Maintenance at Ramses Station had all the decor befitting someone who had been elevated—or likely pushed along the lines of patronage—into such a vaulted position. A sprawling vintage Anatolian rug of blue angular motifs, red spandrels, and golden tulips bordered in deep lavender. A hanging painting by one of the new abstract pharaonists, with its irregular shapes, splotches, and vivid colors that no one could truly understand. A framed photograph of the king, naturally. And some conveniently placed novels by the most recent Alexandrian writers, their leather-bound covers looking as unopened as the day they'd been bought.

Unfortunately, Agent Hamed Nasr noted with the meticulous eye of an investigator, the superintendent's contrived attempts at good taste were subsumed under the humdrum tediousness of a mid-level bureaucratic functionary: transit maps and line timetables, mechanical schematics and repair schedules, memorandums and reports, all overlaid one upon another on washed-out yellow walls like decaying dragon scales. They flapped carelessly beneath the air of an oscillating copper fan, its spinning blades rattling inside its cage as if trying to get out. And somehow, still, it was stifling in here, so that Hamed had to resist the urge to pull at the neckband of his white collarless shirt—thankful, at least, that the dark uniform he wore concealed any signs of perspiration in the lingering heat of late-summer Cairo.

The office's proprietor was seated in a high-backed chair behind a stained, coffee-colored desk. It showed signs of wear, and a fine crack led up one leg where the wood had been split. But its owner had taken care to keep it polished, so that it gleamed under the lone flickering gas lamp in the windowless room. He didn't seem bothered by the unbearable climate. Much like his noisy fan, he prattled on, impervious.

"It's odd that we call it a tram system," he intoned. His finger stood poised beneath a bold nose sheltering a waxed moustache streaked with gray that twisted and curved up at the ends. Hamed was amazed by the man's pomposity: behaving as if he were lecturing first-year students at university—and not speaking to agents of the Ministry of Alchemy, Enchantments, and Supernatural Entities. "It is really a telpher system, when you think on it clearly," he droned on. "Trams are pulled along a single cable line. But like telphers, our cars move independently along any given line, even switching lines at given points much like a train. The original telpher was invented in London back in the 1880s. But once our djinn got ahold of the idea, the mechanics were greatly expanded upon."

"Absolutely fascinating, Superintendent Bashir!" a younger man seated beside Hamed exclaimed. At twenty-four, only four years younger in truth. But the round, clean brown face beneath his Ministry-issued red tarboosh looked as if it belonged on a boy. At the moment, he was rapt with both attention and genuine interest.

"Oh indeed!" The superintendent's head bobbed like some windup toy, eager for the audience. "People have little understanding of how the transit system that connects much of Cairo works. Not to mention what has to be planned for the future. A city of over two million and growing is going to require major works to keep up with its population." He reached for a bronze dish on his desk and jerkily offered it forward. "More sudjukh, Agent Onsi?"

The younger man gave his thanks, gleefully grabbing a few more bits of the sweet—a brown concoction of hardened syrup and nuts that tasted of cloves and cinnamon. The superintendent presented the dish to Hamed, who politely declined. He'd been fighting to get one of the things unstuck from his teeth for the past few minutes.

"Delicious!" Onsi said, crunching down on a mouthful. "Where did you say these were from, Superintendent?"

"Armenia!" The man beamed, drawing out the word. "I visited last year on a development trip with the Transportation Bureau. The government hopes increased modernizations will assure stability for the republic, after so much hardship brokering their independence. While there, I absolutely fell in love with the local food. Sudjukh is by far my favorite."

"Sudjukh," Onsi mouthed as he chewed, his bushy eyebrows furrowing above a pair of round wire-rimmed silver spectacles. "I always thought that was a type of cured sausage."

"Ah!" the superintendent exclaimed, leaning his angular body forward. "You may be thinking of sujuk! The spelling is sometimes similar, though the pronunciation—"

Hamed cleared his throat loudly, coughing into his short moustache.

If he had to sit through a conversation about the dried meats of Transcaucasia, he just might go insane. Or be forced to eat his foot. One or the other. And he liked both his sanity and his feet. Catching the superintendent's attention, he spared a remonstrative glance for Onsi.

They were here on Ministry business, not to spend the morning chatting idly like old men at a coffee shop.

"Superintendent Bashir," he began, trying to smooth the impatience in his voice into something more diplomatic—and scoot a bit of sudjukh from between his molars. "If you could tell us about the problem you're having with the tram?"

The man blinked, as if just remembering why they were there. "Yes, yes, of course," he answered, sitting back into his chair with a huff. He fiddled with the blue-striped kaftan that he wore over a crisp white gallabiyah, the latter complete with buttons and a shirt collar, after the ministerial fashion. Pulling a kerchief from a front pocket, he mopped at the perspiration on his forehead. "It is all such dreadful business," he complained. "Well, there's no way to put this politely—the tram is haunted!"

Hamed opened his notepad, sighing under his breath as he jotted down the word "haunting." That's what had been typed on the file that landed on his desk this morning. He'd hoped the case might turn out to be something more interesting. But a haunting it was going to be. He stopped writing, looking up as his mind worked out what the man had just said.

"Wait, your *tram* is haunted?"

The superintendent answered with a dour nod that made his moustache droop. "Tram 015, that runs the line down to the Old City. It's one of the newer models that came out in 1910. Only two years in service, and we're already having these troubles. God protect us!"

"I didn't know trams could be haunted," Onsi murmured, plopping another sudjukh in his mouth.

Hamed had to agree. He'd heard of haunted buildings. Haunted homes. Even had a case once of a haunted mausoleum in al-Qarafa, which was rather silly when you thought about it. Why make your home a cemetery, then complain about hauntings? But a haunted tram car? That was new.

"Oh, it's quite haunted," the superintendent assured. "Passengers have encountered the spirit on several occasions. We'd hoped perhaps it would just leave on its own accord. But now it's attacked a woman, just yesterday! She was able to escape unharmed, praise be to God. But not before her clothing was all but ripped to shreds!"

Onsi sat gawking until Hamed cleared his throat again. The younger man jumped at that, fumbling out his own notepad to begin scribbling.

"How long has this been going on?" Hamed asked.

The superintendent looked down to a calendar on his desk, tapping the days contemplatively. "This was the first report just over a week ago, from a mechanic. The man has an ill moral character: a drinker and a carouser. His work chief believed he'd arrived at his station drunk.

Almost wrote him up for dismissal, until the passenger complaints began arriving." He motioned to a small stack of papers nearby. "Soon we were hearing from other mechanics. Why, I've seen the wicked thing myself!"

"What did you do?" Onsi asked, drawn in by the tale.

"What any right-standing man would," the superintendent replied, puffing up. "I informed the foul spirit I was a Muslim, and there is but One God, and so it could do me no harm! After that, a few other men took my lead, reciting surahs in the hopes of driving it away. Alas, the vexed thing is still here. After the attack, I deemed it best that I call in those who are more skilled in these matters." He patted his chest in a grateful gesture.

Hamed suppressed the urge to roll his eyes. Half of Cairo flooded the Ministry with trivial concerns, jumping at their own shadows. The other half assumed they could handle everything themselves—with a few verses, some amulets and charms, or a bit of folk magic passed down from their teita. "You say you've seen the entity in question," he prodded. "Could you describe it?"

Superintendent Bashir squirmed. "Not precisely. I mean, well, it's difficult to explain. Perhaps I should just show you?"

Hamed nodded, standing and pulling at the hem of his coat. The superintendent followed suit, leading Hamed and Onsi from the small hot room. They walked down a hallway that housed the station's administrative offices before being herded through the gilded silver doors of a lift, where a boilerplate eunuch stood waiting patiently. "The aerial yard," Bashir instructed.

The machine man's featureless brass face registered no sign of hearing the order, but it sprang into motion—reaching out a mechanical hand to pull on a lever embedded onto the floor. There was the low grumbling of turning gears, like an old man roused from bed, and the lift began to rise. They traveled a short while before the doors opened again, and when Hamed stepped out he had to shield his eyes from the late morning sun.

They were atop Ramses Station where you could see Cairo spread out below: a sprawl of busy streets, spired masjid, factories and architecture that spanned the ages amid the scaffolding of newly rising constructions. The superintendent had the truth of it. The city was growing by the day, from the cramped downtown to the south, to the mansions and welltended gardens in wealthy Gezira. And that was just on the ground.

Because up here was another world entirely.

The pointed steel turrets atop Ramses Station that mimicked golden minarets served as mooring masts for airships. Most of these ships were lightweight dirigibles that shuttled between Cairo and the main port of Alexandria by the hour, discharging passengers from across the Mediterranean and beyond. Some medium-sized crafts sat among them, heading south to Luxor and Aswan and as far as Khartoum. One giant vessel dwarfed the others, hovering impossibly like a small blue oval moon: a six-propeller heavy class that could make uninterrupted trips east to Bengal, down to Capetown, or even across the Atlantic. Most of Cairo, however, got around by less extravagant means.

Corded cable lines stretched across the skyline in every direction, metal vines that curved and bent as they went, interwoven and overlapping the breadth of the city. Aerial trams zipped along their length—leaving bright electric bolts crackling in their wake. The tram system was Cairo's lifeblood, running on a network of arteries and transporting thousands across the bustling metropolis. It was easy to take it for granted when you walked the streets below, not bothering to look up at the rumbling of their passing. But from this vantage, it was hard not to see transit vehicles as a stark symbol of Cairo's celebrated modernity.

"This way, if you please." The superintendent beckoned.

He took the two agents across a narrow walkway like a bridge, away from the airships and the main cable lines, and up several flights of stairs. When they finally stopped they were in a land of trams. Some twenty or more of the cars sat about in neat rows, hanging from cables by their pulleys but otherwise inactive. From somewhere beneath came the sound of other trams in motion, and between the gaps of the platform Hamed could catch glimpses as they streaked by.

"This is one of the main aerial yards," Bashir explained as they went. "Where we put trams to rotate out of service, those needing rest or repair. When 015 started giving trouble, we placed it here."

Hamed looked to where the man was leading. Tram 015 appeared like all the others he'd ever seen: a narrow, rectangular brass box with sectioned glass windows that wrapped nearly all around. It had green and red trim, and two bulbous lanterns on either end encased in cages of densely decorated interlacing stars. The number 015 was embossed in gold lettering that covered a door near the front. As they approached, the superintendent hung back.

"I'll leave matters in your capable hands from here," the man offered.

Hamed thought impishly of insisting he come along and show them how he had bravely stood up to the spirit. But decided against it. No need to be petty. He waved to Onsi and they walked to the car. The door came open at a pull to reveal a small set of steps. There was a gap between the hanging tram and the platform, showing the Cairo streets a far drop below. Trying to ignore the dizzying sight, Hamed placed a booted foot onto the tram and climbed aboard.

He had to duck his tall frame, holding onto his tarboosh, and draw in a set of broad shoulders to clear the narrow doorway. The car rocked slightly at his entrance and jostled again as Onsi came following behind—shorter by at least half a foot but stout enough to be near equal in weight. It wasn't precisely dark inside the tram, but dim. The lamps on the ceiling were on, and the flickering alchemical filaments cast a glare off the silver buttons running down the front of the two men's coats. The crimson velvet curtains at the windows were drawn back, allowing in some sunlight. But there was still a shadowy cast, making the burgundy cushioned seats of the bolted chairs running along either wall seem as black as their uniforms. The air was different too, thicker and cooler than the dry Cairene heat—filling Hamed's nostrils and sitting heavy on his chest. No doubt about it, something was peculiar with Tram 015.

"What's the procedure, Agent Onsi?" he asked.

If the Ministry was going to saddle him with new recruits, he might as well check to see if they'd been trained properly. The younger man, who had been peering about with interest, brightened at the question. "Sir, we should make sure the area is secure and no civilians are in present danger."

"It's an empty tram car, Agent Onsi," Hamed replied. "And I told you, stop calling me sir. You passed your academy exams so you're an agent just like me. This isn't Oxford."

"Ah yes, sir. Sorry, sir." He shook his head, as if trying to clear it of a lifetime of English schooling, which filtered into his accented Arabic. "I mean, Agent Hamed. Ministry procedure says that, taking into account what we've been told, we should make a spectral examination of the area."

Hamed nodded. Trained right after all. He reached into his coat to pull out the small leather case where he kept his spectral goggles. The copper-plated instruments were standard Ministry issue. They fit like eyeglasses, though the pronounced round green lenses were far wider. Onsi had removed his spectacles to slip on his own pair. Eyesight mattered little when it came to the spectral world—which appeared the same to everyone in a haze of startlingly vivid, luminescent jade. The brocaded flower patterns on the cushioned seats could be seen in detail, along with the golden calligraphy that ran along the black window panes. But what stood out more than anything was the ceiling. Craning to look up, Hamed couldn't fault Onsi for his breathy gasp.

The curved ceiling of the tram was awash in a spectral glow. It came from a complex arrangement of cogwheels covering the entire space.

Some of the gears meshed with one another, their teeth interlocking. Others were conjoined by chains into sprockets. They spun and rotated in multiple directions at once, sending out swirling eddies of light. Trams didn't require conductors, not even a boilerplate eunuch. The djinn had created them to run by themselves, to plow along their routes like messenger birds sent on an errand, and this intricate clockwork machinery was their brain.

"I say," Onsi asked, "is that supposed to be there?"

Hamed squinted, following his gaze. There was something moving amid the spinning gearwheels. A bit of ethereal light. He pulled up his goggles and saw it clearly with the naked eye—a sinuous form the color of grayish smoke. It slithered about, like an eel who made its home in a bed of coral. No, that was definitely *not* supposed to be there.

"What's the next step for first encounters with an unknown supernatural entity, Agent Onsi?" Hamed quizzed, keeping his eyes on the thing.

"Perform a standard greeting to ascertain its level of sentience," the man answered on cue. It took a brief awkward silence for him to comprehend that Hamed meant him to perform the task. His mouth made a perfect "Oh!" as he hastily drew out a folded document. Opening it revealed a sepia-toned photo of his beaming face above a blue and gold Ministry seal. "Good morning, unknown being," he said in loud slow words, holding up his identification. "I am Agent Onsi and this is Agent Hamed of the Ministry of Alchemy, Enchantments, and Supernatural Entities. We hereby inform you that you are in breach of several regulations governing paranormal persons and sentient creatures, beginning with Article 273 of the criminal code which forbids trespass and inhabitation of public property owned by the State, Article 275 on acts of terrifying and intimidation of citizens . . ."

Hamed listened stupefied as the man rattled off a series of violations.

He wasn't even certain when some of those had been put on the books.

" . . . and given the aforementioned charges," Onsi continued, "you are hereby instructed to vacate these premises and return to your place of origin, or, barring that, to accompany us to the Ministry for further questioning." Finishing, he turned with a satisfied nod.

Rookies, Hamed grumbled quietly. Before he could respond, a low moaning sounded in the car. There was little doubt where it came from, as the gray smoke had stopped its slithering and gone still.

"I think it understood me!" Onsi said eagerly.

Yes, Hamed thought dryly. And you probably bored it to death. If it was already dead, you might have just bored it back to death.

He was about say as much when there was a sudden terrible screeching.

Hamed moved to cover his ears at the sound, but was sent stumbling back as a jolt went through the tram. He might have fallen flat had he not reached out for one of the stanchions—catching the vertical pole by a hand. He looked up to see the gray smoke swirling furiously like an angry cloud, screaming as it swelled and grew. The lamps that lined the walls flickered rapidly and the tram began to tremble.

"Oh!" Onsi cried, trying to keep his footing. "Oh my!"

"Out! Out!" Hamed was yelling, already heading for the door. At one point, he slipped to a knee as the car shuddered hard and had to pick himself up—grabbing Onsi by the coat and pulling him along. When they reached the stairs something heavy pushed at them from behind, and they went tumbling down in tangle of flailing arms and legs until they were deposited unceremoniously onto the platform. From outside they could still hear the screeching as the hanging craft bucked and jumped.

With a fury, the door slammed shut and all was quiet and still at once.

"I think," Hamed heard Onsi put in from where they lay in a heap, "we may confirm that Tram 015 is indeed haunted."

CHAPTER TWO

Late the next morning, Hamed found himself back with Onsi in the office of the Superintendent of Tram Safety & Maintenance at Ramses Station. Like before, the small space was hot, cramped, and filled with the constant resonance of a rattling fan that pushed out tepid air. There was also more sweet sudjukh, which somehow hadn't melted under the heat and remained tough as ever. He had to give his grudging respect to the candy's resiliency.

"So, it is not a ghost?" Superintendent Bashir was asking. His brow had wrinkled more and more as he listened to their report, until it now looked like crumpled parchment.

Hamed shook his head, working hard at a bit of sudjukh that was beyond chewing. At least this time they'd been offered some tea, and he washed the morsel down with the cool taste of hibiscus and mint. "I've investigated well over a dozen haunting cases and never seen a ghost," he answered. The fact was, in the Ministry's almost thirty years of operation, there'd been no evidence for the existence of ghosts—despite the growing number of spiritualists and self-proclaimed mediums that now flourished in the back alleys of Cairo's souks. Whatever became of the dead, it didn't appear they cared to converse with the living.

"Well, something is haunting the tram," the superintendent persisted. "You saw for yourself." He had the presence to look down at that, allowing Hamed to keep the embarrassment on his face to himself. It was still unseemly to remember how they'd been tossed about yesterday. Not the best look for the Ministry, and he was thankful his skin—the shade of harvested wheat—could not ever possibly show traces of red. Onsi, however, seemed wholly unbothered by the memory.

"Likely the tram is haunted by a djinn," he piped up, helping himself to a second glass of tea while secreting some sudjukh into a pocket.

The superintendent's eyebrows rose. "Djinn? In my tram? You're certain?"

"In these cases, it's almost always a djinn," Hamed replied.

Bashir seemed skeptical. "I've met djinn. Some work for the Transportation Bureau, as you expect. An earth Jann lives on my street. Several djinn, including a very old and powerful Marid, attend my masjid. That creature does not look like any djinn I've encountered. It is rather . . . small."

"Oh, there are more kinds of djinn than the Ministry can even classify," Onsi countered quickly. "Just four centuries prior, the scholar al-Suyūṭī wrote of djinn that caused illnesses in the human mind and body. The early kalam on natural science held—"

"What Agent Onsi means to say," Hamed interjected, before they were led down a rumination on philosophical manuscripts, "is that djinn come in all sorts. So, it's quite possible for one to have taken over your tram."

"Well, what does it want?" Bashir asked.

"Hard to say," Hamed answered. "The djinn we're used to generally choose to interact and live among humans. There are others, Ifrit for instance, who we know keep their distance—most not even staying on this plane. Some we can't even communicate with. Those are often the haunting sort, lesser djinn beyond our classification. Likely, this one was drawn to the magic that operates your tram and has made its home there."

The superintendent sighed lengthily. "Djinn haunting my tram and attacking passengers." He finished with the hand gesture that accompanied the all-too-common Cairo slang: "Thank you, al-Jahiz."

It had been some forty years since the wandering Soudanese genius—or madman, take your pick—had, through a mix of alchemy and machines, bored a hole into the Kaf. The opening of the doorway to the other-realm of the djinn had sent magic pouring out, changing the world forever. Now Cairenes evoked the disappeared mystic at every turn, his sobriquet uttered more often in mockery than praise to complain over the troubles of the age.

Hamed had never understood the phrase's ubiquity. Whether the Sufis were right, and al-Jahiz was indeed a herald of the Mahdi, or, as Copts feared, a sign of the apocalypse, seemed irrelevant. So too, he thought, were the continuing debates on whether al-Jahiz was the same as the medieval thinker of Basra, either traveled through time or reborn. Whatever the truth of it, without al-Jahiz there would be no Ministry.

Egypt would not be one of the world's foremost powers. Indeed, the British might not even have been pushed out if not for the aid of the djinn. And those same djinn had built up Cairo to rival London or Paris. It often seemed that while the country proudly touted its modernity, it yet yearned wistfully for some simpler past.

"Al-Jahiz may have released more djinn upon the world," Onsi put in, as if reading Hamed's mind. "But it's hardly all his doing. Some number of djinn have always lived among us. They appear in too many of our oldest texts to believe otherwise: the *Kitab al-Fihrist,* the *Hamzanama,* and of course, the *Kitab al-Bulhan.* Why, it's commonly believed the old Khedive Muhammad Ali kept a secret djinn advisor, well over fifty years before al-Jahiz arrived in Cairo. His victory over the Mamluks has even been credited to—"

"Before we wander down our national past," Hamed cut in once again—the man was like a stack of history books! "I think it's best I share our proposal for solving your problem." He untied the string holding together the leather folder he carried, and took out a sheet of paper, placing it on the desk and pushing it toward the superintendent. The man took it up and as he began to read, his eyebrows made a steady climb.

"Goodness!" he said at last, mopping at his temples. "This is quite detailed."

Hamed allowed a slight smile. He'd spent half the past day putting together the plan. Every element had been itemized with care. He was a bit proud. Even if the case was only a haunting.

"But this price," Bashir brooded. "So much?"

"Coaxing a djinn of unknown classification from your tram won't be easy," Hamed explained. "Much of the pricing you're seeing is the consultation fee for an elder djinn, a Marid who specializes in functioning as an intermediary. They're about the only class of djinn these entities will listen to. Besides that, we'll need to purchase some basic alchemical elixirs to purify the tram, in addition to a barrier spell—for safety you understand—and assorted other tools. We think that's the best way to assure the job is done effectively."

"It certainly is thorough," the superintendent admitted. "But I'm afraid it won't do."

Hamed's smile slid away. "What? Why? It's a very sound plan." He was somewhat offended. He knew well what he was about.

"Oh, I don't question your abilities, Agent Hamed," the superintendent said soothingly. "I mean this price. I simply can't pay it." Seeing Hamed's startled look he went on. "My office has limited expenditures for this sort of thing. The parliament is ever trying to find ways to cut our budget, yet demands we keep our systems running smoothly. Not to mention the Transportation Bureau is planning construction on several new lines to Heliopolis. There's just no money."

Hamed was at a loss. He hadn't anticipated that response. "I'm sorry," was all he could say. And he was. It was a very well-conceived and written-up plan. "I wish we could do more."

"Ah!" the superintendent exclaimed. "It's interesting you should say that." He reached into a desk drawer and drew out a sheet of paper of his own. "By chance, I was reading this interoffice memorandum on public safety earlier this morning. It was handed down several months ago from the national government and signed off by the Minister of the Interior. It deems any threat to the public good arising from mystical or preternatural occurrences a matter that falls under the jurisdiction of your agency."

Hamed took the paper from the man, trying not to snatch it as it was offered. By chance, was it? As if anyone went around reading months-old interoffice memoranda. A quick scan brought up brief memories of the Ministry lobbying for greater authority over public facilities. He thrust the paper over to Onsi, who took it and began reading in murmurs beneath his breath.

"I believe, since the haunting of the tram is now officially under your agency's dominion," Bashir stated delicately, "that any costs associated with its restoration to a less hazardous state should need come from your *own* funding." He paused in feigned uncertainty. "That is, if I have understood matters correctly?"

"I believe you have, superintendent," Onsi answered, finishing his read.

Hamed shot the younger man an annoyed look, but it was no use. He had gathered as much already. Somebody down at the Ministry hadn't anticipated this possible loophole. They certainly hadn't come across the likes of the wily Superintendent Bashir, either. The man put on a contrite smile that hid nothing before reaching for the bronze dish and offering it forward.

"More sweet sudjukh, Agent Hamed?"

This Is How You Lose the Time War

by Amal El-Mohtar and Max Gladstone

WHEN RED WINS, she stands alone.

Blood slicks her hair. She breathes out steam in the last night of this dying world.

That was fun, she thinks, but the thought sours in the framing. It was clean, at least. Climb up time's threads into the past and make sure no one survives this battle to muddle the futures her Agency's arranged—the futures in which her Agency rules, in which Red herself is possible. She's come to knot this strand of history and sear it until it melts.

She holds a corpse that was once a man, her hands gloved in its guts, her fingers clutching its alloy spine. She lets go, and the exoskeleton clatters against rock. Crude technology. Ancient. Bronze to depleted uranium. He never had a chance. That is the point of Red.

After a mission comes a grand and final silence. Her weapons and armor fold into her like roses at dusk. Once flaps of pseudoskin settle and heal and the programmable matter of her clothing knits back together, Red looks, again, something like a woman.

She paces the battlefield, seeking, making sure.

She has won, yes, she has won. She is certain she has won. Hasn't she?

Both armies lie dead. Two great empires broke themselves here, each a reef to the other's hull. That is what she came to do. From their ashes others will rise, more suited to her Agency's ends. And yet.

There was another on the field—no groundling like the time-moored corpses mounded by her path, but a real player. Someone from the other side.

Few of Red's fellow operatives would have sensed that opposing presence. Red knows only because Red is patient, solitary, careful. She studied for this engagement. She modeled it backward and forward in her mind. When ships were not where they were supposed to be, when escape pods that should have been fired did not, when certain fusillades came thirty seconds past their cue, she noticed.

Twice is coincidence. Three times is enemy action.

But why? Red has done what she came to do, she thinks. But wars are dense with causes and effects, calculations and strange attractors, and all the more so are wars in time. One spared life might be worth more to the other side than all the blood that stained Red's hands today. A fugitive becomes a queen or a scientist or, worse, a poet. Or her child does, or a smuggler she trades jackets with in some distant spaceport. And all this blood for nothing.

Killing gets easier with practice, in mechanics and technique. Having killed never does, for Red. Her fellow agents do not feel the same, or they hide it better.

It is not like Garden's players to meet Red on the same field at the same time. Shadows and sure things are more their style. But there is one who would. Red knows her, though they have never met. Each player has their signature. She recognizes patterns of audacity and risk.

Red may be mistaken. She rarely is.

Her enemy would relish such a magic trick: twisting to her own ends all Red's grand work of murder. But it's not enough to suspect. Red must find proof.

So she wanders the charnel field of victory and seeks the seeds of her defeat.

A tremor passes through the soil—do not call it earth. The planet dies. Crickets chirp. Crickets survive, for now, among the crashed ships and broken bodies on this crumbling plain. Silver moss devours steel, and violet flowers choke the dead guns. If the planet lasted long enough, the vines that sprout from the corpses' mouths would grow berries.

It won't, and neither will they.

On a span of blasted ground, she finds the letter.

It does not belong. Here there should be bodies mounded between the wrecks of ships that once sailed the stars. Here there should be the death and dirt and blood of a successful op. There should be moons disintegrating overhead, ships aflame in orbit.

There should not be a sheet of cream-colored paper, clean save a single line in a long, trailing hand: *Burn before reading.*

Red likes to feel. It is a fetish. Now she feels fear. And eagerness.

She was right.

She searches shadows for her hunter, her prey. She hears infrasonic, ultrasound. She thirsts for contact, for a new, more worthy battle, but she is alone with the corpses and the splinters and the letter her enemy left.

It is a trap, of course.

Vines curl through eye sockets, twine past shattered portholes. Rust flakes fall like snow. Metal creaks, stressed, and shatters.

It is a trap. Poison would be crude, but she smells none. Perhaps a noovirus in the message—to subvert her thoughts, to seed a trigger, or merely to taint Red with suspicion in her Commandant's eyes. Perhaps if she reads this letter, she will be recorded, exposed, blackmailed for use as a double agent.

The enemy is insidious. Even if this is but the opening gambit of a longer game, by reading it Red risks Commandant's wrath if she is discovered, risks seeming a traitor be she never so loyal.

The smart and cautious play would be to leave. But the letter is a gauntlet thrown, and Red has to know.

She finds a lighter in a dead soldier's pocket. Flames catch in the depths of her eyes. Sparks rise, ashes fall, and letters form on the paper, in that same long, trailing hand.

Red's mouth twists: a sneer, a mask, a hunter's grin.

The letter burns her fingers as the signature takes shape. She lets its cinders fall.

Red leaves then, mission failed and accomplished at once, and climbs downthread toward home, to the braided future her Agency shapes and guards. No trace of her remains save cinders, ruins, and millions dead.

The planet waits for its end. Vines live, yes, and crickets, though no one's left to see them but the skulls.

Rain clouds threaten. Lightning blooms, and the battlefield goes monochrome. Thunder rolls. There will be rain tonight, to slick the glass that was the ground, if the planet lasts so long.

The letter's cinders die.

The shadow of a broken gunship twists. Empty, it fills.

A seeker emerges from that shadow, bearing other shadows with her.

Wordless, the seeker regards the aftermath. She does not weep, that anyone can see. She paces through the wrecks, over the bodies, professional: She works a winding spiral, ensuring with long-practiced arts that no one has followed her through the silent paths she walked to reach this place.

The ground shakes and shatters.

She reaches what was once a letter. Kneeling, she stirs the ashes. A spark flies up, and she catches it in her hand.

She removes a thin white slab from a pouch at her side and slips it under the ashes, spreads them thin against the white. Removes her glove, and slits her finger. Rainbow blood wells and falls and splatters into gray.

She works her blood into the ash to make a dough, kneads that dough, rolls it flat. All around, decay proceeds. The battleships become mounds of moss. Great guns break.

She applies jeweled lights and odd sounds. She wrinkles time.

The world cracks through the middle.

The ash becomes a piece of paper, with sapphire ink in a viny hand at the top.

This letter was meant to be read once, then destroyed.

In the moments before the world comes apart, she reads it again.

Look on my works, ye mighty, and despair!

A little joke. Trust that I have accounted for all variables of irony. Though I suppose if you're unfamiliar with overanthologized works of the early Strand 6 nineteenth century, the joke's on me.

I hoped you'd come.

You're wondering what this is—but not, I think, wondering who this is. You know—just as I've known, since our eyes met during that messy matter on Abrogast-882—that we have unfinished business.

I shall confess to you here that I'd been growing complacent. Bored, even, with the war; your Agency's flash and dash upthread and down, Garden's patient planting and pruning of strands, burrowing into time's braid. Your unstoppable force to our immovable object; less a game of Go than a game of tic-tac-toe, outcomes determined from the first move, endlessly iterated until the split where we fork off into unstable, chaotic possibility—the future we seek to secure at each other's expense.

But then you turned up.

My margins vanished. Every move I'd made by rote I had to bring myself to fully. You brought some depth to your side's speed, some staying power, and I found myself working at capacity again. You invigorated your Shift's war effort and, in so doing, invigorated me.

Please find my gratitude all around you.

I must tell you it gives me great pleasure to think of you reading these words in licks and whorls of flame, your eyes unable to work backwards, unable to keep the letters on a page; instead you must absorb them, admit them into your memory. In order to recall them you must seek my presence in your thoughts, tangled among them like sunlight in water. In order to report my words to your superiors you must admit yourself already infiltrated, another casualty of this most unfortunate day.

This is how we'll win.

It is not entirely my intent to brag. I wish you to know that I respected your tactics. The elegance of your work makes this war seem like less of a waste. Speaking of which, the hydraulics in your spherical flanking gambit were truly superb. I hope you'll take comfort from the knowledge that they'll be thoroughly digested by our mulchers, such that our next victory against your side will have a little piece of you in it.

Better luck next time, then.

Fondly,
Blue

A GLASS JAR of water boils in an MRI machine. In defiance of proverbs, Blue watches it.

When Blue wins—which is always—she moves on to the next thing. She savours her victories in retrospect, between missions, recalls them only while travelling (upthread into the stable past or downthread into the fraying future) as one recalls beloved lines of poetry. She combs or snarls the strands of time's braid with the finesse or brutality required of her, and leaves.

She is not in the habit of sticking around, because she is not in the habit of failing.

The MRI machine is in a twenty-first-century hospital, remarkably empty—evacuated, Blue observes—but never conspicuous to begin with, nestled in the green heart of a forest bisected by borders.

The hospital was meant to be full. Blue's job was a delicate matter of infection—one doctor in particular to intrigue with a new strain of bacteria, to lay the groundwork for twisting her world towards or away from biological warfare, depending on how the other side responded to Garden's move. But the opportunity's vanished, the loophole closed, and the only thing there for Blue to find is a jar labeled READ BY BUBBLING.

So she lingers by the MRI machine, musing as she does on the agonies of symmetry recording the water's randomness—the magnetic bones settled like reading glasses on the thermodynamic face of the universe, registering each bloom and burst of molecule before it transforms. Once it translates the last of the water's heat into numbers, she takes the printout in her right hand and fits the key of it into the lock of the letter-strewn sheet in her left.

She reads, and her eyes widen. She reads, and the data get harder to extract from the depth of her fist's clench. But she laughs, too, and the sound echoes down the hospital's empty halls. She is unaccustomed to being thwarted. Something about it tickles, even as she meditates on how to phase-shift failure into opportunity.

Blue shreds the data sheet and the cipher text, then picks up a crowbar.

In her wake, a seeker enters the hospital room's wreck, finds the MRI machine, breaks into it. The jar of water is cool. She tips its tepid liquid down her throat.

> My most insidious Blue,
>
> How does one begin this sort of thing? It's been so long since I last started a new conversation. We're not so isolated as you are, not so locked in our own heads. We think in public. Our notions inform one another, correct, expand, reform. Which is why we win.
>
> Even in training, the other cadets and I knew one other as one knows a childhood dream. I'd greet comrades I thought I'd never met before, only to find we'd already crossed paths in some strange corner of the cloud before we knew who we were.
>
> So: I am not skilled in taking up correspondence. But I have scanned enough books, and indexed enough examples, to essay the form.
>
> Most letters begin with a direct address to the reader. I've done that already, so next comes shared business: I'm sorry you couldn't meet the good doctor. She's important. More to the point, her sister's children will be, if she visits them this afternoon and they discuss patterns in birdsong—which she will have done already by the time you decipher this note. My cunning methods for spiriting her from your clutches? Engine trouble, a good spring day, a suspiciously effective and cheap remote-access software suite her hospital purchased two years ago, which allows the good doctor to work from home. Thus we

braid Strand 6 to Strand 9, and our glorious crystal future shines so bright I gotta wear shades, as the prophets say.

Remembering our last encounter, I thought it best to ensure you'd twist no other groundlings to your purpose, hence the bomb threat. Crude, but effective.

I appreciate your subtlety. Not every battle's grand, not every weapon fierce. Even we who fight wars through time forget the value of a word in the right moment, a rattle in the right car engine, a nail in the right horseshoe . . . It's so easy to crush a planet that you may overlook the value of a whisper to a snowbank.

Address the reader—done. Discuss shared business—done, almost.

I imagine you laughing at this letter, in disbelief. I have seen you laugh, I think—in the Ever Victorious Army's ranks, as your dupes burned the Summer Palace and I rescued what I could of the Emperor's marvelous clockwork devices. You marched scornful and fierce through the halls, hunting an agent you did not know was me.

So I imagine fire glinting off your teeth. You think you've wormed inside me—planted seeds or spores in my brain—whatever vegetal metaphor suits your fancy. But here I've repaid your letter with my own. Now we have a correspondence. Which, if your superiors discover it, will start a chain of questions I anticipate you'll find uncomfortable. Who's infecting whom? We know from our hoarse Trojans, in my time. Will you respond, establishing complicity, continuing our self-destructive paper trail, just to get in the last word? Will you cut off, leaving my note to spin its fractal math inside you?

I wonder which I'd rather.
Finally: conclude.
This was fun.

My regards to the vast and trunkless legs of stone,
Red

RED PUZZLES THROUGH a labyrinth of bones.

Other pilgrims wander here, in saffron robes or homespun brown. Sandals shuffle over rocks, and high winds whistle around cave corners. Ask the pilgrims how the labyrinth came to be, and they offer answers varied as their sins. Giants made it, this one claims, before the gods slew the giants, then abandoned Earth to its fate at mortal hands. (Yes, this is Earth—long before the ice age and the mammoth, long before academics many centuries downthread will think it possible for the planet to have spawned pilgrims, or labyrinths. Earth.) The first snake built the labyrinth, says another, screwing down through rock to hide from the judgment of the sun. Erosion made it, says a third, and the grand dumb motion of tectonic plates, forces too big for we cockroaches to conceive, too slow for mayfly us to observe.

They pass among the dead, under chandeliers of shoulder blades, rose windows outlined by rib cages. Metacarpals outline looping flowers.

Red asks the other pilgrims nothing. She has her mission. She takes care. She should meet no opposition as she makes a small twist this far upthread. At the labyrinth's heart there is a cavern, and soon into that cavern will come a gust of wind, and if that wind whistles over the right fluted bones, one pilgrim will hear the cry as an omen that will drive him to renounce all worldly goods and retreat to build a hermitage on a distant mountain slope, so that hermitage will exist in two hundred years to shelter a woman fleeing with child in a storm, and so it goes. Start a stone rolling, so in three centuries you'll have an avalanche. Little flash to such an assignment, less challenge, so long as she stays on script. Not even a taunt to disturb her path.

Did her adversary—did Blue—ever read her letter? Red liked writing it—winning tastes sweet, but sweeter still to triumph and tease. To dare reprisal. Every op since, she's watched her back, moved with double caution, waiting for payback, or for Commandant to find her small breach of discipline and bring the scourge. Red has her excuses ready: Since her disobedience she's been a better agent, more meticulous.

But no reply has come.

Perhaps she was wrong. Perhaps her enemy does not care, after all.

The pilgrims follow guides down the path of wisdom. Red departs and wanders narrow, twisting passages in the dark.

Darkness does not bother her. Her eyes do not work like normal eyes. She scents the air, and olfactory analytics flash into her brain, offering a trail. At a particular niche, she draws from her satchel a small tube that sheds red light on the skeletons arrayed within. The first time she does this, she finds nothing. The second, her light glints off a pulsing stripe on this femur, that jaw.

Satisfied, she adds femur and jaw to her bag, then banishes the light and wanders deeper down.

Imagine her in utter night, invisible. Imagine the footsteps, one by one, that never tire, never slip on cave dust or gravel. Imagine the precision with which her head swivels on her thick neck, swinging a measured arc from side to side. Hear (you can, just) gyroscopes whir in her gut, lenses click beneath the camouflage jelly of those pure black eyes.

She moves as fast as possible, within operating parameters.

More red lights. More bones join the others in the sack.

She does not need to check her watch. A timer ticks down in the corner of her vision.

When she thinks she's found the bones she needs, she descends.

Far below the path of wisdom, the masters of this dark place ran out of corpses. The niches remain, waiting—perhaps for Red.

Even the niches stop, eventually.

Soon after that, guards set upon her: eyeless giants grown by the sharp-toothed mistresses of this place. The giants' nails are yellow, thick, and cracked, and their breath smells better than one might expect.

Red breaks them quickly and quietly. She has no time for the less violent approach.

When she can no longer hear their moans, she reaches the cavern.

She knows by the changed echoes of her footsteps that she has found the place. When she kneels and stretches forth her hand, she feels ten centimeters of remaining ledge, then the abyss. Strong cold wind gusts past her: the Earth's own breath, or some great monster's far below. It howls. The noise clatters off the bone mobiles the nuns make down here, to remind themselves of the impermanence of flesh. The bones sing and turn, hanging from marrow twine in the darkness.

Red feels her way along the ledge until she finds one of the great anchored tree trunks from which the mobiles hang. She shimmies out upon the trunk until she reaches the bones of some ancient nun, hung by some other.

The countdown clock in her eye warns her how little time is left.

She cuts the old bones free with her diamond-sharp nails and takes her replacements from her pack. Strings them one by one with marrow twine, connecting skull and fibula, jaw and sternum, coccyx and xiphoid process.

The timer ticks down. Seven. Six.

She ties the knots rapidly, by touch. Her limbs inform her that they ache where they clutch this ancient trunk above an unfathomable drop.

Three. Two.

She lets the bones fall into the pit.

Zero.

A rush of wind splits the earth, a roar in darkness. Red clutches the petrified trunk closer than a lover. The wind peaks, screams, tosses bones about. A new note rises above the ossuary clatter, woken by the cavern's wind whistling over precise fluted pits in the bones Red has hung. The note grows, shifts, and swells into a voice.

Red listens, teeth bared in an expression that, if she saw it mirrored, she could not name. There's awe there, yes, and fury. What else?

She scans the lightless cavern. She detects no heat signature, no movement, no radar ping, no EM emissions or cloud trail—of course not. She feels gloriously exposed. Ready for the gunshot or the moment of truth.

Too soon, the wind dies, and the voice with it.

Red curses into the silence. Remembering the era, she invokes local fertility deities, frames inventive methods for their copulation. She exhausts her invective arsenal and growls, wordless, and spits into the abyss.

After all that, as prophesied, she laughs. Thwarted, bitter, but still, there's humor in it.

Before she leaves, Red saws free the bones she hung. The pilgrim Red meant to shape is gone, and the hermitage will be unbuilt. Now Red will have to fix the mess to the best of her ability.

The abandoned bones tumble and tumble and fall and fall.

But don't worry. The seeker catches them before they land.

Dear Red, in Tooth, in Claw,

You were right that I laughed. Your letter was very welcome. It told me a great deal. You imagined the fire glinting off my teeth; knowing your fine attention to detail, I thought I'd put a little devil in it.

Perhaps I ought to begin with an apology. This is not, I'm afraid, the omen you were anticipating; while you listen to my words, you might give a little thought to whose bones are cored and pocked with this letter. That poor pilgrim who might have been! Why leave a self-destructing paper trail when one can enjoy an asset-destroying scrimshaw session and let the wind take a turn tickling some ivory?

Don't worry—he lived a fine life first. Not the life you would have wanted for him, perhaps—unhappy but useful to posterity, harbouring the vulnerable, dimpling the future's punch cards one new life at a time. Instead of building a hermitage, he fell in love! Made glorious music with his fellow, travelled widely, drew tears from an emperor, melted her hard heart, bumped history out of one groove and into another. Strand 22 crosses Strand 56, if I'm not mistaken, and somewhere downthread a bud's bloomed bright enough to taste.

It flatters me to find you so attentive. Be assured that I'll have looked long and hard at you while you assembled my little art project. Will you go still or turn sharply when you know that I'm watching you? Will you see me? Imagine me waving, in case you don't; I'll be too far off for you to see my mouth.

Just kidding. I'll be long gone by the time the wind

turns right. Made you look, though, didn't I?

I imagine you laughing too.

I look forward to your reply,
Blue

BLUE APPROACHES THE temple in pilgrim's guise: hair shorn to show the shine of circuitry curling around ears and up to scalp, eyes goggled, mouth a smear of chrome sheen, eyelids chrome hooded. She wears antique typewriter keys on her fingertips in veneration of the great god Hack, and her arms are braceleted in whorls of gold, silver, palladium, glinting brighter than bright against her dark skin.

Seen from overhead she is one of thousands, indistinguishable from the slow press of bodies shuffling towards the temple: a borehole in the centre of a vast, sun-baked pavilion. No one enters it: Such worshipful heat would wither their god on its silicon vine.

But inside is where she needs to be.

Blue drums her key-clapped fingers against one another with a dancer's precision. *A, C, G, T,* backwards and forwards, bifurcated, reunited. Their percussive rhythm sequences an airborne strain of malware she's been breeding for generations, an organism spreading invisible tendrils through this society's neural network, harmless until executed.

She snaps her fingers. A spark flares between them.

The pilgrims—all ten thousand of them, all at once—collapse, perfectly silent, into one vast ornamented heap.

She listens to the hiss and pop of overheated circuits misfiring in filigreed brains and walks peacefully through the incapacitated pilgrims, their twitching limbs like surf lapping softly at her ankles.

It amuses Blue to no end that, in disabling their temple, in mounting this attack, she has, herself, performed an act of devotion to their god.

She has ten minutes to navigate the temple labyrinth: down the service ladder hand over hand, then one palm against the dry, dark wall to follow its broken lines to a centre. It's cold underground, colder on her bare skin, colder still the deeper she goes, and she shivers but doesn't slow.

At the centre is a boxy screen. It lights up as Blue approaches.

"Hello, I'm Mackint—"

"Hush, Siri. I'm here for the riddles."

Eyes and a mouth—it can't quite be called a face—animate the screen, regard her evenly. "Very well. How do you calculate the hypotenuse of a right triangle?"

Blue tilts her head, stands very still, except for the flexing of her fingers at her side. She clears her throat.

" ' 'Twas brillig, and the slithy toves / Did gyre and gimble in the wabe.' . . ."

Siri's screen blinks with static before it asks, "What is the value of pi to sixty-two decimals?"

" 'The sedge is withered from the lake, / And no birds sing.' "

A fistful of snow skitters across Siri's face. "If train A leaves Toronto at six p.m. travelling east at one hundred kilometres per hour, and train B leaves Ottawa at seven p.m. travelling west at one hundred twenty kilometres per hour, when will they cross?"

" 'Lo! the spell now works around thee, / And the clankless chain hath bound thee; / O'er thy heart and brain together / Hath the word been pass'd—now wither!' "

A flash of light: Siri powers down.

"Further," Blue adds, stepping lightly towards the box, making to lift it into the heavy bag next to it, "Ontario sucks. As the prophets say."

The screen flashes again; she steps back, startled. Words scroll across the screen, and as they do, her eyes widen, and the screen's blue-white light catches on the chrome paint of her mouth as it spreads, slowly, into a ferocious grin.

She clacks her keys one final time before shedding them from her fingers, the sheen from her mouth, the metal from her arms. As she steps sideways into the braid, the heap of ornament shrivels, rusts, flakes, indistinguishable from the fine grit of the cavern floor. The seeker, following after, distinguishes every grain.

Dearest Blue-da-ba-dee,

A daring intrusion! Mad props. I never would have believed your party would risk working Strand 8827 this far downthread until I recognized your distinctive signature. I shudder to imagine an equal and opposite incursion—may causality forbid Commandant ever dispatch me to one of your viny-hivey elfworlds, profusely floral, all arcing elder trees, neural pollen, bees gathering memories from eyes and tongue, honey libraries dripping knowledge from the comb. I harbor no illusions I'd succeed. You would find me in an instant, crush me faster—I'd walk a swath of rot through your verdancy, no matter how light I tried to step. I have a Cherenkov-green thumb.

(I know, I know: Cherenkov radiation's . . . well . . . blue. Never let facts break a good joke.)

But you're subtle. I barely heard the signs of your approach—I won't tell you what they were, for reasons you'll understand. Imagine me, if you want, crouched atop a stairwell, knees to chin, out of sight, counting the burglar's footfalls as she climbs. You're not half-bad at this. Did they grow you for this purpose? How does your side handle this sort of thing, anyway? Did they engender you knowing what you'd be; did they train you, run you through your paces at what I can only picture as some sort of horrific summer camp under the watchful eyes of concerned counselors who smile all the time?

Did your bosses send you here? Do you even have bosses? Or a queen? Might someone in your chain of command want to do you wrong?

I ask because we could have trapped you here. This strand's a prominent tributary; Commandant could field a swarm of agents without much causal risk. I imagine you reading this, thinking you would have escaped them all. Maybe.

But those agents are busy elsewhere, and it would be a waste of time (ha!) to recall them and dispatch again. Rather than bother Commandant with something I could handle on my own, I interceded directly. Easier for us both.

Of course, I couldn't let you steal these peoples' god. We don't need this place in specific, but we need something like it. I'm sure you can picture the work required to rebuild such a paradise from scratch (or even recover its gleam from the wreckage). Think, for a second—if you succeeded, if you stole the physical object on whose slow quantum decomposition this strand's random-number generators depend, if that triggered a cryptographic crisis, if that crisis led people to distrust their food printers, if hungry masses rioted, if riots fed this glitter to the fires of war, we'd have to start again—cannibalizing other strands, likely from your braid. And then we'd be at one another's throats even more.

Plus, this way I can repay you for that trick in the catacombs—with a note of my own! But I'm almost out of room. You like the Strand 6 nineteenth century. Well, *Mrs. Leavitt's Guide to Etiquette and Correspond-*

ence (London, Gooseneck Press, Strand 61) suggests I should end by recapitulating my letter's main thrust, whatever that means, so, here goes: Ha-ha, Blueser. Your mission objective's in another castle.

Hugs and kisses,
Red

PS. The keyboard's coated with slow-acting contact poison. You'll be dead in an hour.

PPS. Just kidding! Or . . . am I?

PPPS. I'm just screwing with you. But postscripts sure are fun!

TREES FALL IN the forest and make sounds.

The horde moves among them, judging, swinging axes, bowing bass notes from pine trunks with saws. Five years back, none of these warriors had seen such a forest. In their home stand sacred groves were called *zuun mod*, which means "one hundred trees," because one hundred were all the trees they thought might be gathered in one place.

Many more than a hundred trees stand here, a quantity so vast no one dares number it. Wet, cold wind spills down the mountains, and branches clatter like locust wings. Warriors creep beneath needled shadows and go about their work.

Icicles drip and snap as the great trees fall, and felled, the trees leave gaps in green that bare the cold white sky. Warriors like those flat clouds better than the forest's gloom, but not so much as they loved the blue of home. They loop the trunks with cord and drag them through trampled underbrush to the camp, where they will be peeled and planed to build the great Khan's war machines.

A strange transformation, some feel: When they were

young, they won their first battles with bows, from horseback, ten men against twenty, two hundred against three. Then they learned to use rivers against their foes, to tear down their walls with grappling hooks. These days they roll from town to town collecting scholars, priests, and engineers, everyone who can read or write, who knows a trade, and set them tasks. You will have food, water, rest, all the luxury an army on hoof can offer. In exchange, solve the problems our enemies pose.

Once, horsemen broke on fortifications like waves against a cliff. (Most of these men have not seen waves, or cliffs, but travelers bear stories from distant lands.) Now the horsemen slaughter foes, drive them to their forts, demand surrender, and, should surrender not ensue, they raise up their engines to undo the knot of the city.

But those engines need lumber, so off the warriors are sent, to steal from ghosts.

Red, hard-ridden for days, dismounts within the wood. She wears a thick gray del belted with silk around her waist, and a fur hat covers her hair, preserving her scalp from the chill. She walks heavily. She broadens her shoulders. She has played this role for at least a decade. Women ride with the horde—but she is a man now, so far as those who give her orders, and follow hers in turn, are concerned.

She commits the enterprise to memory for her report. Her breath smokes, glitters as ice crystals freeze. Does she miss steam heat? Does she miss walls and a roof? Does she miss the dormant implants sewn through her limbs and tangled in her chest that could shore her against this cold, stop her feeling, seal a force field around her skin to guard her from this time to which she's been sent?

Not really.

She notes the deep green of the trees. She measures the timing of their fall. She records the white of the sky, the bite of the wind. She remembers the names of the men she passes. (Most of them are men.) Ten years into deep cover, having joined the horde, proven her worth, and achieved the place for which she strove, she feels suited to this war.

She has suited herself to it.

Others draw back from her in respect and fear as she scans the piled logs for signs of rot. Her roan snorts, stamps the earth. Red ungloves and traces the lumber with her fingertips, log by log, ring by ring, feeling each one's age.

She stops when she finds the letter.

Kneels.

The others gather round: What has disturbed her so? An omen? A curse? Some flaw in their lumberjackery?

The letter begins in the tree's heart. Rings, thicker here and thinner there, form symbols in an alphabet no one present knows but Red. The words are small, sometimes smudged, but still: ten years per line of text, and many lines. Mapping roots, depositing or draining nutrients year by year, the message must have taken a century to craft. Perhaps local legends tell of some fairy or frozen goddess in these woods, seen for an instant, then gone. Red wonders what expression she wore as she placed the needle.

She memorizes the message. She feels it ridge by ridge, line by line, and performs a slow arithmetic of years.

Her eyes change. The men nearby have known her for a decade but have never seen her look like this.

One asks, "Should we throw it away?"

She shakes her head. It must be used. She does not say, Or else another might find it and read what I have read.

They drag the logs to camp. They split them, trim them, plane them, frame them into engines of war. Two weeks later, the planks lie shattered around the fallen walls of a city still burning, still weeping. Progress gallops on, and blood remains behind.

Vultures circle, but they've feasted here already.

The seeker crosses the barren land, the broken city. She gathers splinters from the engines' wrecks, and as the sun sets, she slides those splinters one by one into her fingers.

Her mouth opens, but she makes no sound.

My perfect Red,

How many boards would the Mongols hoard if the Mongol horde got bored? Perhaps you'll tell me once you're finished with this strand.

The thought that you could have trapped me (stranded me, perhaps? Oh dear, sorry-not-sorry) is so delicious that I confess myself quite overcome. Do you always play things safe, then? Run the numbers so precisely that you can reject out of hand any scenario that has a projected success rate of less than 80 percent? It grieves me to think you'd make a boring poker player.

But then I imagine you'd cheat, and that's a comfort.

(I'd never want you to let me win. The very idea!)

I wore goggles, but imagine, please, the widening of my eyes at your sweet interrogation in Strand 8827. Did my bosses send me there! Do I have bosses! A suggestion of corruption in my command chain! A charming concern for my well-being! Are you trying to recruit me, dear Cochineal?

"And then we'd be at each other's throats even more." Oh, petal. You say that like it's a bad thing.

It occurs to me to dwell on what a microcosm we are of the war as a whole, you and I. The physics of us. An action and an equal and opposite reaction. My viny-hivey elfworld, as you say, versus your techy-mechy dystopia. We both know it's nothing so simple, any more than a letter's reply is its opposite. But which egg preceded what platypus? The ends don't always resemble our means.

But enough philosophy. Let me tell you what you have told me, speaking plain: You could have killed me, but didn't. You have acted without the knowledge or sanction of your Agency. Your vision of life in Garden is sufficiently full of silly stereotypes to read as a calculated attempt at provoking a stinging, unguarded response (hilarious, given how long it took me to grow these words), but spoken with such keen beauty as to suggest a confession of real, curious ignorance.

(We do have superb honey: best eaten in a thickness of comb, spread on warm bread with soft cheese, in a cool part of the day. Do your kind eat anymore? Is it all tubes and intravenous nutrition, metabolisms optimised for far-strand food? Do you sleep, Red, or dream?)

Let me also speak plain, before this tree runs out of years, before the fine fellows under your command make siege weapons of my words: What do you want from this, Red? What are you doing here?

Tell me something true, or tell me nothing at all.

Best,
Blue

PS. I'm touched by the research effort expended on my behalf. *Mrs. Leavitt's Guide* is a good one. Now that you've discovered postscripts, I look forward to what you could do with scented inks and seals!

PPS. There's no trick here, no thwart. Give my best to this strand's Genghis. We lay on our backs and watched clouds together when we were young.

Blue sees her chosen name reflected everywhere around her: moon-slicked floes, ocean thick with drift ice, liquid churned to glass. She munches a piece of dry biscuit on deck while the ship's hands sleep, dusts the crumbs off her mitts, and watches them fall into the white-flecked pitch of the waters.

The schooner's name is *The Queen of Ferryland*, carrying a full complement of hunters eager to stack scalps in the hold, hungry for what fur and flesh and fat will buy them in the off-season. Blue's interest is partly in oil, but chiefly in the deployment of new steam technologies: There is a staggering of outcomes to achieve, a point off which to tip the industry, a rudder with which to steer these ships between the Scylla of one doom and the Charybdis of another, onto a course that leads to Garden.

Seven strands tangle on the collapse or survival of this fishery—insignificant to some eyes, everything to others. Some days Blue wonders why anyone ever bothered making numbers so small; other days she supposes even infinity needs to start somewhere.

Those days rarely happen while on a mission.

Who can speak of what Blue thinks on a mission, when missions are often whole lives, when the story spun for her to wield a hunter's hook is years in the making? So many roles, dresses, parties, trousers, intimacies rolled into grasping a berth and bundling into shapeless clothes to keep Newfoundland's winter at bay.

The horizon blinks, and morning yawns above it. Hunters spill over the schooner's side, Blue among them: They sweep across the ice, tools in hand, laughing, singing, striking skulls and splitting skins.

Blue has hauled three skins on board when a big, brash beater catches her eye: It raises its head in threat for all of half a second before bolting for the water. Blue is faster. The beater's skull breaks like an egg beneath her club. She drops into a crouch beside it to inspect the pelt.

The sight hits her like a hakapik. There, in the ice-rimed fur, mottled and marked as hand-pulped paper, spots and speckles resolve into a word she can read: "Blue."

Her hand does not shake as she slices into the skin. Her breath comes even. She's kept her gloves clean, for the most part, but now she stains them red as a name.

Buried in the depths of glistening viscera is a dry piece of cod, undigested, scratched and grooved with language. She hardly realises that she's settled her body onto the ice, cross-legged, comfortable, as if tea, not seal guts, steamed dark and fragrant beside her.

She'll keep the pelt. The cod she'll crush to powder, sprinkle over rancidly buttered biscuit and eat for dinner; the body she'll dispose of in the usual way.

When the seeker comes hard and fast on her trail, all that's left is a smear of dark red on blue snow. On hands and knees, she licks and sucks and chews until all the colour's gone.

Her Silhouette, Drawn in Water

By Vylar Kaftan

1
Lost

These caves have never been friendly.

The tunnel is cold and dark. It's so tight my shoulders crush together. I'm bellying up the slope in my climbing suit. Rough ridges press my stomach flat to the rock, and I dig my gloves into a crevice. I can't return to the swampy passage below—we need to find the next supply print before the bugs do. My wet socks ooze inside my boots, but I can't warm myself until I'm dry. I shiver. The only way out is forward.

Chela has gone ahead. The upper passage glows with her headlamp, outlining the shape of my climb. My own lamp draws an irregular gray shape on the rock wall; everything else is blackness. I move my foot, seeking better traction, and I slip. Pebbles tremble and splash into the muck below, but I'm wedged too tight to fall. My small pack feels like an iron weight.

Light shines at me. Chela's hair hangs down like Rapunzel come to save me. "You okay, chica?" she calls.

Chela is the better climber and survival expert. She says she used to mountaineer on Earth. Without her, I'd be dead.

"Mostly. What's there?"

"Dry spot. Looks safe."

I nod. The bugs like damp places, which most of Colel-Cab is. At least the parts of our prison we've seen . . . or what I remember. I don't remember very much these days. I know tunnels, and more tunnels. Endless crawling, underground pools, and muddy sumps. The painful bites of tiny bugs—or whatever they are. "Bugs" is a valid term when we're the only two people on the planet. We can call them what we like.

And endless darkness. The darkness breaks your mind if you think about it. It claws at you with invisible hands, like a monster lashing out from unseen bonds. It's darkness you can't understand until you breathe it.

At least I'm not alone.

"I got this," I tell her. Defiantly, I wedge my foot and drag myself upslope. She reaches for me, but I ignore her hand as I scrabble to the flat area. I won't let a cave defeat me.

Chela laughs. "¡Qué chévere! Hey, Bee, that was fierce."

I roll on my side, savoring the floor. My headlamp shines on the rough-hewn wall. This tunnel is walkable, which is a welcome relief. It's made of smooth rock, probably man-made by whatever military group worked here. Sometimes we find a sealed metal door, but we've never been able to open one. I don't know who built this place. We're nomads in these tunnels—we go where our jailers print our food.

Chela stretches her arms and chuckles. "I thought you'd get stuck for sure."

I stick my tongue out. "Cabrona. Just because you're skinny . . ."

She laughs again and kisses my cheek. Chela's everything I'm not: tall, light-skinned, and gorgeous. My climbing rock star could model evening gowns, while I look like a boulder she'd lean on. But she loves me, and I love her, and together we'll make it off this planet. Somehow.

"You're brain-damaged, mamita," she says, "so don't waste time calling me names, or I'll hit you harder."

I press my face to the wall, overwhelmed. "I'm glad you're here," I say softly.

She hugs me from behind. I blink, trying not to cry. I barely remember Earth. I don't remember our crime. I just know what Chela told me: we're telepaths, and we're murderers. Four thousand and thirty lives, wiped out in minutes. The guilt eats me alive, like this never-ending darkness.

"Come on, Bee," she says gently. "Keep moving. We need to find the next cache before the bugs hatch."

I nod and force back tears. It's the stupid neck-chip that ruined me. It was just supposed to block my powers, but something went wrong when they installed mine, Chela says. I guess. There's no one else I can ask.

We walk silently in the tall passage, stooping for the low ceiling. I name it the White Walkway. All the passages are specked gray limestone—some rough and natural, some smooth as if carved. Like this one. The rare doors look the same: smooth metal plates with a single handle, like a cabinet. Everything smells awful; it's rust and corpses and toilets all mixed in one. The stink comes and goes in waves, so we can't get used to it.

Colel-Cab is an oppressive planet: silent and dank. Nothing but the endless dripping of water and scuttling of bugs. The toxic water makes us sick. Our cave suits are always damp, and our feet squelch coldly inside our boots. Sometimes we find an underground stream, surprisingly loud, after which the silence throbs in our ears. And sometimes cold wind bites through our suits, hinting at a nearby cavern. Mostly we're lost in an underground maze. A labyrinth with no Minotaur, no golden thread. Just us, trying to survive.

This cave curves through a field of small boulders. The floor becomes rough-cut ahead, despite the smooth walls. "Wait," I say, "there's more of the writing."

Chela looks with me. "I still don't think it's writing."

There are markings on the walls sometimes, never near the doors. It looks like writing or weird floral patterns. I can't explain what's there, but it's like there's a similarity I never quite spot. We don't know who built this place. I like to imagine aliens shaping these caves—perhaps some tunneling species, only semi-intelligent. But we haven't seen proof of anything.

"Well, I want to map anyway," I say, sliding my tablet out of my thigh pocket. I take a picture of the symbols.

"This is a dead planet, honey-Bee. Looks like bug tracks more than anything."

"It feels important."

She shrugs. "If you like."

She's right, but I'm desperate for meaning. I've been mapping as we go. Twice we've lost our data to technical problems—including three weeks ago. And I'm not even sure how long we've been imprisoned here. Chela says eleven months. It's a blur to me.

I slide the tablet away. My stomach twists with guilt. "Chela, why did we do it?"

"Do what?"

"The starship."

Her voice grows tender. "You remember the starship?"

"No, I just remember what you told me. We decompressed a starship."

"Yes. There was a war."

"Yes," I say, faintly remembering. I'm embarrassed I have to keep asking.

"We had to stop that ship. But really, we should've found another way. Worked harder." Her voice turns icy. "We're mind terrorists, Bee. Monsters."

"We're telepaths—"

"We *were* telepaths."

My neck aches, like I've been punched in the head.

"Were."

"You were incredibly powerful. Everyone said you were the best. I think that's why your chip is messed up. They're afraid of you, and I can't say I blame them. I don't know why they put me here with you. Probably a mistake—but here we are. Where we can't hurt anyone."

"Except ourselves," I say.

She takes my hand, and I stare at the ground. Something moves next to us, and we both turn sharply. Three bugs skitter into a crack and drop their lentil-size bugshells. They're still small, but molting is a bad sign.

She yanks my arm. "Move!"

We need the supplies. We clamber over uneven rocks as the path grows rough. I trip and fall, catching myself with my wrists. My knees bruise even through the cave suit. My backpack drags me down. Chela's faster, and she's leaving me behind.

"Wait!" I struggle to one knee, frightened. "¡Chela, espérame!"

"No, abeja, we need it!"

She's right—if we delay, the bugs will wreck the print. It's happened before. It's our only clean water and food, and sometimes we get new clothing or rope or even little distractions. We had a ballerina music box that was my joy until it broke.

But still, I can't do this without her. She's my lifeline. My throat locks and I can't breathe. Darkness surrounds me. I can't think of anything except *I'm alone, she's left me alone; I'll die here alone in the darkness.*

No. I won't think like that. I focus on the music box. That memory, so clear underneath the fog. "Waltz of the Flowers"—that was the song. I force myself to hum. I imagine I'm a dancer, standing up after a fall.

I shakily get to my feet. My only light is my own. I smell

sulfur, which means the bugs are near. I don't notice any, but I have to focus on my footing. Boulders are scattered throughout the tunnel; the cave floor is an obstacle course. The ground is spiky like the inside of a geode. Ahead of me, Chela's headlamp casts wild shadows as she runs. She's risking a sprained ankle. We're close enough to see the beacon flashing orange, a steady pattern against the rocks. A few clicks off to the side, and my heart races. Those are bugs preparing to swarm.

Chela scrambles toward our target, and the clicks intensify. They're louder, summoning more insects. More enemies to steal our food—to starve us.

"Almost there!" she shouts. A wing brushes my face—but it's gone again. Yet another thing we don't understand on Colel-Cab: how bugs go from crawling to flying in seconds. We've seen wings burst from their hairy bodies and grow in a minute flat. Fully grown, they're rabbit size with a four-foot cobwebby wingspan. Like flying mutant roaches. Just one can easily smash a supply print and ruin our rations—and they always come by the hundreds.

I brighten my lamp, using up battery. I scream—not because I'm afraid, but to startle the bugs. "¡Cuidado!" I warn Chela between screams.

Chela shrieks too. It's hard to do a controlled scream; the act of screaming panics you. It's worse than the silence of Colel-Cab. Chela told me about the Rapture—a panic attack specific to spelunking, when you lose your shit completely. Numb hands and feet, heart racing like a locomotive, tremors that tear your finger muscles to pulp. Sometimes I think my whole existence is a never-ending panic attack.

Chela shouts, "Got it!"

I crawl forward, swatting at the insect cloud obscuring Chela. Thankfully these aren't the red biting bugs, but their weaker gray cousins. But they land in my hair, buzz their wings in my face, and seek cracks in my suit to tear open. They shove their antennae up my nose and into my ears. I wave my arms frantically, trying to dispel them and protect the print. Chela bangs the metal box against rock—she has it, the print is safe.

We push through the swarm, not stopping until we reach clear ground. We sit against a wall, huddled with our faces together, holding our treasure close. Soon the sound dies out as the bugs shed their wings. They fall to the floor, then shrink and scuttle into cracks. The silence is overwhelming, and my ears itch. But the threat is gone—for now.

The bugs still terrify me. But I'm curious about them too. I wonder what xenobiologists know about our prison. We've never met anyone working here, and we think that's deliberate. No one would put a closed person near telepaths. It's just Chela and me. All our supplies come from remotely controlled printers.

Chela breaks open the box. Eagerly I ask, "What'd we get?"

"The usual," she says. "Water tubes, protein bars, salt pills. Another clip to replace the one you broke. Ooh, new gloves. Good, mine were torn up."

"Anything we could try to signal with?"

She gives me a dirty look under her headlamp. "Yeah, no. As if we could ever escape."

"What, I'm supposed to give up?"

"You're supposed to enjoy the moment," she says gently, taking my hand. "We aren't getting out, and we can't make base camp. So we may as well adventure—and be glad we're together. That we're not in solitary like telepaths should be."

I look down. I know we've had this argument before. Probably more times than I remember. But I can't give up. I've got to talk to the warden—whoever that is. To explain things: my chip was damaged, and I need my memory back, and I'm really sorry for my crimes.

Chela digs in the print box, scraping the bottom. "Oh, and something else. Hmm. A picture of flowers. A postcard or something." She turns it over in her hands.

"Let me see," I say, taking it from her. The back is blank, but the front shows green leaves and white flowers.

"I guess it's an Earth souvenir. They think we miss it?"

"I do miss Earth," I say, staring at it hungrily.

"Well, I don't," she says, drinking from a water tube and carefully recapping it. "There's no point in missing what we can't have. You're wasting energy and depressing yourself."

"I suppose," I say, slipping the postcard into my pocket. "I still think about it."

"So let me distract you." She takes my face in her hands and kisses me, deeply. Her lips are always soft, even when mine are split and cold. I relax and hold my partner. We're trapped in the depths of Colel-Cab, but at least we have each other.

2
Contact

I know I had a family. My dad died when I was young. My mom worked in a doll factory. She brought home broken, imperfect dolls for me. I'd line them up in my bedroom like an audience. They'd stare at me through missing eyes and wobble on their strangely shaped legs. I knew they were dolls, not people, because I couldn't hear them thinking. For a long time I thought dolls were just better at hiding their feelings.

I don't remember much about being a telepath. I remember my mother carrying me in her arms, running down a hallway, but I don't remember why. I have a clear memory of a car that scared me, some armored black machine speeding past the damaged apartments on my block. I remember my mom's caramel churro recipe, which she made as a birthday treat. I'm fluent in Spanish, but I only spoke it at home. I've loved spaceships ever since second grade, but I don't remember why.

I feel like a silhouette without a self.

At least today we discovered a dry sleeping place—that's not always true. We've returned to that cave, which I've labeled "Scarlet Dome" on my map, to sleep. I'm sick of dull rocks and darkness. I name landmarks to give them color in my mind.

It's an alcove with one entrance, big enough for us to stretch out in. It isn't really nighttime, of course; our tablets say 7:11 a.m. But every time I look, the time and date are different on the tablets. We can't use them as timers. Chela's been estimating days, but she's not sure how accurate she is; she says that people in caves have longer sleep-wake cycles.

We change into the high-tech pajamas we keep in our packs. Chela says they're itchy, but warmer and lighter than silk—she snidely calls them "bata de cárcel." I just find them dry, wonderfully dry. She unfolds our sleeping pads and lays them out. I set out my helmet for a nightlight and turn hers off to conserve the battery. I hate doing it. The cave darkens, as if shadowy creatures encircle us. The claws of the darkness scratch our minds. It happens every time we have to rest—but we need to save batteries, so we give the darkness its due. Chela sleeps and I settle in for first watch.

So many holes in my mind. I remember odd things, like the peach teacups at some party I attended. But when I think about telepathy, my neck spasms. Shame overwhelms me and sometimes I cry. I hope I had a good reason for what I did. I must have. I don't think I'm violent; I'm really softhearted. And I don't want vengeance—I just want my thoughts back. I think if Chela weren't here, I would've killed myself long ago.

I've pressed Chela to fill me in. She must know all about me. But she doesn't like talking about the past—ever. ("Why go over it all again? I envy you, mi abejita, without so much shit on your mind.") She says there's lots I never told her, so she doesn't know the answers.

What she's told me: we met through a secret group. We thought we were resistance heroes, but a telepathic cult was controlling us. "Can't trust a telepath," she always says, and won't say more. She doesn't know when we fell in love—she thinks we always knew how we felt. And we always agreed not to read each other's minds.

Even without my full memory, I know I've never met a woman like her. Chela loves exploring these caves. She wants an adventure—at least, she's making the best of a nightmare. And cheering me up too. I look down at her sleeping figure. She rests on her side, curled like a cat. A long honey-brown curl has drifted across her nose. I tuck the curl back and trace her smooth cheek with my finger. Then I remember the postcard.

I pull out the postcard and examine it, squinting in the dimness. It shows a little white flower—two flowers actually, one mostly hidden. They each have five petals and a pale yellow center. I don't recognize them, though I feel like I should. Maybe I had a garden once. I sniff the postcard, but it just smells like damp paper.

What a strange gift. The wardens decide what we get; from my perspective, supply boxes appear like magic. We get messages on our tablets, and Chela finds the way. For all my mapping, she's much better at navigating. Maybe because she's not trying to find alien histories written in bug scratches.

Something moves nearby. I freeze. Nothing in sight, so I wait. My heart pounds. The darkness presses me, heightening my senses. It crawls into my eyes, my ears and nose, like poison seeking my brain stem. I listen as hard as I can, as if focusing could change what exists. I'm convinced something's there beyond my night-light.

"Chela," I whisper fiercely as my pulse races.

Her eyes flash open, as if she never sleeps. She leaps up, pulls on her helmet, and crouches silently with me.

We wait without speaking. Finally she says, "What is it?"

"I don't know."

Chela takes my hand. Her touch eases my pounding heart. After a minute, her grip eases and the tension leaves my body. She says, "What did you think it was?"

"I . . . don't know. Something?"

"Very helpful, abejita."

I crack a smile. "Okay, sorry. Like . . . I don't know, something was there. Not a bug."

She's silent, then says, "I think you imagined it."

"I . . ." I start to say *I didn't,* but I realize she's right. I'm far more imaginative than Chela. I can invent whole worlds of darkness from a few wall scratches—and she only sees what's in front of her.

She says, "I'm going back to sleep." She lies down, facing away, and is asleep almost instantly.

I watch alone in the near-darkness. Nothing for a while . . . but again I'm convinced something's there. What could be in this place? Aliens? Crazy telepathic aliens, scratching up a wall to talk to me? I laugh at my own imagination. Ridiculous. But as long as I'm fantasizing, I might as well reach out. Try to connect telepathically, which I can't do anymore because of the chip.

I can already hear what Chela will say when I tell her. She'll roll her eyes and tell me I deserved it, the inevitable backwash and headache. What the hell, I resolve to try—to prove to myself I can't do this.

Reaching out hurts, like flinging your brain a thousand feet down on a bungee cord. Such dreadful eyeball pain. This I remember clearly, though I haven't reached out since I was imprisoned. The chip blocks it. So this shouldn't work, and most likely I'll just hurt myself.

I send an inquisitive thought. Nothing—

Then a hammer hits my mind. I pass out.

I wake to a bright light. Chela is rubbing my temples and stroking my hair. She quickly tilts her lamp away from my eyes. Relief washes over her face. "Qué chingados," she says. "What happened?"

"My head," I whimper, regretting my impulse. I roll sideways and vomit.

She wipes vomit off my lips with her sleeve. "You didn't . . ." Her face slides into angry. "You did. Madre de Dios, Bee, that chip will kill you. Don't—"

"Someone is *here.* Someone, something, I don't—"

"No one is here, honey-Bee, no one at all. Have you forgotten? We're in exile."

I sit up. My head spins and I lie back down. "I think it was another mind. Someone real."

"You . . . shouldn't be able to do that."

"Well, I did," I say defiantly.

"If you can, that's bad."

"Why? Maybe it's someone who will help us."

"More likely cops testing your lockdown." Chela cracks her knuckles and spits.

"It didn't feel dangerous," I say slowly, trying to remember. It happened so fast.

"They wouldn't threaten you. They'd use an undercover telepath to scan prisoners. If they reach anyone, they tear them out and screw them down tighter. Or maybe kill them. I don't fucking know."

"It could be help," I say. "Someone to get us off this goddamn planet."

"No one will help us," she says, her voice bitter. "You've forgotten, but they're scared. They hate us. They'll never let us go."

"Well we could fucking *try*!" My voice rings through the cavern. My head throbs and my eyeballs feel like bursting.

Chela doesn't answer. She just glares at the wall. The look on her face makes me wonder if she's right. Maybe we can't win. I should sink into our life here, make the most of it. Like she has.

But I just can't live that way. I whisper, "If I could just remember."

She says, "It's from the installation, honey-Bee. I don't think anyone can fix it now."

"But we can *try*," I insist again.

She sighs. "Please don't reach out. If something happens—" Her voice breaks. She takes my hands and presses them in hers. "If something happens to you, that's the end of me. I can't even think about it without choking up. Prison's an adventure with you. Without you . . . I have nothing."

Her lips brush my forehead. A shiver runs through me. I need her too. Without her . . . I blink back tears. I can't imagine. I'd lose my mind.

She makes a face and sits back. "Abeja, your breath is shit."

I chuckle. "That's because you feed me so much shit." She half-smiles. "Promise me you won't reach out."

"I . . ." I hesitate.

"Promise."

"I can't promise that," I say. "If I think—" She rolls her eyes. "You'll get us killed."

"It's the only hope we have, and you want me to drop it?"

She sighs. "Look, you're exhausted. Why don't you sleep? I'll take watch."

This isn't settled, but she's right—I'm worn to the bone. The presence is gone. I curl up and fall asleep.

When I wake, Chela hands me a mango square—a chewy orange building block containing our nutrition and salts. I'm glad we have decent rations, but I'm so sick of mangoes that I want to burn every tropical tree in existence. To do that, I'll have to escape this prison. I wonder if Chela would enjoy destroying mango trees with me.

I glance sidelong at her. She's eating calmly. She hands me a water tube, and I say, "Thanks for taking care of me last night."

She smiles. "You're welcome, mi cariño. I'm thinking upslope. Get your ass in gear." When we aren't expecting a cache, we keep moving, keep exploring. Chela says it's helped us be ready a few times. Not to mention that anything is better than planting your ass on a cold rock for hours, worrying about your battery life. That's a slow suicide.

After changing into our cave suits, we climb into a tough tunnel with no handholds. We chimney up, bracing ourselves with our butts and feet. My knuckles are always scraped up, even inside my gloves, and my muscles hurt. I still have a nasty headache. But I don't bring up the presence again. Not now, not until I've had time to think.

Chela stops climbing. "Listen," she says.

A pebble drops from the wall by her shoe. Bugs crawl near us—small bugs, no sign of a swarm. Then I hear it: the familiar sound of water. Lots of it, more than I remember hearing before. "A river!"

"Serious water, yeah," she says. "More than these little streams and puddles everywhere. At least it's new."

"We can follow it," I say excitedly. "To—"

She gives me a sharp look. I change my words, saying, "To its source. Maybe the surface."

"I think this place is all tunnels with an extra dose of tunnels," she mutters darkly. "But yeah. Maybe."

As we keep climbing, I wonder: How *did* we kill a spaceship? Did we possess the captain's mind? Did we make the engineer decompress the ship? Or did we send some poor passenger to destroy the ventilation system? I hear the explosion in my head, the scream of four thousand lives snuffed out in minutes, but I don't remember *details* and that bothers me. Shouldn't I be glad it's a blur? How could I live with myself if I remembered it all?

Would it be better if I remembered why it mattered to me?

"Chela?" I ask.

"Yeah?" She's scrambling above me. "Go left—it's easier."

"Thanks. About the war . . ."

She's silent for a minute. "You're thinking about it because of last night, aren't you?"

"Yeah. Were we at war for America? Or an alliance of some kind?"

She sighs. "Telepaths. Against everyone else."

"And we killed innocents."

"Yeah."

"Is this the thing you've said about . . . there are no innocents? Everyone is part of—"

"This is about murder. This is about us telepaths thinking we were immune from human decency."

"But why? Were we persecuted? We must have been—"

She stops and kicks a tiny rock near her. It skitters down past my hand. "We deserve to be here."

"And that's why you want to stay forever?" I ask, taking the harder climb on the right.

"Qué diablo—"

"You do," I insist, catching up to her. "You want to crawl here forever, and keep me for company. You don't want me escaping."

"It's not that, abeja, I'm just so worried about—"

"If I found a rocket tomorrow," I demand, brushing against her arm, "would you leave this planet with me?"

She looks at me. Our headlamps shine against each other, blindingly, but I won't look away. We hold our positions. On her face I see my fears mirrored.

"I stay with you, honey-Bee," she whispers, looking away. "I'm yours. Always."

"Then we try to contact this presence. They might be able to rescue us."

"It's a trap!" she shouts, her voice echoing. "It's the cops, testing you. No one rescues telepaths. Especially not a powerful one like you."

"Well then, *you* try reaching out."

"I'm dead inside!" she says. "I can't even feel the space where I connect."

I'm startled. She's never told me that, not that I remember. "You don't even feel it?"

"Well, I'm not 'the greatest telepath ever,'" she retorts.

"Who says that I am?"

"You," she says angrily. "You, before. When we—" She breaks off.

"Chela," I beg, "mi amor, tell me what you know."

"No," she snaps. "It'll hurt. I'm tired of hurting."

"It hurts not knowing!"

She climbs away from me, spidering up rocks at breakneck speed. There's no way I can follow her.

I sigh. I have to get more out of her, but not while she's in this mood.

We take a side fork, following the river's sounds. It must flow parallel and a little higher than us, across some ridge.

It's a long slog, but physical work relaxes Chela. She'll be kinder.

We spend the day silently, as we sometimes do. I don't feel the presence anywhere, which worries me; are we moving away from it? If it's only in the Scarlet Dome, are we leaving it behind? I've made good notes on my tablet, but I worry about another data crash.

Chela leads us on a roundabout path, bringing us to dozens of dead ends and sumps, but always finding another route to try. She's a natural caver and she's always had a great sense of direction, so I just sketch the pathways and estimate the elevation. I sketch in the Rainbow Passage and the Jade Hanging Rock. We make slow progress across the Feathery Wasteland, with rocks so delicate that our boots crush them to pebbles.

After a long climb, we reach a small cavern where water pours through a gap and drains somewhere out of sight. Chela says it's overflow for the actual river, and she points at a small passage.

"Ready to get skinny, mamita?" she asks. "Make like a snake?"

She seems to be back to her usual self. I nod, then slip off my backpack and hook it over one arm, clutching it like a talisman. We crawl through the passage. It's horribly tight. My boot gets wedged and I can't unstick it. "Pull your foot out," she calls, and I do. The boot stays trapped as I sockfoot through. After helping me up, Chela slinks back down for my boot.

I look around, rubbing my icy foot. This cave holds an underground river, a sizable one, with a spacious ceiling. Water streams past me and disappears into darkness. A small breeze moves in the cave, indicating connected passages. It smells fresh and alive. I don't see any bugs, so I relax against the wall. The nook to one side looks relatively cozy and dry enough for sleeping. I can pretend this cave is comfortable—a place to recover. I name it Tranquility Blue.

Chela returns with my boot. She air-kisses my muddy toes.

"Yuck!" I exclaim, pulling back my damp, stinky foot.

She chuckles. "I didn't *lick* them, silly." She slides my boot on.

I smile. "It's pretty here."

She just nods. We sit for a minute, holding hands. I look sidelong at her headlamp. It shines forward, but beneath it lies her silhouette—faintly, in black drawn on black. She's a ghost of herself in the darkness, like me, and both of us will eventually fade away. I squeeze her hand tightly.

Chela shifts restlessly on her butt. Then she says, "Let's swim. Come on."

"It'll be freezing!"

"I don't care. Let's do it—something different. Look, I still have those chemical warmers from an earlier print. The snap-and-heat kind. We'll be okay. Come on!"

Chela drags me by the arm. I giggle and give in. She shrieks and pulls me into the river. It's deep, with a strong current. The cold water feels like a baseball bat to the stomach.

"¡Chíngate, qué frio!" she screams, and I agree—my toes are going numb. My legs fold reflexively and I hug myself tight. We're only about ten feet from the riverbank. Chela laughs hysterically and throws her arms around me. "Hold me, you dumbfuck!"

I push her off. "Stop swimming, you dumbfuck!"

I'm laughing too—I can't help it, it's contagious. I drag her back to shore and we collapse on the rocks. I'm glad we're alive, feeling pain and joy and everything in between. We embrace and her tongue snakes into my mouth. We kiss fiercely, forgetting everything around us. I could lose myself inside her forever, if I chose.

But my poor feet! "I'm dying now," I accuse her.

Chela laughs in rapid bursts, her hands shaking with chill. "Okay, I'm getting the things out. ¡Espera!"

"I can't; my hands are too cold!" But she'd been right—it was worth it. Every stupid, painful, wonderful minute. Because of her.

We scramble into the nook. Chela pulls out the chemical warmer packets and snaps them with a crack. She shoves one into each of my hands. Immediately warmth spreads through my palms, and I clutch the crinkly packets like the precious gift of fire. She strips my boots and socks, then wraps two warmers around my naked feet. Life pulses into my body. I lie back and close my eyes, letting miraculous heat travel up my arms and legs.

But Chela isn't done. She unzips my climbing suit and reaches inside. I utter an "Eep!" as her cold wrist brushes my bare stomach. Her fingers trace a heart on my lower belly. Then her hand slinks down between my legs.

"For your girlbits," she says, and there's sudden heat. She's shoved a warmer into my pants. I breathe in sharply as my clitoris heats. Warmth shoots like a shock through my nerves—down to my big toes, and up to my cold-swollen nipples. I feel like a drawing of my own nervous system, warm and snug in someone's textbook.

I open my eyes to see Chela's face coming toward mine. Her hair smells of algae. She sets her helmet down for ambient light. She kisses me slowly and caresses my cheeks. She's wrapped warmers around her hands so her touch radiates heat. Her hands trace patterns over my skin—like she's shaping my body with heat. The warmer in my pants becomes almost uncomfortable, and suddenly I don't feel cold anywhere, not even the deep parts of me that have been cold since I can remember.

Chela whispers, "Let me take care of that for you." She peels back my climbing suit, exposing my breasts and stomach. She kisses each breast, like she's greeting them for the day. Then she trails her tongue down to my pubic hair. My back arches in response. I wiggle to help her remove my climbing suit. A few more tugs and I'm free.

I open my legs to her. Her tongue finds me. I gasp with excitement and sheer life—for the adventure that we share. She knows just how to touch me. She brings me to tenseness, my whole body locked, until I push past and drop into perfect relaxation. She adds her fingers—one then two—and with her tongue I climax quickly. I scream into our prison as if ecstasy can free us—and for a moment, it has.

We lie together afterward, our limbs intertwined. I say, "Oh, my darling. Do you want . . . ?"

"No," she says gently. "That was a gift."

"Thank you. I love you. Oh my God, I love you."

"We're good together," she says, brushing a finger over my lips—lightly, like a feather. "We're all that we need. We rescue ourselves."

In this moment she's my world.

After a few minutes, Chela helps me back into my damp suit. The warmers have cooled, but they did their job. I feel better, and Chela looks pleased with herself. She starts exploring Tranquility Blue's dry passages, seeking the river's source. I find more wall scratchings, which I capture in a photo, and I enhance my notes with sketches.

That's when I feel the presence—stronger this time. I suck in my breath. I glance at Chela, whose faint light reflects on distant rocks. She can't see me.

I try to listen to the presence without reaching out. I feel like I remember something about telepathy—that I might hear thoughts without trying. I have to relax and absorb the world in my mind. Lose myself. I close my eyes and breathe

the delicious air, which smells of alien algae. Something alive, and pleasant. I'm alive, like the smell, and so is the surrounding world. We're the same.

:Bee:

What the—

:Danger:

What's dangerous? And how do they know me? The algae scent is gone, overwhelmed by something new—a perfume. I breathe the aroma, wondering what it is. Flowers with a rich depth, like chocolate. I know this smell—it's an Earth scent. Maybe the flower from the postcard?

:Where are you?:

Something about the presence feels desperate. I can't stop myself—I'm never good at boundaries. I reach out and touch another mind. We link for a moment, clasping minds before the hammer crushes my head. I know this voice, and I know it well—but who is it?

When I wake, Chela is holding me in her arms. Her lamp blinds me, and I shield my eyes with a hand. "Bee!" she says tightly. "You didn't. Tell me you didn't."

"Chela, they know me. And I know them."

"It must be a trap, Bee—!"

"What if another telepath is trying to rescue us?"

In a strained voice, she says, "No one can. No ship comes close enough for contact."

"What if they *can,* Chela?"

"No. Not possible."

"Smell the air! Flowers."

She inhales. A moment passes. "No, chica, nothing."

"Chela, why are you convinced it's impossible?"

She looks down. "Even if it *were* possible, there's no chance anyone would rescue us. Hope is useless here."

The scent fills my mind, searching the doors of my memory.

Jasmine.

"Her name is Jasmine." As I say it, I know I'm right. Jasmine's a telepath. We both know her well. The flower on the postcard—the scent.

Chela shakes her head, but I pull her face forward. Her eyes squeeze shut against my headlamp. I say, "Chela. Who's Jasmine?"

She grimaces like I'd hit her. "Bee, this is how they entrap you. Jasmine is dangerous. She's the one who . . ." She chokes and falls silent.

Memories stream back. I see Jasmine's face. A lovely woman, tall and dark, with the whitest smile I've ever seen and tight curls cropped to her head. She always wears . . . some jewelry, something sparkly. I remember kissing her—somewhere, where was that?

Chela shakes me. I've lost time in thought. "My God, Bee, you're going to get us killed. Jasmine is trouble. Don't you remember what I said about undercover telepaths?"

"What do you want me to do?" I ask, my headache churning.

"Play dead. She's testing you. If she finds you've still got power, they'll take you away from me. Or kill you. Please, Bee. You have to trust me."

"But . . ."

She pleads, "Bee. I've been with you from the start. I'll be with you at the end. Please. We can look for a way out, I don't care. But stay away from Jasmine. I need you. I need you here with me, more than you even know."

I don't know what to believe. I say flatly, "Let's map."

Chela sits still and watches me draw, which is unlike her. Eventually she gets up and explores the cave. I don't know what to say. She's been right about most things, aside from saying I'd get used to the nutrition bars. She's never let me down when I needed her.

What do I do? If I hear Jasmine again, she'll reach out to me. I can't even reach out without collapsing. Is it even possible to send back to her? Maybe all I can do is listen. Maybe that's enough.

Troubled, I continue my sketching. There's an alcove I can't quite see, so I go explore it. It's small, with a large central stalagmite that fills most of the space—the Ashen Tower, I decide. I'm sketching the alcove, glancing up, when I see it.

A window.

The Deep

By Rivers Solomon, Daveed Diggs, William Hutson, and Jonathan Snipes

1

"It was like dreaming," said Yetu, throat raw. She'd been weeping for days, lost in a remembering of one of the first wajinru.

"Then wake up," Amaba said, "and wake up now. What kind of dream makes someone lurk in shark-dense waters, leaking blood like a fool? If I had not come for you, if I had not found you in time..." Amaba shook her head, black water sloshing over her face. "Do you wish for death? Is that why you do this? You are grown now. Have *been* grown. You must put those childish whims behind you." Amaba waved her front fins forcefully as she lectured her daughter, the movements troubling the otherwise placid water.

"I do not wish for death," said Yetu, resolute despite the quiet of her worn voice.

"Then what? What else would make you do something so foolish?" Amaba asked, her fins a bevy of movement.

Yetu strained to feel Amaba's words over the chorus of ripples, her skin drawn away from the delicate waves of speech and toward the short, powerful pulses brought on by her amaba's gesticulations.

"Answer me!" Amaba said, her tone desperate and screeching.

Most of the time, Yetu kept her senses dulled. As a child, she'd learned to shut out what she could of the world, lest it overwhelm her into fits. But now she had to open herself back up, to make her body a wound again so Amaba's words would ring against her skin more clearly.

Yetu closed her eyes and honed in on the vibrations of the deep, purposefully resensitizing her scaled skin to the onslaught of the circus that is the sea. It was a matter of reconnecting her brain to her body and lowering the shields she'd put in place in her mind to protect herself. As she focused, the world came in. The water grew colder, the pressure more intense, the salt denser. She could parse each granule. Individual crystals of the flaky white mineral scraped against her.

Even though Yetu always kept herself tense against the ocean's intrusions, they found their way in; but with her senses freshly unreined, the rush of feeling was dizzying. This was nothing like the faraway throbbing she'd grown used to when she threw all her energy into repelling the world outside. The push and pull of nearby currents upended her. The flutter of a school of fangfish reverberated deep in her chest. How did other wajinru manage this all the time?

"Where did you go just now? Are you dreaming yet again?" asked Amaba, sounding more defeated than angry. Her voice cracked into splintered waves, rough against Yetu's skin.

"I am here, Amaba. I promise," said Yetu quietly, exhaustedly, though she wasn't sure that was true. Adrift in a memory that wasn't hers, she hadn't been present when she'd brought herself to the sharks to be feasted upon. How could she be sure she was here now?

Yetu needed to recover her composure. She'd never done something that dangerous before. She had lost more control of her abilities than she'd realized. The rememberings were always drawing her backward into the ancestors' memories—that was what they were supposed to do—but not at the expense of her life.

"Come to me," said Amaba, several paces away. Too weak to argue, Yetu offered no protest. She resigned herself for now to do her amaba's biddings. "You need medicine, child. And food. When did you last eat?"

Yetu didn't remember, but as she took a moment to zero in on the emptiness in her stomach, she was surprised to find the pain of it was a vortex she could easily get lost in. She moved her body, examined its contours. She'd been withering away, and now there was little left of her but the base amounts of outer fat she needed to keep warm in the ocean's deepest waters.

As evidenced by her encounter with the sharks, Yetu's condition was worsening. With each passing year, she was less and less able to distinguish rememberings from the present.

"Eat these. They will help your throat heal," said Amaba, drawing her daughter into her embrace. Yetu floated in the dense, black brine, her amaba's fins a lasso about her torso. "Come, now. I said eat." Amaba pressed venom leaves into Yetu's mouth, humming a made-up lullaby as she did. Water waves from her voice stroked Yetu's scales, and though Yetu usually avoided such stimulation, she was pleased to have a tether to the waking world as her connection to it grew more and more precarious. She needed frequent reminders she was more than a vessel for the ancestors' memories. She wouldn't let herself disappear. "Keep chewing. That's good. Very good. Now swallow."

Spurred by the promise of pain relief as much as by her amaba's prodding, Yetu gagged the medicine down. Venom leaves slithered like slime down her throat and into her belly, and with every swallow she coughed.

"See? Isn't that nice? Can you feel it working in you yet?"

Cradled in her amaba's front fins, Yetu looked but a pup. It was fitting. In this moment, she was as reliant on Amaba's care as she had been in infancy. She'd grown from colicky pup into mercurial adolescent into tempestuous adult, still sometimes in need of her amaba's deep nurturing.

Given her sensitivity, no one should have been surprised that the rememberings affected Yetu more deeply than previous historians, but then everything surprised wajinru. Their memories faded after weeks or months—if not through wajinru biological predisposition for forgetfulness, then through sheer force of will. Those cursed with more intact long-term recollection learned how to forget, how to throw themselves into the moment. Only the historian was allowed to remember.

After several moments, the venom leaves took effect, and the pain in Yetu's hoarse throat numbed. Other aches soothed too. The stiffness all but disappeared from her neck. Overworked muscles relaxed. Sedated, she could think more clearly now.

"Amaba," Yetu said. She was calmer and in a state to better explain what had happened that morning: why she'd gone to the sharks, why she'd put herself in such danger, why she'd threatened the wajinru legacy so selfishly.

If Yetu died doing something reckless and the wajinru were not able to recover her body, the next historian would not be able to harvest the ancestors' rememberings from Yetu's mind. Bits of the History could be salvaged from the shark's body, assuming they found it, but it was an incredible risk, and no doubt whole sections would be lost.

Worse, the wajinru didn't know who was to succeed Yetu. They may not have had the memories to understand the importance of this fully, but they had an inkling. It had been plain to all for many years that Yetu was a creature on the precipice, and without a successor in place, they'd be lost. They'd have to improvise.

Previous historians had spent their days roaming the ocean to collect the memories of the living wajinru before they were forgotten. Such a task ensured that the historian understood who was best suited to take on the role after their own death came. In addition to reaching into the minds of wajinru to log the events of the era, historians learned whose minds were electro-sensitive enough to host the rememberings in the future, and shared that information often and repeatedly with other wajinru.

Yetu never did this. The ocean overwhelmed her even when she was in its most quiet portions, and that was before taking on the rememberings. Now that she was the historian, it was even worse, her mind unable to process it all. She couldn't fathom spending her days traveling across the sea only to burden herself with more memories at the end of each journey. Unfortunately for Yetu, when the previous historian had chosen her, he'd been so impressed by the sensitivity of her electroreceptors that he'd failed to notice her finicky temperament. Yetu loved Basha's memories, loved living inside of his bravery, his tumult. But if ever he'd made a mistake, it was choosing Yetu as historian. She couldn't fulfill her most basic of duties. How disappointed he would be in the girl he'd chosen. She'd grown up to be so fragile.

"I'm sorry," said Yetu. "There's so much to tell you, yet I never know where to begin. But I am ready now. I can speak. I can tell you why I did what I did, and it has nothing to do with wanting to die."

Yetu readied herself to reveal all, to go back to those painful moments and relive them yet again for her amaba's benefit.

"Shhh," said Amaba, using the sticky webbing at the end

of her left front fin to cover Yetu's mouth. "It is in the past. It is already forgotten. What matters is that you are here now, and we can focus on the present. It is time for you to give the Remembrance."

The Remembrance—had it really been a year since the last? A year, then, since she'd seen her amaba? It was impossible to keep precise track of the passing of time in the dark of the deep, but she could ascertain the time of year based on currents, animal movement, and mating seasons. None of that mattered, however, if Yetu wasn't present enough to pay attention to them. The rememberings carried her mind away from the ocean to the past. These days, she was more there than here. This wasn't a new thought, but she'd never felt it this strongly before. Yetu was becoming an ancestor herself. Like them, she was dead, or very near it.

"I didn't know that we were already so close to the Remembrance," said Yetu, unsure she even had the strength to conduct the ceremony.

"Yetu, it is overdue by an entire mating cycle," said Amaba.

Was Yetu really three months late to the most important event in the wajinru's life? Had she failed her duty so tremendously? "Is everyone all right?" asked Yetu.

"Alive, yes, but not well, not well at all," said Amaba.

A historian's role was to carry the memories so other wajinru wouldn't have to. Then, when the time came, she'd share them freely until they got their fill of knowing.

Late as Yetu was, the wajinru must be starving for it, consumed with desire for the past that made and defined them. Living without detailed, long-term memories allowed for spontaneity and lack of regret, but after a certain amount of time had passed, they needed more. That was why once a year, Yetu gave them the rememberings, even if only for a few days. It was enough that their bodies retained a sense memory of the past, which could sustain them through the year until the next Remembrance.

"We grow anxious and restless without you, my child. One can only go for so long without asking who am I? Where do I come from? What does all this mean? What is being? What came before me, and what might come after? Without answers, there is only a hole, a hole where a history should be that takes the shape of an endless longing. We are cavities. You don't know what it's like, blessed with the rememberings as you are," said Amaba.

Yetu *did* know what it was like. After all, wasn't *cavity* just another word for *vessel*? Her own self had been scooped out when she was a child of fourteen years to make room for ancestors, leaving her empty and wandering and ravenous.

"I'll be taking you to the sacred waters soon. The people will want to offer their thanks and prayers to you. You should be happy, no? You like the Remembrance. It is good for you," Amaba said.

Yetu disagreed. The Remembrance took more than it gave. It required she remember and relive the wajinru's entire history all at once. Not just that, she had to put order and meaning to the events, so that the others could understand. She had to help them open their minds so they could relive the past too.

It was a painful process. The reward at the end, that the rememberings left Yetu briefly while the rest of the wajinru absorbed them, was small. If she could skip it, she would, but she couldn't. That was something her younger, more immature self would've done. She'd been appointed to this role according to her people's traditions, and she balked at the level of self-centeredness it would require to abandon six hundred years of wajinru culture and custom to accommodate her own desires.

"Are you strong enough to swim to the sacred waters without help?" Amaba asked Yetu.

She wasn't, but she'd make the journey unaided anyway. She didn't want her amaba carrying her any more than she already had. The memory of Amaba's fins squeezing around her tail fin, dragging her away from the sharks at nauseating speeds, lingered unpleasantly, the same way all memories did.

She understood why wajinru wanted nothing to do with them but for one time a year.

2

It was no longer sung.

For that morsel of mercy, Yetu gave thanks. She understood why all the historians before Basha performed the Remembrance to melody, that impulse to salvage a speck of beauty from tragedy with a dirge, but Yetu wanted people to remember how she remembered. With screams. She had no wish to transform trauma to performance, to parade what she'd come to think of as her own tragedies for entertainment.

Wajinru milled the sacred waters, a mass of bodies warming the deep. Yetu felt them embracing, swimming, sliding against one another in greeting, all of it sending a tide of ripples Yetu's way. The ocean pulsated. The water moved, animated. The meaning behind their name, *wajinru,* chorus of the deep, was clear.

Many wajinru lived far apart, alone or with friends or mates in dens of twenty or twenty-five people. The wajinru had settled the whole of the deep but were sparsely populated. While there was the occasional larger group who lived together, up to fifty or one hundred, there was nothing like the cities Yetu had seen in her rememberings.

For a people with little memory, wajinru knew one another despite the year-long absence. They didn't remember in pictures nor did they recall exact events, but they knew things in their bodies, bits of the past absorbed into them and transformed into instincts. Wajinru knew the faces of lovers they'd once taken, the trajectory of their own lives. They knew that they were wajinru.

Because they tended to live so far apart, when they did gather en masse, it was an occasion of great celebration. Everyone shouted their greetings, swam in excited circles, joined together to dance a spiral. Soon, what had started as something intimate between two or three spread to twenty, then suddenly a hundred, five hundred, then all five thousand or six thousand of them. They moved spontaneously but in unison, a single entity.

It was this same energy Yetu would use to share the History with them.

"I'm relieved you're here," said Nnenyo, Yetu's care-maid during the Remembrance. When Yetu required everyone to hush, he would tell everyone to hush. When she needed stillness, he'd make everyone be still. If words didn't work, he'd compel them softly with his mind: a little nudge that felt to most like a mild, compulsive urge. A cough. A sneeze.

Few had such power of suggestion, but he was getting on, almost a hundred and fifty years old. The average wajinru lifespan was closer to one hundred, and while it wasn't impossible to live for so long, Nnenyo was the oldest wajinru in a long time. He'd learned to harness the electrical energy present in all wajinru minds. That was why he'd been elected to oversee the historians. He was the one Yetu was to inform about the next historian when she discovered who might be capable of taking on the task, and he was the one who'd facilitate the harvesting of memories from Yetu to her successor when the time came. If he was unable, one of his many children would take on the task.

"I'm sorry for the delay. I—"

"Bygones. You are here now. That is what matters. I have a surprise for you," Nnenyo said.

"I don't like surprises," said Yetu. She found it difficult enough managing the quotidian and routine.

"I know," he said. "But I couldn't help it. I'm an old man. Allow me my whims."

Yetu let his words wash over her fully despite herself. The warmth of his tone settling even if the raw sensation of it stung.

Nnenyo was decent. Though he preferred a life in the moment, free of the past, like other wajinru, he recalled more than average. Were it not for his age, he would've been the historian to replace the previous historian, Basha. Yetu was the next best choice.

"So? What is it, then? What's my surprise?" she asked quietly. She needed to save her strength and didn't want to waste energy projecting her voice.

Nnenyo had no trouble feeling Yetu's words despite the surrounding bustle of conversation. Yetu was focusing every bit of her energy on picking his words out of the onslaught of information pressing against her skin. "Ajeji, Uyeba, Kata, Nneti, now," he called with a sharp whistle that pierced through the water.

Yetu wanted to vomit the various food items Amaba had stuffed her with to strengthen her for the Remembrance. Her skin was an open sore, and Nnenyo's call had salted it.

"I apologize," said Nnenyo.

"Do not make such sharp sounds around her," said Amaba, who'd been working quietly near Yetu, minimizing movement in order to lessen the disturbance to Yetu. "Can't you see how it stings her?"

Amaba pampered Yetu now, but it hadn't always been like that between them. Yetu's early days as a historian were marked by endless discord with her amaba. It was only in adulthood that their relationship had settled. Thirty-four years old, Yetu'd matured enough to predict and therefore avoid most quarrels.

That didn't mean there wasn't still hurt. Unlike Amaba, Yetu remembered the past and remembered well. She had more than general impressions and faded pictures of pictures of pictures. Where Amaba recalled a vague "difficult relationship," Yetu still felt the violent emotions her amaba had provoked in her, knew the precise script of ill words exchanged between them.

"Such things don't matter with all of this going on," Yetu said, though it was a lie she told just so Nnenyo didn't feel bad. He was close enough to her that the impact had bombarded her full force.

Amaba looked on the verge of arguing, then seemed to think better of it, returning to her work instead. She was wrapping sections of Yetu's body with fish skins and seaweed to help block out sensation. It wasn't a perfect solution, but it would make the Remembrance more bearable.

Nnenyo's children arrived not long after. They'd been far away to conceal the surprise, so Yetu couldn't discern the shape of it. Of course, the gift was wrapped, but that didn't always matter. Sound traveled through everything, and though a second skin could dull things, it usually wasn't enough to hide something completely.

Ajeji, the youngest of Nnenyo's children at only fifteen, handed Yetu a corpse. Still reeling from the shock of Nnenyo's whistle, she accepted it without pause, question, or upset.

"Don't worry," said Ajeji. "We did not kill it. It was already dead. We just thought it'd make a good skin for your gift."

A vampire squid, strange and complex in form, did make a good disguise, though she hated holding it. She dealt with death every day during her rememberings, and more again when she was lucid enough to hunt for food. For once, she wanted to avoid confrontation with such things, reality though it may be. It never ceased to trouble her that peace depended on the violent seizing and squeezing out of other creatures.

It was perhaps dramatic to compare that to her own situation, but it was true. Her people's survival was reliant upon her suffering. It wasn't the intention. It was no one's wish. But it was her lot.

"Such a beautiful creature," Yetu said, front fins massaging the squid so she could memorize the shape of it. She had not yet determined what gift lay inside, too enamored by the textures of the externals. "I have never touched one or even been this close. Remarkable."

She wanted to cry for the dead thing draped in her front fins.

"You have always been such a tender thing," said Nnenyo as Yetu clutched the vampire squid. "Does it help to know that when we found it, there were no marks upon it? It did not die at the hand of another, as far as we can tell, but peacefully of age."

Yetu nodded. It did help. She didn't understand why everything couldn't be like that. Gentle and easy. No sacrifice. No pain.

Yetu handed the body back to Ajeji, unwilling to break inside the creature's flesh. "What's inside of it?" she asked.

One of Ajeji's siblings—Yetu guessed Kata by the precise, jagged movements—opened up the slit they'd cut in the flesh cut and removed a small, flat object, which she handed to Yetu.

"What is it?" she asked.

"We don't know, but we know how much you like to have old things you can actually hold. It was found here near the sacred waters, lodged inside the skull of a two-legged surface dweller, which itself was inside the belly of Anyeteket," Kata said.

"Anyeteket?" she asked. She hadn't thought of that shark in some time. Anyeteket had only died last year but had lurked in these waters since the first wajinru six hundred years ago. Her age and infamy had earned her a name, which was not an honor bestowed on most sea creatures.

It wasn't common for frilled sharks to be bound by such a limited area as she was, but she had two reasons to stay: One, she'd probably never forgotten the rain of bodies that descended here when two-legs had been cast into the sea so many centuries ago. Sharks didn't usually feast on surface dwellers, but easy meat was easy meat. Two, being sickly, she couldn't travel far to hunt. Wajinru supplemented her diet by bringing her grub.

Yetu was intrigued by the present being offered her. She guessed the two-legs skull inside of Anyeteket had been what had made her so ill all these years. There was a chance the head was one of the first mothers, the drownt, cast-off surface dwellers who gave birth to the early wajinru.

Yetu rubbed the flat object from the skull against the sensitive webbing of her fins to get a better sense of its precise shape. Sometimes, when she came across something she'd never seen before, she could reach her mind out to the History and find it: a tiny detail she'd missed in one of her rememberings.

At first feel, the object resembled a jaw, for there were tiny, tightly spaced teeth, dulled by time. Closer inspection revealed something purpose-made. It was too regular, its edges too smooth, for its origins to be animal. There were complex etchings in it. Teeth marks? Yetu enjoyed the feel of complex indentations against her skin.

"A tool of some kind?" Amaba asked, her voice tinged with desperation. She was anxious for knowledge, any sort of knowledge, keen to fill the various hollows she'd amassed over the past year. The Remembrance was late, and her lingering sense of who the wajinru were had started to wane.

Yetu closed her eyes as she felt a remembering tug her away from the present. Amaba, Nnenyo, and his children were reduced to a distant tingling, and the wajinru who were gathered in the sacred waters felt like a pleasing, beating thrum.

In the sacred waters, there was never color because there was never light. That was how Yetu knew the remembering had overcome her, because there was blurred color. Light from above the ocean's surface peeked through, painting the water a dark, grayish blue. It was bright enough to reveal a dead woman floating in front of her, with brown skin and two legs. There it was, something pressed into her short, coarse hair.

It was a comb, a tool used for styling hair. Yetu flowed from remembering to remembering. She could only find three combs in her memory. The one in her fin didn't seem to be one of them, but its origin was clear. It had belonged to one of the foremothers.

Yetu stared at the face of the woman in her remembering, not yet bloated by death and sea, preserved by the iciness of the deep. She was heart-stilling and strange, her beauty magnetic. Yetu couldn't look away, not even when she felt someone shaking her.

"Yetu? Yetu!"

In the remembering, Yetu was not herself. She was possessed by an ancestor, living their story. Not-Yetu reached out for the comb in the sunken woman's hair and noted the smallness of her own fins, the webbing between the more stable cartilage finger limbs not yet developed. She was a young child. Old enough to be eating fish, shrimp, and so on premashed by someone bigger, but still young enough to need mostly whale milk to survive.

The little hand grabbed the comb, then Not-Yetu was jamming it into her mouth to stimulate and soothe her aching gums.

During such rememberings, Yetu's loneliness abated, overcome with the sanctity of being the vessel for another life—and in a moment like this, a child's life, a child who'd grown into an adult and then an elder, so many lifetimes ago. Yet here they were together, one.

"Yetu! Please!"

It ached to leave the foremother, the peacefulness of being the child, the comb, but she had her own comb now. Nnenyo had chosen his gift for her wisely.

"I'm here. I'm awake," said Yetu, but her words came out a raspy, meaningless gurgle.

"The Remembrance isn't long from now," said Amaba. "You cannot be slipping away like that so often and for so long."

Yetu was going to ask how long she'd been out, but as her senses resettled and acclimated to the ocean, she could smell that everyone was eating now. Hours had passed. It was the evening meal.

The rememberings were most certainly increasing in intensity. Years of living with the memories of the dead had taken their toll, occupying as much of her mind and body as her own self did. Had she been alone, with no one prodding her to get back, she'd have stayed with the foremother and the child for days, perhaps weeks, lulled.

Yetu might like to stay in a remembering forever, but she couldn't. What would happen to her physical form, neglected in the deep? How long would it take her amaba to find her body? Would she ever? Without Yetu's body, they couldn't transfer the History, and without the History, the wajinru would perish.

"Yetu. Pay attention. Are you there?"

It took everything in that moment not to slip away again.

During the Remembrance, mind left body. Not long from now, the entirety of the wajinru people would be entranced by the History. They would move, but according to instinct and random pulses in their brains, indecipherable from a seizure.

They would be in no position to fend for themselves in that state, so they built a giant mud sphere in defense, its walls thick and impenetrable. They called it *the womb*, and it protected the ocean as much as it protected them. Wajinru were deeply attuned to electrical forces, and when their energy was unbridled, they could stir up the sea into rageful storms. It had happened before.

Typically, Yetu was the last to enter the womb. There'd be a processional, and then she'd swim in, finally resting at the center of the sphere.

They were still building. When all of them worked together, it took three days, with no sleep or rest. The meal Yetu had awakened to them eating would be their last. They had to fast before the Remembrance so as not to vomit when the ceremony was taking place and to ensure their minds and bodies were weakened by starvation. That made them more receptive to bending. A historian needed her people's minds malleable to impart the History.

For her part, Yetu feasted, her only companions Amaba and Nnenyo, who alternated shifts every few hours. Nnenyo was off now to gather more food for Yetu and to check on the progress of the mud womb.

Amaba waited silently nearby as Yetu ate. She was still

trying to build her resources. Get her fat up. If she slipped away into her mind during the Remembrance, her people would suffer, experiencing the rememberings without her guidance or insight.

Worse, the Remembrance might subsume her. Reliving that much of the History at once—it might kill her in the state she was in. She couldn't shake the feeling that it already had, that it had been poisoning her for the two decades she'd been the historian.

"Stop fidgeting over there, Amaba. I can feel you," said Yetu. "Why are you so anxious?"

"There hasn't been a day without anxiousness since you took on the History," Amaba said.

"It is different now. More. Tell me, what troubles you? Is it me? Come closer so we might speak proper," Yetu said, surprised by her own request. Closer meant she'd feel the ripples of Amaba speaking more forcefully, but it had been so long since they'd properly talked. She wanted to know what was on Amaba's mind and tell her what was on her own. She wanted to be like other amaba-child pairs, with a relationship unstrained by the duty the rememberings brought. It was never to be, but they could share a moment, at least.

"You have enough troubles of your own. You have the troubles of our whole people. I won't bother you with it. Now quiet. Focus on food and rest. The womb will be ready before you know it, and when it's done, you need to be here. Here, Yetu. You hear me? Here."

Yetu focused on the comb still clutched in her fin. She would ask that it be sewn up inside her in death. It was one of the few tangible things she'd touched of the past, a reminder that the History was not an imagining, not just stored electrical pulses. They were people who'd lived. Who'd breathed and wept and loved and lost.

"You are enamored with that thing," said Amaba, gesturing to the comb, her curiosity plain. Yetu hadn't let go of it since Nnenyo gifted it to her two days ago.

"It is special."

"Your remembering told you what it was, then?" Amaba asked.

Yetu stared out at the working wajinru ahead of her. They were a half mile away, and Yetu could just make out the rumblings of their actions pulsating through the water.

"Yetu? Are you here?" Amaba asked.

"I'm here."

The condemnatory shake of Amaba's head pressed familiarly across Yetu's scales, the burn dulled by its predictability.

"I don't like it when you suddenly stop answering. It scares me," said her amaba.

"You mean annoys you," Yetu said. "Not everything is about the rememberings, Amaba. I'm not a child. Sometimes it takes me a moment to gather my thoughts. Or sometimes I just have no desire to honor your questions with a response."

Yetu felt taken by the same indignation that had often overwhelmed her as a child, inflamed by the slightest of slights. Yetu appreciated Amaba's caring nature, but sometimes her gentle chiding turned into chafing, and Yetu was reminded of all that was wrong between them. Yetu would never be the easy child, nor Amaba the mother to give space. What hopes Yetu had for a connection beyond caretaker and caretaken were squashed. Would she always be just the historian, over time supplanted by the voices of the past?

Yetu shook her head, calming herself down. Amaba was just worried. She had every right to be. It had only been two days since she'd rescued Yetu from sharks. The specificity of the memory may well already be fading for her, but the feel of it, the fear—that stayed.

Amaba whistled softly. Had she been feeling less sensitive to Yetu's needs, she'd have screeched. Such a thing might've killed Yetu. That was the truth. "Why wouldn't you want to answer my question? It is a simple one, no?" asked Amaba. "Do you know what the object Nnenyo and his children gave you is, or don't you?"

"I know what it is," Yetu said, her head beginning to tense and throb. She'd had more interaction in the last few days than she'd had in the past year. Her patience was waning. She could only be the good daughter, the compliant wajinru, and the dutiful historian in short bursts. After a time, the constant conversation and stimulation wore her patience down. She was becoming a sharp edge.

"Well? What is it, then?" asked Amaba, letting her voice get away from her. She spoke loudly enough that Yetu had to swim away several feet. "I'm sorry. Though this would be much less difficult if you answered when I spoke to you, like someone normal."

"Someone normal wouldn't be able to tell you that the object is a comb. Someone normal wouldn't be able to tell you that a comb was a tool the wajinru foremothers used in their hair," said Yetu. "Someone normal would never know these things. Someone normal couldn't fill your hole. You are someone normal, and you don't know anything."

For several seconds, Yetu's amaba didn't speak. She had the look of something wounded, her fins moving in an agitated fluster but her wide mouth puckered shut.

Yetu should've felt guilty, perhaps, for her harsh and bitter words, but instead she soaked up the silence, drunk it like the freshest whale milk.

She didn't mean to be so cruel, but what else was she to do with the violence inside of her? Better to tear into Amaba than herself, when there was already so little left of her—and what *was* there was fractured.

"I'm sorry," said Yetu.

"No need. It is already in the past." Amaba swam closer, so the two were near enough to touch. "I demand too much. Ask too much of you. I don't even understand why I care so much about that stupid, what did you call it? Comu?"

"Comb," said Yetu.

In one of the rememberings, there was still hair caught in a comb belonging to the foremother. Salt water had washed any hair strands from the tines of Yetu's new comb, and now she could only imagine how the bonds of black keratin had once choked the carved ivory.

Yetu didn't explain to her amaba further. She would not be mined for memories yet.

This one knowledge, this one piece of history, it was hers and no one else's.

Nnenyo came back not long later with more food for Yetu, but she'd finally had her fill. Her stomach was bloated and overstuffed, so even though she was hungry, she could not bear to eat another bite.

She had become so ragged, not just since the last Remembrance but over the course of her youth and young adulthood. It all had a cumulative effect, didn't it? She imagined a sunken ship, heavy with cargo, pieces peeling and rusting away year by year like dead scales. Yetu wasn't as hardy as those feats of two-legs innovation, though. She would die, and corpses were not eternal.

"We are almost ready for you to join us in the womb," said Nnenyo.

"Already? So fast?" asked Amaba.

"They are ready for the History. They're working faster than usual, like nothing I've ever seen before."

So much for three days. It had only been two. Yetu wasn't ready.

"It will be fine," her amaba said.

Her stomach twisted and coiled, and her heart raced. She tried to settle herself, to feel the lovely, cool water entering her gills, restoring oxygen to her blood. But she was suddenly short of breath.

"Don't worry, Nnenyo. Like always, she will pull herself together in time," said Amaba.

In the early years, in fact, Yetu had been much worse, unable to keep down food or do such basic things as hold her bowels for more than a few minutes.

"How are you feeling?" Nnenyo asked.

Yetu nodded her head. "I will do what is asked of me."

"You are a blessing," said Nnenyo.

"I am what is required," she said, no warmth left in her even for Nnenyo. Everything tense, she just wanted this whole thing to be over. Fine. Let the Remembrance begin right here, right now, for all she cared, womb or no womb.

"Breathe," said Amaba. "Breathe."

"It hurts," Yetu said, ashamed of the vulnerability. She wanted to flee and be in her discomfort alone, like she'd been this past year. In front of Amaba and Nnenyo, it wasn't so bad, but the whole of the wajinru people would see her in this state. "I'd hoped to be stronger by this point," she said. She wanted there to be more of her, to be steady on her feet, or else the Remembrance would steal what remained of her.

"They don't care if you are strong. Only that you remember," said Amaba. "Do you remember?"

A flurry of tiny bubbles left Yetu's mouth as she sighed. "I do."

"Good," said Amaba. "That is all we ask."

Catfish Lullaby

by A.C. Wise

Part 1
1986

There are stories about him along the Mississippi River from Cottonwood Point all the way down to New Orleans, maybe further still. Every place's got their own name for him—Wicked Silver, Old Tom, Fishhook—but where my people come from, smack dab in the middle of nowhere Louisiana, it was always Catfish John. Depending who you talk to, he's either a hero or a devil, one so wicked even hell won't take him.

—Myths, History, and Legends from the Delta to the Bayou (Whippoorwill Press, 2016)

Caleb lay facing the window, his grandmother's quilt pulled to his chin. From his position, he could just see the persimmon tree in the yard and, beyond it, the screen of pines separating his grandparents' property from Archie Royce's land. Back in the woods, past Royce's and where the ground started to go soft, Caleb's daddy—Lewis's sheriff—was leading a team to drag the swamp for a missing girl.

Caleb had heard Denny Harmon and Robert Lord talking about it at school. They were in first grade, but they'd probably both get held back, so Caleb would be stuck in the same class as them next year. Denny had said Catfish John took the girl.

"My cousin's friend was there. Catfish John came out of the swamp like a gator, mouth full of teeth. He grabbed her with his webbed hands and pulled her into the water."

Denny Harmon had grinned, looking like a gator himself, and looked right at Caleb.

"He probably killed her with a death roll and strung her up by her feet from the trees and slit her throat. He probably let her blood drain into the swamp to feed his catfish family."

Caleb hadn't run to tattle, but Robert held him while Denny punched him in the gut anyway, leaving him wheezing for breath.

"Catfish John likes sissy black boys best," Robert said, leaning close. "He'll leave us alone because we made it easier to catch you."

Mark, Caleb's best friend, found him after Denny and Robert left. Caleb's stomach hurt the rest of the day, but he still didn't tell. If Robert and Denny found out—and they would—it would only make things worse.

His stomach didn't hurt anymore, but he couldn't get Denny's words out of his head. His daddy was out in those woods. What if Catfish John got him? Even a sheriff with a gun could get eaten by a monster.

"I'm telling you who's responsible. Every damn fool in Lewis knows it 'cept nobody else is willing to do a thing about it." His grandfather's voice drifted under the bedroom door, interrupted by a nasty fit of coughing.

"Emmett, hush. Don't bring all that up again. 'Sides, you'll wake Caleb."

"Bet you he's awake anyhow." His grandfather chuckled, the rattling sound of his cough lingering.

Caleb started guiltily as his door opened, light from the hall spilling around his grandmother. It was too late to pretend he hadn't been listening.

"Can't sleep, sweet pea?" His grandmother didn't sound upset.

He sat up, nodding, and she sat on the edge of his bed. Caleb was surprised when his grandfather followed her into the room, crossing to the window to look out toward the trees.

"Did Catfish John kill somebody?" Caleb glanced between his grandparents. His grandmother's mouth made a little o, and the skin around his grandfather's eyes crinkled like it did when he was mad—usually at the government buying up timber from people's land without paying a fair price. "Damn ghost stories." He rested a hand on the window sill. Faint light showed a white scar across the back of his left hand, running from the knuckle of his first finger down to his wrist below his pinky. "That's what keeps folks from going after him. They think old Archie'll put a curse on 'em. Just like his daddy." He sounded like he wanted to spit. Caleb sat up straighter. Did his grandfather think Archie Royce had something to do with the missing girl? There were stories about him too, though not as many as about Catfish John. Gators as big as trucks were supposed to guard Archie's property, and on top of that, the land was haunted on account of some people Archie's granddaddy killed a long time ago.

"What makes you ask about Catfish John?" His grandmother put her hand over Caleb's, her papery white skin a contrast to his warm brown.

Her look flickered past him to his grandfather. She smiled, but the expression went thin at the edges.

"I heard . . ." Caleb hesitated. If he told his grandmother about Robert and Denny, it might get back to them. His grandmother and Robert's nana both got their hair done at Miss Linda's place after all.

"Just something I heard at school." Caleb shrugged, looking down.

"Well, I know a story about Catfish John too." His grandmother leaned forward like she was about to tell a secret, and Caleb looked up again.

"Don't go filling his head with more nonsense, Dorrie." His grandfather spoke without turning from the window. He sounded more tired than upset.

"I want to hear," Caleb said.

"Well." His grandmother glanced at his grandfather, daring him to interrupt. When he didn't, she continued. "When I was little, my mama told me about a man who lived all alone in the swamp."

"Why?" Caleb caught himself too late, but his grandmother didn't fuss at him for interrupting like she normally would.

She smoothed the quilt. That must be why she was letting him stay up late; she was worried too.

"No one knows. There are a lot of stories about Catfish John. Some folks say he was chased out of his home by people who thought he was a bad man. They wanted to hurt him, and he ran into the swamp to hide. Now when my mama's best friend was a little girl, she got lost in the woods and wandered all the way to the swamp. She nearly drowned, but whatever reason he had for being there, Catfish John saved her life."

"But if he saved your mama's friend, then he'd be . . ." Caleb couldn't even begin to guess at his grandmother's mama's age. "He'd be a hundred years old, wouldn't he?" He looked at his grandmother to see if she was fooling him or if she'd smack his bottom for being rude.

"Maybe." She smiled, surprising him, and Caleb didn't see any sign of a trick. By the window, his grandfather made a noise in his throat.

His grandmother kissed Caleb's forehead.

"Try to get some sleep, sweet pea. In the morning, I'll fix

us all a big plate of 'nanner pancakes." She moved toward the door. "Come away from the window, Emmett. Your staring won't do any good."

His grandfather made another noise but followed his grandmother, closing the door behind him. Caleb tried to picture Catfish John saving a little girl. Maybe he'd help Caleb's daddy find the girl who was missing now. It was much a much nicer idea than the story Denny had told.

Caleb came awake to voices drifting from the hall, though he didn't remember falling asleep. Over the trees, the sky was a pearly grey. Not even dawn.

"No, but we found something else." Caleb focused in on his father's voice; he didn't sound happy.

"Might be Evaneen Milton, that girl down from Baton Rouge who disappeared six, seven years ago." His father's voice was rough with exhaustion. "There was barely anything left of her, but she had one of them medic alert bracelets."

"Oh, Charlie." His grandmother made a tutting noise. "Come on. I'll fix us some coffee." Their footsteps retreated down the hall.

Caleb sat up, fully awake now. They hadn't found the missing girl, but they'd found someone else, someone who'd gone missing before Caleb was even born. If that many people went missing in the swamp, maybe Denny was right after all. Maybe Catfish John did kill people, no matter what his grandmother said.

As he turned the thought over, a terrible sound split the air, echoing over the trees and making Caleb's skin pucker with goose bumps.

It was a snarling, wet sound. A scream that wasn't animal nor human but both. Like the swamp itself had found a voice, and it was angry that something that belonged to it had been taken away.

Part 2
1992
Chapter One

. . . nine feet tall, webbed hands, grey skin, mouth turned down at the corners, just like a catfish.

—Myths, History, and Legends from the Delta to the Bayou (Whippoorwill Press, 2016)

Late afternoon light hit the persimmon tree, so the fruit glowed, but all around, the grass was stained with a pattern like roots spread across the yard, a permanent, too-long shadow. Thin tendrils of black wrapped the tree's branches, and the leaves curled at the edges as though burned. Caleb plucked a fruit and pressed his thumb to the skin, black rot oozing from within. Dropping the fruit, he wiped his hand on his jeans.

"I've never seen anything like it." Caleb's father wiped an arm across his forehead, revealing half-moon circles of sweat staining his shirt. Early summer and already his skin bronzed brown-red from hours spent in the yard and on the porch under the eye of the sun.

"Whole thing's going to have to come out. Best burn the stump too, so it doesn't spread."

Caleb toed a blackened patch, half expecting it to smudge like ash, but it stayed put. The stain reminded him of something he couldn't place. Caleb half-listened to his father, thinking how his grandmother would have hated to see the tree go. Her persimmon jelly took the blue ribbon nearly every year at the Lewis County Fair.

"I'll go look for the chain saw," his father said. "Once I get the tree down, I'll need your help hauling it."

Caleb nodded, and all at once, the nagging familiarity clicked into place. The rootlike pattern reminded him of the chest x-ray he'd glimpsed clipped to the chart at the foot of his grandmother's hospital bed, just before the end. She hadn't smoked a day in her life, but her lungs had been threaded with dark shadows. She'd outlived his grandfather but barely, and neither of them had been that old.

As his father disappeared around the side of the house, Caleb followed the shadows twisting away from the tree. They vanished in the pines bordering the property, headed toward Archie Royce's land. A flicker of movement between the trees made him start guiltily as though Archie Royce had caught him staring and now glared back.

Turning his back deliberately on the trees, Caleb pulled on work gloves and began gathering fallen persimmons. He chucked them into the garbage can they'd dragged into the yard, each exploding with a wet splat that was equal parts satisfying and unnerving. The back of his neck itched, and he fought the urge to turn around and see if he was actually being watched or if it was only his imagination. Even if it wasn't Archie Royce, that didn't mean nothing watched him.

Caleb shrugged, rolling his shoulders against the sensation. It struck him that he wasn't even sure what Archie Royce looked like. Lewis wasn't a big town, but even after all the years of his grandparents, and now him and his father, living just on the other side of the trees, Caleb had never seen their neighbor face to face.

There were plenty of rumors of course. One of his father's fishing buddies liked to tell a story about being chased off the Royce land with a shotgun when he was a kid. It could have been Archie Royce or his father, but whoever it was had fired into the air. From what he'd heard, with his skin, there was every chance Archie Royce would keep the gun level when he fired if Caleb ever strayed onto his land.

Archie wasn't the only mystery beyond the trees. Some folks said he had over a dozen kids—all by different women, not all of them willing—holed up on that property. Like his own private cult. Caleb had never seen evidence of them either. The only Royce he'd ever run into was Archie's son, Del. Even though Del looked old enough to be in college or be working at least, all he ever seemed to do was mooch around the Hilltop store, buying liquor and cigarettes. He'd broken in after hours once, but somehow, the charges hadn't stuck, and he'd been back on the streets of Lewis by the next day.

Caleb's main impression of Del was dark hair and a slouching walk. The closest Caleb had ever seen him was last summer when Caleb and Mark had gone to set pennies on the tracks for trains to flatten. Del had been crouched on the old track, running parallel to the new one, half its ties pulled up all the spaces between growing with weeds. At first, Caleb had thought Del was trying to light a fire, but then he'd heard the unmistakable scream of an animal in pain. Caleb had gotten just close enough to see what looked like a possum or a raccoon. Del had it staked to the tracks, his hands bloody like he was flaying it alive.

By the time Caleb and Mark had found someone to tell, it was too late. Del was gone, and he'd cleaned up all the evidence behind him.

"Hey. You hear me?" His father's voice jarred Caleb back to the present. "Sir?" Caleb realized he was standing with a handful of rotten persimmons, staring into the trees despite himself.

"I said, why don't you start in on the branches with these clippers. I'm going to have to run into Buck's for a new chain. This one's rusted through."

"Yessir." Caleb accepted the clippers his father held out.

After a moment, the truck's engine roared to life. Caleb squeezed the handles of the clippers together, and the branch between the blades gave with a dry snap like breaking bone.

Sweat gathered as he worked, his muscles aching pleasantly. Even so, he couldn't help pausing every now and then to glance at the trees. His grandfather talked about Archie's father, Clayton, sometimes, but more often than not, Caleb's grandmother would shush him. Still, it was pretty clear his grandfather hadn't liked the man.

There was a plaque at town hall dedicated to a Reverend Elphias Royce. The family had been in Lewis for generations; they'd practically founded the town, but for all that, no one really seemed to like them as far as Caleb knew. Over the years, the family had grown increasingly reclusive, and the rumors about them nastier. But that's all it was, rumors. Nothing legal stuck, just like Del breaking into Hilltop. It was like the family and even the land had some supernatural force around it.

Caleb gathered the cut branches and dumped the armload in the trash on top of the burst fruit. The black goo in the bottom of the can smelled foul, and Caleb regretted busting them. Burning the tree stump didn't seem like such a bad idea after all. He pictured the flames following the black lines of rot all the way back to Archie Royce's house. Maybe that wouldn't be such a bad thing either.

• • •

Caleb woke to ruddy light blazing above the tree line, bright as dawn but the wrong color. His first sleep-muzzed thought was that his father had decided to burn the stump after all. But that would be a controlled burn and not in the middle of the night. He rocketed up, rushing down the hall to bang on his father's door.

"Caleb, what—" His father's eyes were red with exhaustion; insomnia often ate away his hours until late into the night. He'd probably only just gotten to sleep. "Archie

Royce's place is burning." A sick thrill ran through Caleb. Hadn't he wished that very thing?

Coming awake all at once, his father reached for the phone on the nightstand, twisting the cord around as he gathered his shirt and boots, dressing as he talked. When he hung up, his expression was grim.

"What's wrong?"

His father shook his head, throwing a flannel work shirt over his T-shirt, leaving his boots unlaced.

"Gerry March says it'll take him half an hour to rouse a crew and get over here. That's bullshit." A muscle in his father's jaw twitched. "Archie's got kids in there."

The words sparked guilt over the strange thrill Caleb had felt. Thoughts weren't actions but still.

"The fire won't come over the trees." His father moved toward the door. "If it does, you take the old truck down the road to Ginny Mason's place, and you stay there. You hear?"

"I want to help." Caleb spoke before his brain had time to catch up with his mouth.

His father stopped so abruptly Caleb almost crashed into him.

Even if his father wasn't Lewis's sheriff, he'd still help Archie Royce, no matter what he thought of him. Because it was the right thing to do. Caleb knew he wasn't really to blame just because he'd imagined a fire, but his father's words and his own willingness to help still left him with a feeling of responsibility. Whatever the truth about Archie Royce might be, if he did have kids in there—Del aside—they didn't deserve to die. Caleb stood straighter, adrenaline surging and mixing with his nerves as his father looked him over.

"All right. Let's go."

As his father stepped outside, Caleb's legs turned briefly to rubber; he hadn't expected his father to agree. The truck's engine roared, and headlights flooded the yard. Caleb hurried to catch up.

Caleb's chest remained tight as his father steered onto the main road. The night was silent. No wail of sirens. If their house had been the one burning, trucks would be on the way by now, but because it was Archie Royce's place, Gerry March was content to make excuses and let it burn.

The idea dug at Caleb. No one in Lewis ever took direct action against the Royces, but it seemed they wouldn't take direct action to save them either. He scrabbled for purchase as his father turned hard, slewing the truck onto a barely visible drive. His teeth clicked together as the wheels jounced in worn ruts until his father brought the truck to a halt.

Whip-thin trees framed the burning house. They looked sicker than the persimmon his father had cut down, leaning away as though trying to escape. But if the persimmon was any indication, the trees would be hell to cut down, even diseased. If the fire touched them, would they even burn?

Despite being engulfed, Caleb could see the Royce house had once been grand. He and Mark had never been invited to joyride down the roads at night when other kids from school dared each other onto the property. Seeing the place now, Caleb was glad.

His father climbed out of the truck, leaving the sharp sting of smoke to drift through the open door. Caleb opened his own door and went to stand by the hood.

A beam popped deep in the house, and a section of roof collapsed, sending up a rush of sparks. Caleb lifted his shirt over his nose and mouth. The brightness made a hard backlight to shapes directly in front of the house—a junked car, the remains of a well, and closer to the house, an odd-shaped blot. It took Caleb's eyes a moment to adjust, and even then, his mind didn't want to agree. A girl, standing far too close to the flames.

"Dad!"

His father hoisted his own shirt over his nose and mouth as Caleb pointed. The air wavered, weirdly thick around the girl. It wasn't just the heat rolling off the place; his father moved as though wading through waist-deep water. She didn't react when his father reached her. When he took her by the shoulders, steering her toward the truck, she didn't resist either.

"Get a blanket from the back," his father called, and Caleb hurried to obey. "Take care of her. I'm going to see if there's anyone else."

His father wrapped the blanket around the girl's shoulders and gave her a gentle nudge in Caleb's direction. Caleb watched him walk back toward the flames. The girl's attention remained fixed on the house. He couldn't imagine watching everything he'd ever known burn—his bed, his baseball trophies, the picture of his mother and father and him as a baby sitting on a big striped blanket on the front lawn.

"I'm Caleb." Introducing himself felt stupid given the situation, but if he could get her talking, maybe it would distract her. He lowered the shirt from his mouth. "What's your name?"

The girl ignored him. Caleb looked at her more closely. Smoke and ash streaked her pale skin. Out of nowhere, an odd thought struck Caleb like something coming up out of the swamp. He'd never heard of a woman living at Archie Royce's place; the rumors said all his kids had different mothers who no one ever saw. What if the body his father had found in the swamp all those years ago was this girl's mother?

There was a thinness to her like hunger but deeper. Below the blanket, her feet were bare. She looked about his age, but it was hard to tell. She was at least a head shorter than him, but Caleb was tall for his age. His limbs had been called gangly, and hers had the same thinness but without the awkwardness of knobby elbows and knees that didn't fit.

She clutched something close against her body like she was afraid someone would take it. Caleb could just make out what looked like a figurine roughly the size of a baseball, carved from dark wood. Except when he looked closer, the wood took on a reddish hue, streaked with dark bands like smoke. And as he watched, the bands grew, staining the wood pure black. The reflected firelight must have been messing with his sight.

He blinked, focusing on the girl's face instead. "Are you okay?"

Another stupid thing to say. Of course, she wasn't. He touched her shoulder. She jerked away, startled, but finally turned to face him. Even though the firelight was behind her, her eyes seemed to glow for a moment, and a faint light shone from her skin too. Then the girl blinked, and her eyes were just a normal muddy green-brown. Except she wasn't crying. That struck Caleb as odd. Her house was burning, and there were no tracks in the soot smearing her cheeks.

"Hey . . ." Spooked, Caleb let the word trail.

The girl pivoted on her bare heels, and for a moment, Caleb feared she would sprint back into the burning house. Instead she spat in the dirt at her feet. A sound like the one he'd heard the night his father pulled the bones from the swamp, a sound Caleb would never forget—sorrow and rage—split the air.

Caleb's skin prickled, but movement at the corner of his eye caught his attention. The smoke above the house shifted. As Caleb stared, it formed a face, impossible but distinct and inhuman. The night sky howled again, and beside him, the girl went rigid. Her fingers curled tight around the carving, her lips pulling back from her teeth. Then her head whipped around, a dog scenting deer.

Caleb squinted, trying to see what she saw. A blot of darkness, like she'd been at first, but larger. A man stood near the side of the house, but there was something wrong about his shape.

The girl lurched toward the fire. Instinctively Caleb threw his arms around her to hold her back. Her body hitched like a sob, but the noise that emerged was a keening cry. It was almost music, raw and laced with rage, and it made lightning crawl under Caleb's skin.

The sound went on, a contrast to the wet, red sound howling above the house. The girl's throat worked, reminding Caleb of a pelican struggling with a fish. The noise coming out of her looked painful.

She strained forward again, throwing him off balance. They crashed to the ground, dust billowing around them, adding to the smoke and making Caleb cough. The girl was a knot of sinew, wild and thrashing. Caleb caught her wrists to keep her from hitting him.

All at once, she went still, her breath shallow. Her eyes reflected the light from the house. Burning. Except the angle was wrong, the light behind her. Caleb let go of her wrists with a shout, her skin suddenly hot.

The wail of sirens cut the night, far too late, and the girl slumped, the fight gone. Caleb scrambled to stand. Adrenaline shook him; it was a moment before he caught his breath, a moment longer before he could string together a coherent thought. He got his hands under the girl's armpits and hauled her to her feet.

"I couldn't find anyone else." Caleb's father returned, his voice worn hollow as his expression.

He frowned as though he couldn't quite remember how Caleb and the girl had gotten there. As the fire engine finally pulled into the drive, his expression changed, going flint hard. Caleb watched his father stride toward the splash of red and white lights, ready to give Gerry March hell. When the girl spoke beside him, Caleb jumped.

"Cere."

"What?" Caleb stared at her.

Her voice was smoke-rough, a croak. Light no longer burned in her eyes. Where they'd been muddy green-brown before, they now appeared green-grey like pale moss clinging to a stone.

"Cere." She fixed on him in a way that brought back the electric fizzing beneath his skin. Caleb let out a breath, realizing she'd finally offered him her name.

• • •

Cere perched on the edge of a kitchen chair, hands wrapped around a mug of coffee she'd barely touched. She wore clothes one of the nurses at the hospital had found her—jeans and a ringer T-shirt with Lewis High's bronco in maroon against white.

"Cere's going to stay with us for a while until things get sorted out." Caleb's father put a hand on Caleb's shoulder.

Caleb nodded, but his gaze kept sliding back to Cere. She'd barely acknowledged either of them, not that he could blame her.

"Caleb." His father shook him lightly. "Are you listening?"

"Yessir." The words slid out automatically.

"Good. I have to go make some more calls." There were shadows under his eyes.

It had been a long night, from the fire to Deer Creek Hospital and back here. None of them had slept. Under the kitchen light, away from the smoke and fire, Caleb finally had a chance to get a good look at Cere. Her hair was an odd blonde that was almost silvery. The nurse had worked it into two thick braids that hung over her shoulders. Even for a white girl, she was pale, her wrists showing the faint blue blush of her veins. The pallor was offset by a shock of freckles scattered across her cheeks and nose like a constellation. On top of that, Caleb still couldn't get a good fix on the color of her eyes, which seemed to shift constantly.

Caleb poured himself a bowl of cereal. He placed the box close enough that Cere could reach it if she wanted and then sat at the far end of the table. Cere didn't raise her head. From the far end of the hall, Caleb heard the murmur of his father's voice. He'd been on the phone for hours, trying to track down any other members of Cere's family, but the set of his jaw told Caleb everything he needed to know about how little enthusiasm he had for finding anyone with the last name Royce.

Caleb took a bite of his cereal, finding it tasteless. Within the span of twenty-four hours, less, the world had been turned completely upside down. After Gerry March's team had gotten the fire under control, they'd found Archie Royce's remains in the burned-out shell of the house. Caleb had heard his father mention someone named Ellis who must be another of Cere's brothers. He hadn't heard anything about Del, and it wasn't clear whether their bodies had been found or whether there'd been anyone else in the house.

Cere kicked her heels against the rung of her chair, a restless drumming sound. Caleb abandoned his spoon. The one bite he'd taken already felt like a solid lump in his stomach.

"Do you like baseball?" It was the only thing he could think to say. Cere raised her head. Ignoring her unsettling eyes, Caleb plowed on.

"Our team was pretty good last year. We went all the way

to regional finals. Then Coach Stevens left, and now we suck."

Anything to fill the silence. Cere didn't blink. There was something wrong with her eyes beyond their shifting color. Subtle threads of gold bled into them from the edges. It made Caleb think of the black shadows on the lawn but in reverse.

Caleb shoved his chair back, dumped the rest of his cereal into the sink. To his surprise, Cere followed him down the hall, a pale shadow. He was too stunned to close the door before she slipped past him into his room.

"What are you—"

Cere glanced over her shoulder, stilling him. Caleb held his breath as she trailed her fingers over the bedspread, taking in his books, his trophies, his bat and glove leaning against the closet door. Her hand rested on the photograph of him as a baby with his parents and something coiled tight inside him.

He'd been so young when she died. The picture was the only way he could remember what his mother looked like. He would stare, trying to fix every feature in his mind—her hair carefully smoothed and curled, her skin several shades darker than his, but her eyes just like his own. When he looked at the picture, he could almost remember her laugh, the sound of her voice as she moved around the kitchen while he played on a blanket spread on the floor. Then it would slip again, and her face would blur. Those moments of forgetting were his own personal experience of loss. It was like remembering her death, even though he hadn't fully experienced it at the time. If Cere damaged the picture . . .

He moved to snatch the frame out of her hand as Cere turned her head without moving the rest of her body. It made Caleb think of a bird. Her eyes, the color of Spanish moss now, pinned him, and Caleb's breath stuttered. The gold threads within her irises were unmistakable; they squirmed. She tapped the picture's frame. Everything he'd been feeling uncoiled into guilt. His parents smiling, Caleb between them, a happy family. Even if he'd lost part of it, it must still be more than she'd ever had.

Cere lowered her hand. She turned fully now, facing him. Her voice was still a smoke-rough whisper, every bit as startling as it had been last night.

"I was born to end the world."

• • •

Caleb woke with his heart pounding, convinced the sky was on fire on the other side of the trees. But only stars shone above the pine and oak. Vents sighed with a sudden rush of chill from the air conditioning, and Caleb tugged his blanket higher. Fragments of a dream clung to him. A fat ball of flaming gold crawling into the sky and a great frog or a fish swallowing it whole. There had also been something with scales diving into muck and a woman walking between cypress knees. Her bare feet splashed in shallow water, and she cradled her swollen belly. She glowed.

I was born to end the world.

Even as the images faded, certainty clung to him that the woman in his dream was Cere but older, and the thing she carried in her belly wasn't a child; it was something terrible, darkness and fire, a thing too big to wrap his mind around.

Caleb pressed his ear to the wall dividing his room from Cere's. He was startled to hear a faint murmur, what sounded like "please." The wall under his ear felt hot, the skin of the house glowing like the woman in his dream. He jerked back but not before he heard her window sliding up.

Caleb reached his own window just in time to see a shadow dart across the lawn. Cere. He knew he should tell his father, but at the same time, he couldn't help thinking about the way Cere's eyes squirmed with gold. If she chose to run away, that wasn't his problem. Caleb tried to convince himself, tried to ignore the hammer of his pulse telling him otherwise. He pulled the covers over his head. He was still dreaming; he hadn't seen anything at all.

Biographies

G. V. Anderson

G. V. Anderson's short stories have won a World Fantasy Award, a British Fantasy Award, and been nominated for a Nebula. Her work can be found in Strange Horizons, Lightspeed and Tor.com, as well as anthologies such as The Year's Best Dark Fantasy & Horror. She lives and works in Dorset, UK.

Siobhan Carroll

Siobhan Carroll is a Canadian writer and professor of English at University of Delaware. Her short stories have been published in *Asimov's Science Fiction*, *Lightspeed,* and *Beneath Ceaseless Skies,* among others. In 2020, her fantasy novelette "For He Can Creep" won the 2020 Eugie Award, and was a finalist for the 2019 Nebula Award for Best Novelette, the 2020 Hugo Award for Best Novelette, and the 2020 World Fantasy Award for Best Short Fiction.

Ted Chiang

Ted Chiang's fiction has won four Hugo, four Nebula, and four Locus awards, the John W. Campbell Award for Best New Writer, and has been featured in *The Best American Short Stories*. His debut collection, *Stories of Your Life and Others*, has been translated into twenty-one languages. He was born in Port Jefferson, New York, and currently lives near Seattle, Washington.

P. Djèlí Clark

Phenderson Djéli Clark is the Nebula award-winning and Hugo, Sturgeon, and World Fantasy nominated author of the novel *A Master of Djinn*, and the novellas *Ring Shout, The Black God's Drums* and *The Haunting of Tram Car 015*. His stories have appeared in online venues such as *Tor.com, Daily Science Fiction, Heroic Fantasy Quarterly, Apex, Lightspeed, Fireside Magazine, Beneath Ceaseless Skies*, and in print anthologies including *Griots, Hidden Youth* and *Clockwork Cairo*. He is a founding member of the *FIYAH* literary magazine and an infrequent reviewer at *Strange Horizons*.

Seth Dickinson

Seth Dickinson is the author of the Masquerade series, which includes *The Traitor Baru Cormorant, The Monster Baru Cormorant, and The Tyrant Baru Cormorant*, as well as short fiction published in *Clarkesworld, Strange Horizons, Lightspeed*, and *Beneath Ceaseless Skies*, among others. He has also written for video games, including *Destiny: The Taken King*, and *Destiny 2: Forsaken*.

Amal El-Mohtar

Amal El-Mohtar is an award-winning writer of fiction, poetry, and criticism. Her stories and poems have appeared in magazines including *Tor.com, Fireside Magazine, Lightspeed, Uncanny, Strange Horizons, Apex, Stone Telling*, and *Mythic Delirium*; anthologies including *The Djinn Falls in Love and Other Stories, The Starlit Wood: New Fairy Tales, Kaleidoscope: Diverse YA Science Fiction and Fantasy Stories*, and *The Thackery T. Lambshead Cabinet of Curiosities*; and in her own collection, *The Honey Month*.

Max Gladstone

Hugo-, Nebula-, and Locus Award winning author Max Gladstone has been thrown from a horse in Mongolia and once wrecked a bicycle in Angkor Wat. He is the author of many books, including *Empress of Forever*, the *Craft Sequence* of fantasy novels, and, with Amal El-Mohtar, the internationally bestselling *This is How You Lose the Time War*. His dreams are much nicer than you'd expect.

A.T. Greenblatt

A.T. Greenblatt is an engineer and writer. She won the 2019 Nebula Award for Best Short Story for "Give the Family My Love." She has also have been a finalist for the Hugo Award, the Locus Award, the Theodore Sturgeon Award, and the Parsec Award. Her stories have appeared in *Uncanny, Clarkesworld, Tor.com. Asimov's, Beneath Ceaseless Skies, Strange Horizons, Escape Pod, Podcastle,* and others.

Vylar Kaftan

Vylar Kaftan writes speculative fiction of all genres, including science fiction, fantasy, horror, and slipstream. Her stories have appeared in *Lightspeed, Strange Horizons, Asimov's*, and *Clarkesworld*. Her work has been reprinted in *Horror: The Best of the Year*, honorably mentioned in *The Year's Best Fantasy and Horror*, and shortlisted for the WSFA Small Press Award. She won a 2013 Nebula Award for her novella "The Weight of the Sunrise," as well as a 2013 Sidewise Award for Short-Form Alternate History. She was also nominated for a 2010 Nebula Award for her short story "I'm Alive, I Love You, I'll See You in Reno."

Foz Meadows

Foz Meadows is a genderqueer fantasy author, essayist, reviewer, blogger and poet. Foz is a reviewer for *Strange Horizons*, and has been a contributing writer for *The Book Smugglers, Black Gate* and *The Huffington Post*, as well as a repeat contributor to the podcast *Geek Girl Riot*. Her essays have appeared in various venues online, including *The Mary Sue, A Dribble of Ink and Uncanny Magazine*. She is a four-time

Hugo Award nominee for Best Fan Writer, which she won in 2019; she also won the 2017 Ditmar Award for Best Fan Writer, for which she has been nominated three times.

Mimi Mondal

Mimi Mondal is a Hugo- and Nebula Award-nominated author of science fiction and fantasy and a columnist writing about history, politics, technology and futures. Her novelette "His Footsteps, Through Darkness and Light" was shortlisted for the Nebula Award in 2020. Her first book, *Luminescent Threads: Connections to Octavia E. Butler*, co-edited with Alexandra Pierce, received the Locus Award in Non-fiction and was shortlisted for the Hugo Award in Best Related Work and the British Fantasy Award in Non-fiction, among others, in 2018. Mimi has also been the Poetry and Reprint Editor of *Uncanny Magazine*, a three-times-Hugo-Award-winning magazine of science fiction and fantasy, and an editor at Penguin Random House India.

Karen Osborne

Karen Osborne is a speculative fiction writer and visual storyteller living in Baltimore. She is a graduate of Viable Paradise and the Clarion Writers' Workshop, and won awards for her news & opinion writing in New York, Florida, and Maryland. Her short fiction appears in Uncanny, Fireside, Escape Pod, Beneath Ceaseless Skies, and more. Her debut novel, *Architects of Memory* was published by Tor Books in 2000.

Sarah Pinsker

Sarah Pinsker is the author of over fifty works of short fiction, including the novelette "Our Lady of the Open Road," winner of the Nebula Award in 2016. Her novelette "In Joy, Knowing the Abyss Behind," was the Sturgeon Award winner in 2014. Her fiction has been published in magazines including *Asimov's Science Fiction, Strange Horizons, The Magazine of Fantasy & Science Fiction, Lightspeed,* and *Uncanny* and in numerous anthologies and year's bests. Her stories have been translated into Chinese, Spanish, French, and Italian, among other languages, and have been nominated for the Nebula, Hugo, Locus, Eugie, and World Fantasy Awards.

Cat Rambo

Cat Rambo is a writer and editor of science fiction and fantasy. She has published more than 200 stories, including in publications such as *Asimov's Science Fiction, Clarkesworld,* and *Tor.com,* among others. She won a Nebula Award in 2019 for her novelette, "Carpe Glitter," and was nominated for a Nebula for the short story, "Five Ways to Fall in Love on Planet Porcelain" and a World Fantasy Award for her work with Fantasy Magazine. She is a past president and vice-president of Science Fiction and Fantasy Writers of America.

Shiv Ramdas

Shiv Ramdas is a multi-award nominated author of speculative fiction short stories and novels. He lives and writes in Seattle, Washington with his wife and three cats. In 2020 he became one of only two Indian writers to ever be nominated for a Hugo, a Nebula and an Ignyte Award in the same year. He also gained Twitter fame in 2020 for live-tweeting the saga of his brother-in-law's rice mishap. His first novel, *Domechild,* was India's first mainstream cyberpunk novel. His short fiction has appeared in *Slate, Strange Horizons, Fireside Fiction, PodCastle* and other publications.

Nibedita Sen

Nibedita Sen is a Hugo, Nebula, and Astounding Award-nominated queer Bengali writer from Calcutta, and a graduate of Clarion West 2015 whose work has appeared or is forthcoming in *Anathema: Spec from the Margins, Podcastle, Nightmare* and *Fireside*. She accumulated a number of English degrees in India before deciding she wanted another in creative writing, and that she was going to move halfway across the world for it.

These days, she can be found working as an editor in NYC while consuming large amounts of coffee and video-games. She helps edit Glittership, an LGBTQ SFF podcast, enjoys the company of puns and potatoes, and is nearly always hungry.

Rivers Solomon

Rivers Solomon is a dyke, an anarchist, a she-beast, an exile, a shiv, a wreck, and a refugee of the Trans-Atlantic Slave Trade. Fae writes about life in the margins, where fae's much at home.

In addition to appearing on the Stonewall Honor List and winning a Firecracker Award, Solomon's debut novel An Unkindness of Ghosts was a finalist for a Lambda, a Hurston/Wright, a Tiptree, and a Locus Award, among others. Solomon's second book, The Deep, based on the Hugo-nominated song of the same name by experimental hip-hop group clipping, was the winner of the 2020 Lambda Award and was nominated for a Nebula, Locus, and Hugo award. Faer third book is Sorrowland.

Catherynne M. Valente

Catherynne M. Valente is the New York Times bestselling author of forty works of speculative fiction and poetry, including *Space Opera, The Refrigerator Monologues, Palimpsest*, the *Orphan's Tales* series, *Deathless, Radiance*, and the crowdfunded phenomenon *The Girl Who Circumnavigated*

Fairyland in a Ship of Own Making (and the four books that followed it). She is the winner of the Andre Norton, Tiptree, Sturgeon, Prix Imaginales, Eugie Foster Memorial, Mythopoeic, Rhysling, Lambda, Locus, Romantic Times' Critics Choice and Hugo awards. She has been a finalist for the Nebula and World Fantasy Awards. She lives on an island off the coast of Maine with a small but growing menagerie of beasts, some of which are human.

LaShawn M. Wanak

LaShawn M. Wanak lives in Madison, WI, with her husband and son. Her works can be found in *Strange Horizons, Fireside Magazine, PodCastle,* and *Daily Science Fiction*, among others. She reviews books for *Lightspeed Magazine* and is a graduate of the 2011 class of Viable Paradise.

Fran Wilde

Fran Wilde's first novel, the high-flying fantasy *Updraft*, was published by Tor in 2015, and won a Nebula and Compton Crook Award. *Cloudbound* and *Horizon*—the companion novels to *Updraft*—completed the trilogy in 2017. Her debut Middle Grade novel, *Riverland*, won the 2019 Nebula, was named an NPR Best Book of 2019, and was a Lodestar finalist. Her novels and short stories have been finalists for six Nebula Awards, a World Fantasy Award, three Hugo Awards, three Locus Awards, and a Lodestar.

A. C. Wise

A.C. Wise was born and raised in Montreal, and currently lives in the Philadelphia area. Her short fiction has appeared in publications such as *Uncanny*, *Tor.com*, *Shimmer*, and multiple Year's Best anthologies. Her fiction has won the Sunburst Award for Excellence in Canadian Literature of the Fantastic, and been a finalist for the Nebula Awards, the

Sunburst Awards, the Lambda Literary Awards, and the Aurora Awards, while her work as a reviewer has been a finalist for the Ignyte Awards.

Caroline M. Yoachim

Hugo and three-time Nebula Award finalist Caroline M. Yoachim is the author of dozens of short stories, appearing in *Asimov's, Fantasy & Science Fiction, Clarkesworld,* and *Lightspeed,* among other places. Her work has been reprinted in multiple year's best anthologies and translated into Chinese, Spanish, Polish and Czech. Yoachim's debut short story collection, *Seven Wonders of a Once and Future World & Other Stories,* came out in 2016.

About the Science Fiction and Fantasy Writers of America (SFWA)

Science Fiction and Fantasy Writers of America, Inc. (SFWA) was founded in 1965 by the American science fiction author Damon Knight and was originally named Science Fiction Writers of America. In 1991, the name of the organization was changed to Science Fiction and Fantasy Writers of America, although the acronym SFWA was not changed. In 2013, the members of the organization voted to reincorporate in California, effectively beginning a new 501(c)3 public charity. Activities of the old Massachusetts corporation officially merged into the new California corporation as of July 1st, 2014. Today, SFWA is home to nearly 1900 authors, artists, and allied professionals, and is widely recognized as one of the most effective non-profit writers' organizations in existence. Learn more about SFWA at sfwa.org; you can also follow SFWA on Facebook and on Twitter @sfwa.

About the Nebula Awards ®

The Nebula Awards, presented annually at the SFWA Nebula Conference, recognize the best works of science fiction and fantasy published in the United States as selected by members of the Science Fiction and Fantasy Writers of America. The first Nebula Awards were presented in 1966.

The Nebula Awards include four fiction awards, a game writing award, the Ray Bradbury Nebula Award for Outstanding Dramatic Presentation, and the Andre Norton Nebula Award for Middle Grade and Young Adult Fiction. SFWA also administers the Kate Wilhelm Solstice Award, the Kevin O'Donnell, Jr. Service to SFWA Award, and the Damon Knight Memorial Grand Master Award.

For more information,

visit nebulas.sfwa.org/nebula-conference.

Printed in Great Britain
by Amazon